The North Building

The North Building

A novel of the Cold War

Jefferson Flanders

Munroe Hill Press
Lexington, Massachusetts

Cover design by Mick Wieland Design

ISBN: 0988784084
ISBN-13: 978-0-9887840-8-6
eBook ISBN: 978-0-9887840-9-3

Munroe Hill Press
Lexington, Massachusetts

For Christian, Dana, and Clayton

There is very little that is not wasteful and dismal about war. The only clear, deep, good is the special kind of bond welded between people who, having mutually shared a crisis, whether it be a shelling or a machine-gun attack, emerge knowing that those involved behaved well. There is much pretense in our everyday life, and, with a skillful manner, much can be concealed. But with a shell whistling at you there is not much time to pretend and a person's qualities are starkly revealed. You believe that you can trust what you have seen. It is a feeling that makes old soldiers, old sailors, old airmen, and even old war correspondents, humanly close in a way shut off to people who have not shared the same thing.

– MARGUERITE HIGGINS, from *War in Korea: The Report of a Woman Combat Correspondent*

THE CHOSIN
CAMPAIGN
(Nov.–Dec., 1950)

Marines
Chinese

Yudam-ni

Chosin
Reservoir

Task Force
Faith

Fox Hill

Toktong
Pass

1st Marine
Division HQ

Hagaru

Koto-ri

Funchilin
Pass

Chinhung-ni

To Hungnam
and Sea of Japan

Illustration: Mick Wieland Design

Part One

Washington, D.C.

She kept the newspaper clippings in a manila envelope at the bottom of her cedar hope chest, hidden safely under one of her favorite crocheted sweaters. When she was sure that she would not be interrupted, it took only moments for her to go to the chest in the corner of her bedroom and retrieve the envelope stuffed with his latest columns.

The last day of 1950 found Penny Steele opening that bulky envelope at her dressing table and spreading several long narrow strips of newsprint on the flat surface in front of her. She would have some time to reread them without distraction or fear of interruption for Caleb was asleep in the nursery, Bernice was downstairs in the kitchen preparing dinner, and Matthew was out running errands.

Matthew was pleased with her—she had agreed to attend the New Year's Eve party hosted by Allen and Clover Dulles at their home in Georgetown. It would be difficult for her to stand there next to her husband and smile and listen to the shoptalk of the determined men of the Agency and smile at their inside jokes, but she was resolved to do it. She would wear her latest gown and put on her makeup and her best pearls and brave her way through it—no matter how down she felt, or how much she now hated social events. She owed Matthew that much.

She had not told him that her sense of dread, that some disastrous event was in the offing, had returned. She had not leveled with Dr. Rifkin either, and to avoid her therapist's gentle but insistent questioning ("How have you been sleeping? Do you have any dreams to share?") she had skipped her two last sessions. She had coped during the holidays—a bright smile for her parents when they visited on Christmas Day and a quick kiss and hug for Matthew when they exchanged gifts (a Vacheron & Constantin pink gold wristwatch for her and three new Dunhill shell pipes for him)—and she was sure she could make it through a few more days, perhaps even weeks, until her mood might lift for the better.

She picked up the last column Dennis had written from Korea, from the second week of December, the one headlined "A Valorous March to the Sea." Whenever she read his columns she could hear the sound of his blunt, New York-accented voice in her head. She turned to his opening paragraphs.

December 10 – I was there in Chinhung-ni this morning in the bitter Arctic-like cold to greet the first brave Marines who had fought their way out of a Chinese Communist trap enveloping them at the Chosin Reservoir.

They held their heads high as they arrived in this small, ramshackle Korean hamlet, even though they were exhausted and battered. They had been tested by battle and the extreme elements of wind, cold, and ice, asked to bear conditions almost beyond human endurance. These tired and unshaven warriors with their shoulders hunched over from the biting cold and their faces drawn and wan from fatigue were the vanguard of the First Marine Division commanded by General Oliver P. Smith, some 7,500 men who somehow had survived the concerted assault of the Chinese over the past two weeks.

Surrounded and facing overwhelming odds, General Smith had ordered his Marines and elements of the Army's Seventh Regiment to withdraw from Chosin. They were to march nearly 80 miles to the coast, to the sea, where U.S. Navy ships waited to evacuate them. To reach that safe harbor, his men would have to fight their way from Yudam-ni and Hagaru—obscure towns near the man-made reservoir—down the dirt and gravel-topped main supply route, to the canyon below and Koto-ri, another small hamlet. From there it was another 10 miles of twisting, icy, and contested road before relative safety in Chinhung-ni and then on another 33 miles by truck to the port city of Hungnam.

Yet this was not a retreat, at least not according to the Marines. As far as they were concerned, General Smith had it right when he told this correspondent and other members of the press that you couldn't retreat when you were surrounded, it was a matter of advancing in a different direction.

She stopped reading and closed her eyes and tried to visualize the scene, the winter landscape, the cold, the fear. What must it have been like for the men Dennis wrote about—many of them barely out of high school? Surrounded, trapped, unsure whether they would survive. What kinds of risks had Dennis taken in accompanying the Marines? Had he come under fire? He had always been stubborn and brave to the point of foolhardiness, and she knew he would have stayed as close to the action as he could.

She shivered for a moment. She had seen some of the photographs of the Chosin retreat, the column of Marines trudging through the snow, the mountains rising around them, a barren, unforgiving place. She turned back to his column, remembering how Dennis had told her once that his goal as a newspaperman was to make the reader feel what he felt, to capture in words what he saw around him.

> *The bravery and courage of these men defy description. Surrounded, outnumbered, forced to fight in brutal conditions—heavy snow and nighttime temperatures reaching some 20 degrees below zero where weapons jammed and extremities froze—and short of rations and winter clothing, they faced the worst odds without complaint and overcame them. Many of them survived on nothing more than Tootsie Rolls and jelly beans—the only food that didn't freeze solid.*

> *They never gave up, never lost hope. Not the Marines who broke out of their encirclement at Yudam-ni near the northwest corner of the Chosin Reservoir. Not Lt. Kurt Chew-Een Lee, the tough Chinese-American officer who led a last-ditch relief column through a snowstorm to relieve the besieged men of Fox Company guarding the strategic Toktong Pass. Not the Royal Marines fighting side-by-side with their American allies. Not the supply clerks and cooks and mechanics who picked up rifles and defended the Hagaru perimeter from the enemy. Not New York City-born Private Hector Cafferata who, despite severe wounds, single-handedly held off several human wave attacks on Fox Hill, at one point using his carbine to bat away hand grenades hurled at him like he was Joe DiMaggio hitting fastballs at Yankee Stadium. Not the combat engineers who ignored heavy Chinese fire and placed an air-dropped Treadway bridge across a deep*

gorge at Funchilin Pass, allowing the Marine column to proceed south. None of them gave up.

She stopped reading again and found herself gazing out the bedroom window at the oak and maple trees in the backyard, stripped bare in the winter. She knew at least that Dennis was safe now. Her closest friend in New York, Evelyn Fairchild, had heard from an editor at the *Sentinel* that Dennis had been called back home. Evelyn had been faithfully clipping and mailing his columns to Penny for months. It was hard to find the *Sentinel* on Washington newsstands and Penny didn't want Matthew to know how closely she was following Dennis' coverage of the war; Penny was grateful for her friend's help.

Yet for all of the valor of these men and their officers, too many Marines and soldiers died in the valleys and ridges of the forbidding, near-impassable Taebaek Mountains of northeast Korea. They paid the ultimate price for the arrogance and stubbornness of senior officers in Tokyo who bragged that advancing American troops would be home by Christmas. These same commanders disregarded warnings that the Red Chinese would enter the war if United Nations forces crossed the 38th parallel and advanced north toward the Yalu River and the border with China.

Worse, when it became clear on the ground that we faced an entirely new war with a determined and battle-hardened enemy willing to sacrifice 10 of his soldiers for every one of ours,

General Douglas MacArthur and his staff failed to adjust to these new realities.

General MacArthur revels in taking risks and defying the odds. He bet that the North Koreans would be unprepared for a surprise amphibious assault at Inchon and he was right. He gambled that the Chinese would not risk attacking his advancing armies in the teeth of a Manchurian winter and he was wrong. He lost that bet. And the Marines and soldiers were the ones who paid for his mistake in blood and death.

The lieutenants and captains and majors on Korean battlefields have been, for the most part, magnificent in their inventiveness, bravery, and resolute courage. They have done all that has been asked of them, and more. Yet the men of the First Marine Division, and their now beleaguered comrades-in-arms in the Eighth Army, deserve better leadership at the highest levels of command. That is where they have been failed. I wish that this were not the case, but it is the reality, one that the Secretary of Defense George C. Marshall and President Truman must change. Too much rides on it now. They must act decisively before it is too late, before we see a repeat of the Chosin battle, or worse.

She knew those last few paragraphs of his column would mean trouble for Dennis. She had lived in Washington long enough to know that those who revered General MacArthur, especially his right-wing supporters in the Republican Party, were sensitive to any slights to their hero. Some had even been promoting the General as a Presidential candidate for 1952, although the military setbacks in Korea on MacArthur's watch had quieted such talk.

It was like Dennis to hold MacArthur responsible, by name. She had always loved that about him—he never shied away from telling unpleasant truths, although it often came in the form of a joke or wisecrack. She wondered whether the grim realities of the war had diminished his sense of humor. She hoped not.

She returned the newspaper clippings to the envelope and then placed it under the clothing in the chest. She sat down at her dressing table and found a small pad of paper and pencil. She rarely made New Year's resolutions, but there was unfinished business she needed to resolve in the year ahead. She prayed that she could make progress on her condition, and that she wouldn't need any more extreme treatment, but there was always that possibility. She couldn't delay any longer.

She knew she couldn't wait. She would have to convince Matthew of the moral correctness of what she wanted them to do about Caleb. She had raised it once with him and he had been cool to the idea. He told her that he wanted to think about it, and about all of the consequences. She was sure that he would come around to supporting her wishes. Then she would find a way to bring Dennis to Washington so she could tell him, face-to-face, that he had a son—their child—the consequence of one impulsive, and careless, night of lovemaking in New York.

It had all been so unreal, at first. When she had realized that she was pregnant, after she missed her second period in December and had felt sick on consecutive mornings, she couldn't believe that it was happening to her. It became real as the days passed and she felt the child moving inside her.

She had felt lost, so lost and so vulnerable. She thought, briefly, about ending her pregnancy. She knew there were discreet doctors who for the right price would and could perform an abortion. For whatever reasons, she couldn't bring herself to do that. Her hastily conceived plan was to move to the West Coast and live near her sister, Elizabeth, before she started showing. Once the baby came, she could figure out what to do next.

That never happened, because when she told Matthew the truth early in January, expecting that he would abandon his then-renewed courtship of her, he had surprised her by immediately proposing marriage. She had hesitated before accepting his offer. She worried that he would regret his gallantry later, when the baby came, and he faced the reality of her bringing another man's child into the world.

They placed the engagement announcement in the Washington newspapers in February and were married, in a small ceremony, in early April. Not once had Matthew expressed judgment, and she believed that he had been pleased with the arrival of Caleb not only because of her delight with her baby boy but also because he cared for the child.

It would be hard on him, she thought, to have Dennis Collins back in their lives, but she knew that Matthew would eventually accept her logic. He had always been logical to a fault, a disciplined thinker, willing to accept sound reasoning.

Dennis, impulsive and emotional, still harboring bitterness and resentment toward her, would be another matter. She had never been able to love him in the way he needed her to. She had thrown him over twice and she had treated him thoughtlessly. How could he not despise her? No doubt he thought of her as cold, a heartless bitch, and there was much that was shameful in the way she had treated him. She so regretted that now.

She hoped that he remembered the good times, as well, when they had first started dating, before the war. Those memories were sweet—dancing cheek-to-cheek all night at El Morocco, hurrying through Central Park in a sudden snowstorm eager to get back to her apartment and make love, spending lazy summer weekends on Nantucket where they strolled along Madaket Beach at dusk talking about everything under the sun, even attending the occasional Dodgers game that Dennis dragged her to. Did he think about any of that when he thought of her? Or only the ugly times?

She wished the hurt and the pain they had caused each other could be erased, but she knew there was no going back, no fixing the past. That had been clear when they had seen each other again after years apart and had tried to rekindle their romance. What had gone before was always there, a reminder of failed promises and disappointed love.

Sometimes she wondered if that heaviness of spirit that she felt, that lingering, suffocating dread, was God's punishment for her sins, for her selfishness, for the times in the past when she had betrayed Dennis. When it had really mattered, when any hope of a future with him had hung in the balance, she had deceived him, knowing as she did that somehow whatever there was between them would die. Was she being punished for that? Dr. Rifkin had assured her that it wasn't so, that a loving God would never turn his back on her. She wasn't so sure. Could Dr. Rifkin speak for God?

The news of Caleb would come as a shock to Dennis. How would he react when he learned that she wanted her son to know his father as he grew up? Could Dennis overcome his bitterness toward her and not punish Caleb for the sins of his mother? She hoped that he would eventually understand and accept her idea. He had to. She worried that if she waited to tell Dennis she would lose her nerve. If only she could get him to come and see her, she believed she could say the words to him, the words that would sway him.

She gripped the pen and began to carefully write down what she had to say to Dennis. She wanted to have it scripted out beforehand, so she could make it all clear to him—her regrets, her shame, her desire to repair the harm that she had done. She prayed that he could, in the end, find it in his heart to embrace Caleb, their son, their shared connection to the past and to the future.

One

New Year's Day, a Monday morning. Through the windows of the Lockheed Constellation, Dennis Collins could see Manhattan's distinctive skyline glinting in the winter sunlight as the overnight San Francisco-New York flight began to descend toward Queens and the Idlewild airport. He spotted the Empire State Building and the soaring, idiosyncratic Art Deco spire of the Chrysler Building. As they flew over the East River, the sun reflected off the United Nations Secretariat building, the new blue-green glass skyscraper designed by Le Corbusier that was still under construction. All of it was a welcome sight for Collins, for he was coming home.

As he walked across the tarmac to Idlewild's main terminal Collins glanced around, his eyes slowly adjusting to the morning glare. Inside the building, his brother Frank was waiting. When he caught sight of Collins, a crooked grin appeared on his ruddy face.

In his double-breasted charcoal suit and red-patterned tie, Frank looked sharp, and Collins smiled, remembering how he would kid his brother about being the best-dressed plainclothes detective of New York's Finest. Collins was suddenly conscious of his torn and faded Marine parka, his only warm coat. He should have purchased a civilian overcoat in San Francisco, he realized, and resolved to buy one as soon as he could.

"Hey, Denny," his brother called out. "Happy New Year."

"Happy New Year. Thanks for coming out to pick me up."

"No problem. First time I've ever started the year with a day off. I sort of like it."

"Glad I gave you an excuse to play hooky," Collins said.

They embraced and his brother wrinkled his nose. "Starting early, or didn't you ever stop?"

"You know how I hate to fly," Collins said. "And I didn't get much sleep. I guess I celebrated the New Year on the way."

Collins stopped himself. He didn't have to apologize or explain to his older brother, or to anyone else, about when and where he decided to drink.

"At least you had some decent visibility for your landing," Frank said. "We had heavy fog yesterday and they closed the airport in Newark. Couldn't see fifty feet in front of you in the city."

"We had a nice clear view on the way in. Quite a sight."

"It's a grand city when you see if from the air, ain't it? High time that you were back home."

Collins nodded. He didn't trust himself to say anything more because he was suddenly, unexpectedly, on the verge of tears, overwhelmed by a sudden wave of emotion. Seeing his brother and reaching home had triggered feelings he had kept contained during the longest six months of his life, as he followed the First Division of the Marines through their victories at Inchon and Seoul to their brutal retreat from the Chosin Reservoir.

"Peggy was real excited when you called," Frank said quickly, always sensitive to his brother's moods.

"How is she? And how is Brendan?"

"They're both great. Brendan is looking forward to seeing his favorite uncle. You'll be surprised by how much he has grown. Peggy can't wait to give you some home cooking. We're all really pleased that you're going to stay with us."

"Not for too long," Collins said. "I don't want to get in the way. I'll find a furnished room once I figure some things out. I can't get back into my apartment until June." When he went to Korea, Collins had sublet his place on the Upper West Side to Earl Randolph, a night editor for the Associated Press.

His brother nodded. "You won't be in the way. How was your Christmas? I got your postcard. It must not have seemed like it in Hawaii, with the good weather and all."

"I needed to thaw out."

"That's good, then." Frank paused, hesitating, unsure of himself. Collins knew what he wanted to ask. "It sounds like it was pretty rough over there. From what you wrote in the paper."

Collins didn't say anything. His New Year's resolution—if it could be called that—had been simple: he was going to talk as little as he possibly could about Korea. He figured that was the best way to shake the experience. The more he talked about it, the more the memories would remain vivid. He was already having a difficult time sleeping and when he did doze off he didn't care for his dreams.

"It was hard," Collins said, hoping that his brother would understand. "Very hard." Frank had been a detective long enough to know that there were always things better left unsaid.

Collins had never expected to return to New York in January. He had been recalled to the city by an urgent telegram from his editor, Peter Vandercamp, in the middle of December. It came just days after Collins had joined the evacuation from Hungnam. Vandercamp's message had been brief and to the point: the publisher of the *Sentinel*, Frederick Longworth, had died of a sudden heart attack and the newspaper was in dire financial straits. By the time Collins reached Tokyo a second telegram informed him that the paper would close days before Christmas.

That bad news served to deepen Collins' grim mood. After a brief stay in Tokyo, he began the cross-Pacific trip to Midway. It was difficult to banish the images of the Chosin campaign from his mind as he made the long flight home. Korea had not been his first war as a correspondent—he had covered the Marines in the Pacific—but it had been a different experience. In the island battles of 1944 and 1945 the Japanese had been cut off, isolated without hope of reinforcement, and American victory, while achieved at a horrific cost in lives, was never in doubt. But in Korea, the Marine and Army units that had been confidently pressing north were fighting for their very lives within hours after the Chinese entered the war in November.

Collins spent Sunday in San Francisco with his friend Charlie Adair. They met for an early dinner at Tadich's where they talked movies and baseball. Adair, a Marine veteran, knew better than to inquire too closely about Korea after Collins made a few terse comments about Chosin and didn't elaborate.

After their dinner, Collins took a cab to San Francisco Municipal Airport, arriving in plenty of time for his flight. He shouldn't have spent the money on the airfare back to New York—the train was much less expensive—but he didn't care to wait. He wanted to get back home.

In the first hour aloft, Collins had turned to the copy of *Across the River and into the Trees* he had purchased in Honolulu. He had been saving Hemingway's latest novel for the plane ride and he had looked forward to a large block of uninterrupted time in which to read it. The book started well enough—an opening scene of duck hunting on an iced-over river in Italy, Hemingway sketching the scene without an excess word, and then an encounter between the aging Army colonel and his doctor, signaling that all was not well. Collins admired Hemingway's distinctive, Spartan sentences and authentic and taut dialogue, but he found himself growing irritated as he read further.

Collins was in no mood for dwelling on war memories and failed love affairs. He abandoned the book an hour into the flight, leaving Colonel Cantwell during one of his drunken soliloquies, and decided to get tight himself. He took a few generous pulls on the silver flask that he had tucked in his sweater pocket, enjoying the warmth of the brandy as it coursed down his throat. The lead stewardess gave him a disapproving look. It was not her first silent judgment of the flight. When Collins had boarded wearing his cardigan sweater, frayed button-down shirt, and gabardine trousers she had given him the once over. Collins stared back at her and she looked away. He didn't really care what she thought.

The flask had been a gift to Collins from a Marine captain, Oliver Winslow, a friend. On the third day of December, inside the perimeter at Hagaru when their chances of survival didn't look particularly promising, Winslow had given Collins the flask as an early Christmas present. By then Collins was carrying an M1 Garand rifle himself, as were most of the other combat correspondents. The Chinese Red Army soldiers making nightly assaults on American positions weren't stopping to ask for press credentials. As much as the next man, Collins wanted to live to the morning so he had armed himself.

When he handed Collins the flask, Winslow had joked that every Irishman needed a handy container for his booze. "I bought it at Shreve, Crump & Lowe on Boylston Street last year. It's been gently used, as the saying goes. Almost as good as new."

"The story of my life," Collins said. "Except I can't say that I've been gently used."

In return, Collins gave Winslow his Zippo lighter engraved with the eagle, globe, and anchor emblem of the Marine Corps that he had carried around since Okinawa. Winslow thanked him and slipped the lighter into his parka pocket.

"You do fit the bill for a crazy Irishman," Winslow said. "I'm an expert in spotting the type, you know, because Boston's overrun with them. The proof positive is that you're here when you could be back in Hungnam or Pusan, somewhere warm and safe."

Winslow had been called up from the reserves, leaving a wife and child and prosperous Beacon Hill law practice to rejoin the Corps. Collins thought it was particularly unfair that so many Pacific Theater veterans had been pressed into service. Then again, there was nothing about the conflict in Korea that he could see that was particularly fair.

"It's my job to be here," Collins said.

"Not quite. You're a noncombatant. You ought to clear out of here. No one will think less of you for flying out on the next available transport plane. You're a newspaper guy, remember? And somebody should inform the world about what's really going on here. That's your real job. To tell people how MacArthur and Almond have screwed up royally and to explain that a lot more of us are going to die if the top brass thinks that we can fight the entire Chinese Red Army to a standstill."

"You want to write the column for me?"

"I just did. You can quote me by name. Make sure you add a little poetry. Mention how we proud Marines of the First Division are the citizens of death's gray land."

"Where does that phrase come from? Death's gray land?"

"It's from a poem by Siegfried Sasson about the Great War. An Englishman, despite the name, who had no illusions about the stupidity and horror of war. He won the Military Cross in 1916 for bravery under fire but then refused to return to the front. Sasson sent a letter to his commanding officer, 'Finished with War: A Soldier's Declaration,' that was read in Parliament. I just wish I had his courage. I should send a letter along the same lines to my superiors and to Congress. I don't have the guts."

"You've got plenty of guts."

Winslow smiled slowly. "Well, that's debatable. Is it courage that keeps me here? Or stupidity?" He retrieved an envelope from inside his parka and handed it to Collins. "You can give this back to me when we see each other in Hungnam. Or if that's not in the cards, I want you to make sure it gets to my wife, Beth. If it comes to that, mail it when you get Stateside. I'd like for what I've written to stay private."

"I'll see you soon enough," Collins said, but he took the envelope from Winslow. He could understand why a man wouldn't want his last letter to his wife read by some anonymous military censor.

That night changed Collins' mind about staying in Hagaru. Just after two o'clock Winslow had roused Collins and a few enlisted men, mainly clerks and cooks, from where they dozed by the camp stove in one of the warming tents. Chinese soldiers had breached the nearby defensive line of foxholes and machine-gun placements.

"Grab your weapons," Winslow said. "They're inside our perimeter and coming."

Collins pulled on his fur-lined parka and found his helmet. He picked up his M1, grabbed some loaded clips, and stepped out of the tent, following Winslow and the other men into the half-light. A few other Marines joined them as they cautiously moved toward the sounds of gunfire. Snow was falling rapidly and the cold cut into Collins' face. It hurt to inhale. Their boots made crunching sounds as they broke through the crusted snow. He felt nervous about what lay ahead in the darkness, but the snowfall made it impossible to see more than twenty feet or so in front of them.

Then, without warning, indistinct figures in white emerged suddenly from the dark. Collins fought back his fear. He wondered for a moment whether this was the moment when he would die. Winslow shouted at the Marines to fire and Collins found himself moving into the kneeling firing position and sighting his rifle on the closest figure in front of him. He tried squeezing the trigger only to realize that in his excitement he had left the safety inside of the trigger guard. He flipped the safety off and depressed the trigger and the sudden recoil of the weapon caught him by surprise.

He recovered quickly and began firing as rapidly as he could at the small cluster of Chinese in front of him—men as intent on killing him as he was on killing them—squeezing the trigger slowly as he had been taught. He finished the first clip of eight bullets in what seemed like seconds and quickly slid another into the Garand. He prayed that the carbine wouldn't jam on him, a common failing of the M1 in the extreme cold.

He couldn't tell whether his rounds had hit any of the enemy, but in what seemed like only moments there was no one left standing—just bodies sprawled out awkwardly on the snowy ground in front of them. Collins could feel his entire body shaking from a sudden rush of adrenaline, the shock of the sudden firefight registering on his nervous system.

Later, Winslow took him aside. "Get out of here," he said. "Catch the first outbound flight that you can. This place has become a death trap and it will only become worse when we march out of here. They are all around us and they'll be looking to annihilate us. There's no good reason for you to stay."

Collins knew then that Winslow was correct. There was nothing keeping him there but pride and a sense of loyalty to the men around him. Yet Collins wondered if Winslow had seen something in his face or in his eyes—fatigue, anxiety, perhaps even the fear he was trying hard to mask—that had prompted his friend to again encourage Collins to leave while he could.

"I'll feel like I'm bugging out."

"Is staying here worth your life?" Winslow asked. "You didn't sign up for the duration like we did. No one will think less of you if you leave. You have more than enough to write about now. You know what is happening here and you can tell your readers. You can't do that if you're dead."

Collins nodded reluctantly. He had heard from an aide to General Smith that the Marines would start their breakout to the coast in another day. Collins had no illusions about how dangerous the march south would be.

That was the last time he saw Oliver Winslow, his friend, a man who loved poetry and longed to be back with his wife and son in Boston. Later that day Collins caught one of the C-47 Dakota flights out of Hagaru ferrying wounded Marines to the airstrip in Hungnam. From there he worked his way back up the main road, catching a ride in an Army supply truck ferrying ammunition north. In Chinhung-ni, he waited for the advance elements of the Marine column fighting their way south.

As the men straggled into the village, Collins asked around about Winslow. He had no luck with the first units, but then a captain from the headquarters battalion turned up and told Collins that Winslow hadn't made it past Koto-ri. His men had come under heavy fire when clearing a ridge and Winslow had been killed by a sudden burst of fire from a Chinese machine gun. They had buried him at Koto-ri in a mass grave scraped out of the frozen earth by Marine bulldozers.

Winslow's death had not come as a complete surprise—the officer corps had been hit particularly hard by casualties and Winslow had never shied away from taking the lead when encountering the enemy—but Collins had hoped his friend could have somehow beaten the odds.

He planned to pass along the details of what he learned to Beth Winslow in a cover note that he would send with his friend's last letter. That changed when he was recalled to New York. He figured he might as well travel to Boston and tell her in person. He felt he owed that much to Oliver, to share with his widow what little Collins knew about his friend's last days. He figured that it was the decent thing to do, and sadly, he knew that when it came to Korea, decency was in short supply.

Collins was pulled away from his memories by a question from his brother. "Are we going to be able to hold on?" Frank asked. "The papers say the Reds have started a new offensive and they're driving toward Seoul. The Eighth Army is setting up a defensive perimeter there. It doesn't sound good."

"I don't know what to think," Collins said. He cursed softly at the thought. "If General Ridgway can't get them to hold the line soon, they may have to evacuate the troops to Japan."

"There's talk that if the Russians decide to attack in Germany that we'll need those troops in Europe. People are nervous, Denny, especially the young guys. They know they'll end up in the front lines if we have another world war."

"Let's pray it doesn't come to that," Collins said. He reached into his parka pocket for a cigarette and cursed again when he discovered his package of Chesterfields was empty. Frank silently offered him one of his cigarettes. Collins found his lighter, a replacement Zippo he had bought in Japan at the Tachikawa Airfield PX, and lit up, savoring his first few puffs.

"Makes you wonder if we should be fighting over there in the first place," his brother said. "What do you think? Was it a mistake to send our boys over?"

"I don't think Truman had much of a choice. He figured Stalin was pulling the strings on Kim Il Sung, and if you give Uncle Joe an inch, he'll take a mile. Maybe that was a mistake, but once you're in, you have to see it through."

"Hell of a price to pay, though," Frank said. He gave Collins a light punch on the arm. "You want to get tickets to see Ezzard Charles against this guy Lee Oma at the Garden? It's on the Friday, the twelfth. We could eat dinner beforehand, make a night of it."

Collins had been with the Marines in Seoul when word came in late September that Charles had retained his heavyweight title by defeating an aging Joe Louis in a bout at Yankee Stadium. Collins had been disappointed that Louis, one of his heroes, had been methodically outboxed and battered by the younger fighter—Louis never should have come out of retirement.

"Doesn't sound like it will be much of a fight," Collins said. "Ezzard should flatten Oma early. I think I'll pass."

"You missed a hell of a pennant race," his brother said. "It really was something. The Dodgers had a shot. Last day of the season, all they had to do was beat the Phils at Ebbets Field to force a playoff. I went to that last game, Denny. Ten innings, and then Dick Sisler hit a three-run job and there was no coming back after that. No miracle rally. Then the Yanks win in four against the Phils."

"Stengel has been doing a great job for the Yanks," Collins said. "Can't beat two World Series wins in two years."

His brother snorted. "Give me that much talent and I can manage a ballclub to the World Series."

Collins shook his head. "It only looks easy from the outside. Don't underestimate the difference a skilled manager can make."

"The Dodgers are going to test your theory," Frank said. "What with O'Malley cleaning house, showing Branch Rickey and Shotton the door. I don't get it. We'll see if Chuck Dressen can do any better as the Bums' manager."

Walter O'Malley had bought out Rickey's ownership position with the Dodgers for slightly more than a million dollars. It was common knowledge that the two men detested each other. Burt Shotton had led Brooklyn to two pennants but the mild-mannered manager was one of Rickey's hires, so O'Malley wanted him gone.

"O'Malley let his dislike of Rickey get the better of him," Collins said. "It's a mistake. If I still had a column I'd be writing that."

They had reached the baggage claim area. Collins found his Val Pak folding garment bag and the battered carrying case for his

Royal portable typewriter. With the *Sentinel* shuttered, he figured that the typewriter, once the property of the bankrupt newspaper, had become his souvenir by default.

As they started to leave the baggage area, a man in a dark overcoat and light gray fedora moved purposely forward toward them. The face below the brim of the hat seemed vaguely familiar, but Collins couldn't place it at first. Then he realized, with a start, that it was Andrew Caldwell, an agent with the New York office of the FBI. Frank recognized him as well, because he quickly stepped between his brother and Caldwell.

"What the hell are you doing here?" Frank asked with undisguised hostility. "For Christ's sake, he's just back from Korea. Can't this wait?"

Caldwell spread his arms wide, in a gesture of resignation. "I wish I could, but I can't," he said. He moved closer and Frank reluctantly gave way. Caldwell looked directly at Collins. "We need to talk."

"Is that so?" Collins asked. "What's so damn important that you're bothering me here on my first day back?"

"Matthew Steele."

"Steele? You must be kidding. That bastard? Why would I care to talk about Steele?"

"Let me explain why you should care," Caldwell said. "It's high time that he's made accountable for what he's done, and you're just the man to help us do that."

Collins shook his head. "You've got the wrong guy. I'm not interested."

"Hear me out," Caldwell said. He looked around. "We can talk over there," he said, motioning with his right thumb to an empty, glass-windowed office with a small BAGGAGE CLAIMS sign painted in dark blue letters on its door.

Collins didn't want to go into the office and talk with Caldwell. He couldn't imagine how any good could come of it. Collins had done his best over the past year or so to forget about Steele and Caldwell and all the lousy memories they represented. He knew how federal agents operated, though, and if he didn't talk to Caldwell now, they would follow him and pester him until he agreed to an interview. He might as well get it over with.

He shrugged and nodded and then dropped his cigarette on the floor and ground it out with his heel. Caldwell led the way, opening the glass door and stepping aside so Collins could enter the office first.

Two

A battleship-gray metal desk, a matching file cabinet, and two battered wooden chairs had been crammed into the baggage claims office, leaving little open space. The office looked like it had been used for decades, even though Idlewild—its official name was New York International Airport, but no one called it that—had opened for business in 1947. An abandoned mug of coffee sat on the desktop. Several memos on airline stationary were pinned to a cork bulletin board that had been hung over the desk. From a radio on top of the file cabinet came the sounds of Johnny Mercer and Margaret Whiting singing "Baby, It's Cold Outside." Caldwell reached over and switched the radio off.

"Why don't you sit down?" the FBI agent asked Collins, nodding to one of the chairs.

"No thanks," Collins said. "I've been sitting for hours." He didn't want Caldwell to think that they were going to talk at length. Collins was determined to keep the conversation as brief as possible.

They stood facing each other. Collins glanced through the window and saw that Frank had positioned himself next to the closed door. His brother kept glancing through the glass windows at them, clearly ready to intervene if called upon.

Caldwell took off his hat and placed it on the desk. Being in the confined space of the office with the man brought back a flood of unwelcome memories for Collins. They hadn't spoken since the first day of October 1949, when Caldwell had confronted him at Bellevue Hospital. Collins had been there under the worst of circumstances, and Caldwell had not made it any better.

The federal agent must have sensed what was running through Collins' mind. "Look, I know I said some hard things the last time I saw you. I want to apologize for that. I was angry but you weren't to blame for what happened. It was all Steele's fault, as far as I'm concerned, starting with letting Morris Rose off the hook. You could argue that the girl's death should be on his head as well."

"Her name was Karina Lazda," Collins said.

"Sure. No disrespect intended. Karina Lazda."

Karina had become Collins' lover in that unforgettable last week of September. It was the week America learned that the Soviets had their own atomic bomb, and the week that the Yankees and Dodgers had both battled for the pennant in their respective leagues, and the week that Collins lost whatever illusions that he still had about the world being a just place. Karina had been a refugee, arriving in New York after the war, employed by the United Service for New Americans to help in resettling other so-called displaced persons, or DPs. She had also been a secret, and reluctant, agent for Moscow Center and her decision to break with the Soviets, encouraged by Collins, had gone horribly wrong.

"I'm sorry about what happened," Caldwell said. "We all were. I'd like nothing better than to settle the score on her account."

Collins didn't believe for a moment that Caldwell truly cared about what had happened to Karina. His focus had always been on Morris Rose, a State Department official suspected of subversion who also happened to be Collins' closest friend from childhood. When Morris failed to show up for work in Washington and the FBI had come looking for him, Collins had been less than cooperative. He didn't want to help a politically-motivated witch hunt; he was loyal to his friends, loyal to a fault.

Except Collins had misjudged the situation; he didn't recognize until it was too late that Morris had been working for the Soviets for more than a decade, a true believer in the Marxist illusion, a man willing to betray his country for it.

"What are you doing here, now?" Collins asked Caldwell, eager to finish the conversation. "I don't think you came all the way out here on New Year's Day to apologize to me."

"There have been some developments in the Rose case since you've been in Korea. Bad news for your buddy Matthew Steele."

Collins didn't appreciate Caldwell's sarcasm. Steele, an official with the CIA, could hardly be described as a friend of Dennis Collins. Steele had allowed Rose to escape from New York as part of an elaborate scheme to deceive the Soviets.

"He's no buddy of mine," Collins said flatly. "What's the bad news?"

"Apparently the Soviets figured out what Steele was up to. His plan to feed false information back to Moscow has failed."

"You're sure of that?"

"That's what I'm hearing from Washington."

Collins was dismayed. It meant that there was nothing to show for Karina's death, for her sacrifice—not that Collins believed that any intelligence breakthrough for Steele and his Agency could ever be worth her life, but now the whole episode seemed so pointless.

"Apparently your other buddy, Morris Rose, is riding high," Caldwell said. "He has been spotted in Warsaw and Budapest on a few occasions, always in the company of a pretty girl. A traitor to his country now living the life of Riley. These are credible reports, by the way, from European diplomats who knew him when he was with the State Department. Rose is as Red as they come. What the hell Steele was thinking?"

Collins understood full well why the FBI wanted to pin the blame on Steele. When he defected, Rose had walked away with the Counterespionage Division of the Bureau's closely held list of suspected Soviet agents in the government. It made J. Edgar Hoover and his vaunted G-men look bad, and they held Steele responsible.

"So Steele's plan failed," Collins said.

"It failed big time. Makes you wonder about the entire set-up. If Steele had let us arrest Rose, we could have squeezed him and rolled up the rest of the Reds in the State Department. But Steele was too damn eager to try his Little League hidden-ball trick."

"I don't get where this is going," Collins said. "I don't see where I fit in."

"We need your help," Caldwell said. "We want to dig deeper into what went wrong. Exactly what did Steele tell you? Did he discourage you from cooperating with the Bureau? Did he introduce you to anyone? We need as much detail as you can remember. Chapter and verse. You see, we're not satisfied with his story."

Collins shook his head. "Why would I waste a second of my time on this?"

"I figured you of all people would want to set the record straight. Don't you want someone held accountable for what happened to Miss Lazda?" Caldwell kept his eyes locked on Collins, searching his face for a reaction.

Collins stared back at him. It was true that Karina had been a pawn in the entire episode and Collins had been one, too, but Caldwell just wanted ammunition to use against Steele.

Collins wanted no part of it. He had no desire to remember what it had felt like to watch Karina's life slip away in the moments after she was struck down by a sniper's bullet. He didn't want to relive the pain and anger in the days and months that followed when he fully understood she had been torn away from him. That's all that talking about that week would do.

"How the hell did you know I would be here today?" he asked Caldwell. "My brother was the only one I called about my flight." He wondered for a moment if Frank's phone had been tapped.

"We figured you would be coming home after the *Sentinel* folded," Caldwell said. "The San Francisco office asked Pan Am to let us know when you purchased a ticket to New York."

"I've heard enough," Collins said, ready to end the conversation. He pushed the door open. "I've no use for this."

Caldwell followed him outside, where Frank stood with his arms crossed.

"This could have waited, buddy," his brother said to Caldwell. "He ain't going anywhere. What's the rush?"

Caldwell gave him a hard stare. "It's time to take a close look at Steele. You're a cop. You saw firsthand how he botched the Rose case."

Frank snorted derisively. "From what I remember, you and your partner were supposed to track down Morris Rose. You never did. Never even got close. So who failed?"

Caldwell flushed red with anger. "Steele blocked us every step of the way. He needs to explain why."

"Who cares?" Collins said. "I certainly don't. I want no part of your vendetta."

"You're making a mistake," Caldwell said. He gripped his hat in his hands, struggling to control himself. "Your last few columns from Korea put you back on the radar in Washington. Lots of people in high places aren't happy about what you wrote. Defeatist crap. Questioning the war, attacking General MacArthur. Far from patriotic, if you ask me. So on this Steele thing, we can't force you to assist us, but it would be in your best interests to do so."

"Or what? Are you going to follow me around? Tap my phone? I've done nothing wrong."

"I don't know why you would protect Steele. The bastard doesn't deserve it." Caldwell's face had stiffened with anger. "I've read your columns. You're big on people doing the right thing. Well, it's time for you to step up and do the right thing."

Collins didn't respond. He had other reasons for not helping Caldwell, personal ones. Collins knew that if he did it would look like he was trying to hit back at Penny through her husband. He wasn't about to share that with the FBI agent. It was none of his business. Before he could say anything more, his brother intervened.

"He's not buying what you're selling," he told Caldwell. "So why don't you let us be on our way?"

Caldwell clapped his hat back on his head. "Sure," he said, reluctantly. He looked directly at Collins. "If you change your mind, you know where to find us."

"Don't wait around for that," Collins said. "It won't ever happen. At least not in this life."

They watched the FBI man make his exit, elbowing his way through a crowd of passengers eager to collect their baggage. He disappeared through the far entranceway doors and was quickly lost from sight.

"What's going on, Denny?" Frank asked. "I thought you'd put the Morris Rose thing behind you."

"I thought so, too."

"I had a phone call two days ago at the office that I need to talk to you about."

"A call? Who from?"

"Matthew Steele. I wasn't about to mention it in front of Caldwell after he started in on you."

Collins cursed. "What the hell does Steele want? I can't believe he has the balls to approach me. After what he did?" Collins called Steele some crude names and his brother waited patiently for him to finish.

"He wants to talk with you," Frank said. "I told him in no uncertain terms and in language he probably ain't used to hearing that you had no interest. I give him credit—he didn't hang up the phone."

"What else did he say?"

"He wants you to come down and see him in Washington."

"Did you tell him I was in Korea?"

"He knew that. He also knew you were on your way back to New York."

"Did he say what the hell this is all about? He's the last man on earth I want to see."

"Steele said it had to do about Korea. He wanted to talk about the situation there."

"Is he out of his mind? Why would I spend thirty seconds talking with that son-of-a-bitch about Korea or anything else?"

"I told him as much. Told him not to waste his breath."

They walked in silence through the parking lot, Frank leading the way to the spot where he had parked his Chevrolet sedan. After Collins had put his luggage in the trunk, he climbed into the passenger seat. Frank got behind the wheel.

"I'm sorry you got blindsided by this," his brother said. "I was going to wait to tell you about Steele. I know it brings up a lot of ugly history."

"It does. If he had been straight with me from the start, if he hadn't kept me in the dark, Karina never would have been put at risk. She'd be alive today."

"Then there's the thing with Penny. Hard feelings there, too."

"That's different," Collins said. "I don't blame him for that. That was her choice. Like they say, all's fair in love and war. And like you said once, they deserve each other."

His brother put the key in the ignition, and then paused before starting the engine. "Are you going to stop by the other papers?"

"You mean, will I be looking for a job now that the *Sentinel* is shut? I don't know. I've got enough saved to tide me over. Didn't spend a lot of money during the last six months." He paused, not sure how to express his restlessness. "I've been thinking. I'm not ready to rush back into newspapering. I don't know whether I want to stay in the business."

"Seriously? You want to leave newspapers, Denny?"

"It gets tough being the bystander at all the train wrecks. Maybe it's time to try something else."

"Like what?"

"I don't know. Maybe I'll apply to be a detective. I hear it's a soft job with high pay."

"Funny, Denny. If you're not looking for a job right away, maybe you ought to take a vacation. Someplace warm. Where the girls are friendly."

"I don't need a girl right now, Frank."

"Yes, you do, Denny. You need to laugh a little. Sit on a beach with her. Drink some of those fruity drinks. Maybe even get laid."

"Thanks for the brotherly advice, but I have some other things to do. I have to go up to Boston to see the wife of a friend, a Marine captain I met in Korea who didn't make it back."

"Don't envy you that." Frank leaned forward, his hands on the steering wheel. "So what do you want to do, now? We can go over to Killeen's and have a few beers and talk. Or we can stay there all day drinking and close the place if you want. You've got a head start on me, but I can catch up. Peggy will be pissed when we roll in as drunk as kings, but it wouldn't be the first time and she'll get over it."

"No, we can go to your place now," Collins said. "Maybe stop on the way and grab something to eat." He paused. "I'm glad to be back home. I can't say the last stretch has been good for me. It hasn't. Lots of really bad memories."

"Hey, look on the bright side," his brother said, starting the car and putting it in gear. "You gotta believe that 1951 will be better than 1950. Like Johnny Mercer says, you gotta accentuate the positive and eliminate the negative. Things will work out fine."

Collins nodded in agreement—the New Year had to be better. And why not? Collins was back home, in one piece, with the pain and darkness of Korea far behind him. No more encounters with the thousand-yard stares of Marines who had seen too much combat. No more watching the cruel twists and turns of war tear apart the lives of bewildered Korean peasants. He was lucky. He had walked away before he became a casualty himself.

It was time to shut the door on all of that, and on Andrew Caldwell and Matthew Steele and everything else in his past that was ugly and painful, and to keep it tightly closed.

"You're right, Frank," he said out loud. "Why shouldn't things work out just fine?"

Three

Collins left his brother's home on Friday morning and took the subway to Herald Square. He had spent four days in Brooklyn, sleeping late, reading the papers, and enjoying and appreciating the everyday domestic routines of Frank's family.

On the warmer days, Tuesday and Wednesday, Collins played catch outside with Brendan in the afternoon after he had finished school. When the cold kept them in later in the week, he admired his nephew's baseball card collection, and told Brendan a few entertaining inside-the-clubhouse stories about his Dodgers heroes, Jackie Robinson and Duke Snider.

It was a treat for Collins to sit down to home-cooked meals after months of C-rations and mess hall food. Convinced that her brother-in-law had become too thin, Peggy kept serving Collins seconds until he had to insist that she stop.

At night, Collins waited until Peggy and Brendan had gone to bed before he began drinking with Frank. On Wednesday morning Peggy had been upset by the number of empty Rheingold bottles she found on the kitchen counter. Collins overheard Frank arguing with her later. Sometimes a man needed to blow off steam, Frank told her, and it was better that his brother not spend his nights drinking alone. "He's still wound up from being over there," Frank said. "He needs to relax and having a few beers helps him do that, and having me there helps, too."

Collins figured that Peggy would welcome a day to herself, so he decided to spend Friday in Manhattan. The subway car was crowded and Collins read the morning papers standing up with one hand on the center pole. He started with the *Times*. The front page news was uniformly bad. In Korea, the Chinese Communists had captured Seoul and the Eighth Army continued to retreat south. President Truman told the press that despite calls in Congress to bomb mainland China, he would not do so without a formal declaration of war. General Dwight Eisenhower was reported to be ready to fly to Paris and assume command of the North Atlantic Treaty Organization's military forces.

Collins flipped through the *Daily News* and the *Daily Mirror*. Ike Williams was set to defend his lightweight champion's title against the Argentine boxer Jose Gatica that evening at Madison Square Garden. Ed Sullivan noted in his "Little Old New York" column that actress Merle Oberon had become a redhead. The police raided the Spotlight Cafe on Broadway and arrested three men linked to the mobster Meyer Lansky for taking bets on college basketball. Most of the local stories had been pushed deeper into the papers—the front page headlines all dealt with the worsening international situation.

Collins told himself he wasn't going to brood about Korea. He had been looking forward to his day. He had lunch scheduled at Toots Shor's with Peter Vandercamp, the *Sentinel*'s former managing editor. Then he planned to stop off at the Biltmore Hotel for drinks with Jim Highsmith, a friend he had made in the Pacific, who was in New York on business. Now retired from the Marine Corps, Highsmith ran a small restaurant and hotel in Key West.

The forecast was for clear and cool weather all day, with the temperatures predicted to stay in the high thirties. It was warm enough to walk the streets and take in Manhattan, he decided. When he emerged from the 34th Street station, he found Herald Square bathed in morning sunlight, the familiar crowds jamming the sidewalks, the familiar traffic flowing down Broadway and up Sixth Avenue.

Collins decided to walk north to the *Sentinel* building on West 39th Street. When he arrived there, he found the sign that boldly proclaimed that the newspaper was "the Conscience of the City" was still hanging over the front door.

It had only been a few weeks since the *Sentinel* had been shuttered. Eventually the building would be leased to a new tenant and the sign would be removed. Collins stepped back on the sidewalk and gazed up at the fifth-floor windows, somehow expecting to catch a glimpse of editors and reporters moving about in the newsroom. But no one was talking on the phones or pounding away on typewriters or monitoring the teletype machines. It seemed impossible. The newsroom always began to stir with activity in the late morning as the line-up for the next day's paper started to take shape. That the room had gone silent, permanently, greatly disturbed Collins.

In retrospect, the demise of the *New York Sentinel* was predictable. Many of the city's smaller daily newspapers had run into financial trouble. Ralph Ingersoll's left-wing daily *PM* had folded in 1948. Two years later Scripps-Howard had merged the *Sun*, where Collins had landed his first newspaper job, with the *World-Telegram*. The *Sentinel* had struggled to compete for readers and advertisers with the more popular morning tabloids, the *Daily News* and *Daily Mirror*. When Fred Longworth died, his willingness to subsidize the *Sentinel* died with him.

Collins walked back to Broadway and then turned north. When he reached Times Square, the sidewalks were filled with people enjoying the milder weather—office workers, tourists, shoppers, sightseers. Collins looked around at the theater fronts and the massive neon signs and billboards that dominated the square. The familiar Camel sign was still belching smoke rings, and the garish Bonds billboard remained an eyesore. Little had changed.

He walked north at a relaxed pace as he made his way to Toots Shor's restaurant on 51st Street. When he arrived at Shor's, Collins went through the revolving door into the foyer, where he left his fedora with Thelma, the restaurant's hatcheck girl. The early lunch crowd was already there, most clustered around the circular bar that was the restaurant's signature feature. The tourists would come later, for dinner, hoping to perhaps spy Joe DiMaggio or Jackie Gleason or Frank Sinatra, all buddies of Toots who frequented the place.

Collins listened to the chatter of the regulars around the bar, about the prospects for the Yankees and the Giants and the Dodgers, how great Judy Holliday's performance in *Born Yesterday* had been, whether real estate prices were going to rise, and whether Ezzard Charles could hold onto his heavyweight title. It made Collins feel at home.

When he turned around, he found the large, heavyset figure of Toots Shor towering over him. Shor enveloped him in a bear hug. "Hey, crumb bum," he said. "Great to see you back safe and sound. We were worried about you."

"Thanks, Toots," Collins said. "I'm fine. I was lucky to get back in one piece." Shor had always welcomed Collins to his place, largely because as a boxing fan Toots respected Collins for his brief Golden Gloves career. Collins didn't rate among the restaurateur's favorite newspapermen, a distinction held by Quentin Reynolds, Frank Conniff, and Bob Considine, but he was always seated at a choice table.

"You run into Conniff?" Shor asked. "How is he doing?" Hearst had sent Conniff, a columnist for the *Journal-American*, to Korea as a combat correspondent. Collins had encountered him twice during the campaign for Inchon and Seoul, but Conniff hadn't accompanied the First Marines north as had Collins.

"Saw him a few times. He's keeping his head down."

"Great. Sorry about the *Sentinel* folding. Are you tapioca? Tapped out? I can give you the pencil if that would help."

"No, I'm not flush but I've got some savings to tide me over. I won't have to go on the cuff."

"Not on the cuff," Shor said, feigning hurt at the thought. "I'm not like that raisin cake Billingsley, I don't give anything away. You'd sign for it and I figure you'd be good for it when you get back on your feet." Shor's feud with Sherman Billingsley, owner of the Stork Club, had started years before when Billingsley had fired Shor from his job as a bouncer at the Five O'Clock Club.

"Thanks for the vote of confidence," Collins said. He glanced back toward the front door. "I'm here for lunch with Peter Vandercamp. Seen him?"

"Van hasn't come in yet," Shor said. "You missed the Series, Denny. DiMag was marvelous, like always. That home run he hit in the second game of the Series was a beaut. Tenth inning, wins the game."

"They handled the Phillies pretty easily. The Dodgers would have given them a better Series."

"You Brooklyn guys are hopeless. The Yanks are just too strong. That's not going to change. The front office just sent DiMag the same contract as last year, so I guess we've got the Dago for at least another season." Shor rattled the ice cubes in his glass. "I'm working on a brandy and soda. What can we get you?"

Before Collins could respond he felt a light tap on the shoulder. It was Peter Vandercamp, with his shock of white hair and bushy eyebrows, his appearance unchanged from when Collins had seen him last in June. They embraced awkwardly.

"How are you, Van?" Shor asked.

"I'm fine," Vandercamp said. "And how is Baby?"

Shor beamed. "She's great." Baby, Shor's long-suffering wife, was a former chorus girl and as petite as Toots was gigantic.

"Give her my best, would you?" Vandercamp asked.

"I will," Shor said. "Count on it."

Shor insisted on leading them to a well-positioned table at the back of the dining room, near the fireplace, and called the waiter over to take their drink order before he left them.

"What was that all about?" Collins asked Vandercamp. "How come he treats you like you were the Pope?"

"The Pope? Toots is one of the 'Chosen People' so I don't think he would be catering to the Pope. No, he apparently heard that I was in seminary when I was younger and Baby, who is Catholic, wanted to meet me. We got along famously, and that has worked wonders for me with Toots."

Vandercamp had an intriguing background. He came from a wealthy Old New York family and, to the dismay of his parents, had converted to Catholicism and spent five months in a seminary before realizing that he wasn't called to the priesthood. Vandercamp had gravitated to the newspaper world; Fred Longworth had recruited him from the city room of the *New York Herald Tribune* to become the *Sentinel*'s managing editor. Vandercamp had earned the respect and trust of his colleagues with his encyclopedic knowledge, deft line editing, and gentle sense of humor.

He had been more than just Collins' boss, he had also been his mentor and friend. Vandercamp had fought to keep Collins at the *Sentinel* when it surfaced that Collins had once touted fighters for cash when he was a sportswriter at the *Sun*—a mistake that Collins deeply regretted—and when Collins attracted the attention of the FBI and CIA because of his connection with Morris Rose. Collins had been grateful for Vandercamp's unwavering support.

"What have you been up to?" Vandercamp asked.

"I've been walking around playing tourist. Trying to adjust to being back. I went by 39th Street and the *Sentinel* building was deserted."

Vandercamp shook his head. "I hated to send you that cable," he said. "More bad news at a time when you were in the thick of it. Didn't have a choice. We had to bring you back."

"It didn't exactly make my day," Collins said.

"It was quite a shock to all of us, Fred's death, and the financial collapse of the paper. Who would have thought that we'd be publishing on December 22nd and closed the next day? From what I understand, that let the business office collect the last of the Christmas advertising revenues and pay some outstanding debts."

"When I heard the news I thought about staying in Korea," Collins said. "Maybe catching on with one of the wire services."

"Why didn't you?"

"Chosin was hard. I was looking over my shoulder the entire time. I figured it was time to come home."

"The last column you wrote from Korea, where you met the Marine column marching to the sea, was damn fine reporting and writing. I had Fred Longworth read it in advance, including the tough part about General MacArthur. He told me to go ahead and publish it."

"Was there any question about running it?" Collins asked.

"Not in my mind, but I wasn't the owner. I knew it might cause Longworth some grief. You went straight to the heart of the matter. MacArthur's arrogance, the Marines who deserved better. Like I said, a damn fine column. To his everlasting credit, Longworth thought so, too."

"It wrote itself," Collins said. "You know how that is."

"Accept the compliment, Dennis. You and Maggie Higgins at the *Trib* produced the best reporting from the front, hands down."

"Thanks, Van."

The waiter returned with their drinks and they ordered lunch. Collins chose a club sandwich on toast and Vandercamp asked for the fish special. Vandercamp took a sip of his martini and Collins drank some of his Rheingold.

"Reading anything of interest these days?" Vandercamp asked.

"I tried the new Hemingway on the plane," Collins said. "Too maudlin. Maybe too close to the bone. What about you?"

"Something much lighter. Travel guides for my Grand Tour of Europe. A trip I always promised myself I would take when I was younger but never did."

"Then you're not looking for a paper?"

"No, I'm ready to move on to other things," Vandercamp said. "I've been relatively prudent over the years and so I don't need to return to work unless I wish to. Like every retired newspaperman I'm thinking about writing a book. Nearly everyone else on the *Sentinel* has caught on somewhere. The *Trib* hired Pete Marquis. Hal Diderick persuaded the *Journal-American* to take him on. Some of the nightside crew went to the Associated Press."

"I'm glad that they landed on their feet."

Collins heard his name called and looked over to find Lonnie Marks had come over to their table. The dapper little press agent grinned at him. "I saw you back here and I had to stop by and say hello," he said. "You're fresh back from Korea?"

"That I am."

They shook hands and Collins introduced Marks to Vandercamp. Marks handled publicity for several New York actors and an occasional Broadway show. Collins had met him when he first began writing his column for the *Sentinel* and Marks had always been a great source for show business news.

"I'm sorry about the fate of the *Sentinel*, gentlemen," Marks said. "I've missed reading your column, Denny. Now that you're back in New York which of the papers will you be writing for now?"

"I'm not sure," Collins said. "That's still up in the air."

"Let me know if you need a reference," Marks said. "You've got a lot of fans and I'm one."

Collins thanked Marks. Like most press agents, Marks' stock-in-trade was flattery but Collins still didn't mind hearing that he was missed.

Marks hadn't finished. "I have some great stuff on the new Rodgers and Hammerstein show *The King and I* that's opening in March. They've recruited Gertrude Lawrence, the British actress, to play the role of Anna and a mysterious young man, Yul Brynner, to play the king. Hurry up and get your column back so we can spread the good word." He paused. "By the way, we should get together for drinks and dinner with one of my new clients, Alison Winchester.

She's going to make it big on Broadway. Singing, dancing, acting, she's got what it takes to be a star."

"Sure," Collins said. "Just give me a call." He doubted he would hear from Marks. The press agent had a seemingly inexhaustible supply of young actors and singers who all were, Marks insisted, future stars.

"Must go," Marks said. "I'll be in touch." He nodded to them both and disappeared into the crowd around the bar. There were more people jammed in the front of the restaurant now, and Collins was glad they were at a distance from the lunchtime crowd. Their waiter returned with their food and Collins took a bite of his club sandwich, found the toast was too dry, and washed it down with a gulp of beer. It reminded him that Toots' place wasn't known for its food.

"Lonnie Marks introduced me to Karina Lazda," Collins told Vandercamp, recalling that Friday night at the Stork Club when he had first met Karina. It seemed so long ago, now, a moment lost in his past.

"We've never really talked about her," Vandercamp said. "About what happened."

"We had a week together. We were good together. She died. There's not much more to say." He lifted his beer glass and drank. He regretted having mentioned Karina, because he didn't really want to talk about her.

"But you cared for her." Vandercamp's voice was gentle.

"That I did," Collins said. "I fell hard for her."

"They say it happens, that a man and a woman can fall head-over-heels. Bolt of lightning. The French call it *un coup de foudre*. Can't say I was ever so lucky."

Collins was surprised. In all the years he had known him, Van had never discussed his private life.

"I was married, briefly," Vandercamp said. "You probably didn't know that and I don't advertise it. Jane thought that I loved the paper more than her. She was right. I was working long hours and I came home one early morning and found she was gone. A note on the kitchen table. She packed all of her belongings and took off."

"I'm sorry."

"Nothing to be sorry about. It was a mismatch from the start. I've given it a lot of thought, about where it went wrong. I have learned one thing, you can't let the days and weeks pass without addressing whatever is missing, because you turn around and it has become years. What are you going to do next, Denny? Have you thought about it?"

"I don't know, Van. It seems like everything is up in the air. I'm not sure that I'm ready to go back to covering the fights and baseball and Broadway shows yet. This last stretch was hard, like I told you. I think I need a break. There are other things to consider. Agent Caldwell of the FBI was waiting for me at the airport when I flew in on Monday. They're still looking into what happened back in 1949. Caldwell said my column about MacArthur didn't make me any friends in Washington."

"Unfortunately we live in an age of suspicion," Vandercamp said. "Everyone's loyalty has come under scrutiny, even newspaper columnists."

Collins nodded. During the past year too many newspaper headlines had been about loyalty and suspected Communist subversion. In January, Alger Hiss, a former high ranking State Department official, had been convicted of lying about his role as a

Soviet agent. A month later, a German-born physicist, Klaus Fuchs, confessed to the British that he had passed atomic secrets to Moscow. In May, the FBI picked up Harry Gold, Fuchs' courier, and that summer arrested a New York couple, Julius and Ethel Rosenberg, who the Bureau claimed had run a Soviet spy ring targeting atomic secrets.

In Congress, they had held hearings about Communist penetration of the State Department. Senator Joe McCarthy continued to charge that the government was full of spies without offering any concrete proof. Although the Truman Administration rejected McCarthy's wild claims, the Security Board the president had established kept discharging federal employees on loyalty grounds. That wasn't enough, apparently, because in September both the House and Senate overwhelmingly voted to override the president's veto of the Internal Security Act, a law Truman had called unconstitutional. Collins had been with the Marines outside of Seoul then, and had been dismayed by what was happening in Washington.

"Are you telling me I might run into questions about my politics if I decide to jump back into newspapers?"

"I'm afraid that perceptions do matter," Vandercamp said mildly. "So do reputations. Publishers are nervous about the loyalty question these days. They don't want trouble."

"So what are you saying?"

"It may take some time for you to find something with today's climate. It'd be easier if you wanted to do straight sports."

"You realize how absurd this all is, don't you?" Collins took another drink of his beer and noticed his hand shook slightly as he put the glass down. "I'm no lefty, I just root for the underdog. When did that stop being an American thing to do?"

"I understand. But keep a low profile for a while. Let things settle down. Get some rest. You've paid a cost for Korea. I speak as a friend. You don't look good."

"I know I've been drinking too much," Collins said. "I didn't come back in the best frame of mind." He looked ruefully at the glass of beer in front of him. Vandercamp didn't say anything.

The truth was that Collins had been struggling with his emotions for more than a year, since he lost Karina. He had been angry for most of the winter of 1950, bitter about his betrayal by Morris, about being manipulated and used, and resentful of the lies and half-truths Penny Allen Bradford, the other woman in his life, had told him. He drank too much during that season of discontent. At work, he went through the motions, filing columns that were flat and predictable.

By the early summer he had lost much of his anger but it had been replaced by feelings of numbness and detachment. He went to the Broadway openings, wrote about the Dodgers' poor start, covered the burgeoning gambling scandal that threatened to implicate the Mayor, and looked for the quirky human interest stories that Peter Vandercamp favored, but he took little pleasure in what he had once loved doing.

When the war started in Korea, Collins had persuaded Vandercamp that the *Sentinel* should send him there to cover the fighting. Collins figured he could find a renewed purpose in telling the Korean story. He secretly hoped that he could lose himself in the routine of reporting and writing and in the adrenaline rush of covering combat.

He got it wrong, of course. Collins hadn't found a new purpose in Korea. By Chosin, he had realized that he didn't really want to see any more of war. He returned from Korea in worse shape than when he left, physically exhausted and emotionally tapped out.

Collins broke the awkward silence. "I know I should go on the wagon," he told Vandercamp. "I'm planning to do that. I need to get away. I have a few things to resolve first, though. I have a trip to Boston and then afterward I'm going to take a vacation."

"If there's anything I can do, let me know," Vandercamp said.

"Thanks, Van. I appreciate it."

Collins didn't spot Toots Shor anywhere near the front of the restaurant after they had finished lunch and were ready to leave. He retrieved his hat and followed Vandercamp out into the street. They shook hands and Vandercamp gently detained Collins for a moment with a hand on his coat sleeve.

"You'll figure it out," he said. "I have faith that you will find your way."

"I'm glad that you do. Have faith, that is."

"I do. And one other thing. When you were a boxer, back in your Golden Gloves days, I'll bet your coach told you to keep jabbing away and eventually you'd get a chance to land a hook. That's what you need to do, Denny, jab away for now, buy yourself some time."

"I'm not sure the metaphor holds up, Van, but I get your point. And thanks for the advice."

Vandercamp nodded his farewell to Collins and then slowly made his way up 51st Street, heading east, slightly hunched over, as he negotiated his way through the crowded sidewalk. Collins lit up a cigarette and stood there for a moment, taking a few puffs, thinking about his conversation with his friend.

He appreciated Van's closing pep talk. It was true that as a boxer you learned to get up off the canvas after you'd been knocked down, and to keep punching away even when you were behind on the scorecard. Anything could happen as long as you stayed on your feet.

Collins had learned those lessons in the ring, but he wasn't convinced that they held up in life. Sometimes standing there toe-to-toe and taking a drubbing didn't get you anything more than a lot of cuts and bruises. Sometimes it was better to get out of the ring, to take a break, to get away. Collins liked that idea. It sure beat taking an unnecessary pounding.

Four

Collins always thought of F. Scott Fitzgerald when he walked into the Biltmore Hotel and glanced up at the ornamental bronze clock prominently placed over the Palm Court entrance. Fitzgerald had made the clock famous as a rendezvous spot for couples in his short story "May Day," and lovers were still meeting there some thirty years after the story had appeared in *Tales of the Jazz Age*.

But no one was lingering under the Biltmore clock when Collins arrived at the Palm Court. It was too early in the day for a romantic rendezvous, he figured, and the restaurant looked nearly deserted. The maître d' led Collins to the far side of the dining room where Jim Highsmith awaited him at a corner table. Highsmith, a lanky, deeply tanned man with a salt-and-pepper crewcut, wore a brown-and-tan houndstooth suit that was clearly too lightweight for January in New York.

He greeted Collins with a firm handshake. Highsmith, a Marine Corps major, had been the executive officer of a tank battalion when Collins first met him on Okinawa in 1945. Collins had followed the tankers as they rooted out Japanese defenders in the caves that honeycombed the island's southern highlands with cannon fire and flamethrowers. It had been hard fighting, the dirty, thankless, often grisly work of war. He had been impressed that Highsmith refused to demonize the Japanese. "They've been misled," he told Collins. "Taught that the emperor is divine and that sacrificing themselves for him is glorious. I'm sure some of those poor devils out there may be having second thoughts, now, but their officers shoot anyone trying to surrender."

Highsmith became one of the Pacific Theater veterans, along with Charlie Adair, that Collins had stayed in touch with after the war. Highsmith had landed in Key West, his wife Marta's hometown, after he left the Corps in 1945. They had bought a restaurant and small hotel on Amelia Street and things had gone well—a gregarious host, Highsmith had a talent for the business—until his wife came down with cancer and died a year later.

Highsmith waved Collins into the empty seat opposite him. "My father brought me here for lunch when I was fifteen years old," Highsmith said. He leaned back in his chair and gazed up at the ceiling above them. "Nothing has changed. The place still looks like a miniature Grand Central concourse. Same skylight and mirrors and there's no question that they had to keep the palms."

"Classic old New York," Collins said. "I didn't know you had spent any time in the city."

"My branch of the family is originally from Upstate," Highsmith said. "Near Albany. The Bank of New York still handles my finances. It gives me a reason to visit every so often to take care of banking matters."

A waiter appeared and Collins thought about switching to coffee for a moment and then ordered a beer. Since he had eaten lunch, it wasn't like he would be drinking on an empty stomach.

"I talked with Charlie on the phone a couple of days ago," Highsmith said. "He told me that you spent some of Sunday together in San Francisco."

"We had a good time," Collins said. "Got caught up. Wished I could have stayed for New Year's Eve but I had a ticket for the overnight flight back."

"Charlie said you didn't want to talk much about Korea."

"That's true," Collins said. He shook his head. "It was the worst I've seen, Jim. Sheer insanity. All those men killed or wounded because of the towering arrogance of that megalomaniac sitting in the Dai Ichi building in Tokyo."

"Easy there," Highsmith said. "That's pretty strong stuff. You might want to tone that down a bit."

"You can't be a MacArthur fan."

"I'm not, but I don't think all the blame lies with him. Truman and Marshall agreed to send him across the 38th parallel, after all. He wouldn't have moved north without orders to do so."

They were interrupted by the waiter. He poured Collins' Rheingold into a glass and replaced Highsmith's bourbon and water. Collins took a few sips of the beer and then moved his glass closer to the middle of the table, where he would have to stretch to reach it. That would help him slow down a bit.

Collins waited until the waiter was out of earshot. "Orders or not, who would be arrogant enough to send men to fight in that weather and think they could succeed? Many of the M1 carbines jammed. Mortar rounds fell short because the charges didn't work properly in the cold. The casualties from frostbite and exposure were staggering. But MacArthur insisted on pushing on to the Yalu. And then he split his forces with sixty miles of mountains between the Eighth Army and the Tenth Corps. I may not have graduated from West Point, but I know that violates sound battlefield tactics. There's a reason he did it, but it's a sorry reason."

Highsmith didn't respond. Collins could see that his friend was uncomfortable with the drift of the conversation.

Collins glanced over at his beer glass and resisted the urge to reach for it. "He did it because he could. I'm convinced that

MacArthur ordered the advance because he saw a chance to make history. After Inchon, he figured the Supreme Commander for the Allied Powers didn't have to follow the book. The laws of war, the laws of physics themselves no longer applied. And if MacArthur said the Chinese weren't going to enter the war, they weren't."

"He made some mistakes," Highsmith said. "But he was trying to end the war as fast as possible."

"He told the troops they'd be home by Christmas," Collins said. He reached over for his glass and took a drink. "I don't think they thought that meant coming back home in a coffin, though."

"You need to let it go. You can't carry it around with you. That isn't healthy."

Now that he had started, though, Collins didn't want to stop. He took another sip of his beer. "Chosin could have been another Little Big Horn, you know. The Army units on the east side of the reservoir were wiped out for all practical purposes. It was touch and go for the Marines. The Chinese almost succeeded in cutting off Litzenberg's Seventh Regiment at Yudam-ni. Thank God there was an airstrip at Hagaru for resupply. They flew out four thousand wounded men. I was on one of the last flights out."

"Lots of things go wrong in war," Highsmith said. "We made our fair share of mistakes on Okinawa, too."

"This is different, Jim. The Chinese are willing to trade ten, twenty, thirty men for one American. I talked to some Marines who thought the Chinese soldiers were drugged up—they were wearing tennis sneakers and quilted jackets in temperatures that dropped to twenty below and they kept attacking, charging right into concentrated machine-gun fire. If we didn't kill them, the frostbite and exposure did. But they kept coming."

He paused, aware that across the table, Highsmith was intently studying him. "I keep thinking about what this friend of mine said to me at Hagaru, just before the breakout to the coast. He told me he wished he had the guts to quit. Talked about Siegfried Sasson, this British officer in the First World War who refused to go back in the trenches and sent a letter to his commander to that effect. My friend, a captain from Boston named Oliver Winslow, didn't write a letter. He stayed with his men."

Highsmith nodded. "Like I would have, or Charlie Adair. If you ask me, I think we need to take the gloves off. President Truman should let the Air Force hit the Yalu River area hard and take out the bridges, the roads, the staging area, even if they have to bomb Chinese territory." He looked over at Collins. "What happened with your friend?"

"He didn't make it. Oliver died halfway through the retreat. He gave me his last letter for safekeeping and I'm heading to Boston to deliver it to his wife next week."

"That's tough. He have kids?"

"One. A young son."

Highsmith grimaced. "I always hated writing letters home when I lost a man in my unit, especially when I was sending it to a young mother."

"After I see Beth Winslow I'm going to take a break," Collins said. "My newspaper folded, so I'm without gainful employment for the moment."

"Charlie told me," Highsmith said. "Come down to Key West. I'll put you up and if you're feeling ambitious you can help me out around the hotel and restaurant. You'll get out of the cold for a spell. Have you ever been to the Keys?"

"No farther south than Miami. I went down to Vero Beach the last two years for spring training with the Dodgers. And I've read *To Have and Have Not*, if that counts."

"The town has changed a lot since Hemingway's time. We haven't seen much of him of late. He's not popular with the locals, you know, since he walked out on Pauline and his kids back in '38. The tourists think everyone loved Papa, but that's not the truth." Highsmith leaned back in his chair. "You should come down. It'd be a great change of pace. The people are marvelous, really friendly. I can guarantee no snow or ice. No honking taxis. You can get out on the water and fish and in the Gulf of Mexico it seems like the day after God created the earth—peaceful, unspoiled, timeless."

"I appreciate the offer," Collins said. "Even if I suspect that Charlie put you up to it. There are a few things I need to do. That trip to Boston. A few more people to see here in New York. I want to figure out what's next."

"Figure it out in the sun. We've got plenty of room. It's just me and my daughter, Maria, taking care of things, and an extra set of hands is always welcome."

"It'd qualify as honest work, wouldn't it?"

"It would. I'm not saying that we're living in paradise, mind you. There's gambling, whoring, drinking, cockfighting, what you'd expect when you've got a naval base taking up half the town and you're only ninety miles from Havana. So it's not all peaches and cream. This reporter for the *Key West Citizen* wrote about the gambling in town and got beat up for his troubles."

"Sounds familiar."

"All things considered, though, it's a great place. If you come down, we can catch the car ferry over to Havana and go watch a ball game or two. The baseball's not bad. I'll hand it to the Cubans, they take it seriously. They know the game."

"You ought to be running the Key West Chamber of Commerce, Jim. You make a great pitch."

Highsmith grinned. "As a matter of fact, I joined the Chamber. Been encouraging them to promote the town more."

Collins heard his name called out loud. Pee Wee Reese, the shortstop of the Brooklyn Dodgers, approached their table. Collins introduced Highsmith to the slightly built ballplayer, who looked more like an unassuming insurance salesman in his twenties than the captain of a major league baseball club. Reese explained that he had stopped by the Biltmore to meet a friend from Louisville visiting New York.

"Haven't seen you around, Denny," he said. "You disappeared in mid-season and then I saw in the paper that you had gone to Korea. You and Jimmy Cannon both went."

"That's true," Collins said. "We both went over." He didn't like always being lumped in with Cannon, the veteran *New York Post* columnist, but he had learned not to let it bother him. "I've been back a week. Sorry I wasn't around to see the end of the season. You guys made quite a run for the pennant at the end. Almost like '49."

"Almost but not quite."

Collins respected Reese as much as any player in baseball. It wasn't just his skill on the diamond, but also his character. When Branch Rickey signed Jackie Robinson to a contract with the Dodgers and broke the color line, Reese—a Kentuckian, a Southerner—could have given the Negro player the cold shoulder. Instead, Pee Wee accepted him as a teammate and eventually as a friend. In spring training in 1947, Collins had watched as Reese had crossed the practice diamond and welcomed Robinson with a firm handshake. Reese later admitted to a few of the beat writers that it was the first time he had ever shaken hands with a Negro. Collins figured that Reese made up for the bastards in baseball like Ty Cobb and Enos Slaughter who were proudly racist.

Reese was also a damn good ballplayer. When it came to shortstops, Collins ranked Reese only behind Lou Boudreau, the recently hired player-manager of the Boston Red Sox, and perhaps Phil Rizzuto of the Yankees, who had just won the American League's Most Valuable Player Award.

"So how are you?" Reese asked. "I guess you've been worrying about more important things than baseball the last few months. Pretty rough going over there."

Collins nodded. "I'm hoping it will get better." He didn't want to talk about Korea. "My brother Frank tells me that you had a great inside-the-park homer in that last game at Ebbets with the Phillies. He said the tenth inning, when Sisler hit one out, was a heartbreaker."

Reese shook his head. "What can you do? That's baseball. So are you back in New York to stay? Are you coming down to Vero Beach for spring training?"

"Not sure," Collins said. "But thanks for asking. What do you and the guys make of losing Branch and Burt in one fell swoop?"

Reese shrugged. "Like I just said, what can you do? Mr. Rickey did great things for us and we'll miss him. Dressen knows the club from before he went over to the Yankees and now he's back. He'll do a fine job."

"That's because he's got the right guy as captain."

"Thanks, Denny. I appreciate that." Reese quickly checked his wristwatch. "Hope to see you down in Florida," he said, ready to leave.

"Another reason to come down and stay with us," Highsmith said to Collins. "We could drive up to Vero Beach for a weekend and catch some of spring training." He reached in his coat pocket and found a business card and handed it to Reese. "Look me up if you get any free time. If you like fishing, there's some great action on the flats. I've got a boat and I know a few hot spots."

"Thanks," Reese said. "They keep us on a pretty tight leash, but I appreciate the offer."

After Reese had left, Collins asked Highsmith if he followed baseball.

"Not as closely as my daughter," he said. "Maria's the fan in the family. During the season, I look at the box scores now and then for the Red Sox, to see how Ted Williams is doing. I've gone fishing with him a couple of times. He's a good man. A Marine, you know." He rose to his feet and Collins followed suit.

"Call me when you're ready to come down," Highsmith said. "I think even a big-time newspaperman like you could use some rest and relaxation. It's a chance to get recharged. You'd be surprised how much better life seems after a day of fishing for bonefish and a dinner of black beans, rice, and plantains chased by a few bottles of Hatuey."

Collins was tempted by the offer. Escaping from the cold weather was an appealing idea and staying in Key West for a few weeks would certainly lower his profile. "I may take you up on the idea," Collins said. "I'll call you if I decide to come down. But Boston is next. First things, first."

Five

A delicate, wispy fog lingered in the air outside Grand Central Terminal on Thursday morning when Collins arrived. He was dead tired. He had been jolted awake, gasping in fear, by a vivid nightmare at four o'clock in the morning. In his dream he found himself alone inside the defensive perimeter at Hagaru, surrounded by the frozen bodies of dead Marines, dreading the moment when a wave of Chinese soldiers would charge his position.

Then he heard the sound of distant bugles and cymbals and whistles and thousands of ghostly figures in padded white-jackets emerged from the falling snow in front of him, screaming and yelling as they came. Collins aimed his M1 and tried to fire it, but he had left the safety on, and even after taking it off the weapon jammed on him. As he fumbled with his rifle, the wave of attackers breached the barbed-wire fence in front of him and he flinched at the glint of bayonets moving toward his body as the American position was overrun. That was when he awoke, drenched in sweat, his heart pounding furiously.

He knew his nightmare had been triggered by his trip to Boston and the memories it stirred up of Oliver Winslow and the night Collins had joined him in fighting off the enemy unit that had penetrated into the Marine encampment. It took twenty minutes before he had settled down enough to fall back into a fitful sleep.

Once he reached Grand Central, Collins bought a cup of hot, dark coffee and drank it slowly. When he passed through the Grand Concourse, he looked up at the mural of nighttime constellations overhead. He had always admired the painting with its gold stars glittering against a cerulean blue sky, inviting commuters and travelers alike to pause and appreciate the artistic depiction of the zodiac in the vaulted ceiling. It was sad, he thought, that so few people stopped to glance above.

He boarded the seven o'clock train to Boston and took a window seat. He began skimming the morning papers quickly as the train pulled out of the station. It appeared that the Eighth Army had slowed the Chinese advance. General Ridgway's leadership in the field was apparently making a difference.

He stayed away from the bar car on the ride north, although he was thirsty. He didn't want to show up smelling like a distillery at the Winslows' Beacon Hill home. Beth Winslow had asked to meet him there when they had talked briefly, and haltingly, on the phone.

The train arrived at South Station on time. Outside the terminal a cold wind blew in from the northeast, and Collins pulled up his coat collar. He could see his breath in the air, and he was grateful the taxicab that he hailed had a working heater. After Korea, he had resolved that he would never again complain about the temperatures in New York or Boston, no matter how cold he might feel. There was no comparison.

The numbing, penetrating cold that he had encountered in the Taebaek mountains was unlike anything he had ever experienced. It cut into exposed flesh like a thousand stinging knives. The frigid air made it hurt to breathe in deeply, and frostbite threatened exposed noses and ungloved hands.

He was early for his appointment with Beth Winslow so he told the cab driver to take him by the Public Garden and the Common. As they sped past the snowed-over Common on their way to Beacon Hill, he thought about all the times he had come to Boston to watch the Dodgers or Yankees play the Braves or the Red Sox. He glanced over at the Common and caught a glimpse of the skaters on the Frog Pond, a scene out of a Currier & Ives print. In the distance, the sun glinted off the golden dome of the State House.

He had the driver let him off at Beacon and Park so he could walk the last few blocks to the Winslows' townhouse. When he knocked on the solid brass doorknocker, a tall young woman opened the door. It was Beth Winslow—Collins immediately recognized her from a snapshot that her husband had once shown him in Korea. She had a narrow, angular face with a prominent aquiline nose and slate blue eyes. No beauty, Collins thought, but attractive in her own, composed way. Winslow had grown up with her; their families had adjacent summer homes on Lake Winnipesaukee and Oliver once explained to Collins that everyone had expected them to marry one day and it had seemed the most natural thing in the world when they did.

"Welcome, Mr. Collins," she said. "I've been expecting you."

She took his coat and hat and led him into the drawing room. A dark red Kerman carpet with a graceful medallion design covered the polished wood floor, and a small couch, two wing chairs, and matching end tables were arranged around a small fireplace where a blaze flickered. In the far corner, a mahogany grandfather clock ticked away the time.

Collins noticed two large portraits hanging on the wall of forbidding looking men dressed in frock coats, no doubt Winslow patriarchs of the eighteenth century. He studied the canvasses for a moment but he failed to find any resemblance in their pinched faces to Oliver.

They sat in the wing chairs, facing each other. She offered Collins coffee, which he accepted, and she poured a cup from a carafe sitting on the end table. He noticed that she was drinking tea.

"I'm sorry it took me a few weeks to get here," he said. "As I said on the phone, I promised Oliver at Hagaru that I would deliver his letter to you if anything happened to him."

"Why you, Mr. Collins? No offense intended, but I wondered why didn't Oliver choose one of his fellow officers to safeguard the letter?" She had what Collins had heard described as an upper class mid-Atlantic accent, not as distinct as, say Katharine Hepburn's, but still quite noticeable.

"I was flying out of Hagaru. There were no guarantees that anyone who stayed would make it through to the coast. Your husband figured that I'd have a better chance of making it back than one of his fellow officers."

"I see."

Collins found the envelope in his inside jacket pocket. He didn't see any point in dragging things out so he handed it to her, without comment. She placed it on the side table next to her.

"I don't know what you've been told about Oliver's death," he said. "Should I share with you what I've learned?"

"Please. They've told me very little, only that he died on the march from the reservoir. Killed in action. I understand it was a bit chaotic."

"It was. I waited for the Marines as they arrived in Chinhung-ni near the end of the march. I asked around and finally ran into one officer who told me that Oliver's unit had come under heavy enemy fire when clearing a ridge. He was killed by a machine-gun burst. They buried him in Koto-ri."

"So he died quickly?"

"From what I was told, he did." Collins fumbled for words, knowing that whatever he said would be inadequate, but hoping to give her some comfort. "Your husband was a fine man, respected and admired by anyone who spent time with him. His men would follow him anywhere. They could see how he put them first."

"Thank you," she said. "I apologize for being brusque with you earlier. This has been very difficult for me. I still don't understand why Oliver had to go back to war. He served his country in the Pacific, and I thought that was more than enough for one lifetime."

Collins remained silent. He didn't really know what to say, because he agreed with her. It was patently unfair that so many of the Marines called to duty in Korea were veterans of the fight against the Japanese.

"I can stay here with you as long as you'd like," Collins said, glancing over at the envelope on the side table. "Or I can leave you now so that you can have some privacy."

"Please stay," she said. "I'll want to talk after I'm finished reading it."

She carefully opened the envelope and unfolded the letter and began to read. Collins looked away, not wanting to watch, wishing he was anywhere else in the world but in that hushed drawing room, sitting with a young widow reading her husband's last letter. He could hear the grandfather clock rhythmically ticking away and he busied himself studying the portraits.

Since Thanksgiving of 1950, thousands of young women like Beth Winslow all over the country had been confronted with the awful reality that their husbands or boyfriends had been killed. It must have been particularly difficult news to bear, Collins thought, when it had seemed in early November that the war was nearing a quick end.

Collins knew from personal experience that, as his brother Frank had once reminded him, life went on. But it was a different life, one always shadowed by the sense of what could have been and those possibilities now lost. He did not envy what Beth Winslow faced in the days and months ahead. Oliver had told Collins about his life in Boston: his son, now three years old, the homes on Beacon Hill and in New Hampshire, his thriving law practice. All of that ordered existence was gone, now, and his widow would have to pick up the pieces and fashion something new.

She cleared her throat and looked over at him, blinking back tears. "I must thank you again for bringing me this," she said. "I was officially notified that I had lost Oliver in December. We held the memorial service at the Church of the Advent a week later, just before Christmas. It was so strange. We were married in that church. It bothered me that he was buried in Korea, so far away, but I imagine there was no other choice at the time."

"There wasn't," Collins said.

She looked at the unfolded pieces of paper in her hand. "This makes it real, in a way. The letter helps me better understand what he went through. He knew that he was not going to make it home. Oliver could always size up a situation. Did you know anything about what's in the letter?"

Collins shook his head.

"My husband was a gifted man, a scholar. Oliver read deeply in military history and he loved the outdoors and certainly knew how to read a map. In the letter, he has nothing but praise for General Smith and his fellow Marines but he holds the senior commanders, especially General Almond and General MacArthur, responsible for what happened. He considers them culpable, guilty, for placing the First Division in an untenable position."

"That reflects what a lot of us believed at the time," Collins said.

"In the letter Oliver has asked me to find some way to expose what happened. To force an accounting." She paused, her young face suddenly hard and unyielding. "He has included a message that he wants me to deliver to those responsible for the conduct of the war. So I will do that, Mr. Collins. I plan to go to Washington and see whomever I can in the Department of Defense and force them to listen to what Oliver wanted them to hear."

Collins didn't say anything, but he knew that she could tell from his expression that he didn't think much of the idea. The grandfather clock began to chime, momentarily interrupting them. Beth Winslow waited until it finished before she spoke again.

"Do you agree with my husband, Mr. Collins, about what happened at Chosin? About who bears responsibility?"

"I do," he said. "I wrote one column directly criticizing the high command in Tokyo. But I'm just a newspaperman, a civilian, not an officer with combat experience, so I don't know that it counted for much."

"Do you support what Oliver has asked me to do?"

"Do I support it? I think your husband was a man of great courage. I admired him. I understand why he would want his message heard. But I'm afraid that you will find no takers for it at the Pentagon."

"Why do you say that?"

"I don't think that questioning the judgment of generals will work. Not when the questioner is a captain in the reserves who is jumping the chain-of-command. That's not the way it's done in their world."

She fixed an unflinching gaze on him. "I'm not in the military so I could care less about the chain-of-command. I'm an American citizen, and I learned in civics class that the military answers to its civilian leaders. Did you know that during the Revolution the Massachusetts militia elected their own officers?"

"I don't disagree with any of that. I guess I see it as a noble gesture, but—" He didn't want to finish the thought.

"A waste of time. Futile." She refolded the letter carefully and put it back into the envelope. "I have the luxury of time, something my husband no longer does. So I will honor his request and deliver his message. I will ask Senator Lodge tomorrow to arrange an appointment for me with someone in authority at the Pentagon. I trust that having the senator make the request personally should open some doors."

Whether or not Beth Winslow was aware of it, Collins thought, she couldn't have picked a better intermediary with the military. Henry Cabot Lodge Jr., a major in the Army Reserves, had served with distinction in Europe. He had been the first senator since the Civil War to resign his seat to return to active duty. Armed only with a revolver, he had accepted the surrender of a four-man German patrol in Italy. Lodge had been returned to the Senate by Massachusetts voters in the 1946 election.

"That will definitely get the attention of the brass at the Defense Department," Collins said.

"I hope so," she said. "Did you have anyone waiting at home for you, Mr. Collins? A wife? A steady girlfriend?"

Collins shook his head, hoping that he could avoid the subject, but she waited for him to speak. "I guess it made it easier on me, in a sense," he said. "I was freed from the worry that if something happened to me that it would cause someone else great pain. I have experienced that loss, of losing someone I love, suddenly, unfairly. I wouldn't wish that on anyone. On the other hand, I found myself envying men like your husband who had someone back in the States waiting for them."

He didn't want to tell her the full truth, that he had been in no mood for romance or love after Karina's death, that he had been left numb for months. By the time the memories had started to grow less painful, he was on a plane on his way to Korea to cover the war.

"Will you be returning to Korea?"

"No, I won't." Collins surprised himself with his own sudden certainty. "I've seen enough of war."

"Oliver says in the letter that you're a very brave man," she said. "He said that he would trust you with his life."

Now it was Collins' turn to look away, embarrassed by the tears that had come, unbidden, to his eyes. "I treasured him as a friend," he said. "Please let me know whatever I can do to help you." There wasn't anything else he could say.

She gazed at him directly, intently, and Collins felt as if she was measuring him in some way. "I recognize that this is a great deal to ask, Mr. Collins, but would you join me in Washington when I call on the Department of Defense? It will be suggested that my husband was not himself when he wrote this letter, but we both know better. You were with him. You can speak to his state of mind, how he was thinking clearly, that he was lucid, rational. That should count for something."

Collins hesitated, not sure what to say. She was correct that her husband's mental and emotional stability would be questioned, although he doubted that it would be done openly to her face. She would be politely received and she would be pitied.

In the end, nothing would change. It was true that MacArthur's imperial arrogance and Almond's ambition had cost the lives of thousands of American soldiers and Marines, he thought, but in the end O. P. Smith and his commanders had averted a disaster and so a true reckoning could be avoided. MacArthur was untouchable, backed by his fellow West Pointers (known by the cynics in the military as the West Point Protective Association) and supported by numerous right-wing Congressmen.

Yet Collins couldn't refuse her. If she wanted him there when she faced the Defense Department officials in Washington, he would have to be there. He owed that to Winslow and the other men who had been left behind in those hastily dug graves in Hagaru and Koto-ri and Hungnam.

"I would be honored to accompany you," he said. "Oliver was one of the finest officers I ever knew. His men would have followed him to the gates of hell. And when he handed me your letter he was calm and collected. He damn well knew what he was doing."

She leaned forward to touch his hand lightly in acknowledgment, pleased with his answer.

"Thank you," she said. "Shall I call you at the newspaper when I have the time and date of my appointment?"

Collins shook his head and explained that he was no longer with a newspaper. He wrote down his brother's phone number in Brooklyn on one of his old business cards and gave it to her.

"I will try to make this a very quick visit to Washington," she said. "I don't want Alexander left alone even for a few days. I had him stay with my mother today. I didn't want him to see me until I had a chance to compose myself. Do you understand?"

Collins nodded.

"Someday, when he is older, I would like you to visit us and tell him about his father. Alexander should hear about Oliver from his father's dear friends, not just from me."

Collins told her he would be glad to. "I've written down the titles of some of the poems he used to recite," he said. "Would you like me to send them to you? So your son knows them?"

"No need," she said. "I've heard those poems a thousand times." She stopped for a moment, fighting back tears. "This will be very strange, delivering his message. But Oliver knew I would never be one to shirk from doing my duty. I suspect he knew the same about you, Mr. Collins. In any event, we will do our duty, won't we?"

"We will," he said. "Count on it."

Collins found a shabby bar near South Station where he could kill time before his train left for New York. The bartender was a slight, ginger-haired man with a ruined face and eyes that looked like they had seen their own share of hard things. Collins had him pour a draft beer and he took it with him to a side booth where he wouldn't be disturbed. He didn't feel like talking.

He lit a cigarette and took a sip of beer. Bing Crosby was playing on the jukebox, singing "Far Away Places," and the lyrics gave Collins pause. He knew plenty of Americans in Korea who were stuck in "far away places with strange sounding names" that weren't calling to them, like the song claimed, and to a man they couldn't wait to get home. Collins had met Crosby once in 1946 at the Stork Club just after the singer had become a part-owner of the Pittsburgh Pirates. He had liked the famous crooner. They had chatted about the Pirates' prospects and Crosby's other passion, golf, and Collins got a fairly well-received column out of their talk.

There was a couple in the booth next to him and even with the jukebox playing Collins could overhear them. The man was waiting for a departing train and his companion was clearly unhappy about his upcoming trip.

"I hate it when you leave," the woman said. "The apartment feels so empty. And I'm so lonely."

"It's only two weeks," he said. "I'll try to wrap up business as fast as I can and get back."

"I wish you didn't have to go."

"We've been over this before. It's part of the job."

"I'm sorry. I just wish it wasn't like this."

"I know, baby, but I'll be back here before you know it."

She said something in a low voice that Collins couldn't hear and the man laughed. "Well, that gives me quite an incentive to finish up early and get back here."

Collins looked at his watch. The memories and emotions that the day had surfaced had added to his sense of exhaustion. He hoped he had given Beth Winslow some comfort with what he could relate about her husband's last days, even if he had offered her the sanitized version, stripped of the fear and desperation that they had all felt.

Collins figured that anyone who had lived through Chosin would struggle to come to grips with the dark, vivid memories. Once dusk came and the Corsairs could no longer fly and strafe and bomb the Chinese forces, the assault would come. There was an awful savage beauty as the attacks began; the Marine mortarmen shooting phosphorus shells to illuminate the battleground; red and blue-green tracer rounds seeking targets in the dark. Then the sounds of battle: the bugle calls and whistles and cymbals as the Chinese infantry advanced, and the bark of carbines, Browning Automatic Rifles, and machine guns being fired; the hoarse yells of men; the screams of the wounded and dying carried by the wind.

Just thinking about it made him nervous. He could feel the sweat trickling under his armpits and he knew his heart rate had begun to climb. Who wasn't a secret coward on those nights when Death came calling with no regard for class or rank or experience? When it snuffed out the light of life in so many young men? Collins recalled the soaring sense of relief he felt on the day he left as the overloaded Dakota's twin engines strained and roared and the plane slowly, and finally, lifted clear off the improvised Hagaru runway.

His next few nights would be difficult, he knew, interrupted by nightmares and a lingering sense of dread that he would find hard to shake.

He would help Beth Winslow make the rounds at the Pentagon, bringing a message that no one there wanted to hear. That would close the book on his time in Korea, he decided, in a particularly fitting way—it would be a painfully screwed-up exercise, just like the war.

Maybe then he could take up Jim Highsmith's offer and spend a month or two in the Florida sun, fishing in the Gulf, laying back and taking it easy. He could return to New York when he had figured out what he wanted to do with his life. It was simple, actually, and for now it made sense.

Six

It had been more than a year since Collins had been in Sardi's, but when he arrived there for dinner on Tuesday night, he found the place virtually unchanged, the same as he had left it, and he liked that. The hundreds of caricatures of Broadway stars and New York celebrities framed in black were still hanging on the walls, including the huge one of former Mayor Jimmy Walker placed over the door. The restaurant was already crowded with noisy, happy customers, many grabbing an early dinner before heading off to a nearby show.

Vincent Sardi credited his success to the caricatures, first drawn by an eccentric White Russian artist named Alex Gard. Show business types loved admiring their pictures on the walls. Because of the caricatures, and the restaurant's location just off Times Square, Sardi's naturally attracted a more theatrical crowd than did the Stork Club, Toots Shor's, or the 21 Club.

Collins was at Sardi's only because Lonnie Marks, the press agent, had called him earlier in the week to remind him that he had agreed to drinks and dinner. "Alison Winchester is eager to meet you," Marks said. "She's a big fan, loves your column."

"You should be using the past tense. I no longer have a column."

"You will, though, I'm sure of that. How about the Stork at six?"

"How about someplace else?"

"I thought you loved the Stork," Marks said. "Did you have a falling out with Sherm?"

"Nothing like that. It just has gotten old. Same faces, same stories." Collins had no intention of telling Marks why he had been avoiding the Stork Club. There were too many bad memories there; too many ghosts from the past.

"Let's make it Sardi's, then. See you tonight at six."

Collins figured it would get him out of his brother's house for most of the evening and so he agreed. He put on a clean shirt and his blue suit and headed to Manhattan.

He didn't stand at the front of the restaurant for long. Vincent Sardi's son, Cino, who was now running the place, hurried over to greet Collins. They shook hands and the younger Sardi slapped Collins on the back.

"Great to see you," he said. "I read every single one of your columns from Korea, Dennis. You made me feel like I was there. I was in the First Division during the war, and it's been hard to sit here while they're getting roughed up."

Collins nodded. "I'm hearing that from a lot of Marines," he said, thinking of Charlie Adair and Jim Highsmith. He knew better than to call them "former Marines," because the saying was "once a Marine, always a Marine." Cino's loyalty to the Corps was well-known. Any Marine in uniform who found his way to Sardi's would be seated at a prime table and comped a round of drinks. Yankee right fielder Hank Bauer, a tough Marine veteran with two Bronze Stars and two Purple Hearts, supposedly had never been presented with a check at Sardi's.

"Are we past the worst of it?" Sardi asked Collins. "Can we hold off the Chinese?"

"I think so. Everything I've heard about General Ridgway is positive. I've got my fingers crossed that he can stabilize things."

"That last column you wrote was quite something. I'm glad someone had the guts to call out the top brass."

"Thanks," Collins said. "But that didn't take any guts. I was just doing my job."

"Let me know if there's anything I can do for you, Dennis. You need to run a tab? Just say so."

Collins thanked him but declined the offer. No doubt Cino Sardi had assumed the closure of the *Sentinel* had left Collins short of cash. Before his retirement Vincent Sardi was famous for extending credit to struggling actors and singers. Show business was a tough business. Even famous entertainers could find themselves out of work for months at a time.

Cino led Collins to one of the choice tables facing the front, already occupied by Lonnie Marks and an attractive young blonde woman. Collins guessed that she was in her mid-twenties; she had her hair styled like Betty Grable, with a side part and two victory rolls in the front. He wondered, for a moment, if she also had legs as shapely as the movie star's, and found himself grinning at the thought.

"Glad to see you're in a good mood," Marks said. He quickly introduced Collins to the actress.

"Lonnie mentioned that you remembered me from *South Pacific*," she said. "I'm flattered that you did because I had such a small part in the show."

"But a memorable part," Marks said quickly. He avoided eye contact with Collins, for good reason, because Collins wouldn't have remembered Alison Winchester from the chorus of *South Pacific* and Marks knew it. Collins wasn't about to call him on it, of course, and embarrass the girl by suggesting, in so many words, that she wasn't memorable.

"What show are you in now?" Collins asked the actress. "I'm just back in town so I'm not up to speed on what's playing."

"I guess I'm in between shows," Alison said. "I have an audition for that new musical, *Make a Wish*, coming up."

"I'm in between papers," Collins said. "So we have something in common."

Before she could respond, one of the waiters approached the table. "A message for you, Mr. Marks." He handed the press agent a folded piece of paper. Marks opened it and read it quickly.

"Oh dear," he said. "I'm going to have to run. A minor emergency with a friend." He quickly rose to his feet. "I insist that you two stay and have dinner. On my tab. I apologize for being pulled away, but don't let me ruin the evening."

Collins had to grin as he watched Marks collect his coat, shake hands with Cino, wave to a few friends (real or imagined), and exit the restaurant. It wasn't hard to figure out what he was up to. Marks was an amateur matchmaker. He loved to brag about how many romances he had started with an introduction or two.

"How well do you know Lonnie?" Collins asked the girl.

"Not that well, but he's always been very helpful."

"Please don't take this the wrong way, but do you happen to be unattached?"

She nodded. "I am," she said. "I'm not seeing anyone at the moment."

"Nor am I, so I think this might have been a set-up on Lonnie's part. He loves playing matchmaker. I'll bet his emergency was manufactured. It wouldn't surprise me to find that his message was a blank piece of paper."

"Sounds like you have some history with him," she said. "How long have you known him?"

"Long enough that he would choose a very pretty blonde if he was trying to arrange a blind date for me. Which, I guess, he has."

She responded with a throaty laugh. "Thank you for the compliment," she said. "He knows your tastes, then? Blondes over brunettes? Is that because gentlemen prefer blondes?"

Collins smiled. The musical, *Gentlemen Prefer Blondes*, was still playing at the Ziegfeld Theatre two years after opening on Broadway with Carol Channing starring in the role of Lorelei Lee.

"I'll plead the Fifth on that," he said. "Did Lonnie lure you here under false pretenses? A story about how you could meet and charm a newspaper columnist who could promote your career?"

"He did just that," she said. "Lonnie should have asked me before trying to set me up, because I'm not dating right now. My divorce hasn't come through officially and I'm a bit gun-shy." She paused. "It's not that I don't find you attractive, Dennis. I do. But I'm not ready to see anyone."

"We're in the same place, then. Lonnie assumed that since I was single and back in town, that he should make some introductions but I've sworn off romance for the time being."

"We might as well eat," she said, "especially since Lonnie is paying."

They had a relaxed, friendly dinner. She had the Canelloni à la Ripley, French pancakes stuffed with meat and covered with Sardi's white sauce, and Collins ordered the Supreme of Chicken, his favorite Sardi's dish because of its layers of asparagus tips and chicken. During dinner, Collins kept the conversation focused on Alison and she quickly opened up. She had to be as lonely as he was, he decided. He had learned early on that if you kept asking the right questions, people would talk at length. Alison was no exception. He easily deflected any questions about his own life and she didn't seem to notice that she ended up doing most of the talking. Collins learned that she was from a small town outside Pittsburgh, that her real name was Alice Wolenski, and that she wasn't a natural blonde. She had come to New York just after V-E Day and had landed minor parts in a few Broadway musicals, including *South Pacific*.

The city offered everyone the chance for reinvention, he thought. She had left her hometown hoping to establish herself on Broadway with a new persona. He wasn't any different. Dennis Collins had crossed the East River determined to succeed, drawn by the chance to write for the sports pages of the *New York Sun*.

After her third glass of white wine, Alison Winchester confided to him that her biggest mistake in life to date had been her city hall marriage to a jazz trumpeter who was always surrounded by women but claimed he was crazy only about her. She had believed him.

"I caught Victor with one of my girlfriends in our bed seven months later. The bastard had the nerve to tell me that he just couldn't help himself." She looked across the table at him. "So why have you sworn off romance?"

"A string of bad luck. I kept chasing the wrong girl and finally wised up. Then the right girl came along and I lost her. Just one of those things."

"Sorry it didn't work out."

"I'm used to disappointment, I'm a Dodgers fan."

"Tell me about it. Remember that I'm from Pittsburgh and the Pirates haven't had a winning record since Mae West was a brunette."

They were good friends by the time Cino sent after-dinner drinks over to their table, compliments of the house. Collins thought about inviting Alison to continue the evening at El Morocco or the Club Versailles but decided against it. He really wasn't ready for romance and he didn't want to send her the wrong message. The last thing in the world he needed was a complicated personal life, and she didn't strike him as the kind of girl who would be happy with a casual relationship. So he found her a taxicab in Times Square and waved good-bye as it sped off into the night, swerving to avoid a city bus, and then disappearing into the flow of traffic.

In the morning, Beth Winslow phoned from Boston to tell Collins that Senator Lodge had arranged an appointment for her to meet with an Assistant Secretary of Defense. The meeting was scheduled for mid-afternoon on the Friday of the following week. He wrote down the details and they agreed to meet at the entrance to the Pentagon at one o'clock. Collins figured he could take the early train to Washington and, after the meeting, stay the night in a hotel.

In the early afternoon he borrowed his brother's Chevrolet and drove over to the Evergreens Cemetery. He had put off coming there, but he knew it was something that he needed to do. He parked by the entrance. It was cloudy, with a bite in the air, and he spotted only a few visitors inside the fenced grounds.

Collins slowly made his way through the rows of gravestones. He had been there only once before on a snowy February day almost exactly a year ago. It took him two tries before he located the small granite marker inscribed with Karina's name.

He closed his eyes and tried to remember what Karina had looked like, the shape of her face, her dark eyes, the quizzical smile that she had used as a first line of defense. He held onto the few vivid memories that he had of her, how she had coolly assessed him when he came to the Center to interview some of the displaced persons, how she had lost herself in their lovemaking the first time they went to bed, how she had clung to him in the moments before a sniper's bullet had ended her life.

It was easy to romanticize their time together. It had been so brief, and so intense. They were still strangers, tentative lovers not completely sure about each other, who ran out of time. Their affair had felt like an intense wartime fling, all caution abandoned in the pleasure of the moment, little thought given to the morrow. For Karina that made sense. After witnessing the horrors inflicted on Poland by the Nazis and the Soviets during the war, had she really ever escaped the sense of living on the edge?

He found it ironic that the very week he met Karina had also been the week that Penny Allen Bradford had chosen to reenter his life. He had been alone for years and then, suddenly, he found himself with competing claims on his heart. There was a further, bitter irony in that he lost them both by the end of that week. It ended with Penny when he discovered that she had deceived him, hiding her prior connection with Matthew Steele. And Karina had died on a New York street, executed by a Russian with a high-powered rifle.

Collins spent fifteen minutes at Karina's gravestone, lost in thought, before he walked back to the entrance gate. He sat in Frank's car and smoked a cigarette. He wondered if anyone else had visited Karina's grave in the past year. Perhaps a colleague from the Center where she had worked had made the trek out to Brooklyn, but he doubted it. It bothered him that she could be forgotten so quickly, that all that was left of the passionate and courageous young woman that he had fallen so hard for was a small granite marker in an obscure corner of the cemetery. She deserved better.

After dinner that evening, Collins and his brother sat at the kitchen table and drank a few beers. It was clear that Frank had something on his mind.

"I had an interesting discussion at work today," Frank said. "Captain Pearson of the Red Squad invited me to his office and we talked about all sorts of things. Like about my younger brother and his buddy Morris Rose and any other pinkos that might be family friends. I didn't appreciate the attention, Denny. Is there something going on I should know about?"

"Absolutely not," Collins said. "I'd tell you if there was."

Collins didn't like his brother's news. The New York Police Department had monitored radicals, anarchists, left-wing activists, Communists, and other political "subversives" with its own homegrown intelligence unit since the start of the century. It had been called the Italian Squad, the Radical Squad, and now it was known as the Red Squad. The members of the Red Squad didn't worry too much about civil liberties. They employed informers and, some claimed, agent provocateurs in looking to disrupt radical groups. Collins figured that with the current political climate it was open season on anyone suspected of Communist leanings, however that was defined, or of disloyalty.

"You don't want to have the Red Squad interested in you," Frank said. "If I had to guess, it's that prick Caldwell. Payback for you turning him down."

"What did you tell Pearson?"

"That you're the most loyal American since George M. Cohan. That your friends are newspapermen, baseball players, and guys you met during the war, and that when you go out on the town, you date good-looking showgirls who think Karl Marx is the brother of Chico, Harpo, and Groucho."

"Funny. Sounds like you laid it on a bit thick."

"That's the only way to play the game. But here's the problem, Denny. This is just round one. They've obviously started a file on you and the only reason for that has to be the Bureau asking them to. Talking to me sends a message to you. It won't be long before they start asking you questions and harassing you in small ways. Tailing you. Talking to your friends and neighbors. Having a friendly chat with your boss. You get the idea."

"So what do you think I should do?"

"It would be a great time to get out of town. Take a vacation. Let Pearson and his boyos forget about you."

"So you're telling me I should run away from this? That I should disappear for a while because if I don't, I'm looking at a witch hunt?"

"Look, Denny, you're the one who thought MacArthur shouldn't have pressed his luck and kept heading north when the Chinese Reds showed up. It's no different. A tactical retreat."

"It's lousy to give in to the Caldwells of the world."

"You're not giving in. You're staying a step ahead. While you're away, I'll see what I can do to persuade Pearson that he's been fed a bogus story about you, get him to close the file."

"Okay," Collins said. "I'll give Jim Highsmith a call. When I go to Washington next week maybe I'll keep heading south to Key West."

"That would be smart," Frank said. "By the way, Peggy tells me that you went over to the Evergreens Cemetery today."

"I did."

"Please take this the right way," his brother said. "You need a break, and not just to keep Captain Pearson off your case. You went from what happened with Karina to covering the damn war in Korea and then delivering bad news in Boston. Too much that's negative. It's time for accentuating the positive, remember?"

"I hear you," Collins said. "Loud and clear."

Later, he called Jim Highsmith in Florida. They chatted for a few minutes and then Collins explained the purpose of his call. "The offer still open? Still looking for some help? I've been thinking about it and the idea of a working vacation has been growing on me."

"That's great," Highsmith said. "You're more than welcome. When can you get down here?"

"Next week," Collins said. "I volunteered to accompany Captain Winslow's wife on a visit to the Pentagon. She has some questions for them. I thought I'd fly down your way once we're done."

"Just give us a call when you're ready to make your escape," Highsmith said. "I can meet you at the Miami airport. And good luck to you and Mrs. Winslow when you tackle the deskbound warriors."

"Thanks," Collins said. "I have a feeling we're going to need it."

Seven

Collins didn't really know the city of Washington all that well. It was an American League town, and when he was covering baseball he didn't get to the District of Columbia very often because the Dodgers didn't play the Senators. When he traveled with the Yankees, it was to Boston or Cleveland or Detroit because the Red Sox, the Indians, and the Tigers were pennant contenders. The Senators weren't. As the wry saying about the Washington ballclub went, "First in war, first in peace, and last in the American League."

He'd been to the tourist spots—the White House, the Capitol, the Lincoln and Jefferson Memorials—and he had climbed to the top of the Washington Monument for the bird's-eye view of the city and the Potomac and the Virginia suburbs beyond, but he had never really explored the capital city in depth and learned its rhythms and customs.

He knew what he didn't like about Washington. He didn't care for the massive stone-and-concrete New Deal federal buildings with their neoclassical pretensions. They seemed too imperial, too grandiose, with their bas-relief sculptures and chiseled inscriptions. Of course, Franklin Roosevelt and his supporters believed in remaking the government and the new structures represented the physical manifestation of their quest for centralized power, something you couldn't do with modest buildings fashioned out of colonial red-brick.

It had been drizzling in New York when Collins boarded the early train, and it was cloudy in Washington with temperatures in the forties when he arrived. On the long train trip south, Collins had avoided the bar car and when he arrived at Union Station he figured a few quick beers and a sandwich in the main concourse bar was a fair reward for his discipline.

He took a taxi from the train station to the Pentagon. The route took him around the Capitol building, then past the Jefferson Memorial and the Tidal Basin, across one of the twin bridges over the Potomac and finally to the entrance of the Pentagon. The massive limestone-faced building dominated the landscape on its side of the river.

He waited in the front lobby for Beth Winslow. She had stayed with friends in Virginia and she turned up fifteen minutes before their scheduled appointment, elegantly turned out in a gray dress, light blue sweater, and high heels. She looked like an officer's wife, a woman familiar with the cocktail parties and formal dinners of the military elite, and Collins suspected that she had deliberately dressed the part. Beth Winslow wanted to be taken seriously and she wasn't a woman to be intimidated.

A stocky, red-faced Army colonel named Ralph Harvey introduced himself and escorted them down several long hallways. Harvey ushered them into the office of Hilton Rutledge, an Assistant Secretary of Defense, according to the embossed nameplate on the door of his office suite.

When they passed into his inner office, Rutledge came out from behind his desk to greet them and shake hands. If Collins had passed Rutledge on the street he would have guessed that he was an executive of some sort, or a banker—well-dressed, discreet, skilled at handling difficult situations, at delivering bad news. When Senator Lodge called the Pentagon on Beth Winslow's behalf to arrange her visit, Rutledge had been the logical choice to handle the grieving widow.

Once they were seated, Beth Winslow got straight to the point. "As I told your secretary on the phone," she said to Rutledge, "I shan't take up much of your time. I appreciate that you have rearranged your schedule in order to see me."

"You have my condolences on the loss of your husband," Rutledge said. "We are all in his debt."

"Thank you. If his sacrifice is to have any meaning, certain truths have to be acknowledged. Oliver wanted them known, so that costly mistakes would not be repeated. That's why I'm here."

"You will forgive me, Mrs. Winslow," Rutledge said. "I'm not sure I fully understand. This is something your husband related to you before his death?"

"Mr. Collins delivered Oliver's last letter from Korea to me. My husband was determined that no more lives would be thrown away, heedlessly wasted."

"I see," Rutledge said. He exchanged a quick glance with Colonel Harvey. "Do you have this message from Captain Winslow with you?"

"I do. I would like to read you the pertinent passages from his letter to me."

Rutledge nodded and picked up a fountain pen and placed a legal pad on the desk in front of him, ready to take notes.

Beth Winslow slowly opened her handbag and retrieved the letter Collins had brought to her. She carefully unfolded it and paused while she scanned the handwritten lines. She looked up from the paper at Rutledge and studied him for a moment before she spoke. "My husband was not an overly emotional man," she said. "Oliver was an intellectual, in the best sense of that word. He was reasoned and measured in the way he practiced law, and I believe that he would never let emotion overly influence him." She turned back to the letter. "Here is what he wrote," she said, and began to read out loud.

Beth, please read the following to anyone in authority who will listen.

None of us understood over the past weeks why we were advancing north into arctic weather. Was it to gratify the ego of the Supreme Commander in Tokyo? Was that worth the life of a single Marine?

Worse, we were sent into harm's way with little regard for the men. Not all of us have the proper winter clothing and gear. Our weapons freeze when the temperature drops fifteen or twenty degrees below zero, as it has most nights. We are fighting an implacable enemy, one who does not seem to care how many of his own men are sacrificed, about the human cost.

I haven't attended the Army War College, but I know a losing tactical proposition when I see it. We should not be fighting this war in the way we are. We are playing into the hands of the Chinese Communists, who would like nothing better than to engage in a war of attrition. We will run out of men long before they do. Why would we ever repeat the mistakes of the French and British on the Western Front?

In the past few weeks I have found myself questioning the orders I have been given. As a Marine officer I am expected to say "aye aye" and execute those orders. I have done so, but I have thought about resigning my commission. I did not do so only because I could not abandon my men. They deserve whatever I can do to help them make it to the coast, to safety, and so I have resolved to see it through with them.

I know that some may question my patriotism for expressing these sentiments. Let me address that. The Winslows have fought for this country since the Battle of Bunker Hill. My ancestors were at Yorktown and Gettysburg and my father served on General Pershing's staff in France. I despise the assault on personal liberty and freedom that lies at the core of Communism, but I do not think it is unpatriotic to suggest that we have chosen the wrong place and the wrong time for armed confrontation. And it is deeply disturbing to read that General MacArthur has suggested involving the likes of Generalissimo Chiang, a tin pot dictator, in opening a new front in mainland China or in bringing Nationalist troops to Korea.

It is on the behalf of my men that I have written these words, in the hopes that the leadership of this marvelous nation will heed them, will consider our current course and have the courage to change it before any more decent Americans are sacrificed in a war that is being fought on our adversary's terms, not ours.

There was a long silence after she finished. Collins glanced around the room. Rutledge had his eyes fixed on the legal pad on his desktop. Harvey wore a grim look, and he appeared to be studying a framed print of George Washington in his general's uniform hanging on the far wall of the office.

Collins understood their discomfort. The Pentagon had never been run as a democracy. Junior officers from the Reserves weren't supposed to challenge decisions made by the military's most decorated leader—nor call attention to his lapses in judgment.

"I recognize that what Oliver has written may not please many people here," Beth Winslow said, breaking the silence. "I'm confident that the other men who were there, who survived the Chosin campaign, would corroborate what my husband has written."

She gazed over at Collins. "Mr. Collins was there in Hagaru with my husband. I asked him to come with me today. He can tell you what he saw and he can tell you about Oliver's state of mind. Then I would hope and pray that you would draw your own conclusions and act in the best interests of the men still in Korea, and in the best interests of the country."

Rutledge scribbled a few more words on his pad and then looked up and nodded. "Thank you for your candor, Mrs. Winslow," he said. "This must be very difficult for you."

"My conscience will be clear," she said, staring at Rutledge. Collins could see that she was not a woman who would shy away from hard things. There was something flinty about her, an uncompromising Yankee toughness handed down from generation-to-generation. She was not going to make it easy for Rutledge.

"Do you have anything to add?" Rutledge asked, directing his question to Collins. It was clear to Collins that the man had no desire to hear any more, but that he felt obligated to ask. Collins figured he had nothing to lose by telling the truth—he would be, at the least, keeping faith with Oliver Winslow and the Marines of Chosin.

"Captain Winslow gave me the letter just before I flew out of Hagaru," he said. "I hoped that I could return it to him when he reached the coast. That didn't happen, so I delivered it to Mrs. Winslow when I got back to the States. I can't disagree with anything he wrote. It matches what I saw when I was there."

"You are not a veteran, are you?" Colonel Harvey asked.

"I am not. I covered Saipan and Okinawa and I reported on Inchon and the Seoul campaign last fall. I don't speak as a military expert, just as someone who has observed a fair amount of combat."

"And you agree with Captain Winslow's assessment?" It was Rutledge, his pen poised above the legal pad, again ready to write.

"I believe that it reflects the views of many of the officers of the Tenth Corps. They felt that there was a disregard for the realities on the ground by the high command in Tokyo and that General Almond's unwillingness to deviate from his orders made a bad situation worse. They couldn't understand why they were ordered to advance north as they began encountering Chinese regular units in considerable strength."

"In your opinion," Harvey said with an edge in his voice. He made little attempt to hide his disdain.

"It's what the officers in the field believed and what they told me," Collins said. "Why would I invent that?"

Harvey looked like he had swallowed something sour. He hadn't got the answers that he wanted, that was for sure. In covering the military, Collins had learned that donning an officer's uniform didn't automatically make a man any smarter or any more competent. Nor did attending West Point or Annapolis or Quantico guarantee that he could lead men. For every Oliver Winslow or O. P. Smith there was an arrogant martinet or ambitious and politically-savvy climber who had been promoted beyond his abilities. Collins had the distinct impression that Harvey fell into that second category.

Rutledge hadn't written anything more on his pad. "Thank you, Mr. Collins," he said. He put his pen down. "We appreciate your sharing your impressions with us."

Rutledge looked over at Beth Winslow, weighing his words before he spoke. "Mrs. Winslow, war is a terrible thing. It is an inescapable fact that men will die and that other men—fallible men I should note—will have given orders that will have led directly or indirectly to their death. I can promise you that my staff will review and research the situation and will report to me directly about their conclusions. This is a highly sensitive matter, as you can imagine, and I am confident Colonel Harvey and his colleagues will handle it with the requisite confidentiality."

He rose to his feet and came out from behind the desk and moved into the center of the office. Rutledge glanced at his wristwatch and then turned to Beth Winslow.

"Mrs. Winslow, I know the Secretary of the Navy would like to have a few words with you. If you will please come with me, I'll escort you to his office." He looked over at Harvey. "Why don't you and Mr. Collins wait here, Colonel?"

Moments after Beth Winslow and Rutledge had left the room, Harvey turned to Collins. "Did you encourage her to come down here for this?" he asked in an accusatory tone. His face was flushed.

"Just the opposite. I told her coming here wouldn't make any difference."

"You're no innocent, Collins. You know about the fog of war and what can go wrong. General MacArthur has made his mistakes, but so did Grant and Pershing and Patton." Harvey's face had grown even more flushed. "If I were you, I would encourage Mrs. Winslow to return to Boston and get on with her life. She has made her point." He stared directly at Collins. "Am I making myself clear?"

"Tell her that yourself," Collins said. "I'm not going to carry your water for you."

"I never cared for your type," Harvey said. "Hanging around the troops like a vulture so you could sensationalize and twist things so you could sell more newspapers. And when it got truly dangerous, you didn't stick around. You left. I read that column you wrote about Chosin. You talked about honor and duty and courage, but you have no idea of what those words really mean. You disgust me."

That was when Collins lost his temper. He felt his anger rising and his heart pounding and he found himself grasping Harvey's uniform jacket and slamming the heavier man into the wall with a resounding thud.

"Don't lecture me about courage," he told him, pinning him against the wall with both hands. "You sorry son-of-a-bitch. You sit on your ass here while men with real courage are fighting for their lives because you and the rest of the desk jockeys don't have the guts to challenge MacArthur."

Collins released him and took a step backward. He brought his clenched fists to chest-level, ready to block any punches that Harvey might throw, but Harvey apparently didn't want to fight. He straightened his uniform jacket, adjusted his tie, and then spoke, avoiding eye contact with Collins.

"I'm going to let this episode pass," he said. "I can smell the booze on your breath. You're an embarrassment. When you've had a chance to cool down, you'll regret what you've said here today."

"That will be a cold day in hell," Collins said.

"So be it, then. I meant every word I said. You're a vulture."

They were interrupted by a knock on the door. Harvey walked over to open it and Rutledge and Beth Winslow came into the inner office. Collins noticed that she had put on white gloves and she was clutching a long, leather box in her hands.

"They've awarded Oliver the Silver Star," she said to Collins. "For bravery in Korea." She opened the lid of the box to show Collins the ribbon and medal nestled inside. Her eyes glistened with tears.

"He was a courageous man, and a good man," Collins said.

He didn't doubt for a moment that Oliver Winslow deserved the Silver Star, but he wondered about the timing of the award of the medal to his widow. When Senator Lodge asked for the appointment for Beth Winslow, did the bureaucracy cast about for ways to disarm her? He silently cursed his own cynicism.

There was no bringing Oliver back, after all, and if honoring his courage and valor gave some comfort to his widow and his family, then Collins couldn't question it. The irony, of course, was that had he survived Oliver would have argued that there were other Marines more deserving of the medal, men who had done more, made a greater sacrifice. On that point, at least, Collins knew Oliver Winslow would have been completely wrong.

Outside the Pentagon a hired car and driver waited to take Beth Winslow on the brief ride to Washington National Airport. She turned to Collins before she got into the car.

"I want to thank you, Mr. Collins, for all you've done."

"Please call me Dennis."

"Dennis, then. I want you to know how deeply I appreciate your help and support. I understand why Oliver trusted you as a friend."

"I'm sorry that we met under these circumstances," Collins said. "Oliver had been eager for me to come and visit in Boston after he returned home. I would have liked that."

She bowed her head for a moment, struggling with her emotions. When she looked up, she had regained control. "What's next for you, then, Dennis? Back to New York?"

"A change in plans for me. I'm flying down to the Keys. I'm going to help a friend with his restaurant and hotel. Catch some sun. Go fishing. Unwind."

She motioned to the sunny vista of the Potomac to their east. "It can't have been easy, coming back and trying to reconcile all this with what you experienced over there."

"I had the option to fly out of the combat zone," he said. "So I count myself as lucky. I'm here, unlike many of the men who had to march to the coast, and the ones who are still stuck there, holding on for dear life."

"You've done what you could," she said. "That's what counts."

He thanked her and asked her to let him know if there was ever anything he could do to help. "Oliver used to kid me about how the Irish were loyal to a fault, but I'd like to think it's not always a fault."

"I shall," she said.

He watched her as the car pulled away, her head held erect, giving no sign of the despair and sadness she had to be feeling. He told himself that when he began writing again he would make sure that Oliver Winslow's message wasn't lost. It might not change anything and MacArthur and his coterie might remain in command in Tokyo, but at least Collins would know that he hadn't given up, that in some small way he had honored Winslow and the others who had been sacrificed to ambition and arrogance in the snows of Korea.

Eight

Collins closed his eyes and tried to clear his mind during the taxicab ride back across the Potomac to the center of the city. He had a room reserved at the Willard Hotel on Pennsylvania Avenue, just a few blocks from the White House.

He had stayed at the historic hotel once before, in May 1941, when he covered the Joe Louis-Buddy Baer heavyweight title fight at Griffiths Stadium. It had been a memorable bout; Baer, a giant of a man, had surprised Louis in the first round with a huge left hook that knocked the Brown Bomber through the ropes. Louis climbed back into the ring and battled back to eventually win the fight when, after being knocked down three times in the sixth round, Baer could not answer the seventh-round bell.

Collins told himself it was better to reminisce about past boxing matches than dwell on his afternoon at the Pentagon—the all-too-vulnerable look on Beth Winslow's face as she studied her husband's Silver Star, the disgust and fear reflected in the eyes of Ralph Harvey when Collins had pinned him to the wall in Rutledge's office, and Hilton Rutledge's detached, too-smooth professionalism. Collins knew that Oliver Winslow's message would be smothered by the Pentagon bureaucracy—he had known that with certainty before he set foot in Washington—but that didn't make it any more palatable.

After checking in at the Willard's dark yellow marble front desk and declining any help from the bellman, Collins pocketed his room key and picked up his canvas overnight bag and set off for the elevator bank. Before he had gone five feet, he was confronted by the unwelcome sight of Andrew Caldwell standing in the lobby. Collins knew immediately it was no coincidence that the FBI agent was there and it angered him. He figured he might as well confront Caldwell directly and so he walked over to him.

"Look what the cat dragged in," Collins said. "Why the hell are you following me?"

"Good afternoon to you, too," Caldwell said. "Appreciate the warm welcome."

"I told you that I wanted to be left alone."

"Greta Garbo says the same thing."

Collins was in no mood for jokes. "Why don't you tell me what you want and I can tell you once again to go pound sand."

"Your trip to the Department of Defense with Mrs. Winslow not work out so well?"

"What of it?" Collins didn't care for Caldwell's tone. Caldwell must have followed him from New York to Washington, which would have required approval from his higher-ups at the Bureau. Was only Caldwell watching him? Had other federal agents been instructed to watch his movements in the city? Collins didn't understand why his visit with Beth Winslow to the Pentagon would attract such attention.

"You're a hard man to figure out," Caldwell said. "I can see how helping out Mrs. Winslow appears to be the right thing to do. You were friends with her husband and you felt obligated. But in January when I asked you to help us, to help your country, you didn't see that as the right thing. That's passing strange."

Collins shook his head in disbelief. "Help my country? You must be joking. I told you at Idlewild that I wanted no part of your petty bureaucratic squabbles. I'm not going to help you settle old scores."

Collins gripped the handle of his bag and started to move toward the elevator bank at the far end of the lobby. Caldwell stepped in front of him with his hands palms up.

"Wait a minute," he said. "Hear me out."

Collins put his bag down. He figured that he might as well listen to what Caldwell had to say; the federal agent might reveal whatever it was that had become important enough for him to follow Collins to Washington.

Caldwell stared at him disapprovingly. "Since our discussion on New Year's Day, I've asked around about you. In fact, I've become a bit of an expert on Dennis Collins. I learned that there was quite an internal debate within the Defense Department last year about whether to grant you press credentials for Korea. Whether you could be trusted with secret information, troop movements, that sort of thing. Your childhood buddy defected to the Reds, and there was your liaison with a foreign national. To say nothing about how the whole episode ended."

"Are you going to get to the point with this?"

"Sure. From what I can gather, someone in the CIA had vouched for you on the loyalty question. Managed to convince the right people in the Pentagon that you weren't a security risk. Pushed them to approve your going to Korea as a correspondent. You can imagine how curious that made me."

"This is all news to me."

"Well, here's more news. Turns out that your guardian angel was none other than Matthew Steele. He was the one who vouched for you. And that made me even more curious. I do a little more digging. I find out that Steele married your ex-girlfriend, Penny Allen Bradford, now Penny Steele. The whole thing is a bit too cozy for me. Something wrong about it. I'm just a simple guy but I get curious when things don't add up right. So maybe you can tell me what's going on."

"There's nothing to tell. I haven't seen Steele since October of 1949."

Caldwell grinned. "So I take it you weren't one of the wedding guests?"

Collins found the handles of his bag and picked it up. He tried not to show any anger when he spoke. "Are we done? I really don't want to waste any more time on this."

"Bear with me. I think I know a little about human nature. I gave you a chance to get back at the guy who was responsible for the death of a woman you say you loved. You didn't take it. If it were me, I'd be eager for payback. So when you pass up the opportunity, and I find out that this guy is calling in favors for you, it doesn't sit too well. Something going on that's not on the up-and-up."

"If you and the Bureau want to investigate me, be my guest. I have nothing to hide." He thought for a moment about challenging Caldwell over siccing the Red Squad on him, but decided against it—Caldwell would probably be pleased by Collins expressing his annoyance over the move. "I don't know if the story you're telling me about Steele is true. If he did intervene, maybe he felt guilty over what happened in New York."

"Maybe. Or maybe you cover for Steele, and he covers for you."

"Think what you like," Collins said.

Caldwell may have been about to say something more, but Collins didn't wait to listen. He turned his back on the FBI agent and walked slowly over to the elevator bank. He pushed the button to summon the car. Caldwell must have decided to give up on continuing their conversation, because Collins found himself alone in the car when the doors closed.

Once he was in his room, he took off his suit jacket and hung it in the closet. He found his flask in his overnight bag and poured some brandy into a glass. He took a sip and felt the warmth of the liquor flowing down his throat.

There was a knock at the door. Collins placed the drink down on the sitting room table and went to the door and opened it. Standing there in the hallway was Matthew Steele. Somehow it didn't seem all that strange for Steele to turn up, Collins decided, not after his confrontation with Caldwell in the lobby.

Steele gazed at him through wire-frame glasses, his blue eyes as wary and unreadable as last time they had met. He had noticeably aged, though, with gray strands now interspersed in his brown hair and he didn't look healthy—there was a sallow quality to his skin.

"What the hell do you want?" Collins asked, giving the man a hard stare. He didn't feel any need to be polite with Steele. He had no use for him, and he didn't care if Steele knew it.

"I'd like to talk with you," he said.

"Talk."

"In private. Can I come in?"

Collins reluctantly opened the door and Steele moved quickly into the room. His gray Brooks Brother suit hung loosely on his thin frame, and Collins figured that he had lost ten, perhaps even fifteen, pounds.

"You've ignored my calls," Steele said mildly. "I'm sure that your brother passed my messages along. He's the responsible type."

Collins looked at him with distaste. "Why wouldn't I ignore your calls? You have to know what I think of you. That hasn't changed one iota. I hold you largely responsible for what happened in New York."

"I understand that," Steele said. "Nonetheless, I have something to discuss with you and I would appreciate it if you would hear me out."

Collins wanted to tell him to get lost, but Caldwell's appearance in the lobby was enough to make him hesitate. Steele might be able to shed some light on the FBI's sudden interest in Dennis Collins.

"I can give you a few minutes," Collins said. "As much as I'd like to kick you out, I have some questions of my own I want to ask you."

Steele moved into the sitting room and found a chair. Collins sat down across from him and picked up his drink from the table. He took a sip and waited for Steele to say something.

"I can imagine that your reception today at the Pentagon with Mrs. Winslow was respectful and measured," Steele said. "And in the end, I assume that you were politely ushered out of Hilton Rutledge's office with the promise of a committee to look into Mrs. Winslow's concerns. Was the FBI agent in the lobby inquiring about that?"

"You saw us?"

"I did. Agent Caldwell of the New York field office."

"How did you know about the meeting with Mrs. Winslow? And why is Caldwell so convinced that you and I are somehow buddies?"

"I'm afraid I may be responsible for the Bureau's interest in you, and consequently in Mrs. Winslow. I suspect that they have been monitoring you since you returned from Korea. They apparently would like to pin what happened in New York and its aftermath on me."

"Its aftermath?"

"The defection of Morris Rose."

"You've got that right," Collins told him. "Caldwell is eager to hang you out to dry. He wants me to help out, but I've told him no."

"Why, may I ask?"

"I could care less about their desire to settle old scores. I won't rehash what happened if I don't have to." Collins put his glass of brandy down on the table. "I have another question. Caldwell said you had intervened on my behalf with the military so I could go to Korea. Vouched for me on security grounds. Is that true?"

Steele nodded. "I did."

"Why? I don't get it."

"I owed you that. Your country owed you that. And I knew you would report the truth about what was happening there. That would also be a contribution you could make. As it happens, I was on the phone with Fred Longworth a few days before he died. We talked about your columns from Korea, especially the ones from Chosin, and how they got to the heart of the matter. How honest they were. Sad, that Fred should go before his time. He had just turned fifty. A tragedy for his family, and for the *Sentinel*."

Collins wasn't about to let Steele divert him from his line of questioning. "The FBI really wants to pin the failure in New York on you. They're saying ugly things about you, hinting that maybe your loyalty isn't what it should be. You didn't answer my question. Why are they so eager to discredit you?"

"To put it in baseball terms, I believe they see me as the clean-up hitter for the Agency when it comes to counterintelligence. Pull me out of the line-up and my team is weakened. Hoover wants to fill any resulting vacuum with his own people. If he could have his way, all intelligence matters, foreign and domestic, would come under the control of the Bureau. Under Hoover's personal control, in practice."

"What about the rumors that Hoover might become baseball commissioner and replace Happy Chandler?" Collins asked. "While it would be terrible for baseball, it'd be good for the country."

"I agree. Unfortunately it will never happen. Hoover wouldn't give up the power he has now even if he is a baseball fanatic. I do wish he would take the job and take Senator Welker with him. Did you know Welker has continued to scout baseball players even while in the Senate?" Steele shook his head in wonder. "Can you imagine that? Welker says he never met a ballplayer who was a Communist. That's a great comfort, knowing even the lefthanders in baseball are loyal."

"More so than newspaper columnists, it seems. Agent Caldwell apparently thinks I'm a bit suspect. Has the Red Squad in New York poking around about me. By the way, he told me there have been sightings of Morris Rose in Warsaw and Budapest. Is that true?"

"Caldwell told you that?" Steele seemed surprised. "It's true. He's just repeating what we've shared with the Bureau. We forwarded them that information on Morris. It was supposed to be held in confidence."

"And Ruth Rose?"

"Moved back to New York. She's doing secretarial work for the Fur and Leather Workers Union. She filed for divorce from Rose after he wrote and told her that the marriage was over."

"So you're opening and reading her mail?"

"The FBI, not us." He reached into his right jacket pocket and produced a pipe. "Mind if I smoke?"

"Suit yourself," Collins said.

Steele pulled out a small tobacco pouch from his other jacket pocket and quickly filled his pipe. Collins decided he would have a cigarette himself and lit up a Chesterfield. Steele took the first puff from his pipe, and the aroma of Virginia tobacco—tangy and somewhat sweet—quickly filled the room. "There have been other developments of note," he said, "ones that Caldwell wouldn't know about. Last summer a Russian diplomat, Vadim Ivanovich Tolstoy, walked into our embassy in Helsinki to defect. We've learned a lot from him. Tolstoy was stationed in Berlin after the war and says he knew Anatoli Yatov there."

Collins stiffened in his chair. Just hearing Yatov's name was enough to disturb him, to call up ugly memories. One of Moscow Center's top agents in the United States, Yatov had controlled both Morris and Karina and had ordered Karina's assassination.

"This diplomat is named Tolstoy, like the writer?"

"A distant relative. Vadim Tolstoy has been a career diplomat. Stops in Ankara, Berlin, Oslo, Helsinki. A bureaucrat from what we can gather, good at paperwork. Tolstoy has identified Yatov from some photographs we had of visitors to the Stasi building in East Berlin." Steele reached into his inner jacket pocket and produced an envelope. He offered it across the table to Collins.

When Collins reluctantly opened the envelope he found a small black-and-white photograph inside—a blurred image of a dark-haired middle-aged man who looked vaguely Eastern European. The picture had been taken at street level.

"The mysterious Mr. Yatov," Steele said. "We've learned a lot more about him since New York. In Berlin he headed a small group that specialized in eradicating so-called threats to the state, particularly Social Democrats and trade unionists who wouldn't toe the Party line. According to Tolstoy, Yatov worked for the NKVD's assassination squad during the Spanish Civil War. Yatov personally liquidated several high-ranking members of the Partido Obrero de Unificación Marxista in Barcelona. 'Eliminating anarcho-Trotskyist counter revolutionaries' was the euphemism at the time, I believe. So he's no newcomer to wielding terror. His approach to Karina Lazda was quite in line with his normal operating procedure."

"Has Yatov been spotted in Moscow? Or in Eastern Europe?"

"No," Steele said. "I don't think he returned to the Soviet Union. Why should he? The only people who might identify him by sight—Rose and Miss Lazda—had been removed from the scene. No doubt he established a fresh legend, a new false identity, and continued to run his network."

"You're looking for him, then."

"That I am. I will find him, eventually, if he is in the United States."

"And then what?"

"He will be brought to justice," Steele said. "One way or the other."

Collins put his glass down and looked at Steele with distaste. "So what is it that you want with me?" he asked. "You didn't come here to talk about the good old days."

"I have a proposal, of sorts." Steele paused, and Collins was surprised to see him licking his lips nervously. It wasn't like Steele to display such obvious signs of anxiety. "What if I could give you an opportunity to tell your story, about what happened in Korea, where it might do some good?"

Collins slowly shook his head. "I only came down here because of a man I admired and respected, Oliver Winslow. His wife asked me along, to corroborate Oliver's message. I had no expectations that our visit would change anything. I didn't think that George Marshall will recommend that the president fire Douglas MacArthur based on what Mrs. Winslow and I had to tell his underlings."

Steele reached into the inner left pocket of his jacket and produced another envelope. He opened it and pulled out and unfolded a newspaper clipping. He read aloud: "Yet the men of the First Marine Division, and their now beleaguered comrades-in-arms in the Eighth Army, deserve better leadership at the highest levels of command."

"It was true when I wrote it," Collins said. "It's still true."

"But it's not the entire story, which is much worse. You didn't write about what happened to the Army units that were east of the Reservoir. The men who were cut off and virtually annihilated by the Chinese. You didn't write about what the officers thought of the orders they had been given. Nor how long we can continue to fight the Chinese on their terms. That story should be told, without pulling punches, to those in power. The men who can change the way this war is being conducted. I want to give you that chance."

"Even if I thought that would make a difference, which I don't, why should I believe anything you say? Why would I ever trust you again, after the way you lied to me and manipulated me in New York?"

"I did what was necessary. I couldn't tell you what we were doing at the time, couldn't take the risk that you might inadvertently tip off Rose to our plans." He held his pipe in one hand, contemplating it for a moment. "I deeply regret Miss Lazda's death. I misjudged the situation. You may not believe me when I say this, but I carry the burden of that failure with me."

"So you admit that your scheme failed," Collins said. "That's what Caldwell said. The Russians smoked it out. Which means Karina died for nothing."

"She did not die for nothing," Steele said with sudden passion. "She died trying to stop something she believed was fundamentally evil. She understood what Yatov represented. She didn't hesitate when she thought she could stop him. I'm asking you to do something very similar. I want you to tell your story, about what you saw at Chosin, to a few senior officials, in the hope it will provoke major changes in the way we are conducting the war."

"Why me? Can't you find some of your Agency people to do that?"

"We didn't have anyone at Chosin. General MacArthur has minimized our presence in the theater. You were there. You can give an unvarnished, objective account."

Collins shrugged. "Try a clipping service. They should have copies of my columns from Korea."

"Nothing beats an eyewitness account."

"What's your angle in this? Is this a chance to jam a stick in MacArthur's spokes because he never trusted the OSS and now feels the same about your new outfit? Is it because he won't take your advice and relies instead on his buddy General Willoughby, the genius who kept insisting the Chinese hadn't moved south of the Yalu in significant numbers?"

"Some of my colleagues who would like nothing better than to derail MacArthur and Willoughby. But that's too narrow a goal, in my view."

"Too narrow?"

"There's a bigger picture to consider. Chosin and the drubbing the Eighth Army is now taking are a foretaste of what happens when you attempt to fight on the enemy's terms and on his terrain. Pitched battles with the Chinese Red Army? In the winter when our air superiority counts for less? Insanity. We don't need new commanders who will repeat the same mistakes. We need a fresh approach."

"That may be so," Collins said. "But I did what I could. I'm done. I'm spending the rest of the winter someplace warm."

"That's your choice," Steele said. "I won't argue the point. But I have one other request, something more personal."

He took a quick puff on his pipe. "This is quite difficult." He coughed nervously. "Penny would like to see you while you are in Washington. She's been sick and I think it would cheer her up."

"Sick? Is it something serious?"

Steele shifted in his seat, clearly uncomfortable. "She has been suffering from depression. It started after Caleb was born, last summer."

"You have a son?" Collins told himself that he shouldn't be surprised—it was logical that Penny and her new husband would have children—but it was a jolt to hear it said aloud. There had been a time when he had dreamed of starting a family with her. "Congratulations."

"Thank you. He's been one of the few bright spots for us of late."

Collins downed the last of his brandy and then spoke. "With all due respect, I don't see how my seeing Penny would help matters. We didn't part on the best of terms. You know that full well. Seeing me would just stir up a lot of painful memories."

"I thought so, too," Steele said. "I have consulted with her doctor. She thought that if it was something Penny asked for, then I shouldn't stand in the way." His pipe had gone cold, and he tucked it back into his jacket pocket. "You can imagine that I don't welcome this, considering the history."

"But here you are asking me to see her."

"I am. If the visit lifts her spirits, then it's worth whatever awkwardness and discomfort it may cause me."

Collins could see how uncomfortable Steele had become. He had avoided direct eye contact with Collins ever since they had turned to talking about Penny. Was it jealousy? Did Steele worry that Penny was having second thoughts about the choices she had made? As far as Collins was concerned all that was done and over. Although she had been the first woman he had ever loved deeply, any feelings he had for her were gone.

"When would you like me to stop by?" Collins asked.

"Tomorrow. Join us for lunch. She's at her best early in the afternoon."

"I'd planned to take a flight to Miami tomorrow," Collins said.

"She wouldn't blame you for refusing," Steele said. "But she hopes that you'll be willing to look past what has happened. I believe that she wants to unburden herself about some things."

"I don't need her apologies."

"You may not need them," he said, "but she may." Steele paused. "I must warn you, in advance. She has struggled of late, and she looks the worse for it. I wouldn't want you to be unprepared for that. She's very sensitive about it."

"I understand," Collins said. "We're all getting older. I looked a lot better this time last year."

"Does that mean you'll come and see her?"

"I think it would be a mistake."

"Penny doesn't. She would have come here, to the hotel, if I had let her. She's too fragile for that."

Steele had changed, it seemed to Collins. He was less sure of himself, the arrogant edge that Collins remembered had faded. Or perhaps Collins was fooling himself and the man hadn't changed at all. Nonetheless, Collins believed Steele about the situation with Penny. Collins didn't bear her any ill will, not any longer; if visiting her briefly might help in Penny's recovery, it would be mean-spirited on his part to refuse.

"I can take a later flight," Collins said.

"Penny will be pleased," Steele said. "Thank you." He offered Collins a slip of paper. "Here's our address. Can we expect you around noon or so?"

Collins nodded. "I'll be there," he said. "Even if I'm not sure that it's such a great idea."

Nine

Matthew Steele's Hoban Road residence proved to be an imposing Tudor Revival mansion with half-timbering decorating its exterior walls, rows of narrow windows, and a prominent chimney. The three-story house was set well back from the street, its well-tended grounds ringed by a black wrought-iron fence. Through the bare maple, elm, and black oak trees on the property Collins spotted a carriage house, in matching Tudor styling, situated some fifty yards behind the main structure.

Collins had the cab driver let him off at the entrance to the residence's circular driveway. He walked past a Packard convertible coupe parked in the driveway, its dark-blue finish gleaming in the sun.

He ignored the brass door knocker and rang the doorbell instead. He waited patiently as he heard someone inside fiddling with the lock. When the door swung open, Steele stood there, wearing a cream-colored tennis sweater over a button-down shirt. They shook hands and Steele moved to one side to let Collins enter.

"Thanks for coming," Steele said. "Appreciate it."

He led the way into a large, elegant living room decorated with restrained good taste. A backless sofa stood against one wall, and the room had several upholstered chairs and two small dark wood tables.

Steele appeared nervous and Collins couldn't blame him. "Why don't I get Penny?" he asked rhetorically. "I'll be right back."

Collins found himself tensing up. He had not seen Penny since that ghastly October night at the Stork Club when he had said some very harsh things to her. He had been angry and bitter and he had wanted to hurt her.

When Penny entered the living room, with Steele a step behind, Collins rose to his feet. She moved toward him, smiling, and took his right hand in both of hers and held it tightly for a long moment.

"Hello, Dennis," she said. "I'm so glad that you could come to see us."

She wore a sheath dress with a double strand of pearls, and Collins could see that she had lost weight. There were faint dark shadows under her eyes that her makeup couldn't completely conceal. He suddenly remembered taking her to dinner at El Morocco one night in 1940 when she wore a fashionable azure cocktail dress and had her blonde hair swept up in the latest style. Every man in the place stared at her when they arrived and she had glowed that night, fully aware of how fabulous she looked. Collins saw little of that Penny in the exhausted woman in front of him.

"It's been some time," he said. "More than a year."

"Yes," she said. She nervously pushed a strand of her hair away from her forehead. "More than a year and so much has happened. I could never have imagined how much things would have changed for me."

"I understand that congratulations are in order," Collins said. "For your son, Caleb. Your husband told me about him. That's wonderful."

She brightened at the mention of her child. "Thank you," she said. "Caleb's an adorable little boy, if I say so myself. Of course, I'm not the most objective person."

"Penny thinks that Caleb hung the moon," Steele said. "And the stars, too, for that matter."

"I just wish that I was feeling better and could be a better mother to him."

"He knows you love him," Steele said directly to her, almost as if Collins wasn't there. "That's what truly matters. When you're feeling better you'll be able to spend more time with him."

She sighed audibly. "You keep saying that, but it hasn't happened. It makes me so sad."

There was a prolonged, uncomfortable silence. Steele suggested that they move into a small adjacent room for lunch. There were places set for three at a round table covered by a damask tablecloth. Steele motioned for Collins to sit across from Penny. A middle-aged woman entered the room with a silver coffee service. She poured coffee for all three of them and then left the room.

"I hope I get a chance to meet your son today," Collins said to Penny.

"You will," she said. "We can see him in the nursery, after lunch. Bernice, his nanny, is there with him now. When I left them he was playing happily with his toys and his blocks."

"Caleb loves his blocks," Steele said. "I'm betting that he'll grow up to be an architect."

"How are things at the newspaper?" Penny asked Collins.

"Big changes," Collins said. He explained the circumstances of the *Sentinel*'s closure and Penny listened with a slight frown.

"That's horrible," she said. "I can't imagine Dennis Collins without a newspaper to call his own." She brightened. "Which paper will you be writing for, now?"

"Actually I'm trying to figure that out," he said. "Not sure what I'll be doing next. I'm planning to take a break from newspapers and spend some time in the sun."

Collins felt strangely calm sitting across from her. He was pleased to find that he wasn't stirred by her at all. Whatever love he had once felt for her—and if he was honest, there had been as much bitterness as love—had vanished. They had lost whatever connection there had once been between them.

The woman returned to serve them salads. Penny earnestly tried to carry the conversation. "Have you been to any of the new Broadway shows?" she asked Collins. "Have you seen *Guys and Dolls?* It had great reviews. Matthew brings the *New York Times* home from work and I try to keep up with the theater."

There was something brittle in her manner, something forced. She was trying too hard, Collins thought, which wasn't like her. The Penny he knew in New York could effortlessly manage small talk.

"Can't say I've seen anything on Broadway yet," he said. "I left for Korea in the early summer, so I have some catching up to do. I did bump into Lonnie Marks the other day at Toots' place and he says that there's a great Rodgers and Hammerstein musical coming this spring, *The King and I.*"

"That sounds just like Lonnie, always promoting someone or something. I would love to see the show. Rodgers and Hammerstein are so brilliant."

Before she could say anything more, a phone began ringing elsewhere in the house. Steele rose to his feet. "I'm expecting a call," he said. "If you'll excuse me."

There was an extended silence after he left the room. Collins took a sip of his coffee and waited for Penny to speak. She would get around to whatever she wanted to say to him when she was ready. He was sure of that.

"To my surprise, I find that I miss New York," she said and dropped her eyes. "It's so vibrant there, so alive."

"A marvelous city," Collins said. "You realize it best when you're away from it for a while. You should come up when the weather is better and see some of the shows."

"I would like that," she said. She rubbed her hands together briskly, another nervous gesture Collins remembered from the past. "I just need to get my energy back. Matthew has been wonderful in making sure that I see the best doctors. I visit Dr. Rifkin now two or three days a week for therapy. She's a Jungian. Therapy is all new to me and I know I have a lot to learn. Then I also see Dr. Sollers, who is on the Georgetown faculty. He arranged treatment for me last fall when I had to go into the hospital."

Collins was silent for a moment. It was clear that for some reason Penny wanted to share the details of her medical condition and its care with him. He waited for her to continue.

"Did Matthew tell you that I had to have electroshock last fall? We were at wit's end. Matthew's therapist, Dr. Frader, was more open to the idea and Dr. Sollers made a very convincing case. He was concerned that without the electroshock that I might do something dire."

Penny poured herself more coffee in a fresh cup and set it down next to her. She was so preoccupied that she didn't realize that she now had two cups on the table in front of her.

"The shock therapy worked, for a time," she said. "I felt like myself, like the old Penny. I became a much better mother to Caleb and a better wife. But then, after Christmas, I started feeling blue again. Dr. Sollers felt that I had been making progress and thought it might be a temporary setback, but now he seems convinced that I've had a relapse. He recommends more sessions of electroshock."

"What did your other doctor, your therapist, say?"

"Dr. Rifkin hasn't told me what she thinks, but I believe she has reservations."

"Why is that?"

"The treatment has some side effects. For me, it's taken the form of memory loss. The summer of 1950 simply vanished, as far as I'm concerned."

"You didn't miss much," Collins said, hoping to make a joke of it, but Penny didn't smile or laugh.

"Dr. Rifkin worries about my loss of memory. I imagine that's because so much of the therapy is helping me explore my past." She paused to drink some of her coffee. "As I think I told you, my therapist is a Jungian and Matthew sets great store by Dr. Jung's theories. He met the great doctor in person—they were introduced by Allen Dulles, one of Matthew's colleagues—when they were in Switzerland during the war. Matthew has seen his own therapist ever since."

Collins nodded, somewhat surprised that Steele would agree to psychotherapy. He didn't seem like the kind of man who would. Did Steele find it offered a release from the tension of the secret world he operated in? Was it a way to address whatever conflict he might feel about his role at the Agency?

"I am making progress," she said. "I'm beginning to know myself better. I just wish I could shake this sadness that comes over me. If I could only understand what lies behind it, and resolve the conflict. I so want to get my old self back."

"It sounds like you are doing the right things for your health," he said.

"I wanted to see you, Dennis. There are things I want to talk about. Dr. Rifkin thought it would help if I could. I am so pleased that you were willing to come see me."

"When I saw you last, I said some very harsh things," he said. "I blamed you for things that weren't under your control."

"I deserved it," she said. "I deceived you."

"It's over and done with," Collins said. "There's no need to dwell on it."

"I want you to forgive me," she said.

"If you feel you need forgiveness, consider yourself forgiven," he said. "I don't deny that I was angry about what happened. But I've figured out that staying angry would consume me if I let it, so I've left that behind."

"Are you bitter at all, Dennis? About Karina?"

"I'm more resigned than bitter. I can't change the past, no matter how much I want to."

"We cannot change the past, but perhaps we can make amends."

He shrugged. "As I told your husband, I'm not particularly interested in rehashing what happened. I'd rather just not talk about it."

"Matthew has been very good to me," she said quickly. "I could never do what he has done for me. I'm too selfish. I know you don't think highly of him, Dennis, but you are wrong. He does the right thing. You two are much more alike than you realize."

"That may be so," Collins told her, but the truth was that he didn't believe her for a moment. Steele was all calculation, playing the angles, keeping his eye on the prize, whatever it might be.

He was about to say more when Steele appeared in the door to the living room. "I'm back," he said. "Time for the salmon?"

Steele told stories about life in Switzerland during the war as they turned to the main course of cold salmon with sour cream and dill sauce. Collins noticed that Penny picked at her food and ate very little. He saw that Steele quietly encouraged her to eat some of the salmon, but she stopped after a bite or two.

After lunch, Steele suggested Penny take Collins to the nursery to meet their son.

"Yes, let's do that," she said. "Dennis, would you like to come with me?"

He followed her up the staircase and down a hallway to a spacious nursery on the second floor. Caleb Steele was sitting on the carpeted floor, playing with a plastic truck and a pile of colored wooden blocks. He had thin dark hair, an upturned nose, and dark brown eyes.

Collins got down on his knees and the boy looked up from his blocks and contemplated him for a long moment. Then he gave Collins a toothless grin of delight. Collins smiled back at him and Caleb reached out and gave Collins one of the wooden blocks. Collins thanked him and placed the block on top of another. The child selected another block and again handed it to him, and Collins thanked him again.

"He certainly knows how to make friends," he said to Penny.

"I didn't know you were so comfortable around children," she said.

"Sportswriters are just big kids who like games. It's no wonder that the editors call Sports the toy department."

As Collins sat on the nursery floor and played with Caleb, Penny settled into a rocking chair next to her son's crib. They talked, quietly, as Penny asked him about the *Sentinel* and what his last year had been like. He could tell that she was genuinely curious, and she relaxed as they spoke, becoming more animated over the course of the conversation. Yet he still felt that at times she had to make a considerable effort to stay engaged.

Once she started to say something but then hesitated and instead gave him a wan smile.

"Is everything okay?" he asked.

"Sure," she said. "Everything's fine."

Bernice returned to the nursery to announce that it was time for Caleb's nap. After Collins had tousled the boy's hair and said good-bye, they made their way back downstairs.

"It is wonderful to see you, Dennis," she said. "I so wanted you to meet Caleb."

"He's a handsome boy," he said. "Lots of energy."

"I wish I felt better so that I could keep up with him. On my good days I try to play with him as much as I can. To make up for the days I can't."

Steele was waiting for them in the living room. He exchanged glances with Penny and Collins thought he saw her shake her head, as if to say "no," but he couldn't be sure.

"So you've met the apple of her eye," Steele said.

"I have," Collins said. "And he's as handsome and smart as advertised."

"Thank you," Penny said. "I'm starting to feel a bit tired so if you'll excuse me, I think I will follow Caleb's lead and take a nap."

She took Collins' right hand in both of hers and said good-bye. Then, holding the railing, she slowly climbed the steps to the second floor.

"Before you go, Dennis, I have one item to discuss," Steele said. "Why don't we sit in my office and chat for a few minutes?"

"All right," Collins said.

Steele led the way into his book-lined study. Sunlight streamed into the room through two wide leaded-glass windows. A substantial mahogany desk had been positioned near the windows. Collins noticed that there were a few books stacked on the desktop, including a Catholic missal. A photograph of Penny in a silver-edged frame was placed by the window.

"The desk was my father's," Steele said. "And my grandfather before him. It will be Caleb's someday."

He motioned for Collins to sit in one of two wingback chairs arranged across from the desk and he occupied the other. He leaned forward, his hands on both knees.

"How does Penny seem to you?" he asked. "I'd like your honest appraisal."

"You know that she doesn't look good. She seems fragile, a bit scattered. She's been through a lot, apparently, and it shows. It's sad to see her like this."

"She's been sick for some time, now. I've had her seen by the best doctors. They believe that her depressive state may have been triggered by her pregnancy."

"Penny told me about her therapy," Collins said. "And the electroshock. I assume that there wasn't much choice in the matter."

"There was not," Steele said, defensively. "We were concerned that she might harm herself. She wasn't eating, she wasn't getting out of bed in the morning. We got her into the hospital and after several sessions she came out of her funk." Steele looked directly at Collins. "I'm worried that she's sliding back, now. I hate the idea of her going back into the hospital."

Collins shifted in his chair and remained silent. He wasn't going to be drawn into a conversation about Penny's medical options.

"You said we needed to talk," Collins said. "I don't want to miss that last flight to Miami."

"This won't take long," Steele said. "The telephone call I took earlier? I've been able to arrange an opportunity for you to tell your story to someone who matters. If you'll agree, we'll go see him in a few days. Unfortunately we will have to travel some distance, but I will pay for the expenses of the trip, and we'll have you back here by the end of next week."

"A trip of some distance? It would help if you would just give it to me straight. Who is it that I would meet?"

"General Eisenhower. I thought he would be back in Washington next week, but it turns out he won't. So if you agree to it, we'll fly over to Paris and meet him there. Through his chief-of-staff, he has agreed to see us. Informally, of course. I should know exactly when tomorrow and we can make the travel arrangements."

"Why Eisenhower? He's been placed in charge of Europe, not Korea."

"That's today. But he may be asked to assume command in Korea if the situation worsens and if MacArthur must be replaced."

"There are a lot of ifs. Truman and Marshall are just as likely to keep him on in Paris."

"I don't dispute that, but Eisenhower is likely to be in the thick of things no matter what happens. You came to Washington with

Mrs. Winslow knowing that she wouldn't really be heard. This won't be the same. General Eisenhower will listen. I promise you that."

"And why should I do this?"

"Because it may save lives," Steele said. "Isn't that why you assisted Mrs. Winslow? This would be a chance to change things. Don't you want that?"

"I do." Collins hesitated. He did want the story of what really happened at Chosin to be heard by those in power, by anyone who could influence the course of the war in Korea, but he didn't trust Steele. "If I were to do this, there would be some conditions."

"I'm not sure what you mean."

"Five hundred dollars a day for my time." Collins watched Steele intently, waiting to see whether the man would flinch at his demand, but Steele's expression didn't change. "It's not for me, because I won't take your money. But I have something you want and I figure you will pony up if it's that important to you. The money will go to the United Service for New Americans as a donation to help refugees coming to New York. A gift in memory of Karina Lazda. And I want it coming out of your pocket, not the Agency's."

Karina might still be working at the organization's Center for displaced persons on the Upper West Side if Steele had leveled with Collins from the start. Collins would have made sure that she was kept clear of any danger. But Steele had hidden the truth from him.

"You see, I don't trust you," Collins said. "You burned me once badly and I won't allow that to happen again. This way even if it turns out that your motives aren't as patriotic as you claim they are, it's not a complete loss—the money will at least have helped some of the DPs start a new life."

Collins figured he had every right to be suspicious. He wondered whether Steele had used Penny's illness as a way to keep Collins in Washington longer. Was it a scheme to buy time for Steele to convince Collins to go to Paris with him? Or was it all on the level? Whatever the case might be, Collins wouldn't take anything Steele said at face value. Fool me twice, shame on me.

"I wouldn't expect you to believe me when I say that I have come to deeply regret what happened with Miss Lazda," Steele said. "I treated her, and you, as means to an end. That was wrong."

Collins shrugged. "Talk is cheap. That's why I'm asking for the money."

Before Collins could say anything more, Steele walked over to his desk. He opened the top drawer and pulled out a checkbook register and sat down and wrote out a check, which he handed to Collins. It was made out to the "United Service for New Americans" for $2,500. In the lower left corner Steele had written "To honor the memory of Karina Lazda."

"Five days paid in advance," he said. "You can mail it to them."

"And if we're done in less than five days?"

"I won't ask for my money back," Steele said. "I've agreed to your terms, and now I have some of my own. First, you may not tell Penny about this financial arrangement of ours. Second, while you're in Washington, you'll stay here in our guest house so that you can see Penny when she feels up to it."

"I agree to the first condition," Collins said. "That won't be a problem. The second will. Staying here will be damn awkward."

"Only as awkward as you choose to make it," Steele said. "I've seen today how your presence makes a difference to her. She's more engaged than I have seen in months. She dressed up for you. She's making an effort." He paused, embarrassed. "I should be jealous, I imagine, but I'm not. I'm just glad to see she can fight against her dark moods when she tries."

Collins carefully folded the check in half and placed it in his suit coat pocket. "I'm going to stay at the Willard another night," he said. "I'll come by here after lunch tomorrow."

"So we are set, then?" Steele asked. "You agree to my terms?"

"I'll stay in your guest house," Collins said. "And you'll get your dog-and-pony show for Ike. For what it's worth."

Ten

After his return to the Willard Hotel, Collins placed a long-distance call to Jim Highsmith. While he waited for his connection, he watched the rush-hour traffic below on 14th Street and Pennsylvania Avenue from the vantage point of the bay window of his corner room. Highsmith answered after three rings.

"It turns out I have a few more things that I need to attend to," Collins told him after they had exchanged greetings. "I'm staying in Washington for a bit longer. I'll explain when I see you."

"How did your meeting with the Pentagon brass go?"

"Beth Winslow's a brave woman. They listened to her politely, but it's clear nothing will happen."

"You did your duty. That's what matters."

"I'm looking forward to seeing you in Key West. I'm sorry about the delay."

"You'll get here when you get here," Highsmith said. "Maria will be disappointed. She loves it when I have friends come and stay. It provides some excitement."

"I don't know how exciting I'll be, but I look forward to the visit," Collins said. "It'll take me a week or so to finish up business here. Then I'll come down your way. I'll give you a call when I have a better idea of the timing."

After they hung up, Collins rummaged through the desk to find some hotel stationary. Then he composed a brief cover note for Steele's check to the United Service for New Americans. In the note, Collins explained that the donor, Matthew Steele, wished to remain anonymous and that his gift, in memory of Miss Karina Lazda, should be used to help refugee families begin their new lives in the United States. Collins added that he hoped that the Center could use a small portion of the money to find some appropriate way to recognize Karina.

He addressed the envelope to the Hotel Marseilles on 103rd Street, the Center's location in New York. He would leave it with the front desk clerk to post when he checked out in the morning, before he took a cab to Steele's house.

No matter the outcome of his meeting with General Eisenhower, he knew that at least one good thing would come out of their trip. Steele's donation to the Center wouldn't in any way balance the books, but it was something, Collins told himself, and it meant that Karina Lazda could still influence the world in some small but significant way.

When Collins returned to Hoban Road in the late morning, he found Matthew Steele waiting for him. "Penny is resting," Steele said. "She says she isn't feeling very energetic. She does want to see you again, later today if possible."

Steele brought him to the carriage house at the back of the property, a smaller one-story version of the main house. It had a bedroom, a sitting room, and a bathroom, all with high ceilings.

"You'll have privacy here," Steele said. "There's a telephone with a separate line if you need to make any calls."

"Any idea when we're traveling to Paris?" Collins asked.

"Yes, we now have a time certain for our meeting with Ike. We'll leave tomorrow and fly overnight to France. Our appointment is two days hence." Steele glanced at his wristwatch. "Before we go, I'd like you to visit the Kremlin with me."

"The Kremlin?"

"Our nickname for the Agency's headquarters. It's a complex of buildings on Naval Hill, just across from the State Department on E Street. Some employees are in temporary buildings down by the Lincoln Memorial, but the Kremlin is the heart of the operation. There's someone I'd like you to meet there, my boss, Allen Dulles, the deputy director of plans. He expressed an interest in having a brief chat."

Collins had heard of Dulles, a New York lawyer who was known for his service in the Office of Strategic Services during the war with General "Wild Bill" Donovan. Collins was more familiar with Allen Dulles' brother, John Foster Dulles, a prominent establishment Republican who had been appointed to the U.S. Senate by Governor Dewey when the incumbent, Robert Wagner, stepped down because of illness. The elder Dulles brother couldn't hold the seat, though, losing a special election to Herbert Lehman in 1949.

"I don't see why not," Collins said. He wondered exactly what Steele had told Dulles about their shared history.

"Capital," Steele said. "Why don't we head over there now?"

It took only ten minutes to drive from Steele's house to the CIA complex on E Street. This Kremlin wasn't what Collins had expected; it felt more like a college campus than the headquarters of a government intelligence agency. Three Federal-style red brick buildings sat in a U-shape around a well-manicured lawn. Collins could see the Potomac River below them to the west and the Lincoln Memorial to the south. Steele parked the Packard in an empty space near the East Building, the largest of the structures. At the entrance to the building, Steele showed his identification card to a guard who waved them through.

"Allen's office is on the first floor," Steele explained. "Our new director of Central Intelligence, General Walter Bedell Smith, sits just up the hallway. His friends call him Beetle, but I haven't heard anyone here use that nickname yet. To say that General Smith has a bit of a temper would be the understatement of the century. He doesn't suffer fools kindly."

Collins followed Steele down a long corridor until they came to an office with double doors. After knocking on the nearest door, Steele opened it and they entered Allen Dulles' office, which could have been that of a college dean with its crowded bookshelf, desktop crammed with folders, and strong smell of pipe tobacco. Dulles fit the image of an academic with his tweed coat, wire-rimmed glasses, neatly trimmed white mustache, and close-cropped hair. Collins estimated that he was in his late fifties or early sixties.

He shook hands firmly with Collins when they were introduced and invited him to sit down in one of the two black captain's chairs facing his desk. Steele took the other chair.

"I'm pleased to meet you, Mr. Collins," Dulles said. He fiddled with the bowl of his Dunhill pipe until he was satisfied that the tobacco was tamped down properly. "I appreciate this opportunity to get to know you." He lit the pipe and took a long puff. Collins had always been secretly amused by the rituals of pipe smokers. They seemed to get as much pleasure out of preparing the pipe as they did from smoking it. That would never work for Collins—when he wanted to smoke he didn't want to wait.

Dulles took the pipe out of his mouth. "Matthew shared the background about what happened in New York in 1949, and I've been fully briefed on Trojan Horse. I know how deeply he regrets what happened."

Steele coughed slightly. "Trojan Horse is our internal name for the operation involving Morris Rose," he told Collins.

Collins didn't respond. He hoped Steele hadn't brought him there with the idea that they would discuss Morris Rose or anything to do with him. Collins was done with that.

"You can brief me on Trojan Horse activities later," Dulles said to Steele and turned back to Collins. "I understand that you'll be joining Matthew on his vacation to Paris and will stop by and pay your compliments to General Eisenhower."

"I didn't know it was a vacation," Collins said. "I've agreed to tell General Eisenhower about what I saw during the battle of Chosin Reservoir."

"It's a vacation only because it's not an official visit," Steele said quickly. "I won't be there representing the Agency in any formal capacity."

"How long were you with the Marines in Korea?" Dulles asked.

"I went ashore at Inchon," Collins said. "And I followed the First Division through the liberation of Seoul and then their transport by sea to Wonson in late October. I was with General Smith's staff throughout the Chosin Reservoir campaign. I left his headquarters at Hagaru, just before the breakout south."

Dulles carefully placed his pipe down on the desk. "I believe President Truman compared Chosin to Xenophon's retreat and said the Marines beat old Xenophon by a mile when it came to the fight. I agree. The Greek mercenaries didn't have to face twenty-below-zero weather and the Persians weren't as tough as the Chinese. Have you read *The Expedition of Cyrus* about the march of the Ten Thousand to the sea, Mr. Collins?"

Collins shook his head. The truth was that he had not heard of Xenophon before President Truman's widely quoted comment and had only a vague sense of the story and its historical context.

Dulles paused momentarily to remove his eyeglasses; he cleaned them with his handkerchief. Then, after putting them back on, he spoke again. "Xenophon was an accidental commander. The Persians had fomented dissension in the ranks of the Greeks after Cyrus the Younger, their employer, had been killed in battle. The Spartan leader of the mercenaries, Clearchus, was lured to a conference where he was taken captive and later executed. After this treachery, Xenophon took command of the Ten Thousand and led them on their long and perilous march to safety and home."

Steele nodded. "There is that wonderful description of the Greeks reaching the mountain summit at Teches and the cry rising from their ranks of *Thálatta! Thálatta!* 'The sea! The sea!' They glimpsed the Black Sea in the distance and knew they were nearing home."

"What should not be lost," Dulles said, "is that the march of the Ten Thousand began as a story of subversion. Had Clearchus been more alert to the maneuvering of the Persians, he never would have been tricked."

"Do you see subversion involved somehow in Korea?" Collins asked, confused, not sure what parallel Dulles was trying to draw.

"Stalin stands in the shadows behind the Chinese intervention," Dulles said. "They would not have entered the war without his backing. Nor would the North Koreans have invaded last summer. I talked with Dr. Jung about Stalin at one point. Jung thought he was a modern Genghis Khan, a brute intent on dominating. Stalin spent most of his adult life fighting the Czar and Jung said that we often become the thing we fight the hardest. He thought Stalin might even declare himself Czar at some point."

"Perhaps a Czar in everything but name," Collins said. "His fellow Communists might be a bit touchy about that."

"I can imagine," Dulles said. "What was the point of the revolution if you end up with a Red Czar? As to your upcoming trip, I'm sure General Eisenhower will appreciate hearing your account of what happened. Whether or not this is a scheme by Stalin to divert us from Europe will become clear over time."

"I'll gladly talk to anyone who can change the way we're fighting the war," Collins said. "Matthew thinks General Eisenhower may be one of those men."

"Let's hope that he is," Dulles said. "I would like to chat when you return from Paris." He paused for a moment. "Writers make very good intelligence officers, you know."

"I'm not volunteering for that role," Collins said, somewhat stiffly.

"Of course not," Dulles said. "But the fact remains that journalists have the skills and temperament for the work. They're curious by nature. They collect facts and make sense of them. And they have some insights into the workings of the human heart. Did you know that Daniel Defoe was a British spy?"

"I did not."

"Defoe was a fascinating man. A merchant, an embezzler, a soldier, a novelist, and the first truly modern journalist. He spied on behalf of William of Orange and although he never wrote about his exploits, I imagine his creative skills came in handy. I believe we can learn from literature. Conrad better understood the motives of double agents than our in-house experts do, in my opinion. Take that short story of his, 'The Secret Sharer.' I don't think there's a better description of the mental strain imposed on an agent-in-place." He shifted his attention to Steele. "Matthew, can we turn to the more practical? What progress have you made on the Trojan Horse follow-up?"

"I've widened my inquiry beyond the ways Trojan Horse might have been compromised," Steele said. "The leakage of secret information appears to be more widespread. Some of our recent setbacks in Korea may be linked to intelligence flowing from Washington to our adversaries. I'm convinced now that it is not only the Soviet agent named Homer who's involved, but also perhaps others."

"You continue to have access to the Arlington Hall decrypts?"

"I do. Meredith Gardner won't be intimidated by Hoover."

Dulles turned to Collins to explain. "Gardner runs the code-breaking shop over at Arlington Hall. Unfortunately Mr. Hoover has blocked any Agency access to decoded cables. Matthew has been kept fully informed, however, in large part because he has been a technical advisor to the project. So we know what we need to know. Mr. Hoover believes that we're ignorant of the investigation into Homer—a Soviet agent stationed in the British embassy during the war—but we're not. In fact, thanks to Matthew, we may be the only ones with the complete picture."

"Excuse me," Collins said. "I'm not cleared for classified information. I don't understand why you would discuss this in front of me."

"I rely on Matthew's estimation of character and he tells me you can be trusted," Dulles said. "The fact, Mr. Collins, is that you paid quite a high personal price because of our failure with Trojan Horse.

I believe that you have a right to know how we are seeking to repair some of that damage."

Collins nodded, but he couldn't help but wonder about the motives of Dulles and Steele. Did they hope to flatter him, to make him feel that he was one of them? Was the idea to persuade him to present the approved Agency view of what should be done in Korea to General Eisenhower? Yet Collins wasn't sure what that might be—Steele had been silent about what he should say in Paris about the Chosin campaign.

"Here's the latest update," Steele said to Dulles, handing him an accordion file folder tied with black ribbon. Dulles, carefully untied the folder and retrieved a single sheet of paper from it. He briefly scanned the paper and then looked up at Steele thoughtfully for a moment. Then Dulles read the document a second time.

"Fascinating," he said. "Have you shared this with anyone else?"

"You're the first and only one to see it," Steele said.

"Good. Let's keep it that way for now. I think you should pursue this avenue with some urgency." Dulles glanced over at Collins. "Matthew and I must keep some of our cards hidden, for the moment. The time may come when we can include you."

"I understand," Collins said.

"By the way, Allen," Steele began, "I plan to stop by Kim Philby's house after we leave here and let him know that I will be out of town for a few days on my vacation. As a professional courtesy."

"Splendid," Dulles said. "Do brief our colleague in full."

"I shall. Just as we discussed."

Dulles again returned his attention to Collins. "I'd be interested in what you think of Mr. Philby. He's our intelligence liaison—our elegant and dashing liaison—with the British here in Washington.

Perhaps you can give me your impressions of him when you tell me about your talk with General Eisenhower."

"I may be able to stop by after I return, although I'm a bit overdue on a vacation I'm planning to take in the Keys."

"I'd be grateful if you can find the time," Dulles said. He waved his hand toward the door. "I'm cut off from the field these days, stuck at a desk, so it's a distinct pleasure to hear about what is actually going on beyond these walls."

Dulles rose to his feet, making it clear that the interview was over, and then followed them to the door of his office. He gave Steele a collegial pat on the back.

"Good luck on your trip," he said. "Good hunting, Matthew."

As they walked back to Steele's car, Collins thought about Dulles' soft-spoken charm and display of erudition. Collins reminded himself not to be fooled by it; Allen Dulles was no gentle Mr. Chips. He was a hardened OSS veteran with a history of clandestine operations against the Nazis where people were killed in cold blood when the mission demanded it.

Their adversary had changed, but Collins didn't believe for a moment that Dulles, or Steele, of any of their Agency colleagues would flinch from making hard, life-and-death choices when the circumstances called for them. Collins had suffered the consequences of that harsh calculus once before, he reminded himself, and he had no desire to repeat the experience.

Eleven

They drove north from the CIA's E Street complex and followed Massachusetts Avenue until they reached the Cathedral Heights neighborhood where Kim Philby lived. On the way there, Steele explained that Philby had been sent to Washington in October 1949 to serve as the liaison between the British Secret Intelligence Service and the FBI and CIA. Although Philby was an officer of the SIS, he was listed as first secretary at the British embassy.

"Philby comes from an unorthodox background," Steele said. "His father, St. John Philby, served in the Indian Civil Service and charted Saudi Arabia's Empty Quarter from the back of a camel. Wrote a book about it. Married a slave girl given to him by the Saudi King, then converted to Islam in 1930 and took the name Hajj Abdullah. Remarkable story."

"The son has taken a more conventional path."

"He has, although he's nicknamed after Kipling's Indian spy. His full name is Harold Adrian Russell Philby."

"I take it he's expecting your visit?"

"He's at home this afternoon. I told him I'd stop by for a quick drink. Philby likes to entertain. A quite sociable man."

Philby lived on Nebraska Avenue, near the campus of American University. The houses and lawns in his neighborhood were well-maintained and the wide streets were lined with large oak and maple trees.

Philby greeted them politely when they arrived at his front door. He matched Collins' mental picture of an upper-class British civil servant: a tall, fair-haired man with regular features, polished manners, and a reserved demeanor. Collins guessed that he was in his early forties. Philby ushered them into his living room and suggested they try a glass of the Talisker Scotch he was drinking.

"It's from the Isle of Skye," Philby explained. "Robert Louis Stevenson called it the king of drinks."

"With a recommendation like that, we'd be foolish not to join you," Steele said. Philby poured them both a glass and invited them to sit down. Collins found that the Scotch had a sweet and somewhat smoky taste with a slight bite.

They were interrupted by the arrival of another man, who Philby introduced as Guy Burgess, a second secretary at the embassy. "Guy is my lodger," Philby said. "He's also a friend of many years standing."

Burgess' dissolute appearance was a surprise. While also fair-haired, his face was puffy and he had none of Philby's sleekness. Burgess smelled strongly of alcohol and tobacco and sweat. His fingers were yellow from nicotine and stains marred Burgess' suit jacket and pants—but, strangely, his black patent leather shoes were shined to perfection.

Burgess hurried over to the array of bottles on the side table and, uninvited, poured himself a glass of Talisker. He sat down in an upholstered chair and crossed his legs at his ankles.

"Are you gentlemen veterans of Wild Bill's regime?" Burgess asked. "I've heard the Agency is crammed full of Donovan's cronies." His tone was challenging, almost hostile. Collins figured that Burgess had already downed a few drinks.

Steele nodded. "As it happens, I served in Switzerland, with Allen Dulles. Perhaps you know Allen?"

"I know of him," Burgess said. "By all accounts, another misguided American romantic. I suppose that he's directing his energies against the Soviets now, like some hyperactive Boy Scout."

"Guy, really," Philby said with a pained look on his face. "I know Dulles and he's not at all like that."

Burgess shrugged and took a generous gulp of his whiskey. "And what connection to Dulles do you have?" he asked Collins. "Are you also in the spy business?"

"I'm a newspaperman," Collins said. "Just back from Korea."

"Dennis also covered the Pacific campaign," Steele said. "Saipan and Okinawa."

Collins found Burgess' bloodshot eyes trained on him. "Then you have experienced the folly of that megalomaniac MacArthur," Burgess said. "He came close to sacrificing the entire American Army, didn't he? Served him right, in my book, for his arrogance. Not that you should be fighting in Korea in the first place. It passes all understanding why you would defend that corrupt dictator Rhee and his wealthy landlord friends. They were all in bed with the Japanese, you know. Now they've just changed masters."

Philby shook his head disapprovingly. "Perhaps you should write a letter to the editor of the *Manchester Guardian*, Guy. I doubt that our friends want to hear you ranting on about this."

"It's a free country," Collins said. "We're used to people ranting."

"I agree," Steele said. "Mr. Burgess should feel free to express his views openly. I believe that quite a few in my own shop might agree with him on some of his points."

Burgess didn't seem pleased with Steele's comment. "Well, then I would hope that people in your shop would recognize that America can't expect to throw its weight around without a violent counterreaction. Neocolonialism is just colonialism with Coca-Cola, not any better. If your idea is to establish your own empire, now that's the sun has set on ours, you're in for a harsh lesson. You're not the only one with an arsenal of atomic bombs. The Russians have them now, too."

Steele seemed more amused than offended by Burgess. "Our involvement in Korea isn't driven by neocolonialism. It's the consequence of some errors of judgment on both sides. In the end, though, when the North Koreans came south they didn't leave us much choice."

"Nor us," Philby said. "Attlee made it clear from the start that we would support you."

"You've sent brave men," Collins said. "I met some of your Royal Marines at Hagaru. They had been part of Task Force Drysdale and fought their way through a place they called Hellfire Valley to reach Hagaru, where General Smith had established his headquarters. Then they stepped into the defensive line and helped beat back the Chinese."

"We're quite good when it's time to battle the local wogs," Burgess said. "That's what a century or two of misbegotten imperialism will do for you. I'm sure our boys displayed the proper stiff upper lip. The playing fields of Eton and all that."

"I don't know anything about that," Collins said. "I just know courage when I see it. Anyone who was at Hagaru will never forget what the Royal Marines did."

The room became silent. Steele gave Collins a slight nod, a signal that he had appreciated his rebuke of Burgess.

Philby broke the silence, looking to smooth things over. "One of the differences between us is how we express our patriotism. What did Churchill say, 'One people separated by a common language'? We tend to understatement, but in the end we do pull together for king and country. 'This sceptered island' and all that."

Burgess turned to Collins, suddenly defensive. "You should know that I have a signed copy of Winston's speeches presented to me at Chartwell in October 1938 by the great man himself. That impresses even the High Tories, although it probably wouldn't satisfy the bloody McCarthyites."

"I have no more use for McCarthy than you do," Collins said.

"But the senator has some powerful backers," Philby said. "They say McCarthy has dated two of Ambassador Kennedy's daughters. They also say Kennedy's son, a war hero, will be running for the Senate next year. Quite a family. The father was a bit of an America Firster, wasn't he?"

"He was," Collins said. "But he lost his oldest son in the war and Jack Kennedy, the one in Congress who may run for the Senate, was badly wounded in the Pacific."

"You were a Chamberlain man yourself before the war, weren't you, Kim?" Steele asked.

Collins could see Steele's pointed remark had caught Philby off guard. "I wasn't the only one to think that Winston was a bit of an alarmist and that Neville's more diplomatic approach to the Germans would be more productive," Philby said. "I was wrong, but I was far from alone in my misjudgment."

Burgess grinned, displaying his stained and uneven teeth. "I guess not everyone appreciated Winston the way I did, from the very start."

Philby reached over and gripped Burgess' right arm firmly. "We don't want to detain you, Guy, any longer. Why don't you carry on with your own business?"

"Right-o," Burgess said. "It's off to the trains, then. There's the most marvelous O-gauge model train set in the basement below. Our line would be the envy of British Rail." He saluted them with his glass and then downed the remaining whiskey.

They watched in silence as he left the room. Philby waited until they heard Burgess descend the stairs into the basement before he spoke.

"My apologies, gentlemen," he said. "Guy so enjoys making a dramatic first impression that he sometimes forgets himself. He delights in playing the provocateur."

"It takes all types," Steele said. "Isn't that the saying?" He swirled the Talisker in his glass, studying it. "As it happens, I won't be around for a few days, Kim. I wanted to let you know. A quick trip to Europe. Dennis will be joining me."

"What's the occasion?" Philby asked. "More than sight-seeing, I would imagine."

"A fact-finding mission," Steele said. "We're flying to Paris to consult with some of our French colleagues and compare notes on a Soviet illegal of interest. And Dennis will brief some of the brass there at Allied headquarters about what he saw in Korea."

"That's a bit of a thankless task." Philby looked over at Collins, openly appraising him. "I covered the Spanish Civil War for the *Times*. I can't think of a nastier invention by man than that of modern warfare."

"You'll get no argument from me on that," Collins said. "And the war in Korea has been particularly nasty."

"There's nothing like a first-hand account," Steele said quickly. "Uncensored. It may prove of some value for our commanders in Europe if the balloon goes up again there."

"God forbid," Philby said, "but I agree. And you say you're discussing Russian agents with the French?"

"That we are," Steele said. "I think we may be nearing a breakthrough." He contemplated the whiskey in his glass for a moment, reflecting. "Have you ever heard of a Soviet operative named Anatoli Yatov? He's First Directorate. A rather violent reputation. Part of the assassination squad the Soviets sent to Spain."

"Yatov? Can't say that I have."

"We believe he's in the United States, running agents. Yatov may even be handling a Washington cell. The French have compiled quite a dossier on him, which they have agreed to share with us. Photographs of the man, details on passports he has used in the past, some of his operational methods. If the stuff is as good as the French say, we'll be able to narrow our search for him."

"Good luck on that, then," Philby said. "Let's hope they have something concrete on the fellow." He turned to Collins. "Do enjoy the City of Light, Mr. Collins. Still a bit chilly there, but the food and wine should more than make up for it."

Steele stood, ready to leave, and Collins followed suit. Philby followed them outside to the Packard.

"So when do you take off on your trip?" Philby asked Steele.

"Tomorrow," Steele said. "We'll meet with the French the day after our arrival. Dennis will brief later in the afternoon. That's our schedule for now."

Philby shook their hands briskly. "Bon voyage, gentlemen," he said. "Please give me a call when you return, Matthew, so you can fill me in on what you've learned from your trip. His Majesty's government will happily pay for the first round."

"What did you think of our British colleagues?" Steele asked Collins as they drove back to the house on Hoban Road.

"Burgess is actually attached to the British embassy? That's on the level? He's the strangest diplomat I've ever met, if that's the case."

"He is at the embassy. I'm not quite sure who in the Foreign Office protects him. Burgess is a notorious homosexual, you know. I think he's made a pass at every handsome young man within the District of Columbia. He apparently believes diplomatic immunity exempts him from the local sodomy laws."

"Perhaps he has family connections? He did drop Churchill's name."

"Not from what I've heard," Steele said. "They say he's brilliant when he puts his mind to it. Can quickly review ten memorandums and fashion a coherent summary in a few minutes."

"He struck me as a mean drunk," Collins said. "I prefer happy drunks."

"I'm surprised that Philby doesn't intervene," Steele said. "Tell his friend to take a bath and get his suit cleaned and pressed. The contrast between the two of them is remarkable. But growing up with St. John—or Hajj Abdullah—as your father might very well inure you to the eccentric and strange. By Philby family standards, maybe Burgess isn't that shocking."

Steele briefly took his eyes off the road to glance at Collins. "You didn't care for Philby, either, did you?"

"Was it that obvious?"

"No, you disguised it well. I'm getting to know you better, Dennis. To read you."

"I can't point to any one thing Philby said that makes me dislike him, but I do," Collins said. "He's smug and that rubs me the wrong way. I've learned to trust my instincts about people, and you're right, I don't care for him. And do you like him?"

"Kim Philby's intelligent, well-read, and we're colleagues so I should, shouldn't I? But in the year or so that I've known Philby, I've never had a single glimpse of who the man truly is, what he believes. He's all charm and calculation." Steele paused and smiled. "Yes, I'm also a man who calculates, but I do so for a reason. I believe that it matters who wins this struggle we are engaged in and that our vision of liberty and individual freedom is closer to how God intends us to live. Philby would most likely find those sentiments sentimental and quite embarrassing. In poor taste."

"That's not much of an endorsement," Collins said. "It sounds like you don't care for him, either."

"Truth be told, I don't," Steele said. "When it comes to Kim Philby, I think your instincts are pretty damn good."

Collins welcomed the chance to retreat to the privacy of the Steele's guest house. He took a shower and shaved and changed into a lightweight shirt and slacks. He was reading a copy of the *Washington Star* when there was a light knock on the door and it opened slightly to reveal Penny Steele.

"May I come in?" she asked.

Collins wordlessly motioned for her to enter the sitting room.

"I wanted to talk to you in private," she said. "I know you and Matthew will be traveling tomorrow and I didn't want to miss my chance while I'm feeling somewhat better. So I got my courage up and so here I am."

Collins didn't say anything. He wasn't sure quite what to expect, because Penny had been so changed by the events of the recent past.

"I've not been feeling well for some time," she said. "It's been hard on Matthew. I haven't been much of a wife and a mother, and I'm not a very good patient. When I was younger, there were a few times when I would feel the blues, but never like this. They're blues that won't go away. I wake up and that sadness is still there, hanging over me. At times, I wonder what the point is. Am I being punished for something? Why can't I shake it?"

"I don't think you're being punished."

"You may find this a bit strange. Matthew and I are both taking instruction with Father Loughlin at Holy Trinity."

"Instruction? To become a Catholic?" Collins tried to keep a neutral expression on his face.

"Father Loughlin isn't a Quaker." She laughed nervously. "I know what you're thinking, Dennis. You grew up in the church and you're a skeptic and so it has no mysteries for you. It's not the same for us. There is a promise of grace there that is incredibly appealing. When Matthew first suggested we attend Holy Trinity, I thought he might be angling for an exorcism. For me." She smiled at her own joke. "To banish my melancholy demons. I think Matthew would convert to Mohammedism if he believed that it would cure me."

"I'd stick with Father Loughlin. You won't have to pray to Mecca five times a day."

"You find humor in almost everything, don't you?"

"It's the Irish in me," he said. "You know that. We joke to keep the tears from falling."

"I'm so glad that you're here," she said. "There are some things we need to talk about. Could we do that?"

"I'm all ears."

"This is so difficult. It's about Caleb, and how you two share a connection." She rubbed her hands together briskly, as if she wanted to warm them up, a signal of her nervousness.

"I don't understand."

"There's no easy way to say this, Dennis. I'm sorry to spring this on you. You see, you are Caleb's father."

He wondered for a moment whether she had slipped into some sort of delusional state. Was she fantasizing, mixing up the real and the imagined? He scrutinized her closely, not sure what signs of possible mental imbalance to look for.

"Caleb's father? How can that be?"

"That one time we made love," she said. "In New York at your apartment, in September. We were careless and I was unlucky. It had to be you because there was no one else. I didn't know that I was carrying Caleb until December."

"You're sure?"

"I'm sure. You've seen him, Dennis. Didn't you notice the clear resemblance? The dark hair? The eyes?"

"I wasn't looking for one," he said. "How would I have known? You never told me. Now I don't know what to say."

He remembered the night well enough. They had come back to his apartment after dinner at Maison Henri, both of them a bit tight, and had gone to bed and it had been like old times, when they were lovers before the war. They were good together that way, always had been. But then, later, things fell apart.

"I'm sorry you had to learn about Caleb this way."

"Why didn't you tell me before? For Christ's sake, why did you keep it a secret?"

"I wanted you to know," she said. "If things had been different between us. . ." Her voice trailed off. "Remember how we ended?"

"That wouldn't have mattered."

"If I had told you we both know that you would have asked me to marry you, to make me an honest woman. If I had been scared enough and weak enough to say yes, then what? Every time that you looked at me, you would have been reminded of the past, of how that week in New York ended. Would you secretly blame me for Karina? After all, if I had not kept things from you, if I told you about my relationship with Matthew, things might have turned out differently."

"You never gave me a chance to decide," Collins said flatly.

"How many ghosts can a marriage hold? No, I made the right choice at the time."

"Did Matthew know before he married you?"

"Of course he did," she said, coldly. "As soon as I realized that I was pregnant, I told him. That was in early December, when we were back in Washington. We announced our engagement in February and we planned to get married in June, in the National Cathedral, but when I started showing we realized we couldn't wait. So we had a ceremony in April, just for my parents and a few friends. And then Caleb showed up in June."

"So why tell me now?"

"For when Caleb is older." She paused. "When I started feeling poorly, Matthew and I talked about it. I believe that Caleb should know the truth about who his father is. I thought that if you knew you would want to have contact with him over the years ahead—first as a friend of the family—and that it would be less of a shock when the time comes."

"What did your husband think of this idea?"

"He has agreed. Matthew was reluctant at first, but he knows how much this matters to me."

Collins didn't know how to respond. He had never expected to be confronted with the news that he was the father of Penny's child. "So what now?" he managed. "What do you propose that I do?"

"That's up to you. I would hope that you would spend time with Caleb. I want you to get to know him."

"Why did you wait until today to tell me?" he asked. "What if I had flown off to Florida yesterday? Why didn't you tell me then?"

"I lost my nerve," she said. "But if Matthew had not been able to persuade you to take this trip to Paris with him, and to stay here with us in Washington for a few days, he promised that he would tell you about Caleb himself."

Collins shook his head. "I need some time to think about this, Penny. I'll acknowledge Caleb as my son if and when the appropriate time comes. I'm not sure what else makes sense."

"Do you hate me for this?" she asked. "Do you hate me for what I've done?"

"No," he said, softening. "How could I? You did what you thought was right at the time. I don't blame you. I have to take responsibility for my own actions. I'm just not sure where we go from here."

"Would you be willing to talk to Matthew about it? About how it could work? When you're on the trip together?"

Collins nodded. "It's a conversation we must have at some point, so we might as well have it. I can imagine that it will be very hard for him, maybe harder for him than for me."

"Matthew will do the right thing," she said. "Please talk to him. You'll see. He will want what's best for Caleb, and in his heart, Matthew knows that this is it. I have no doubt that it is."

Twelve

They took an overnight TWA flight from Washington to Paris. Collins and Steele sat across from each other in aisle seats, but Steele showed little interest in conversation. Collins didn't really want to talk either. He had resolved not to raise the question of Caleb; he wanted Steele to broach the matter first.

So Collins tried to sleep during the flight, reclining his seat as far back as it would go. One of the stewardesses, a tall brunette with bobbed hair, offered him a pair of earplugs and it helped muffle the roar of the engines and he finally managed to doze off.

He woke when the plane began its descent outside Paris and he was surprised to find morning light streaming through the clouds. Collins caught a brief glimpse of the Eiffel Tower, the great white basilica of Sacré Coeur on Montmartre and then the Seine River and the city spread out below as they made their way toward Le Bourget airport.

It was his first visit to Paris, and Collins regretted that he would not have the time to explore the city. He was there with one purpose, and it wasn't to visit the Latin Quarter and the Eiffel Tower and the Louvre and drink absinthe in Les Deux Magots. He promised himself that he would return, but sightseeing would have to wait for a later day.

Once they had passed through passport control and had collected their luggage, Steele led the way through the crowded airport terminal. A driver was waiting by the front glass doors holding a sign that read MR. HANNAY and Steele beckoned for Collins to follow him over to the man.

"I imagine that Lord Tweedsmuir wouldn't have objected to our borrowing the name," Steele said. "We are here on somewhat of a covert mission."

Collins had to grin. Lord Tweedsmuir was better known as John Buchan, the author of the spy thriller *The Thirty-Nine Steps*, which had featured his Everyman hero Richard Hannay. The film version had made Alfred Hitchcock's reputation as a director. Buchan had finished his career as governor general of Canada and Collins remembered seeing a newsreel of his state funeral when Buchan died in 1940.

They drove south from the airport through St. Denis and soon arrived at the more densely-populated parts of Paris. Six years after the end of the war, Collins spied few if any signs of the conflict that had engulfed Europe. Paris had been spared, thanks largely to its German military governor, Dietrich von Choltitz, who had disobeyed direct orders to destroy the city before the Allies arrived. The townhouses, apartments, and private mansions along the cobblestoned streets gave no indication that violence had ever come to this cosmopolitan and cultured place. Of course it had, Collins knew. The Gestapo had a prison on the Rue de Saussaies in the Eighth Arrondissement and the SS occupied 84 Avenue Foch. Thousands of French Jews had been rounded up and sent to the Nazi death camps.

During their flight over, Collins had skimmed through a tourist guide to Paris, so he recognized the broad expansive plaza of the Place de la Concorde when they arrived there. It had been the site for the main guillotine during the Terror, and was now dominated by an Egyptian obelisk in its center.

Their driver pulled up in front of the Hôtel de Crillon, where a uniformed porter opened the car door and carried their luggage into the hotel. Steele explained that he preferred to stay at the Crillon because of its historical connection to America. Ben Franklin had negotiated the first treaties between France and the United States there, Woodrow Wilson and the American delegation had planned the League of Nations in its rooms, and General Eisenhower had made it his headquarters after the Allies liberated Paris in the summer of 1944.

"Of course Ike and his staff replaced the German high command at the Crillon," Steele said. "To the victors go the spoils."

The lobby had an understated elegance with its marble floors and walls, crystal chandeliers, and antique furniture. The desk clerk greeted Steele warmly and dispensed with a formal check-in. Steele explained that they wouldn't need the porter to take their bags to their rooms and the clerk nodded and handed both of them room keys.

After they had collected their luggage and were walking back through the lobby to the elevator, a voice called out Steele's name. They turned around to find a slim, dark-haired man in a finely tailored blue suit striding over to greet them. After he had embraced Steele, kissing him on both cheeks, the man introduced himself to Collins as Phillipe Gillain of the Service de Documentation Extérieure et de Contre-Espionage, the French equivalent of the CIA.

"I must inform you, Matthew, that you and your colleague were tailed from the airport to here," Gillain said. "There are at least two men now watching the hotel from across the Place de la Concorde, so I think it's safe to assume that you will have company anywhere you go in the city."

Steele nodded gravely. "What do you know about them?"

"They are Czechs. They were apparently waiting at the airport, as was one of my men who spotted them. He had seen them before at the Czech embassy. I'd hazard the guess that they're working on behalf of the Russians. They'd have no interest in you otherwise."

"How did they identify us?" Collins asked. "We weren't the only Americans on the flight. How did they know we were coming?"

"An excellent question," Gillain said.

"They must have been tipped off," Steele said. He did not appear disturbed by the thought. In fact, Collins thought, he seemed strangely pleased. "There may be a photograph or two of me in Moscow Center's files."

"Is there anything you would like us to do?" Gillain asked. "We can make it uncomfortable for them, if you wish."

"No, I don't think that is necessary."

"I see," Gillain said wistfully. "It's a shame, though. The Czech agents here under diplomatic cover are a tough lot. I would welcome a chance to deliver them a stiff message."

"Understood," Steele said. "I'm sure you'll get your opportunity to badger them, just not today."

"How shall we handle your visit? Security, that is?"

Steele suggested that Gillain instruct his team to follow them at a discreet distance. "That is, if you can spare the men."

Gillain responded with an expressive shrug. "Of course."

"Let the Czechs follow us. I would ask you to intervene only in the most extreme circumstances. If they tried something clumsy."

Gillain waved his hand in a gesture of dismissal. "They would attempt direct action only out of desperation. Their Russian masters recognize that we could not allow such an affront to our sovereignty—an attack on our American colleagues on the streets of Paris. It would prompt a most unpleasant response." He considered the matter. "Are you expecting such trouble? Are you prepared for such an attempt?" He reached into the pocket of his suit-jacket. "I can lend you some artillery if you like. You call it artillery, do you not? I believe I can find a Luger for you, which I know you prefer, Matthew." Gillain grimaced to indicate what he thought of Steele's preference for German firearms.

"I assume that your team will be outfitted appropriately?" Steele asked.

"But of course."

"Then I will decline your kind offer and rely on the good offices of your Service."

They agreed to meet for dinner at seven o'clock. "I can assure you that you'll like the restaurant, Chatard's," Gillian said. "The food is *magnifique*."

"How could it not be?" Steele asked. "We're in Paris, after all."

The drive from the Hôtel de Crillon to the restaurant took ten minutes. Chatard's occupied the ground floor of a two-story eighteenth century building on the Rue Duret, a narrow side street just off the Avenue Foch.

As they entered the restaurant, Collins heard the distinctive strains of Edith Piaf's "La Vie en Rose" coming from a nearby record player. He had seen the waif-like Piaf in New York, at the Versailles, in 1949, before the tragic airplane accident that had taken the life of her lover, the middleweight boxer Marcel Cerdan. Collins had heard that she was back in Paris, working with a young songwriter named Aznavour, and wondered if Piaf would sing in a New York club again anytime soon. He somehow doubted it—her memories of Cerdan were probably too closely fused to the city for her to want to return just yet.

Phillipe Gillain greeted them in the cramped foyer of the restaurant. He quickly peered over Collins' shoulder toward the street.

"I assume that you were followed here? By your Czech comrades?"

Steele nodded, surprising Collins who had not spotted any obvious signs of surveillance on their way to the restaurant.

They occupied a corner table, near the back of the restaurant, facing the front entrance. Collins had to smile: in New York restaurants it was the gangsters who insisted on sitting where they could see anyone entering the place. He imagined that Frank Costello, who ran gambling in all five boroughs, would have approved of their positioning.

Gillain quickly ordered aperitifs of Ricard Pastis for them. "The Czechs are surprisingly diligent today," he said. "I've stationed one of my best men just outside the door so we will not be disturbed here." He took a sip of his drink. "It is pleasant to be back in Paris, no? Like the old days. Do you plan to call on the ambassador while you are here, Matthew?"

Steele turned to Collins to offer an explanation. "I was stationed here briefly after the Liberation. Our office was on the Champs-Elysées, above Madame Pinson's dance studios. A short walk from the Crillon. I did not stay for too long, unfortunately, because duty called me to Berlin." He addressed Gillain. "We will not intrude upon Ambassador Bruce on this visit."

"Did the ambassador work with you in Switzerland during the war?"

"No, Bruce was based in London so we didn't have much contact. I understand he is quite competent."

"That he is."

They were interrupted by the arrival of the rotund owner of the restaurant, Monsieur Chatard, attired in his toque and white chef's blouse, and he seemed quite pleased at finding Phillipe Gillain in his establishment. He snapped his fingers and instructed a waiter to bring a bottle of chilled white wine, and then conferred with Gillian about their meal, which they decided should start with salads and fresh chestnut soup, feature an entree of Sole Meunière with vegetables, and finish with an apple tarte tatin.

"So what can I do for you, Matthew?" Gillian asked after he and Chatard had finished setting the menu. "You were suitably vague on the telephone."

"I have a favor to ask," Steele said. He produced a buff-colored envelope from his inner suit-jacket pocket and slid it across the table to Gillain. "This is the dossier on Anatoli Yatov of the First Directorate. He has surfaced in Berlin and New York, most recently. I've included a photo, the only one we have." Steele paused. "I would greatly appreciate it if you would keep an eye out for him here. He may surface in Paris at some point."

"And should we encounter this Yatov?"

"If you could watch him discreetly, and then contact me. I'll come over and we can mount a joint operation to neutralize him. He has been operating as an illegal—no diplomatic cover—and he has ordered at least one assassination in the U.S., so in my book that makes him fair game."

"It's like that, is it?"

"I'm afraid so," Steele said. "If such a joint undertaking will compromise you or the Service, I will understand. You can alert me if he appears in Paris and I will settle matters without involving you any further."

Gillain studied Steele closely. "There is an element of the personal in this?"

"Nothing that would cloud my professional judgment."

"I see. I trust your judgment, Matthew. You will have whatever assistance you may need if and when that day arrives."

Steele raised his wine glass in appreciation. "*Merci.*"

"*De rien.*"

Collins had remained silent during the conversation, confused by what Steele had said. Steele had told Philby that the French had a dossier on Yatov, but Gillian clearly had never heard of the Russian. Why had Steele misled Philby? It didn't make sense.

"Dennis is here to brief General Eisenhower on the situation in Korea," Steele said.

"You were in Korea recently?" Gillain asked Collins.

"I left in December," Collins said. "After the Marines were evacuated from Hungnam."

"A difficult time, no?"

Gillain took a silver cigarette case from his pocket and, after clicking it open, offered a Gauloise, to Collins, who took it. Collins found his Zippo and lit both of their cigarettes. Steele was already puffing on his pipe. Collins took a quick puff and found the Gauloise had a strong, almost harsh, taste.

"A very difficult time," Collins said. "The Chinese intervention caught us by surprise."

"You know we are fighting the Reds in Indochina and General de Lattre did win a formidable victory over the Vietminh at Vinh Yen. Now we ask for American bullets and bombs, but we understand that your State Department counsels caution."

"They are concerned about becoming overextended, because of Korea," Steele said. "And I think some in Washington are not eager to defend colonialism of any sort in Asia."

"That is understandable," Gillain said. "It was simpler before, no? The Boche was the enemy and we knew that we had to defeat him, to expel him from France. In Asia it was the Nipponese. We all agreed on that. Now, not so simple. While there are no Reds in Prime Minister Pleven's cabinet, the Communist Party remains strong here. The truth is that I cannot be sure that my own Service has not been penetrated. It is a different world we live in now." He glanced over at Steele. "All we can do is stand by our friends. That's the way to make things simple again."

Phillipe Gillain had accurately described the food at Chatard's—it was magnificent, and Collins felt sated and sleepy when they returned to the Crillon. Steele pulled him aside and suggested they have a brief chat. They sat in an alcove off the lobby where they would be undisturbed. Collins expected Steele might want to talk about Caleb, but instead he started the conversation by discussing their upcoming meeting with General Eisenhower.

"We have an hour with the general in the morning," Steele said. "As busy as he is, I'm pleased that he has carved out that much time for us."

"Have you met him before?" Collins asked.

"Once or twice. He's very direct. No nonsense. He's also very sharp and doesn't miss much. They say he plays a very good hand of poker."

"I don't," Collins said. "Too easy to read my face, I guess."

"I don't plan to say much, Dennis. The idea is for you to tell him what you saw. He needs to hear what really happened."

"I plan to," Collins said. "I didn't come all this way to sugarcoat the situation." It seemed like a good time to ask Steele about his conversation with Gillain on the topic of Anatoli Yatov. "You confused me at dinner. In Washington, you told Philby that you were coming here to get what the French had on Yatov. But it's clear that Gillain had never heard of him."

"That is true."

"And why the hell would the Czechs, or the Russians, care about what we are doing here?"

"Two questions with perhaps the same answer. You must bear with me. Our primary mission is to see General Eisenhower. A secondary goal of mine was to see if we showed up on the radar of the Soviets when we arrived in Paris. We have. That tells me something. This is an unscheduled, unofficial visit. Only Phillipe and General Eisenhower's aide were alerted that we were coming."

"And you trust Gillain?"

Steele smiled. "You're beginning to think like an intelligence officer, Dennis. Yes, Phillipe is trustworthy." He paused and put down his pipe. "It's time you knew more about the complete state of affairs. I'm on a bit of thin ice right now. There are some in Washington trying to lay the failure of Trojan Horse at my feet. When General Smith took over the Agency he decided to lower my profile. My office was moved from the East Building to the North Building, away from Smith and Allen Dulles. A public exile, as it were, to the far reaches of our American Kremlin. A message being delivered about my standing in the Agency, the equivalent to being sent to the attic without supper."

Steele walked over to the window and gazed out at the lights of the Place de la Concorde. "I have spent much of the last year trying to figure out how Trojan Horse was compromised after Morris Rose defected. It should have worked. We had convinced Moscow Center that we desperately wanted to retrieve the list of suspected Soviet agents that Rose had taken from the FBI. A perfect set-up to begin using the agents we had left off the list, the ones we had turned and could use to pass back any information we wanted the Russians to have. But they didn't bite. It became painfully obvious that somehow they knew."

"Someone told them?" Collins asked. "Or perhaps something else made them suspicious?"

"Someone told them," Steele said. "I am sure of that. It became more complicated last fall when the Agency began fielding complaints from Generals Walker and MacArthur that the North Koreans and Chinese appeared to know what moves we were about to make in the field, that they had advance knowledge of our tactical war plans. The prevailing wisdom was that the generals were making excuses, looking to blame someone else for their own mistakes. I wasn't so sure. It seemed to me that whoever had tipped off Moscow Center about Trojan Horse might have done the same with the intelligence about Korea. I began asking a series of questions. Who had access to those military plans? Who also knew about Trojan Horse? I always kept access to the Trojan Horse files to a limited few, and even then only a handful of men knew the full extent of what we had planned. I figured that a process of elimination might lead us to the source. So I focused on the gatekeepers, those with access to numerous streams of information."

Steele reached into his inside jacket pocket and pulled out a square of folded yellow legal paper. He unfolded it and showed Collins that it was covered by a spider's web of lines connecting names written on the page.

"This is my crib sheet," he said. "I began with those men in Washington with knowledge of Trojan Horse and possible access to military intelligence. My list initially included Hoover, Tolleson, and Lamphere from the FBI. From the Agency, Hillenkoetter, Smith, Dulles, and myself." He smiled. "I was able to rule myself out. And I learned that at least one other person, Kim Philby, apparently knew something about Trojan Horse."

"Had you shared the details of Trojan Horse with the British?"

"I had not. It seems that General Smith at some point passed along a general outline of the operation to Philby. No names, of course."

"But the Russians wouldn't need names," Collins said. "They'd immediately recognize that it was Morris and that the list of agents that you had fed him wasn't complete and therefore genuine."

"Correct. I needed more than that, however. From decrypted cables we knew that the Soviets had a source with the code-name of Homer in the British embassy in Washington in 1944 and 1945. The Brits worked up a short list of suspects. They narrowed it down to two candidates, Paul Gore-Booth and Donald Maclean. 'Homer' in Russian is a near-anagram for Gore, so they began with Gore-Booth, but it's become clear that Maclean is a better fit. The cables mentioned that Homer often visited New York and Maclean had traveled there to see his wife, who was pregnant and staying with her mother in the city. Maclean was with the embassy until September 1949, when he returned to England. Then the Foreign Office gave him the American desk, which meant that he had access to all of the stuff on Korea when war broke out in the summer of 1950."

"But he wouldn't have known about Trojan Horse if he left in September," Collins said.

"Exactly. Trojan Horse occurred after his departure and there was no way he would have known about it. It dawned on me then that there might be more than one agent in Washington supplying secrets to Moscow Center. Maclean might very well be Homer but he wasn't around to learn about Trojan Horse. So it had to be someone else. Then some of the later cables mentioned an agent code-named Stanley, a recent arrival. What if both Homer and Stanley were betraying us? Maclean was here when Homer was active. Stanley started showing up later, after Philby entered the picture."

"You think Stanley is Philby?"

"I do," Steele said. "Which is why I told him that little story about the French having the goods on Yatov. I believe that Yatov may be Philby's controller. If he is, Philby would have told him about our trip, and it would explain why the Czechs were waiting for us at Le Bourget."

Collins found it hard to accept Steele's theory. Could it be that two senior British officials in Washington had passed secrets to the Soviets? It seemed too fantastic to believe. Was Steele trying to find someone else to blame for the failure of Trojan Horse? To repair his own reputation at the Agency? To move back to the East Building, as it were?

"Can you prove any of this?" Collins asked. "Because frankly speaking, your theory of two agents in the upper echelons seems fairly outlandish."

"Lord knows that it is outlandish," Steele said. "Proving it will be difficult, but it can be done. I have some evidence, but I need more. I have learned something of great value from this trip, from finding the Czechs waiting for us at the airport."

"You believe that Philby is responsible?"

"I do. And mentioning Anatoli Yatov to him seemed to have set everything in motion. Yatov may very well be the key. If I am correct, if we can connect Yatov to Philby, then we have Philby dead to rights."

"Several big ifs."

"I've seen bigger," Steele said. "And my instincts tell me that Comrade Yatov is our man."

Thirteen

The Hôtel Astoria, the location for General Eisenhower's Paris headquarters, was a commanding structure on the Avenue des Champs-Elysées topped by two domes and featuring elaborate exterior balconies. Collins could tell that Steele was in a good mood as they arrived on time for their appointment, just before ten o'clock. Steele explained that the Astoria was known to Parisians as the "Kaiser's Hotel" because it had been built in the German style before the First World War and the Kaiser had planned to live there once his armies conquered Paris.

"It's a temporary spot for Ike and his people," Steele said. "They're building a permanent facility in Rocquencourt, out in the suburbs."

An Army major, Campbell Kerr, met them in the Astoria's lobby. He escorted them past the military police, and led them to Eisenhower's office. Steele nodded to Collins to enter first. As they advanced into the office, a lean man with sparse, graying hair and a ruddy complexion strode across the room and extended his hand to Collins. "Eisenhower," he said. They shook hands and Collins introduced himself.

He had seen Eisenhower once before in New York at the Waldorf, just after the general became president of Columbia University in 1948, but had never met him. Eisenhower looked fit in his freshly pressed uniform and seemed both taller, and somewhat younger, than Collins remembered from his newspaper photos. Collins thought ruefully for a moment of his own threadbare brown suit and nondescript necktie and hoped he wasn't making a poor impression on the general.

Eisenhower and Steele exchanged greetings. "Glad to have one of Beetle's men visit us," Eisenhower said. "I think he's the right man to run Central Intelligence. Certainly not shy about taking the reins of command."

"General Smith is not shy," Steele said. "And how do you feel about being back in uniform?"

"I hadn't expected to be called back from my plow," Eisenhower said. "But even when I was at Columbia I was still technically in the army. When you have the rank of General of the Army you never truly retire. I've got a simple job, now. The Secretary of Defense tells me that I'm here to keep the Soviets out, the Americans in, and the Germans down."

Collins and Steele sat on a small couch facing Eisenhower and Kerr who occupied wooden captain's chairs. Steele immediately broached the purpose of their visit.

"I thought it was important for you to hear details about what happened at the battle of Chosin from an objective eyewitness. Mr. Collins covered the campaign for the *New York Sentinel* and much of what he will relate to you hasn't been in the newspapers or in the intelligence reports about the fighting."

"We are half a world away from Korea," Eisenhower said. "It really isn't part of my current brief."

"Yet you may be called upon for advice and counsel concerning Korea. You may be asked to return to Washington in a command capacity at some point. The idea is to provide you an independent source of information about the situation."

"Courtesy of the Central Intelligence Agency," Eisenhower said. "Proof that, unlike General MacArthur, I should rely on your intelligence assessments in the future and support the full funding of your Agency."

"I am here on my own initiative," Steele said. "This is not an official Agency presentation. Mr. Collins volunteered to make the trip. We are both here on our own time, and on our own dime."

"Beetle doesn't know you're here?" Eisenhower gave them a broad grin. "I doubt that highly." He shifted his gaze to Collins. "And you volunteered?"

"I did. I figure that I have an obligation to some of the men I met in Korea who didn't make it back." He briefly told Eisenhower the story of Oliver Winslow and how Collins had traveled to Washington with his widow to relay his Winslow's message about the conduct of the war. "I didn't expect our visit would change anything. The chain of command doesn't particularly appreciate advice from junior officers. Mr. Steele has convinced me that this mission has a better chance of success."

"Is your editor aware that you are directly lobbying the senior officer corps?"

"I don't have an editor to answer to at the moment. The *Sentinel* went under, ceased publication, just before I returned from Korea."

"That's a shame. As I recall, your publisher was an internationalist."

"He was," Collins said. "I didn't have anything to do with the editorials, though. I just wrote my column."

"So why don't you tell me the story you came here to tell," Eisenhower said.

Collins nodded and took a deep breath. He began by recounting his experiences with the First Marines at Inchon and Seoul and then described the advance up the coast from Hungnam toward the Chosin Reservoir in November. On Thanksgiving Day the troops had been served a traditional American holiday meal of turkey, mashed potatoes, and cranberry sauce, but it was already so cold outside that the gravy froze on the plate before a man could get a fork of food to his mouth.

"I tagged along with the Tenth Corps as it moved north," Collins continued. "We didn't realize that the Chinese had encircled the advance units, nor that the Army's 31st Regimental Combat Team, which had been sent to the east side of the Chosin Reservoir, had also been surrounded. Thank God that General Smith ordered the construction of a crude airstrip at Hagaru, where he set up headquarters, over the objections of General Almond, who thought it would slow down the advance north. Smith ignored him. His staff told me that Smith didn't believe the intelligence coming from Tokyo. He was convinced that the Chinese forces posed an imminent threat."

General Smith's by-the-textbook tactics for preparing an effective defense eventually paid off, Collins explained. By developing and guarding the narrow and winding main supply route, and taking and holding the high ground whenever possible, Smith was later able to concentrate his forces in one place, in Hagaru, after the Chinese attack began. The Army units on the east side of the Chosin were the most exposed. Their commander, Colonel Allan MacLean, had left them spread out in several small hamlets. The Chinese hit them hard.

"General Almond flew in by helicopter to the front positions on the east side of the reservoir on November 28th," Collins said. "I talked to some of the men who were there and who witnessed the meeting between Almond and Lieutenant Colonel Don Faith, an officer who later replaced MacLean. Almond insisted that Faith should keep attacking north. He told Faith that he shouldn't let a group of laundrymen stop him."

Eisenhower shook his head and rose from his chair. He stood there for a moment, rocking on his heels, and then gestured for Collins to continue.

"They say General Almond awarded Colonel Faith a Silver Star on the spot, pinned it to his parka, and did the same to two other officers. Almond liked to award battlefield medals. After Almond left in the helicopter to fly back to Hagaru, Faith ripped off the Silver Star and threw it in the snow. He was overheard saying, 'What a damned travesty.'"

"None of this has been in the newspapers," Eisenhower said.

"It hasn't," Collins said. "I wasn't there to see it with my own eyes so I didn't write about it. I trust the men who told me the story but who knows? They were in bad psychological shape when I talked to them."

Eisenhower cleared his throat. "And you believe the story?"

"I do," Collins said. "By insisting on they continue to advance, General Almond had sentenced Colonel Faith, and his men, to death. Faith knew it. Their one chance of survival was a quick withdrawal to Hagaru. They might have kept the Chinese off the ridges above them with their mounted Bofor guns long enough to reach the Marine encampment."

Instead, Collins explained, when Colonel Faith attempted a breakout south on the first day of December, it was too late. Faith was killed and his Task Force Faith convoy stopped by the Chinese. With most of their officers dead, many of the enlisted men abandoned their vehicles and scattered into the nearby hills and ravines. Some sought escape on the ice of the Chosin Reservoir. Collins had witnessed the shattered remnants of the 31st RCT stumble into Hagaru. A determined lieutenant colonel, Olin Beall, had ventured out on the reservoir's ice and rescued almost three hundred survivors. He also discovered many soldiers who had died of their wounds or had frozen to death.

At General Smith's headquarters in Haragu, Collins said, it was impossible to tell what was happening beyond the defensive perimeter. The Marines in Yudam-ni, to the northwest, had also been encircled. They managed to fight their way out of the trap and Collins witnessed their march into Hagaru on the night of December 3rd, singing the Marine Hymn.

"The Chinese kept probing at night, trying to overwhelm us at Hagaru. I witnessed one such an attack when a small group of Chinese slipped through our lines and were beaten back by supply clerks and cooks and anyone else who could handle a rifle." Collins decided he wasn't going to say anything about being one of those hastily assembled defenders.

He explained how he left Hagaru on a C-47 flight the next day. From the air he could see the marks the battle had left on the nearby ridge lines, the dead bodies of the Chinese scattered across the hilly terrain, the pockmarks in the snow of the foxholes dug by the Marines, and the burned-out vehicles near the perimeter of the Marine encampment.

Collins had flown to Hungnam. From there he hitched a ride aboard a supply truck heading north to Chinghung-ni. That small town had become the jumping-off point for the First Battalion of Marines to move north to link up with their comrades moving south from the Chosin. "It took General Smith's forces almost forty hours to fight their way south to Koto-ri," Collins said. "The cold never let up. It was snowing heavily when the First Battalion attacked the Chinese on Hill 1081 to relieve the pressure on the column retreating south."

"I saw some of the photographs of the march in *Life* magazine," Eisenhower said. "The terrain is about as hostile and barren as it gets. A very brave group of men."

"Those photos were taken by David Douglas Duncan," Collins said. "A very brave man. He stayed with the Marines through the entire withdrawal."

"And what conclusions have you drawn about Chosin?" Eisenhower asked. "Speak frankly, please, Mr. Collins."

Collins took another deep breath. "A mistake from start to finish. General MacArthur never should have sent the Marines north that late in the fall and when we started encountering veteran Chinese troops, he should have halted the advance. In my opinion General Almond ignored the intelligence because he wanted to please MacArthur and that doomed Task Force Faith." Collins shook his head. "Oliver Winslow had it right. We shouldn't fight on their terms. We won't win a war of attrition."

Eisenhower nodded. "I have become convinced that the most dangerous man to have around is the 'yes man.' He will blind you to the flaws of your plans and to curry favor with you he will withhold his true opinion. I'm afraid that Douglas has surrounded himself with just such a group of admirers. As you probably know, I was his aide in the Philippines between the wars. I have seen the phenomenon first hand. It was partially the reason for my departure from Manila."

"We ought to see if the Chinese would accept a return to the status quo," Collins said. "A truce of some sort. Otherwise a lot of American boys will die in trying to push the Chinese out of Korea."

"Had we stopped at the 38th parallel in October the Chinese might have stayed out," Eisenhower said. "On the other hand, it's understandable why Douglas wanted to push north. Destroying the North Korean army would have allowed the creation of a unified country and that would have avoided the problems we're encountering with a divided Germany."

"I know some officers who thought we should have bombed across the Yalu when we moved north," Collins said, remembering his conversation with Jim Highsmith.

"General MacArthur wanted to hit the Chinese Army on both sides of the Yalu," Eisenhower said. "The Joint Chiefs told him that they couldn't commit the Air Force to such a strategy without endangering our position in Europe. We just don't have enough planes. The same issue with additional troops. Sending the 82nd Division to Korea would have left us without a ready reserve if the Soviets made a move in Germany."

Eisenhower stopped to reflect for a moment. "When I was Army chief of staff I told Congress that we needed to leave a division or two in Korea. They wouldn't listen. If they had, if they hadn't been in such a god-awful rush to bring our boys home, there wouldn't have been a war. I'm convinced of that. It didn't help that Acheson decided to tell the world that Korea was outside our hold line. An invitation for aggression."

"What do you make of our tactical position in Korea now?" Collins asked.

"From what I gather, General Walker recognized that he would have jeopardized the entire Eighth Army by trying to make a stand north of the 38th parallel. He pulled us back to a defensible line, although I doubt he characterized in those terms when communicating with Tokyo. We're fortunate that General Ridgway could step in when Walker was killed. Ridgway seems to have stabilized the line."

Eisenhower looked at Collins and then Steele. "Gentlemen, I appreciate your traveling quite some distance to see me. Mr. Collins, I'm particularly grateful that you would pursue this matter as a private citizen and that I was able to hear your first-hand report."

"As far as I am concerned, you have more than fulfilled whatever debt you owed Captain Winslow," Eisenhower said. "I promise you that I'll whatever I can to avoid any repetition of this tragedy. We're letting the Soviets know that we can hit them harder than they can hit us should they decide to test us here, in Europe. As to Korea, I agree that we must avoid a war of attrition. Whether I'm called upon to address that question is another matter." He paused. "Right now I have to worry about the Fulda Gap."

"The Fulda Gap?" Collins asked.

"There are two corridors of lowlands near the border with East Germany. An ideal route for invasion. We need a strong enough defense there so that if Stalin decides to move west, we don't have T-34 tanks rolling down the Champs-Elysées within days." He walked over to the closest window and looked out. "The Arc de Triomphe has had a magnetic appeal to dictators, I'm afraid. God help us if that day arrives. If we continue to signal our resolve here, we can convince Stalin the cost of his moving against us militarily would be too high."

Eisenhower glanced over at Major Kerr. "Perhaps you could treat Mr. Collins to a real cup of coffee," he said. "I'd like a private moment with you, Mr. Steele, if I might."

Collins spent fifteen minutes with Kerr drinking coffee—brewed from Chase & Sanborn roasted beans brought from the States, Kerr boasted—and waiting for Steele to finish his meeting with Eisenhower. When Steele arrived in the lobby, he flashed a satisfied smile, and thanked Kerr for his help in arranging their visit. Once outside on the street, Steele looked around to make sure that they could not be overheard.

"A productive morning," he said. "The General found you quite credible. He joked that we should replace military intelligence with a few hand-picked combat correspondents. You apparently confirmed much of what he had feared about the situation in Korea and its impact on the morale of the men. He is convinced, by the way, that the Marines at Chosin saved the Eighth Army from destruction by holding up the Chinese advance and decimating many of their best units. They kept us from losing the war right then and there."

"What does it mean in concrete terms? For the men there?"

"I can't say. While General Eisenhower is quite influential, it may require a change in administrations to alter course. The election is only eighteen months away, and there's talk that Ike may run for the presidency himself."

"Do you think that he will?"

Steele thought for a long moment. "If he concludes that the country needs him, he will. He's being encouraged to run by a fair number of people." He paused. "You can include me in that group.

As I just told him, there are no better alternatives. Ike laughed and said that if that was the case he truly feared for the country."

That night, after a quiet dinner at the Crillon, Steele mentioned that he planned to visit a nearby church, the Église Notre-Dame de l'Assomption, and wondered if Collins cared to join him.

"Sure," Collins told him. "Close enough that we can walk? I'd like to stretch my legs."

"It's close," Steele said. "Let's walk."

Pierre, the agent Gillain had stationed at the front door, didn't like the idea. He suggested that instead they take a cab, because if they went on foot it might prove difficult to keep an eye on the Czechs and make sure they kept a proper distance.

Steele argued briefly with Pierre, but eventually agreed that they should go to the church by car. When Collins exited the Crillon, hundreds of street lamps illuminated the Place de la Concorde; looking down the Champs-Elysées, he could make out the Arc de Triomphe in the distance. Above them, the sky was clear and he could see the moon. Collins regretted that Steele had let Pierre talk him out of their walk.

It was only a few minutes by taxi to the church, which stood on the corner of Rue Saint-Honoré and Rue Cambon. "The Poles in Paris come to this church to worship," Steele said. "They've made it their own." Collins caught a glimpse of a large dome looming overhead in the dark. They crossed a small plaza and climbed the steps to the entrance of the church.

"If our Czech friends have bothered to follow us, they will be intrigued by this visit," Steele said.

As they entered the church, Collins reflexively dipped his fingers in the holy water in the font. He made the sign of the cross and bowed slightly to the crucifix above the main altar at the front of the church. Steele followed suit.

They sat down in a pew near the front of the church. Several hundred feet above them the interior dome of the church featured a scene of the Assumption, a logical choice for a church named after that moment in New Testament history, Collins thought.

They sat there in silence. Steele stirred slightly and then got on his knees to pray. Collins wondered for a moment what Steele would pray for. The success of their mission? Better health for Penny? The state of his own soul?

As he considered the scene—the candles glittering in the darkened church, Steele on his knees in prayer—Collins had to give the man credit for his unpredictability. He glanced to the back of the church where a dark-haired man was now occupying the last pew. One of the Czechs shadowing them? Or one of Gillain's men? Or just a believer seeking the same comfort in worship that Steele had?

By the time they were ready to leave, the man in the back had disappeared. Steele paused once they were in the vestibule, the door to the nave shut behind them. "I almost feel sorry for the Czechs. If they report that I stopped here, then Moscow Center will want to know why. They'll assume that I had a rendezvous planned with an Agency asset, possibly a Pole, and they'll raise hell with the Czechs when they claim they saw no one else enter. 'Confusion to our enemies,' isn't that the saying?"

As they emerged from the church, Steele leading the way, Collins caught a flash of motion and heard the sound of a car revving its engine. He turned to see a Citroën speeding down Rue Saint-

Honoré toward them. He caught the shiny glint of a gun muzzle from the vehicle's front left window. Collins didn't hesitate, on instinct pushing Steele down to the ground and then diving after him, just before several gunshots rang out in succession. They slammed into the masonry of the column above them, splintering stone.

Collins could feel his heart pounding and then a sudden exhilaration—the shots had missed them—mixed with fear. Was there more to come? Would there be armed men on foot coming after them?

"Let's get back inside the church," he whispered to Steele, who had stayed flat on the ground next to him.

Keeping low, Collins crawled back to the church entryway and found the relative safety of the vestibule. Steele followed right behind him. Collins was surprised by his own calm—perhaps his experience in Korea had hardened him to the sensation of being shot at. Then he noticed his hands were shaking uncontrollably.

Steele brushed his clothes off. He was breathing heavily and his face was pale. "We can't stay here," he said. "There has to be a back exit. Let's find the priest."

They hurried through the chapel to a side door. It was locked. Steele pounded on it and called out loudly in French until someone inside responded. A few moments later a craggy-faced priest in a cassock appeared. Steele said something to the priest in rapid French and the man nodded and motioned to them to follow. He led them down a long narrow corridor and through a small kitchen before indicating a door where they could exit.

It was quite dark outside and they moved silently along the street, avoiding the streetlamps, until they reached a busy thoroughfare. Steele hailed a cab and asked the driver to take them to the Place de la Concorde. When they reached the broad plaza Steele instructed the driver to circle the obelisk twice before he finally told him to pull in front of the Crillon. He silenced any questions from the cabbie by handing him a wad of francs.

Phillipe Gillain was waiting in the lobby, a grim look on his face, pacing back and forth. He strode over to them.

"Pierre called me at home to inform me of the attack," he said. "I cannot believe those stupid bastards took a shot at you."

"First time in years for me," Steele said. "It certainly concentrates the mind."

"What happened to the gentlemen's agreement that intelligence officers were off limits?" Collins asked Steele.

"They clearly aren't gentlemen."

"They may be Czechs, but they are acting like Bulgarians," Gillain said. "Crude and violent. We will now have to treat like them like Bulgarians."

"I need to make some arrangements," Steele said. "We will need to adjust our travel plans. Can I ask for your assistance with this, Phillipe?"

"Of course," Gillain said. "I will station a team of my men here at the hotel throughout the night in the event the Czechs have completely lost their minds and decide to make another try."

Steele excused himself and pulled Gillain to the side. Collins waited while they talked. When they were done conferring, Gillain made his farewells and left the Crillon. Steele suggested that he and Collins spend a few minutes together in private. They found a quiet spot in the lobby and sat facing each other in glided armchairs.

"I haven't thanked you properly," Steele said. "If you hadn't pushed me to the ground at the church—" He didn't finish the sentence.

"Lousy shots," Collins said. "Wouldn't have hit either of us. I think I could have done better and I've only had a half-day of instruction from a Marine sergeant with a M1911 pistol and the M1."

"I'm grateful, nonetheless."

Collins shrugged. "Glad to be of service."

"We have been somewhat removed from the foxholes, haven't we?" Steele began. "Hotels like the Crillon and the Astoria seem a million miles from the action. So does the E Street complex. Don't be fooled by the peaceful surroundings, because the struggle goes on, only it's hidden in the shadows. The Soviets have learned that they can accomplish a great deal by infiltrating their agents into the corridors of power. Only occasionally will they employ violence overtly to achieve their aims—like the attempt to eliminate us tonight."

"Us? I don't think they were gunning for an out-of-work newspaper columnist. You were the target."

"No doubt," Steele said. "Although I suspect that there's a file on you now in a Moscow Center office just off Dzerzhinsky Square."

"Maybe they can compare notes with the FBI and the Red Squad in New York. They also seem to be building files on me."

"Quite a day," Steele said. "Quite an evening. It does encourage reflection. Do you believe in coincidences? I don't. I think that you were meant to be there tonight to keep me out of the line of fire. I've seen other times when the right person is there to intervene. I think that's the hand of God guiding our destinies. We are only given slight glimpses of his design, now and then. Was it a coincidence that you and I connected through Penny? Or that you are the father of her child? Or that you and I were thrown together on this journey?"

Collins shook his head slowly, not convinced. "Where you see the hand of God, I see our own actions, our own decisions, at work. We determine those aspects of our destiny that aren't caused by the randomness around us. The accidents of fate. I've seen two Marines advance against machine gun fire where one was hit and the other wasn't and I didn't see anything divine about it. Just dumb good luck for one man and bad luck for the other."

"Penny must have told you that we're both taking instruction with Father Loughlin," Steele said. "I know the church does not have all the answers to these questions, but over the ages they have considered them. The tension between free will and predestination and how we are responsible for our actions here on earth. It's hard to take God out of that equation."

"I can't imagine the God of Sister Roberta or of Father Hanratty—the Catholic God of my childhood—putting His thumb on the scale one way or the other," Collins said. "I wish I could believe that, but I can't."

Steele leaned forward. "You may believe that you have arrived here in Paris randomly and I may think that your arrival is not by chance, but we can agree that we can, and must, act when the moment calls for it. We are called to intervene, if and when we can. We have that responsibility. That is the imperative we share, is it not?"

"It is," Collins said.

"We haven't talked about Caleb."

"We haven't. I've been waiting for you to raise the topic."

"Fair enough. It came as quite a shock to you, no doubt. Penny insisted on telling you the truth. She thought it was the right thing to do."

"And you? Did you think it was the right thing to do?"

"As you can imagine, I had mixed feelings. But it's done. I wonder how you feel now about the situation."

"It's awkward as hell," Collins said. "It's given me a lot to think about. I'm not sure where we go from here."

"It can be quite simple. Caleb will have a father and a stepfather. He won't be the first boy to find himself in those circumstances. Nor will you and I be the first to have to sort out the mechanics of a somewhat tangled family situation. Please know that Penny and I want you to decide the nature of your relationship with Caleb and we'll do what we can to make it work."

"That's not going to be easy. I have to get my life in better order first before I can figure out where Caleb fits in. All of this has caught me by surprise. It's nothing I ever expected."

"I understand. Penny does as well." Steele removed his eyeglasses so he could rub his eyes. He put his glasses back on before he spoke again. "We can talk more about this later. For now, please stay in your room with the lock bolted. No use in tempting fate twice in one evening. I will stop by in the morning when it is time to leave. Let's plan on six o'clock."

"Tempting fate?" Collins asked and then laughed. "We'd have to agree on what it is before I could tempt it."

Fourteen

When Steele knocked lightly on his hotel room door at six o'clock, Collins was already wide awake, packed, and ready to go. Steele was right about one thing, Collins thought, getting shot at certainly concentrated the mind. Even though he had not slept much, Collins didn't feel fatigued. He was on edge.

Phillipe Gillain and two fit young men were waiting for them when they stepped off the lift. They escorted them to the front door of the Crillon where Gillain paused to quickly murmur commands to his men. The French agents exited first, providing a human shield of sorts for Steele and Collins as they followed them outside.

A Ford sedan and a small truck waited in front of the hotel, engines running, and two other men in dark peacoats stood with their backs to the hotel's entrance, intently watching the traffic circling the Place de la Concorde. Collins saw that one man carried a rifle and the other was cradling a Thompson submachine gun in his arms. It was clear that Gillain's contingent had prepared for any attempted attack by the Czechs during the trip to Le Bourget.

Collins and Steele seated themselves in the back of the sedan and Gillain took the front passenger seat. Two of the agents in peacoats climbed into the truck. The vehicles accelerated quickly and pulled into the traffic flowing through the Place de la Concorde.

"I've made the arrangements," Gillain said to Steele. "As you requested."

"Splendid," Steele said. "Was Archie available?"

"Yes. She has a new plane, a Stinson, waiting at Le Bourget that she's eager to show off."

Steele offered Collins an explanation. "A slight change in plans. We're going to stop in London first en route to the States. We've lined up a pilot who will fly us from Paris to Croyden airfield this morning. After we transact some business, we'll take Pan Am's evening flight to New York and arrive the following morning. I trust that will not prove too much of a disruption of your plans."

"What about the flight to Washington we're supposed to take this morning?" Collins asked.

"Phillipe has handled that. We're listed on the passenger manifest. As far as Pan Am is concerned, we will have boarded that flight. I don't care to have our side-trip public knowledge."

"And the purpose of this visit?"

"A chance to catch up with some old friends. Compare notes." Steele leaned back in his seat. "I'm confident that you will find it an enlightening experience."

Gillain turned his shoulders so he could see them both and addressed Steele. "You'll see Julian, then?"

"We shall. Julian and I had a brief conversation last night."

"Ah, then please give him my regards. Tell him that he is long overdue for a visit."

"I shall."

"And be careful, Matthew," he said. "Whatever you're up to back in Washington, you have stirred up a hornet's nest."

The trip to the airport proved uneventful—no cars trailing them, no sign of the Czechs—but Collins wasn't disappointed. He had little appetite for any more drama.

Gillian and two of his agents accompanied them on a hurried walk through the terminal to a door marked PRIVÉ. Gillian led them through the door and down a corridor to a set of double doors, which opened to the outside, and quickly bid them farewell.

Twenty yards away, on the tarmac, a jeep was idling. Its driver was wearing a leather pilot's jacket and a dark olive baseball cap. When he got closer, Collins could see it was a female in the driver's seat. She smiled broadly when she spied Steele.

"Haven't seen you in a while, Colonel Steele," she said. Her voice suggested the English upper classes to Collins. Her aquiline nose was balanced by sensual lips.

"Archie, you know that rank was a temporary wartime arrangement. No need for formalities. Please call me Matthew." He nodded toward Collins. "Dennis Collins, a colleague."

The woman took Collins' outstretched hand and shook it vigorously.

"Artemis Fraser, but known as Archie. Glad to be flying Americans. My recent jobs have all been headed eastward, and I couldn't pronounce any of my passengers' last names. Steele and Collins I can manage."

"Archie was in the RAF Air Transport Auxiliary," Steele explained. "She flew Tiger Moths, Dakotas, Hurricanes, and Spitfires—all sorts of aircraft—from the factory to the airfield."

"The Spitfire is a lovely plane," Fraser said. "A woman's plane, if I may say so, quite responsive to a lighter touch. Like my Stinson. It has a lovely feel in the air when you're at the controls."

"Archie has been very helpful in providing transport for various different people," Steele said. "Situations where regular air service won't do."

She smiled. "After the war I wanted to keep flying and I figured there would always be a call for a pilot willing to fly on short notice and into tight places, places that might get tricky. I was correct. Matthew's colleagues have kept me quite busy."

She drove them at top speed to the portion of the airport with the smaller, general aviation aircraft. She pulled up near a corrugated steel building and led them over to a sleek plane which reminded Collins of the L-5 spotter planes he had seen in Korea.

Fraser invited them to climb in and stow their luggage in the back of the cabin. Then she went forward to remove the chocks under the wheels. Once she was back in the cockpit, Fraser was all business, conducting her preflight check with what Collins regarded as an admirable thoroughness.

Collins didn't look forward to the prospects of a flight in a small aircraft over the English Channel, but it was immeasurably better than the prospect of, say, flying in a helicopter, which he had done once in Korea. He had hated every moment sitting in the glass-enclosed bubble with the rotors—which he was told were the equivalent of the wings for a helicopter—rotating above him and shaking the craft.

"We have a lovely day to fly," she said, almost as if she was reading Collins' mind. "It should be calm all the way to London."

Their flight from Le Bourget to Croydon airport south of London took almost three hours. They flew over the sunny French countryside and then approached the Channel, a sudden expanse of blue-gray water appearing on the horizon. Below them Collins spotted a few fishing boats amidst scattered whitecaps but there was little else to see.

Fraser piloted the plane to the mouth of the Thames, and then followed the silver thread of the river as it twisted its way, ribbon-like, to the west. They arrived at the outskirts of the city of London and flew over a series of bridges before reaching the famous landmarks of the Tower of London, St. Paul's Cathedral, and the houses of Parliament. Fraser guided the plane into a graceful bank and headed south. Within minutes the landing strips of Croydon came into view and Fraser began communicating with the air controllers. After a smooth touchdown, she taxied the Stilton to a nondescript hanger. A faded sign on the side of the building proclaimed it to be Croyden General Aviation.

Fraser switched off the engine. "So we're back to 'this blessed plot, this earth, this realm, this England' in one piece." She glanced over at Steele. "Let me know if you need anything more. Otherwise I'll head back to Le Bourget."

"We're set, thanks. Have a safe return trip."

Fraser helped them with their luggage before climbing back in the Stilton. She restarted the engine and pulled away, heading back toward the main runway. Collins heard the crackle of the radio as Fraser began communicating with the control tower.

When they entered the building's lobby area, they found a slight, well-dressed man of perhaps forty waiting for them. He shook hands with Steele and introduced himself to Collins as Julian Farnsworth. He cut a dashing figure with his tweed coat and cravat. Collins had heard that the British Secret Service, like the OSS, had recruited largely from elite colleges and from the well-bred, and Farnsworth certainly seemed to fit the part.

"I'm the advance guard, here to welcome you," Farnsworth said to Collins. "Didn't think I'd have the dubious pleasure of working with Matthew again, but you know what they say about bad pennies."

"I've turned up again, have I?" Steele laughed. "Julian and I had our fair share of adventures in Switzerland. He was our liaison in Berne."

"And Matthew was the leading light for Oh So Social," Farnsworth said. "Along with Allen Dulles, of course."

"Guilty as charged."

"Was that Archie Fraser that flew you here?" Farnsworth asked.

"It was."

"Remarkable girl." He turned to Collins. "Her father, Lord Fraser, doesn't quite approve of her adventurous existence. But Archie has done what she has wanted since she was sixteen. They say she's one of the better pilots around, male or female."

"So what's our schedule?" Steele asked.

Farnsworth explained that they would lunch at his flat in Pimlico and that he had arranged for Steele to meet with a colleague from MI5 in the afternoon. "You should have enough time to get out to Heathrow to catch your flight. I would have invited you to my club for lunch, but you said you wanted to stay under the radar."

"We do. By the way, Phillipe sends his best. He is hoping you can visit him."

Farnsworth beamed with pleasure. "How is he faring? He's a good man. Always liked Phillipe. Some of my colleagues blame his crew for helping Jewish refugees evade the blockade and reach Palestine. It wasn't humanitarian on their part, mind you. The French haven't cared for our growing influence in Lebanon and Syria and figured they could rock the boat a bit by helping the Jews."

Farnsworth led them to a gleaming tan Bentley sedan parked just outside the entrance to the terminal. He drove them at top speed into London, zipping past cars, black cabs and double-decker buses.

Farnsworth paid no attention to the posted speed limit, but Collins had to concede that he was quite skilled behind the wheel.

As they drove through London's streets, Collins saw occasional gaps in the line of row houses and piles of rubble and collapsed walls in the space where the buildings had been. In a few places there was scaffolding and construction or repairs underway.

"Matthew told me that this is your first visit to London," Farnsworth said. "So I thought you should see some of this on the way. When visitors discover that Big Ben and the Tower of London and Westminster Palace are intact, they don't realize the extent of the damage caused by the Blitz and the V-1s and V-2s. The estimates are that the Luftwaffe destroyed a million homes. They obliterated the docks in the East End. It's sobering. You look at the damage done to London and you realize that we must prevent another war, especially now that our adversary has his own atomic weapons."

Farnsworth pulled the Bentley into a parking space in front of a Georgian-style brick home. He led the way up the steps and unlocked the front door. Collins had expected an elegant residence and he was not surprised by the high ceilings, polished wooden floors, thick Persian rugs, and expensive furniture that he found inside.

They followed Farnsworth into a small parlor.

"Whiskey neat?" he asked. "It's Glenfarclas, so it's better without the soda." Farnsworth went to the sideboard and poured their drinks. There was a platter of roast beef sandwiches and a bowl of homemade potato crisps waiting for them on the dining room table. Collins found he was quite hungry and he joined Farnsworth in enjoying a sandwich. He noticed that Steele ate sparingly, hardly touching his food.

"So you were quite mysterious when you called from Paris last night, Matthew," Farnsworth said. "A quick stop here for lunch, a meeting with MI5, and then back to the States, you said."

"That's the idea. Feliks Hawes is available to meet us?"

"He is, although he thought it quite irregular. No meeting recorded on his calendar, no indication of the topic, a rendezvous in a public house."

"But he will meet us?"

"He will. The Britannia in Kensington at three o'clock. To quote Feliks, 'No bloody Red would dare venture into pub called the Britannia,' but he wants you to keep a sharp eye out for followers anyway."

"The Russian embassy is over on Bow Street, is it not?" Steele asked and Farnsworth nodded.

"How far is that from the pub?" Collins asked.

"Their embassy is in Whitechapel, so I would estimate four or five miles," Farnsworth said. "Far enough that you shouldn't bump into one of Feliks' bloody Reds by accident."

"By the way, our visit to Paris proved quite valuable," Steele said. "It corroborated something I have been concerned about now for more than a year. I wanted to brief you directly and privately. I hope you'll be able to act as the voice of reason in the days ahead on some pressing security matters."

"That sounds somewhat alarming."

Steele reached into his briefcase and produced a dossier. He slid it across the table to Farnsworth. "We don't have a great deal of time together so I will get to the point. We're convinced that Donald Maclean of the Foreign Office is Homer, the Soviet penetration agent. The pertinent details are in the dossier. The more I've studied this, the more it makes sense. Maclean was trusted with the most sensitive information both in Washington and as head of the F.O.'s American desk."

"And you say you are convinced of this? Of Maclean's involvement?"

Steele nodded.

"Then let's say that after I study this file I conclude that you are correct about Maclean," Farnsworth said and paused. "As you could full well imagine, there would be significant resistance to this idea within the Foreign Office. You're asking them to believe that one of their own top men has gone bad. It's true Maclean's personal behavior has been an embarrassment of late. An incident in Cairo, nonstop drinking, and bizarre episodes here in London—he supposedly sexually importuned some large, African doorman at one of the hotels and was knocked down for his trouble. That can all be chalked up to the strain. A mental crack-up. Dry him out, dust him off, and put him back in harness."

"I'm afraid there's more," Steele said. "I want to make it clear that what I have to tell you now is my theory alone, at the moment. It may not be easy to accept either. What did you make of the Volkov matter?"

Farnsworth gave Steele a puzzled look. "Volkov? That was in September '45." He turned to explain to Collins. "Konstantin Volkov, the deputy head of the NKVD in Turkey, walked into our Istanbul consulate one fine morning, looking to defect and offering to give us the names of the Soviets' agents in Turkey and Britain. A treasure trove of information. We could have crippled their networks. Except that before we could extract any pearls of wisdom from him, Volkov was bundled off to Moscow. We moved too slowly and lost the opportunity."

"Do you know who was tasked to handle his defection?" Steele asked. "From London?"

"I don't. I was in Berlin at the time. As were you, as I recall."

"It was Kim Philby, then the head of your Russian desk. Apparently Philby took his sweet time in getting to Istanbul. Word reached Moscow Center before Philby's arrival, because a bandaged Volkov was seen being loaded aboard an Aeroflot plane at the airport. Philby told the consular people that he had been delayed by the holidays."

"What are you suggesting?"

"That Philby's tardiness allowed the Russians to remove Volkov." Steele paused. "A deliberate delay. There's more. Philby recently oversaw an operation designed to insert insurgents into Albania. The idea was to foment an insurrection against the Communist regime. Not well thought out, but it didn't have to end the way it did. The Albanian secret police were waiting at the insertion point."

"I can believe it about Maclean," Farnsworth said. "He strikes many of us as unstable, but Philby is different. He was a success on the Russian desk, and I hear he is quite popular in Washington. Some believe that he is in the chase to become our top man before the end of the decade. Kim Philby a traitor? That's a bit hard to swallow."

"It is my theory at this point," Steele said. "Mine alone. I think the Soviets have exploited two inside sources—Maclean and Philby."

"So what do you want me to do with this?" Farnsworth asked.

"Prepare the way. A word to the wise with your senior people, perhaps, that you know the Americans are beginning to focus on

Maclean as the chief suspect for Homer. That you have learned this through informal channels. As for Philby, I'd like you to wait. I'll telephone when it's time for you to have another conversation with your superiors."

"God, I hope you are wrong about Kim," Farnsworth said. "Maclean will be bloody bad enough. But Kim? A disaster."

Steele suddenly winced in pain. He rose to his feet. "Can you point me to the bathroom, Julian? An upset stomach, I'm afraid."

Farnsworth led Steele over to a nearby corridor and they disappeared into the interior of the house. While he waited, Collins studied a large portrait of a beautiful young auburn-haired woman in a formal, dark blue evening dress, her bare shoulders covered by a thin shawl. There was the hint of a smile on her slightly turned face.

"My mother," Farnsworth said, returning to the room. "Quite the beauty in her day. It's a John Singer Sargent, painted in 1898, just after she married my father. At the time her friends cautioned her about being painted by Sargent. The saying was that with a Sargent portrait you placed your face in his hands. Clever, no? My mother ignored the warnings and I'm glad she did. He did capture her spirit and verve. I keep it here in the Cambridge Street house because she loved the city, not so much the country life. Unlike my wife, who is happiest with her dogs and horses in Sussex."

"Which do you prefer, the city or the country?"

"The city. I guess that makes me my mother's son." He took another sip of his whiskey. "How long have you been working with Matthew?"

"I've known him since 1949. I can't say that we're colleagues in the sense that you mean."

"I see," Farnsworth said with a tone that suggested that he didn't. "Can't go wrong with Matthew in the field. He worked wonders during the war. During one operation he crossed into Germany carrying a false Swiss passport and brought out a technician who had built one of the Wehrmacht's mechanical coding devices."

"I didn't know that he'd done covert work. Directly, I mean."

"On a few occasions he did. I understand that Dulles also tasked him with handling relations with the Zionists. They had some operatives in Switzerland and an extensive network in Eastern Europe. Their intelligence proved quite valuable. They trusted him once they realized that he shared their distaste for Whitehall's policy on Palestine. He got a reputation as a bit of a Zionist himself. That made him somewhat *persona non grata* in some circles. It was rumored that he had steered funds to Haganah. Never substantiated."

"American money?"

"That was never clear. There were wild stories about confiscated Nazi gold. Who knows? If he had, it certainly would have reflected Matthew's strong sense of justice."

Collins understood why Farnsworth and Steele would have become fast friends. They came from the same social class and they were both intellectuals who had found intelligence work a way to engage with the world, to test theory against practice. No doubt they thought of themselves as the secular equivalent of the Knights Templar, defending the West not against Saladin and his warriors but against Stalin and Moscow Center.

They heard the distant sounds of a toilet flushing, of pipes banging, and a faucet being turned on and off. A few moments later Steele appeared in the doorway, looking pale and drawn.

"The travel must be getting to me," he said. "Not feeling quite up to snuff."

"Come have another splash or two of the whisky," Farnsworth said. "It's a sure cure for whatever ails." He consulted his gold pocket watch and frowned. "Only have another ten minutes or so before it's time for you to leave for your rendezvous with Hawes."

Steele returned to the table. "I do have some other information I would like to share," he began. He handed Farnsworth an envelope identical to the one he had given Phillipe Gillain. "Inside you'll find details on Anatoli Yatov of the First Directorate. A photo and his biography. It's not much, but it's a start. Should Yatov darken your doorstep, I'd like to be informed."

"Is he connected to the leaks in Washington? To Philby?"

"That's my working hypothesis. When Yatov was based in New York we know he was handling at least one agent in the State Department. It's highly likely that he's the contact for any high-level penetration agents."

"So I take it we should be particularly attentive if this Yatov fellow turns up anywhere in the vicinity of Donald Maclean."

"Exactly. In which case I'll catch the next available flight here so we can resolve this together."

"In which case, I'd like to tag along," Collins said to Steele, surprising himself. "If Yatov does surface, I want to help in any way that I can."

Steele frowned. "Dennis has a personal interest in the Yatov matter," he explained to Farnsworth. "Some unpleasant business in New York. Things went wrong. Largely my fault." He glanced over at Collins. "I'll need to clear it with Allen. Considering the circumstances, I think that he will agree to your further involvement."

"We'll do our bit here," Farnsworth said.

"I would never expect anything else," Steele said, "but it's a comfort to hear you say so."

Fifteen

They took an indirect route to the Britannia public house and their rendezvous with MI5's man, Feliks Hawes. After they left Farnsworth's flat, Steele had them walk two blocks before he hailed a cab. He instructed the driver to take them to the corner of Exhibition Drive and Kensington Road by Hyde Park. Steele kept a close watch out of the rear window of the car, clearly concerned about whether they had been followed from Farnsworth's place.

"No signs of trouble," he said quietly.

Their driver, a silver-haired man with a prominent nose, glanced back over his shoulder at them, his curiosity obviously piqued, but he didn't say anything.

At Hyde Park, they walked through the closest entrance and followed the path for about a thousand yards before the Albert Memorial came in sight. Steele had them halt at a park bench that faced Kensington Road. As they sat on the bench, Steele scrutinized everyone passing by on the roadway. Collins was surprised at how drawn and tired he looked. The long flights and the change in time had clearly caught up to him.

While they waited, Steele explained that he had encountered the MI5 official they were meeting, Feliks Hawes, once before, in 1947. He had briefed Hawes on what he knew about a Russian diplomat who had been stationed in Berne and then had been assigned to the Soviet embassy in London. Hawes spoke Russian fluently. He had a Polish father and an English mother and had adopted his mother's surname when his parents separated. His father, a colonel in the Polish Army, had been murdered by the Soviets at Katyn Forest in

1940 along with much of the Polish officer corps. Hawes had enlisted at seventeen in the Royal Commandos and served in Egypt, Crete, and Italy. When he returned to England, he had been recruited into counterintelligence.

"Clearly Hawes has no love for Russians," Steele said. "He has a reputation for being a very effective interrogator. I certainly wouldn't want to end up on his wrong side." After another five minutes of sitting and monitoring the pedestrians passing by, Steele appeared satisfied that they hadn't been tailed.

"Time to go," he said.

They strolled through the park to the wrought-iron Queens Gate exit and then walked along Kensington High Road. They arrived at the Britannia, a two-story brick building which was tucked in on Allen Street, some fifteen minutes early. The pub's Victorian interior featured dark wood paneling, framed cartoons, and a deceptively large common room. The place was quiet, with only a few mid-afternoon patrons. A small fire blazed away in a stone fireplace, bringing welcome warmth.

They ordered pints from the publican, and Steele selected a table in the corner of the pub, where they could watch the door and where they wouldn't be overheard.

Steele examined the wall behind them and smiled. "It's a Gillray," he said, inspecting a framed caricature. "By the looks of it, an original. A satirical portrait of King George the Third. Do you like cartoons, Dennis?"

"Some. I've always liked Bill Maudlin. I thought Willie and Joe were great. Maudlin caught what it was like in the field for the average GI during the war."

"Herblock's my favorite. He has certainly pegged Joe McCarthy, with that five o'clock shadow. Of course Herblock's politics are a bit too left for me, but he's got McCarthy's number."

"Unfortunately not enough people do," Collins said.

"We'll win despite him," Steele said. "There will always be those who try to profit politically from this struggle. The difference is that we can stop the McCarthys of the West through the ballot box and the courts. In the Worker's Paradise there's no way to remove a Beria."

"You have more confidence that McCarthy will get his comeuppance than I do."

"Remember Primo Carnera? The bigger they come, the harder they fall."

Collins had to laugh. Primo Carnera, a gigantic Italian heavyweight fighter, had defeated a string of weak pushovers in the early 1930s. Then he beat Jack Sharkey with a sixth-round knockout in a heavyweight title fight. There were rumors that Carnera was mobbed up and that Sharkey was paid to take a dive. When Carnera got into the ring at Madison Square Garden in 1934 with a real boxer, Max Baer, it was no match. The giant fighter hit the canvas eleven times in eleven rounds. Some cynics claimed that Primo had tanked, but Collins was convinced the bout was on the level and that if Carnera fought Baer a hundred times, he would lose a hundred times.

A minute or two later a man in his late twenties wearing a well-tailored, pin-striped chalk suit entered the Britannia. He carried an elegant black leather briefcase and an umbrella. He could have passed for a successful stockbroker stopping off at the pub after an early day in the City, London's financial district. Collins noted the man's high

Slavic cheekbones, his strong jaw, and his piercing, focused eyes as surveyed the room slowly before he walked over to their table. Steele extended his hand.

"Matthew Steele. We met back in '47."

Hawes shook Steele's hand. "I remember." He glanced over at Collins, his eyes watchful.

"We should be left undisturbed for our chat," he said to Steele. Hawes had a husky tenor voice. "The regulars don't show up until later. I'll fetch myself a drink and we can talk."

When Hawes returned to the table with a pint of ale, Steele introduced Collins simply as his colleague and explained that they had already seen Julian Farnsworth. "Julian indicated that we could be frank with you," Steele said. "And that you would hold our conversation in confidence."

"Understood," Hawes said. "This is an informal meeting, then. No notes taken." He took a long drink from his mug. Collins could sense the toughness underneath the man's surface polish. "What can I do for you, Mr. Steele?"

"An exchange of views, of information of some importance."

"I would welcome that," Hawes said. "Julian wouldn't have called me if it wasn't something of importance."

Steele nodded briskly. "All right, then. To begin, there have been repeated warnings from defectors like Krivitsky and Gouzenko, and would-be defectors like Volkov, that your Foreign Office has been penetrated by the Soviets. After reviewing the facts, we have concluded that a Foreign Office official, Donald Maclean, has been an agent for the Soviets operating out of your Washington embassy."

"Heard there was an investigation under way of leaks from Washington," Hawes said. "Would love to take a crack at Maclean, but the security lads over at the Foreign Office are quite protective of their own."

"The day may come, however, when you are summoned to help out on the investigation and forewarned is forearmed. There's more, unfortunately. The flow of secrets from Washington continued after Maclean returned to England in '49. I now believe that Kim Philby, the first secretary at the embassy, the liaison with our intelligence services, has also been working for the Soviets."

Hawes raised his eyebrows, clearly skeptical. "Kim Philby? That's a new one. He's one of their rising men, isn't he? Some say he's in line to inherit the keys to the kingdom some day."

"Which shouldn't put him above suspicion," Steele said. "Philby is funneling information to Moscow Center. What evidence we have is largely circumstantial, but I hope soon to have more concrete proof."

"A full and abject confession from Philby is what you need. Otherwise Lord This or That and his colleagues will bend over backwards for him. They will try to ride the high horse on this—they'll argue that a man of Philby's background couldn't possibly be a subversive. He's a charter member of the club, their club."

"Then we'll have to get Philby to confess," Steele said. "If we can catch him in the act, so to speak, he may be willing to talk."

"I wouldn't bet on that," Hawes said. "Not if Philby is a true believer. No doubt the Soviets have at some point presented him with the Order of Lenin. Just to admire for a few moments, and then back in the box. But it makes Philby one of them, the medal to be kept secret, hidden away, until that glorious day arrives when the hammer and sickle is flying over Whitehall. I don't see him talking."

"Klaus Fuchs talked," Collins noted.

"That he did. But he was a babe in the woods when it comes to the spy game. He gave the Soviets scientific information for what, a few years? It's not like that for the men we're talking about. Maclean. Philby. Probably recruited just out of Cambridge. How long is that, twenty-five years ago? Do you think either of them will turn their back on a commitment of such long standing?"

"Perhaps not," Collins said. "Or perhaps they have become tired of the deception and the fear and would welcome a way out. Things may look quite different to a forty-year-old man with children than they did to an idealistic undergraduate."

"It's possible," Hawes conceded.

"They must have doubted over the years whether they had made the right decision. The purges, the show trials, the attack on Finland, the Hitler-Stalin pact, the terror Stalin uses against his own people. It's not a pretty picture. Why would anyone want to be a party to that?"

"I'd like to ask Kim Philby that question, and many others," Hawes said. "Assuming that he is a spy, nothing can happen unless those in authority confront that reality and let us go after him. Not everyone is as suspicious as I am, mind you. My own outfit continued to affirm Fuchs' security clearance. MI5 gave him the equivalent of a clean bill of health eight times. Eight bloody times. You must understand what we're up against."

"We fully understand," Steele said. "I face skepticism as well in Washington. It's why I'm here unofficially."

Hawes cleared his throat. "Then you'll understand why I have to tread very carefully. Even making unofficial inquiries about Maclean or Philby will stir up trouble at the Foreign Office and SIS. Trouble I don't need."

"There's something you could pursue," Steele said. "It falls under old history, so you should be able to research it quietly without drawing too much attention. During the war, Philby handled the agents of the Dutch underground. I think if you take a hard look at the operational files, you'll find that many of those operatives loyal to the House of Orange were caught or killed by the Gestapo soon after they returned to Holland. The Communist agents in the Dutch underground had much better luck."

"And you think Philby had a hand in that?"

"I do," Steele said. "We know that Moscow Center was looking to strengthen the position of the Reds in Holland. Why not have Philby sabotage the competition, the Dutch loyalists? The NKVD and the Gestapo were quite chummy between '38 and '41 until Hitler decided to turn on the Russians, so it wouldn't have been hard for Philby to pass along the necessary information."

"I can look into that," Hawes said.

"There's a similar pattern with Philby and his involvement with Albanian agents more recently. The Albanian security forces seem to always know where the agents are being inserted and they show up in force. I have some reports on that I can share with you."

Hawes swallowed a mouthful of ale. "The more detailed information you can send, and the more I can dig up here, the better. I prefer to be armed with facts when I head into an interrogation. That is, if I get the chance and I told you, that's dodgy. Philby's one of theirs, you know."

"There's one other matter," Steele said. "By any chance, have you stumbled across a fellow named Anatoli Yatov? First Directorate. Spain, Berlin, then New York and Washington."

Hawes frowned. "I have. The name conjures up bad memories. I was sent over to Warsaw in 1946, on loan to SIS. An official in the Ministry of Public Security, Jakob Borowski, wanted to defect and I was supposed to talk him in because he had once been friends with my father. Borowski had been sickened by the persecution of Home Army officers and by the police state that was being created. When I met with Borowski he was looking over his shoulder every two minutes. He was worried about this Yatov fellow who was rumored to be coming from Berlin on official business. Yatov's reputation for brutality preceded him. I reassured Borowski and set up another meeting, where I was going to give him his false papers and the details of the escape route."

"What happened?" Collins asked.

"He never showed up for the meeting. The word we got was that Borowski and another Ministry official who were thought to be lacking sufficient enthusiasm for the new order had been invited to a meeting at headquarters. Yatov had walked in with a revolver and shot them—one after another—at close range. *Genickschluss*, a single bullet in the nape of the neck, the approved Moscow Center solution for traitors. Then Yatov walked out of the room, cool as a cucumber, his job done." Hawes shook his head. "An object lesson for the rest of the lot in the Ministry, I imagine. They must have been watching Borowski and realized he was going to defect. Not sure what the other chap had done. In any case, I flew back to London since I had no reason to stay."

"That fits what we know about Yatov," Steele said. "As it happens I have a photo of him that you can have. If you could keep an eye out, I'd appreciate it. Unofficially, of course."

Steele handed Hawes an envelope, and after Hawes removed the print, he studied it for a long moment. "Ugly little brute. We can certainly watch for him. If he turns up, what then?"

"If you could alert Julian, he'll take it from there."

"All outside official channels?"

"That would be best."

Hawes slid the photo of Yatov back into the envelope and secured it in his inner jacket pocket. He emptied his mug. "There's one small condition for my cooperation. I'd like to have first crack at any action involving Yatov on British soil. Unofficially, of course."

Steele considered Hawe's offer for a moment. He looked over at Collins. "We've already got a fair number of volunteers who want to help out unofficially. Another can't hurt."

"Done, then," Hawes said, reaching across to shake Steele's hand.

Hawes suggested that he should leave the Britannia first. "In the unlikely event that I was followed here, I'll draw any Bolshies watching along with me."

"As you wish," Steele said.

They waited fifteen minutes after his departure before they left the pub. A light rain had begun to fall as they walked back to Kensington High Street to find a cab for the trip to the airport.

"Hawes wouldn't be fooled by either Maclean or Philby if he gets the chance to interrogate them," Steele said. "If he gets the chance. Another one of those ifs."

"And Julian? Where does he stand?"

"He'll arrive at the same conclusions, but it'll take him longer. Harder for him to accept that Trinity College men are betraying their own."

"Do you think Yatov might be in Paris or London?"

"It's unlikely," Steele said. "I believe that he has remained in the United States, but I can't be certain and I don't want to prematurely close out other possibilities. If he does surface in Europe, it will make moving against him somewhat more complicated, but it can be done. It will be done."

They had reached Kensington High Street and Steele came to a stop. Collins reached out to grasp his sleeve.

"You will remember that when it's time to harpoon this white whale, you've agreed that I can play a role."

Steele was amused. "So I'm Ahab in your eyes, am I? Should I call you Ishmael?"

"Clever," Collins said. "I didn't read the entire book but I do remember 'Call me Ishmael.' I just want to be there and do what I can to bring Yatov down."

"You shall. I promise. And fortunately for you, Ishmael was the only crew member of the *Pequod* who survived."

Part Two

Washington, D.C.

By early March, Penny realized that she was nearing a darker place. She felt like she was slipping down a long tunnel into darkness and there seemed to be no way to climb back up and reach the light.

She craved sleep. It was the one and only time where she could hide from all of it; where she could forget her troubles and welcome the escape into nothingness. She remembered when they studied Virgil in her high school Latin class and read about the river Lethe; how those in the underworld who drank from its waters would lose their painful memories and could be reincarnated without remembering any of their past hurts. The idea appealed to her, to wipe out all of the sadness and pain, to start over again. She would be freed from her concerns, past and present.

It became her guarded secret, the way she felt, what she thought. She knew that she should tell no one. She lied to Dr. Rifkin about the dreams that she was having. She reported only a dreamless sleep, a slumber untroubled by the ghosts of her past or the torments of the present. Dr. Rifkin might have had her suspicions, but Penny kept doggedly to her story. Her therapist seemed at a loss without Penny's dreams to interpret and Penny's brief, factual accounts of her daily routine, coupled with her obvious lethargy, didn't give her doctor much to work with at their sessions. The truth was that Penny had tired of the questioning, the analyzing, the talking. Would it really bring her to the core of her sadness and help her heal? Or was it a mistake to even begin therapy? Why surface all the painful things in her life? Was silence such a bad thing?

On her good days she managed to function, to read to Caleb and to help Bernice around the kitchen. If she was feeling particularly energetic she would have dinner with Matthew and listen to him talk about the political situation in Washington. Even then she tired too quickly and found herself longing to crawl under the covers and sleep.

She worried about Matthew. He couldn't shake the cold he had been fighting since before his trip to Europe. He seemed to have lost his appetite and he stayed in his study until late at night reading files and writing.

He had returned from his trip without Dennis Collins, saying only that Dennis had gone back to New York and would let them know when he had settled on what he wanted to do about Caleb. She had masked her disappointment and had been careful not to ask too many questions about when Dennis might visit them again. Whenever she looked out of her bedroom window at the carriage house, now dark and empty, she wondered when he would reenter their lives.

She would not rest until they had negotiated a way to make Dennis part of Caleb's future. Matthew said Dennis wanted time to think things through, but she worried that he was exacting some sort of delayed revenge by making her wait for his answer. Then she felt ashamed for thinking that about him.

She recognized that Dennis had changed. He told her once that fatigue and cynicism were occupational hazards of being a war correspondent. Now he seemed hardened, more closed off than before, hiding behind a polite exterior, his true feelings hidden. She couldn't predict what he would do now, like she could in the old days, when they were lovers.

Her bad days were very dark. She felt guilty over her neglect of Caleb. She thanked God that Bernice was there to watch over him. She hated the way Matthew looked at her, his concern and fear so evident, whenever she mentioned how tired she felt. She dreaded his close scrutiny. Did he suspect that she had begun to slip back into the darkness?

She wouldn't tell Dr. Rifkin about her recurring dream, the one that had come to her a year before and then had returned to her in the past weeks. It bothered her that she couldn't remember all of its details. She could recall that in the dream she wandered through their house and was frightened to find all of the rooms had been emptied of furniture. She would run up the steps to Caleb's room, expecting to see him crawling on the floor, but the nursery would also be bare, stripped of toys and his crib.

From her bedroom she would look out into the backyard and she would see Matthew, Dennis, and Caleb standing together looking up at the house. Her son would be between the two men, each holding one of his hands, and he would be wearing a bewildered look, a little boy lost. She would realize that they couldn't see her on the second floor and rather than waving to them she would step away from the bay window.

She did remember that in this dream she felt strangely at peace, untroubled, detached from what was happening around her. She wondered if she had died and Matthew, Dennis, and Caleb had been drawn together because of it. If Father Loughlin's description of the afterlife was accurate, there was nothing to fear. If he was proven wrong, and nothingness awaited her, at least she would have escaped her pain and worry.

She knew better than to ever share her dream with Matthew. Dr. Sollers had been talking to him about another round of ECT and she feared that they would use her dream as a reason to justify hospitalizing her for more shock treatment. She could not stand that. She lost a piece of herself, of who she was at her core, every time it was administered. She felt numb and frozen afterward.

Inside the hope chest, next to the envelope with Dennis' newspaper clippings, she had hidden a bottle of sleeping tablets. There was another secreted in the drawer in her night table. Matthew had removed all of the pill bottles from their medicine cabinet at the end of January but he didn't know that she had her own cache of Veronal and Nembutal.

She would keep the tablets hidden. They were her escape. As long as she knew they were there, she could bear the pain and the sadness for now. There would be an end to it, she was sure. There had to be, one way or the other.

Sixteen

On their flight back to New York, with most of the nearby passengers fast asleep, Steele had revealed to Collins how he planned to move against Kim Philby. His hope, he told Collins in a hushed voice, was to quickly build a convincing case that Philby represented a significant security risk. At a minimum, Steele said, that would force his removal as the British intelligence liaison in Washington.

"Allen has already warned our key men to be careful about what they share with Philby," Steele said. "We can't control his access to other American intelligence, though, and it's the Department of Defense materials that are of greatest concern."

"Can't you warn the military?"

"It's not that easy. If the intelligence goes through the embassy, Philby sees it." Steele smiled thinly. "The Brits are fighting side-by-side with us in Korea, so I hardly think we can stop sharing our plans with them. No, Philby has to go."

"And how do you propose to do that?"

Steele explained that penetration agents of long standing sometimes became careless and let their guard down. Philby might have grown lax and kept government documents—cables, memos, maps—or other evidence of his secret work somewhere in his house.

"We need to get into his house when he isn't there," Steele said. "A thorough search of the place. At the moment, Philby is confident that all eyes are elsewhere. If we can find some top secret stuff in his house, we'll have him. Then we can see if we can leverage that to trap Yatov."

Steele added that with his current status ("suspended in limbo in the North Building") he could expect no assistance from the Agency. Even if he had been in better standing, Steele thought it highly unlikely that he could win official sanction for a break-in at the residence of an intelligence officer from America's closest ally.

"I hoped that you and your brother might help me," he said. Collins had wondered why Steele kept referring to "we" and now he had the explanation.

"You want us to search Philby's house?" Collins made no attempt to keep the incredulity out of his voice even as he tried to match Steele's hushed volume. "Are you serious, Matthew? We aren't intelligence operatives. You're asking us to break the law."

"I know that your brother is a cool customer," Steele said. "And you've acquitted yourself well under fire. After Okinawa and the Chosin campaign I would think a quick reconnaissance mission inside a deserted house wouldn't worry you. It'll take no more than an hour or so."

"You don't plan to come along on this reconnaissance mission?"

"I would like nothing better, but I can't take the risk. It would be a disaster if I were to be apprehended in Philby's house."

Collins knew it was not a matter of Steele shying away from danger but of simple logic. Steele had been thinking that way for so long, dispassionately weighing the costs and benefits of any action, that it had become second nature for him.

"And if Frank and I do this and we're caught?"

"You'll pose as carpenters or plumbers, so you'll have a believable cover story. There would be no overt connection to me, or to the Agency. Philby might suspect something was up, but he couldn't be sure."

"And if the police don't buy that story, wouldn't Philby recognize my name on the arrest report?"

Steele sighed. "Dennis, you and your brother will be carrying false identification. Driver licenses with false names. I would hope that you could talk your way out using the workman ploy. If you do get arrested, I'll get you bailed out quickly. I'm confident we could get the charges dropped, after a decent interval, with a word to the wise to the correct people. If we can't, the authorities will not have your real identities."

"You've planned for this for some time, haven't you?"

"I have a greater sense of urgency, now," Steele said. "After Paris, I believe that Philby suspects that I suspect. We need to move on this search quickly before he covers his tracks."

"So if Frank and I were to help, when would you need us?"

"A week or so after we get back," Steele said. "I need to make sure that Philby will be out of his house for a long enough period of time that you can look around. Will you help?"

"I figure Philby set us up for the Czechs in Paris," Collins said. "You may have been the target but they were also shooting at me. In for a penny, in for a pound. I'd like to give Feliks the chance to ask Philby some hard questions and this seems a good way to make that happen. So I'm in. I'll let you know if Frank is willing to go along."

Collins told himself that he had his eyes wide open. He thought the risks were worth running to expose Philby as an agent and possibly to strike at Anatoli Yatov, however indirectly. That alone was enough incentive for Collins.

After his return from London, Collins slept for most of the next two days. He didn't want to bother Frank and Peggy so he took a room at the Hotel Tudor on East 42nd Street and hung the "Do not disturb" sign on the doorknob. He ordered room service when he woke up from his first ten hours of sleep and had a hamburger and a few beers. He didn't start feeling like himself until Thursday.

He phoned Frank and arranged to meet him at Toots Shor's. Collins was drinking a beer at the circular bar, waiting for his brother, when he felt a tap on his shoulder. He turned around and found Lonnie Marks grinning at him.

"There you are," Marks said. "I've been looking around for you for a few weeks. Where have you been?"

"Traveling. Washington, mainly."

"You look tired, my friend. Burning the candle at both ends?"

"I'm fine," Collins said. "What do they say, there's plenty of time to sleep when you're dead?"

"A cheery thought. I was looking for you because I'm throwing a little farewell party for Lionel Graham. Do you know him?" Marks didn't wait for an answer. "One of my favorite clients. He has landed a role in one of Warner's films and so Lionel's heading out to Los Angeles. We're sending him off in style next Thursday at the Stork. I hoped you could come. Alison Winchester is going to be there. She tells me you two hit it off that night at Sardi's when I couldn't stay."

"We did. She's a sweet girl." Collins decided not to give Marks a hard time about his matchmaking. "If things were different I'd be calling her for drinks and dinner."

"What does that mean? I hope you don't mind me asking?"

Collins knew that Marks would have asked even if Collins did mind. "My personal life is a bit complicated at the moment. Until I get it straightened out, I need to keep things simple."

"I see," Marks said. "Mysterious as always. Do let me know if there's anything I can do."

"I appreciate it. Afraid I have to work this one out myself."

"Listen, Denny, you've always treated me with respect. I feel that I owe you. I can't say the same for some of the other columnists. If there's anything I can do, put in a good word for you at one of the papers, just let me know."

"Thanks. I don't think the Vatican will be considering me for sainthood any time soon but I'll let you know if I need any testimonials." He paused, wondering how to phrase what he wanted to say to Marks. "With my situation like it is, you might want to think about finding another eligible guy to go to dinner with Alison."

Marks shrugged, dismissing the idea. "Alison could dine out every night of the week with a new guy if she wanted to. She doesn't have any trouble attracting men. It would be nice to see her end up with someone who can appreciate her for more than the way she fills out a dress."

"There's an awful lot to appreciate about her," Collins said. "It's just the wrong time for me to be the one doing the appreciating. It's my loss." He looked at Marks directly. "And you can tell her that, if you think it's a message she would want to hear."

"Sure, Denny," Marks said. "I think she'd like to know that under other circumstances you'd be interested."

Frank Collins passed Marks on his way into the restaurant. Collins asked for a quiet table in the back, and once they were seated and had their drinks, he gave his brother an abbreviated account of his trip to Paris, explaining the situation with Steele and Kim Philby.

He told Frank how Steele believed that the British intelligence officer had done a great deal of damage by passing documents to the Russians. "He thinks Philby warned Moscow that the FBI list that Morris took with him was a plant. He also believes Philby has been passing military information as well—what we have planned in advance on the ground in Korea. Two very strong reasons to stop him, among others."

"Are there more reasons?"

"Personal reasons. Steele believes that Philby's controller is Anatoli Yatov, the one who was handling Morris."

"The bastard who murdered Karina," Frank said grimly.

"If Steele exposes Philby, it hurts Yatov. Who knows, it may even flush him out into the open. There's something else. Philby tipped the Russians that Steele was going to be in Paris. They sent some relatively incompetent Czech thugs after us who tried, and failed, to bury a round or two in us."

Frank whistled softly. "They're playing for keeps."

"They are. As far as I'm concerned the only difference between Yatov and Philby is that Philby speaks English with a Cambridge accent. His hands are just as bloody."

Collins glanced around to make sure that they couldn't be overheard before he broached Steele's idea of searching Philby's house for incriminating documents.

"I would like your help to get into the house," Collins said. "It's a bit risky, and it could mean trouble for both of us if it doesn't go right."

"By getting into the house, I assume you mean breaking and entering. I think that's what the district attorney would call it. You're asking me to help you commit a felony."

"I am," Collins said. "It's a last resort and we'd do this only to prevent a greater evil."

"And you're willing to accept the consequences, if things go bad? You're convinced it's worth it?"

"To stop Philby? And Yatov? Yes, it's worth it. So are you in?"

"If you need me for this, I guess I am." Frank hesitated. "Steele doesn't have anyone he can use in Washington? Local talent?"

"Steele isn't the most popular man in Washington today. His own agency keeps him at arm's length. He doesn't seem sure of who he can trust. The two of us are outside that circle, so there's less risk in using us."

"So what does Steele see as the risks?"

"We could get caught by the police when we're in the house. Steele will arrange for false IDs, so at least they won't have our real names if we're arrested."

Frank smirked. "Are you kidding? If we do it right, we'll be in and out with no one the wiser. We have a bit of an advantage—I'm a cop and I know how cops think. I also know the stupid mistakes the bad guys make that get them caught and we'll steer clear of them."

"Can you get us into the house without breaking any windows?"

"Do you mean, can I pick a lock? Sure. I can borrow a few tools from a guy I know. He's gone straight, at least for the time being. I'll explain that I want to show one of the new detectives how a lock gets picked."

"One other risk. It's possible that the Soviets are watching Philby and might object to uninvited visitors at his house. That's extremely unlikely, though, according to Steele."

"Whose track record on predictions isn't the best, from what I remember. So we need to be prepared for all eventualities. Safest course is to stake out the house and wait a while before we go in, make sure we haven't been followed, that there isn't surveillance on the place. How much time will we have once we're in? Does Steele know?"

"At least an hour, maybe two. We'll pose as plumbers if the police should come by."

"That plumber story might work for the neighbors, but I don't know about the cops. There's an alternative story. I could show my badge and explain that I'm doing a little moonlighting on the side. A rich businessman in New York thinks his wife is seeing this guy Kim Philby on the side when she visits her sister in Washington. I've been hired to retrieve some love letters that she sent Philby. The rich guy wants to use the letters for grounds for the divorce. I'll explain that we only came for the correspondence."

"And what about me? How do you explain me?"

"You're my out-of-work younger brother and I'm helping you out by including you in on the job."

"Not bad," Collins said. "Maybe you missed your calling. You could be writing dime store crime novels, like Mickey Spillane. But would your story be convincing enough that they would let us walk?"

"It might be. We'd be hoping for professional courtesy. Hell, I've seen cops look the other way on a lot worse things than unlawful entry."

"And if they don't buy it?"

"We hope that Steele has some clout left. Friends in high places. But I sure as hell hope it doesn't come to that. Just tell me that you trust this guy, Denny. I can't help but remember what happened the last time you got mixed up with him."

"I don't know that I could ever completely trust him," Collins said. "Not after what happened with Morris and Karina. But we want the same thing now, to expose Philby and hurt Yatov. On this I do trust him, as strange as that might seem. I think I have a better sense of who he is, and what drives him."

"I hope you're right. If it turns out that Steele is wrong about this British guy, and he isn't spying for the Soviets, then we'll have crossed the line for the wrong reasons." Frank grunted. "There are a few things I'll need. I'll call Steele so he can have them for us when we get there."

A waiter appeared in front of their table. "You have a call, Mr. Collins," he said. "You can take it up front, in the side room, if you like."

Collins made his way to the telephone, puzzled by who would be phoning him. The mystery caller turned out to be his longtime accountant, Jacob Stein.

"Figured I'd find you at Toots' place," Stein said. "Is there something going on I should know about?"

"Like what?" Collins asked.

"I don't know. The federal agents that came to see me this morning wouldn't say exactly what it was either, but they had a lot of questions about your finances. Whether there had been any large payments in the past year to your account."

"Was one of them named Caldwell?"

"Yes, that's the name. He did most of the talking, and the other agent just stood there giving me the evil eye."

"What did you tell them?"

"The truth, that your primary source of income in 1950 was your *Sentinel* salary and that you picked up a few bucks for that magazine article you did for *Collier's*, the one on Inchon. Nothing more."

"What did Caldwell say to that?"

"Then he wanted to know about 1949. I told him that it wasn't much different, that your income didn't change much."

"Did that satisfy him?"

"He made some comment about how the money might be off the books. I told him that I dealt with all types and that you were the last guy in the world that I'd figure for any funny business. Caldwell shook his head and said that if you were squeaky clean the Bureau wouldn't be asking about you. He wanted to know me if I would tell you about their visit and when I said yes, he smiled. Not a nice smile. What's going on, Dennis?"

"Caldwell is out to deliver a message," Collins said. "He wants to demonstrate that the Bureau can poke around in my life anytime that they want. That they can make trouble for me."

"What's this all about?"

"Nothing for you to worry about. It's complicated. They want me to help them attack the loyalty of someone in Washington who they don't like. It's wrong and I won't play ball with them. No matter what they may have insinuated, I'm not on the Comintern payroll. In fact I'm not on any payroll at the moment."

"You don't want to make that a habit. Not being on a payroll. And I've been reading your column long enough to know that you're not some sort of subversive, unless pulling for Pee Wee and Jackie Robinson has become un-American. By the way, how's the job search going?"

"It isn't," Collins said. "I have a few personal things I need to get squared away first. Then a vacation down in the Keys, where I can figure out what's next. It may be a couple of months before I'm back in the saddle."

"Speaking as your accountant, a couple of months is about what you can afford. But I think taking a break is a good idea, Denny."

Collins thanked him for alerting him to Caldwell's visit. "Do me a favor, would you?" he asked Stein. "If Caldwell does come back, tell him that I don't care if J. Edgar Hoover has been asking about my finances, for any more information they'll need to get a warrant. Tell him that my lawyer will be happy to discuss the matter with him."

Stein whistled. "Okay, Denny. I'll give him the word. You've got a lawyer, now?"

"No, I don't have a lawyer—not yet at least—but Caldwell doesn't know that."

"I'm glad to see some things haven't changed. You're not afraid to throw a brushback pitch or two."

"Sometimes you have to," Collins said. "Can't let them dig in at the plate, can we?"

When he returned to the table, Frank was starting his second beer.

"You know a good lawyer?" he asked his brother. "Someone really sharp?"

"Now what?"

"It's Caldwell again. He showed up at my accountant's office and started asking lots of questions. Dropped hints about me getting payments off the books. He's letting me know there's a cost for not ratting out Steele. If he keeps pushing, I'll need a lawyer who can tell him to get lost if he can't produce a warrant. I want Caldwell thinking twice about trying any more bully boy tactics."

His brother thought for a moment. "Sounds like you need your own bulldog, a sharp criminal lawyer, someone not afraid to talk tough. Irish. A member of the right tribe for dealing with the Bureau. I know just the guy for you. Terry Sullivan. I'll give him a call and explain that J. Edgar has taken a dislike to my little brother and that you'll be contacting him if the Bureau decides to turn up the heat."

"Thanks," Collins said. "I appreciate it."

"It's not just for you that I'm going to call," his brother said. "I want to have Sullivan lined up for both of us if Steele's scheme works out as well this time as it did last time around."

"There's one other thing," Collins said. "I'd like you to keep this between us for now."

"You got it."

Collins told him about Penny's revelation that Caleb was his son, and how she wanted him to play some role in the boy's life, and how Matthew Steele had accepted the situation with surprising grace. Frank listened intently and Collins could tell that he didn't like what he was hearing. His brother had never warmed up to Penny and had always resented her sway over Collins.

"It's strange at best," Frank said when he finished. "I'm happy for you being a father but the circumstances are damn irregular. It's a hell of a thing to drop on you a year after the fact. Are you sure that he is yours?"

"I know you've never cared for Penny but she wouldn't lie about this. I don't doubt it, the times and dates match up. I've met the boy—he looks like my son, like a Collins."

"Why tell you now?"

"She regretted keeping the truth from me. She thought she had wronged me."

"You say Penny has been depressed. Is she thinking straight about this? I mean, why not keep her mouth shut? It would make life a lot less complicated for her and for you."

Collins leaned forward. "That doesn't matter now. Caleb is my son and I'm not going to shirk from my responsibilities."

"It'll be messy, you know that. No matter what Steele says now, it won't be an easy thing for him, having you around." His brother frowned, a look of suspicion on his face. "Tell me that it's completely over between you and Penny and this isn't her scheme to get you back."

"I swear to you that it's over. We're wrong for each other, and we both know it. This is about Caleb, plain and simple."

"I'll take you at your word," his brother said. "And I'll hand you this—you're certainly living an interesting life. Sometimes it just seems a bit too interesting."

When Collins got back to his room in the Hotel Tudor, he called Beth Winslow's number in Boston. The phone rang a few times before she answered.

"I wanted to check in and see how you were doing," he explained. "I know it's been a while."

"Thank you for calling, Dennis," she said. "I was thinking about you just the other day. I was wondering whether you had begun writing for another newspaper."

"Not yet," he said. "In fact, I wanted you to know that I've spent some time in Washington doing what I could to make sure Oliver's message got through and that I think we're making some headway."

"That's marvelous," she said. "I appreciate it. I will confess that I've been worried about you, about your adjusting to being back here."

"I'm fine," he said. "The longer I'm back, the easier it gets."

"Are you in Florida?"

"Not yet. Still in New York. I have a few more things I need to do. Then I'm off to the Keys."

"Don't put it off for too long," she said. "Everyone needs a vacation now and then."

"I've come around to that way of thinking," he said. "I'll drop you a postcard when I get there."

Seventeen

Their call to action from Steele came two days later, on Wednesday. He asked Collins and his brother to come to Washington on Friday, when Kim Philby and his family would be out for the evening and the Nebraska Avenue house would be vacant for several hours.

"Plan to stay over with us, Dennis," Steele said. "Penny would like to talk with you, and you can spend some time with Caleb."

"Sure," Collins said. "I can stay Friday and Saturday night. I'll let my friend in Florida know that I'll be catching a flight from Washington to Miami on Sunday morning."

On Friday, Collins and Frank caught a morning train to Washington, arriving at Union Station in the late afternoon. Steele met them in the waiting area. He looked haggard and tired, with dark circles under his eyes, and Collins wondered if Penny's depression had deepened.

"I know we last met under difficult circumstances," Steele told Frank after they shook hands. "As your brother knows, I deeply regret what happened to Miss Lazda."

"You miscalculated," Frank said. "I get how that works. For what it's worth, I thought you should have given it straight to Denny from the start. But I blame Morris and I blame Yatov for Karina, not you. Denny understands how I look at it. I wish I had taken a shot at Morris when I had the chance."

"I wanted to clear the air," Steele said.

"You have. No hard feelings on my part."

Steele wasn't done. "I appreciate what you and Dennis are doing. It's for a good cause."

"I wouldn't be here if I didn't think it was. And I'm supposed to look out for my brother when he gets in a jam."

"I hope this doesn't fall into the category of a jam," Collins said. "Just a simple break-and-enter job."

"I have procured the van that you asked for," Steele said to Frank. "And the overalls."

Frank laughed at the puzzled look on his younger brother's face. "I made some advance arrangements. We'll play the role of plumbers, called in on an emergency basis to fix a leak in the kitchen piping. Or at least that's our story."

"I have Virginia driver's licenses for the two of you," Steele said. "Frank and Dennis Ryan."

"That's original," Collins said.

"Better that you don't have to worry about remembering new first names," Steele said. "It's easier."

"Our initial cover story is that we're there to fix the plumbing," Frank said. "An emergency call. That's what we tell a snoopy neighbor who comes by to check. If it's the cops, we've got the moonlighting detective story as a back-up."

As he drove them to Hoban Road, Steele explained that Philby and his family would be dining out that evening in Georgetown with James Angleton, one of the Agency officials, and his wife. Guy Burgess had left Washington to visit a friend in New York City. Philby's house would be empty for several hours. Once they were in his house, Steele suggested that they concentrate on his study, his bedroom, and anyplace else that they thought Philby might think to hide documents or other sensitive materials.

When the Philbys left the Angleton residence Steele promised that he would call. "I will ring the phone in Philby's house three times and then hang up," he said. "You'll have about ten minutes to clear out after the call. That's about how long it will take him to drive back home."

"Where will you be when you make the call?" Collins asked.

"Near the Angletons," Steele said. "As it happens, I'll be visiting a friend who lives across the street from them, so I'll be Johnny-on-the-spot."

Frank opened his suit jacket to reveal his shoulder holster and the butt of his service revolver, a Colt Police Special .38. "So you know, I'm ready for most anything."

Steele shook his head. "I'd advise you to leave that behind."

"What about the Russians? We saw what they're capable of back in New York. What if they're watching Philby's place?"

Steele shrugged. "Don't be concerned about that. Any Soviets here would be giving Philby a wide berth. They don't want to ever be seen anywhere near him during daylight hours."

"If it's all the same to you, I think I'll keep it with me," Frank said. "Like they say, Mr. Colt made all men equal, and I'd prefer to be on equal footing if Ivan or Boris or Anatoli Yatov shows up."

"Suit yourself," Steele said. "I've checked and neither the Philbys or the neighbors have dogs, so that's one less thing to worry about."

When they reached Steele's house, Collins noticed that a gray, unmarked delivery van was parked on the street near the driveway entrance. "That's the rented truck," Steele said. He checked his wristwatch. "You have about an hour before you need to arrive at Philby's house. I left the overalls and gloves in the carriage house. Try not to disturb anything inside the house. They have children, so Philby may not notice a few things out of order, but be particularly careful to leave things as you found them when you search his study and bedroom."

"And if he notices afterward?" Collins asked.

"I guess it depends on whether you do find something or not. If the house is clean, it most likely means that he has been expecting greater scrutiny and has prepared for it."

"And if we find something?"

"Bring it back with you. That will be the proof we need."

"If documents are missing, Philby will know immediately that the game is up."

"He will, won't he?" Steele smiled. "That's 'a consummation devoutly to be wished' and we can only hope to be that fortunate."

"What's with Steele?" Frank asked Collins as they drove to Nebraska Avenue in the rented truck. "Has he been sick? He looks terrible—his color is bad and he's lost a lot of weight."

"Maybe the trip over to Paris and back knocked him down," Collins said. "He was fighting a cold the entire time. And there's the problems with Penny. That will take a lot out of a man."

Frank snorted. "Better that it's him rather than you that's taking the beating." Collins didn't say anything—his brother had never thought Penny was the right woman for him.

It only took ten minutes for them to reach Nebraska Avenue. They parked the van up the street about fifty yards from Philby's driveway and waited fifteen minutes or so before moving the truck in front of his house.

Collins led the way into the backyard. Frank followed him carrying a large canvas tool bag. A large stand of elms screened them from sight from the north.

"If the police show up now, we're here to work on their clogged kitchen sink." Frank held up a large plumber's wrench. "Very unlikely that we'll attract that sort of attention. Let me do the talking if we are interrupted."

Frank grunted softly in satisfaction after inspecting the back door lock. "This shouldn't be too difficult," he said. He pulled a tension wrench and a long metal lock pick out of the canvas bag and dropped to his knees so he could work on the lock.

Collins watched nervously as his brother fiddled with the tools. He looked back over his shoulder several times to make sure that they had remained unobserved. They were hidden from view by the elm trees and several nearby bushes.

His brother exhaled sharply and rotated the wrench until there was a clicking sound. He turned the doorknob. "We're in," he said.

Frank instructed Collins to hide the canvas bag with the lock pick set somewhere in the bushes behind the garage. "There's no way to hide the fact that these are burglary tools," he said. "Let's not make it easy for the cops if they don't buy our story."

"Keep your gloves on," he added. "No prints. If you need to turn on the light when you enter a room, make sure to turn it off when you leave."

They moved through the house quickly. Frank went to the second floor to search Philby's bedroom and Collins made his way to Philby's study.

Collins rifled through Philby's desk and was disappointed to find nothing of interest—a few folders with household bills and some blank stationary but no government documents of any sort. He began to check the books in the one large bookshelf in the room, but stopped when he saw a film of dust had settled on top of them.

His brother appeared in the doorway of the study. "Clean as a whistle upstairs in his bedroom," he said. "I checked his suits and jackets in the closet and found nothing. Nothing under the bed or in the dressers. No obvious hiding places."

"Nothing here of interest, either," Collins said. "It doesn't look like he uses the study much. Let's check out the basement together."

Frank went first down the steps from the kitchen, switching the light on, and Collins heard him whistle softly when he reached the bottom of the stairs.

"That's some train set," he said.

A large plywood table was set up in the middle of the basement and on it were model train tracks arranged in a figure eight. Two miniature locomotives, each with its own passenger and freight cars and caboose, occupied the tracks.

"They're Lionels," Frank said. "O-gauge. I looked at buying a set for Brendan. They're not cheap."

In the far corner of the basement there was narrow door. Collins tried the doorknob and found it locked. He looked over at his brother.

"I think I can open that with my pocket knife," Frank said. He went to work on the lock. It took only a minute before he had the door open and flicked on a light switch. The interior room filled with a red glow from the overhead light and Collins saw that it was a darkroom, with a sink, chemistry trays, and an enlarger. Bottles of developer and fixer lined a small shelf. In one corner of the room there was a table with a set of lamps clamped above it. A Leica camera sat on the table.

"It's a professional set-up," Frank said. "What you would need if you were photographing lots of documents."

The telephone rang loudly upstairs, startling them. It continued to ring and Collins looked over at his brother, who was listening intently. The phone rang five times and then stopped.

"Five rings," Collins said. "Steele said that he'd end the call at three rings."

"You think we should stay?"

"I'm not sure it's worth the risk. We checked his study and his bedroom and we've found a set-up here to take photos. I think we should get out now."

"I was hoping you would say that. I'm getting a bit antsy. We've been here long enough."

They left through the back door; Frank inspected the lock to make sure there were no signs of his handiwork with the lock pick. Collins went behind the garage and retrieved the small canvas tool bag. Frank took the lead as they walked slowly to the front yard.

"Take your time," he said. "We're working guys finishing a plumbing job. No rush, no hurry."

Frank got into the driver's seat of the van and Collins hopped in beside him. They drove out of the neighborhood slowly. Friday evening traffic on Nebraska Avenue had picked up and Frank flipped on the radio. They listened to Louis Armstrong sing "When the Saints Going Marching In" and then the Duke Ellington orchestra playing "Take the 'A' Train."

"Great music," Collins said. "It reminds me that I haven't been back to the 52nd Street clubs in a while."

"You're the one going to Florida," Frank said. "As soon as you're back in the city, we can hit the jazz clubs and catch a couple of Dodgers games."

"I'd like that," Collins said.

"Will you move here later? To Washington? So you can be close to the boy?"

"I don't know. That's one of the questions I need to answer."

"I do want to meet your son," his brother said. "Didn't think this was the right time."

"It isn't," Collins said, "but I'd like Caleb to get to know his crazy uncle Frank."

After they put Frank on the overnight train to New York, Steele and Collins drove back to Hoban Road.

"You're sure it was a Leica," Steele said, repeating a question he had asked earlier when Collins and his brother had initially described the basement darkroom. "A screwmounted Leica?"

"I'm not a photographer or a camera salesman so I don't know the exact model," Collins responded. "It was definitely a Leica. I saw the name on the top of the camera."

"Did you look to see what type of film? Were there boxes of undeveloped film in the room?"

"I didn't see any. The phone rang and we decided it was time to go. I'm sorry I can't give you any more details."

"It's enough," Steele said. "In my mind, it's enough. Philby has expensive photographic equipment in his basement that could be used for microfilming."

"Or that could be used for taking pictures of his children."

"You don't need a Leica for that. It's three hundred dollars for the camera and lenses alone."

"I'll grant you that it seems fishy," Collins said. "But we didn't find any documents. Nothing official."

"He's careful," Steele said. "But not careful enough. If he were my agent, I would never let him keep photographic equipment at home and certainly not a Leica. It raises too many questions. I'm surprised that Yatov would allow it."

"If Yatov is in the picture."

"He is," Steele said. "Trust me. He is."

In the morning Collins spent twenty minutes outside playing with Caleb, helping him toddle around the Steele's backyard. Penny sat in a lawn chair with a wide-brimmed straw hat sheltering her from the sun and they talked quietly.

"I'm glad you're back," she said. "I didn't realize that you were returning to New York and not Washington after the trip to Paris."

"Your husband had us change flights," he said, not sure whether Steele had told Penny about their intermediate stop in London. "It was a nice gesture on his part because it saved me a trip from Washington to New York."

"We didn't finish our talk. I need to make sure that you have forgiven me. Not only for how I treated you in the past, but also for the way I handled the situation with Caleb."

"I forgive you," Collins said. "Wasn't that clear?" He tried to keep his annoyance out of his voice. He wondered how many times he was going to have to tell her that he wasn't angry with her over the past.

"Are you sure?"

"Penny, why would I lie to you about that? You've asked me twice and I've told you twice. I forgive you and I don't see how any good can come out of rehashing what happened."

"Don't be angry with me. It's important that we're at peace with each other."

"I'm not angry," he said, softening. "I've had a chance to think about it, and what's done is done. I don't blame you for Caleb and I understand why you wouldn't have told me about him. So you can rest easy."

"Thank you, Dennis."

"Is there anything else? Ask away."

"No, I feel much better. I thought you might be punishing me."

Collins shook his head, exasperated. "No, Penny, I don't want to punish you. I want to figure out what I should do next and how I can make a living and how Caleb can fit into my life. I have no desire to cause pain for you."

After they returned to the main house, Penny took Caleb upstairs to the nursery and Steele asked Collins to come to his study. Sitting in one of the wingbacked chairs was a balding, heavyset man, who Steele introduced as Guy Myers, a member of the Agency's counterintelligence staff.

Myers nodded to Collins. "Allen Dulles has briefed me on your background, Mr. Collins."

"I thought you should hear about what Dennis stumbled across in Philby's basement," Steele said. He didn't explain why Collins was in Philby's house and Collins decided he wouldn't volunteer anything about his presence there.

"Philby has a pretty elaborate photo lab set up down there," Collins began. "A darkroom with high-end equipment, as good as anything we had at the newspaper, and a Leica camera."

"Did you see any documents?" Myers asked. "Or photographic prints?"

Collins shook his head. "Nothing like that. The darkroom was immaculate. Everything in place."

"And the rest of the house?" It was clear that Myers knew about the search Collins and his brother had performed.

"Nothing. We only had time for a quick run through. We could have easily missed something."

"Did you spot a safe anywhere in the house?"

"No," Collins said. "Neither of us saw a safe."

Myers turned to Steele. "So Philby has a photo lab in his basement and an expensive German camera. That's curious, but there are many possible explanations for it. Maybe photography is his hobby."

"Perhaps," Steele said. "Is it a coincidence that Philby owns the exact camera that you'd select if you were filming documents? It's not a Kodak Brownie for taking shots at a birthday party. Then there's the Albanians, and Volkov, and the leaks from Washington. What about the fact that only Philby knew about my trip to Paris and we suddenly had company at the airport when we arrived? That doesn't strike you as suspicious?"

"We can't jump to conclusions. Can you be sure that others within the Agency didn't know about your visit to Paris? Or maybe the Czechs had the airport staked out for someone else and spotted you." Myers shook his head. "I'm far from convinced of Philby's wickedness. You know he wrote a memo suggesting that we review the Foreign Office personnel in their Washington embassy, past and present, for candidates for Homer. Does that seem like something a Soviet agent would do? Point us directly toward Maclean? No, that isn't logical."

"Then there's Burgess," Steele said. "What do you make of that relationship?"

"It's strange," Myers said. "I'll grant you that. Apparently they are friends of long standing. But, again, would a Soviet agent invite someone like Burgess—a known homosexual—into his house? Do you really believe Moscow Center would countenance that? To have someone as disreputable as Burgess, an obvious target for blackmail, that close to a penetration agent and possibly attracting unwanted attention from the security apparatus? I think not."

"So you won't consider surveillance on Philby?" Steele asked. "Just to monitor his movements for a few weeks?"

"Sorry," Myers said. "There's just not enough there to warrant that sort of effort. It's not like we have the manpower to mount such an operation anyway. And I think we can agree this isn't something we want to ask our friends in the Bureau to undertake. Do we?"

"No, that would be a mistake." Steele thought for a moment. "If I can surface more concrete evidence, will you be willing to take this up the line, to General Smith, and higher if necessary?"

"Depends on the evidence," Myers said. "And in my professional opinion, you've lost perspective on this, Matthew. With all due respect, I think you've fallen in love with your theory about Philby and you're trying to force fit the facts that you have to match up with it. And you believe that lurking behind all this clandestine activity is Anatoli Yatov. "

"I don't believe I mentioned his name," Steele said.

"You didn't. You didn't have to. Your theory about Yatov running penetration agents in Washington is well known. Ergo, you think Yatov is handling Philby. I think you're wrong on both counts, and again I think your preconceptions have colored your judgment."

"You don't think Yatov is in the States?" Collins asked Myers.

"I don't. After the Trojan Horse episode I imagine that he was recalled to Moscow. I doubt that he survived the scrutiny that would inevitably follow such a botched operation. He has been purged, no doubt, or sent off to Siberia." Myers spoke with certainty. Collins could see that Myers was the sort of man who, once he had made up his mind, would stubbornly defend his position. Steele had his work cut out for him if he hoped to convince Myers of Yatov's involvement.

"Anatoli Yatov survived the bloodletting in Moscow in '38 and '39," Steele said. "Hundreds of NKVD agents were killed on the flimsiest grounds, but he went unscathed. And he has survived all of the purges since. He's always performed with ruthless efficiency. I think he is still here running agents."

"And some people believe in ghosts," Myers said. "That doesn't mean that they exist. I'm not a superstitious man. Until Yatov turns up in Times Square on New Year's Eve or is seen flying a kite near the Washington Monument, we can safely assume that he's not here." He rose to his feet, nodding to Collins. "And if you will both excuse me, I must run. I have a standing tennis match on Saturdays with Kurt Braustein. You remember Kurt, don't you, Matthew?"

"I do indeed," Steele said. "Worked with him in Berlin. Give him my regards."

"Those were the days, weren't they?" Myers gave them a weak smile. "You could look right across Brandenburg Square and see your flesh-and-blood adversary. Nothing ghostly about that in the least."

Eighteen

Collins had grown tired of waiting in airports and of sitting through long flights. He drank two beers at a restaurant in the National Airport, and then had a few more on the flight to Miami. He had skipped breakfast so while he wouldn't have described himself as tight by the time they landed, he also wasn't feeling any pain.

Once inside the terminal, he looked around for the tall figure of Jim Highsmith without any luck. Then he spotted an attractive, dark-haired girl dressed in a starched white shirt and khaki pants who was holding a handwritten "Highsmith Inn" sign. As he walked over to greet her, Collins could see she had a light olive complexion, dark brown eyes, and remarkably beautiful features. A simple silver cross hung on a chain around her neck. He guessed she was in her mid-twenties.

Collins introduced himself and was rewarded with a broad smile.

"I'm Maria Highsmith," she said. "I'm your driver for the ride back to Key West. My father sent me because he was tied up at the restaurant. But don't worry, I promise we'll get there a lot faster with me driving."

"Is that a promise or a threat?"

"Funny," she said. "Consider it a promise."

After he had collected his luggage, she led the way to the airport parking lot and he followed her to a dusty, wood-paneled Dodge station wagon. The intense tropical heat made Collins feel dizzy and he fought back a sudden wave of nausea.

She drove them south on Le Jeune Road, passing through Coral Gables and picking up Route 1. Collins shielded his eyes from the sun with his right hand. His head was hurting and he felt queasy, but he figured that he would brave it out until his stomach settled. After they drove through Florida City and reached the start of the Keys, he finally admitted to the girl that he felt sick and he asked her to pull in at a roadside restaurant just outside of Key Largo.

He left her in the dining area at a wooden table and hurried to the men's room, a shabby cubicle of a room with a chipped porcelain sink and a toilet. Collins proceeded to get sick, vomiting into the toilet bowl, hating the feeling. Afterward he washed his hands and face in the sink and dried himself off with some paper toweling.

Maria waited at the table, her eyes watchful, as he made his way slowly back over to join her.

"How are you feeling?" she asked.

"A bit rugged. My own fault. Drinking on an empty stomach and the heat must have got to me."

"That will do it," she said. "I ordered toast and coffee. You should drink a few glasses of water before you eat the toast. It will help settle your stomach. Then the coffee."

"Maybe not."

"It works wonders," she said. "Believe me, we see lots of people who drink too much in the restaurant and this is what Miguel recommends to them for treating a hangover. Trust me."

"Miguel?"

"Our bartender. If anyone would know, he would, wouldn't he?"

"You have me there. I guess Miguel would know."

A middle-aged waitress brought them a side order of toast and two cups of coffee. Collins ate slowly, washing the toast down with the water. Maria added two spoons of sugar to her coffee before she drank it; Collins took his black.

"Are you feeling well enough for conversation?" she asked.

"Sure. My condition has stabilized. I don't think you'll need to drive me to the emergency room."

"That's good," she said. "Because the closest hospital is in Homestead, twenty-five miles away, and it's probably not up to New York standards. I think it only has ten beds."

"I'll survive," he said.

"Can I ask you a question?"

"Ask away."

"My father thinks I should have gone to college," she said. She tucked a wayward strand of hair behind her left ear. "I don't see why. I've always loved reading and I've always been able to learn whatever I need to on my own. I didn't see how going off to school with two hundred rich girls was going to improve my mind or my life. What do you think?"

"I think I'll stay out of this one."

"Are you a college man?"

"No such luck," he said. He drank some more of his coffee. It was surprisingly good. He was starting to feel better. "I guess you could say that my classroom was the city room of the *New York Sun*."

"So you didn't go to college. Hasn't hurt you a bit, has it?"

"I guess I've overcompensated by reading a lot. Someone once told me that when you have educated yourself you're an autodidact. Always wanted to work that word into a column, but never got the chance. I would have liked to go to college, but once I caught on at the *Sun*, I loved what I was doing too much to stop. And now it's too late."

"Too late? How old are you, Mr. Collins?"

"Maybe you should think about getting into newspaper work yourself. You're certainly curious enough and you're not shy about asking personal questions."

"You didn't answer my question."

He laughed. "I'm thirty-five."

"You look younger," she said. "Thirty, tops."

"Thanks, I'll consider that a compliment. And how old are you, Miss Highsmith?"

"Twenty-two. Just had my birthday last month. And please call me Maria, and I'll call you Dennis, because we're not too worried about the formalities in Key West."

"Fair enough," he said.

"My father says that you're a very interesting man. That's one of his highest compliments, by the way. I'll bet you have some great stories to tell. New York newspaper columnist. War correspondent. Dad said something about you competing in Golden Gloves so that means you know how to box. I was wondering what you might be like when he said you were coming down to stay with us."

Collins grinned. "I'm beginning to take your side on the college question. I don't think Sweet Briar or Mount Holyoke would have been ready for your directness, and vice versa. Not particularly ladylike."

"That has nothing to do with being a lady," she said sharply. "Whenever I hear someone talking about ladylike behavior, it usually means they don't like whatever it is that you're doing and they're hoping that using the phrase will stop you."

"I guess I'm at a disadvantage," he said lightly. "No one ever talks to me about ladylike behavior, so I wouldn't know. But you can keep asking questions, it's a free country."

"My dad didn't tell me that you were funny," she said. "I thought you'd be very serious."

"I'm Irish," he said. "That's how we look at the world. Keeps us from crying in our beer."

"I tried to read James Joyce," she said. "*Ulysses*. I couldn't stand it. The librarians laugh at me because I borrow so many books and return them quickly. I'll try fifteen or twenty pages and if the book doesn't interest me, then I drop it. *Ulysses* I found useless."

"Now you're the funny one," Collins said. "And if it's any consolation, I never warmed up to Joyce, either."

"You were in Korea, weren't you? What was that like?"

He looked over at her across the table, at her innocent, trusting face, and knew he didn't want to talk about the war with Maria Highsmith. There was nothing he could say about it that wasn't, in the end, ugly. Anyone who had been there understood, and those who had not, could not understand. He picked up the check that the waitress had left for them.

"Sure," he said. "I was there. It was tough." He drained his coffee cup before he spoke again. "Why don't I pay and then we can get back on the road?"

"I get it," she said. "You don't want to talk about Korea."

Collins didn't say anything but took the check over to the counter and paid. Once they were back in the station wagon and on Route 1, Collins broke the silence. "I made a New Year's resolution to stay off the topic of Korea. I'm trying to keep to it. That's why I ducked your question. Sorry if I was a bit abrupt."

"I understand," she said. "My dad is that way about the last war. If I ask him about Okinawa he clams right up."

"Why don't we talk about something more pleasant. Your dad said you liked baseball."

"He did? It's true, I'm the real fan in the family."

"Who do you root for?"

"Dad took me to some ballgames in Washington when he was stationed at Quantico so I guess I'm a Senators fan but I read the box scores for all of the games."

"Any favorite players?"

"Ted Williams, because my father has been fishing with him and because he's a Marine. And Jackie Robinson, because I admire how brave he is."

"Good choices. Robinson is a lot easier to interview. Williams doesn't care too much for the press. But I'd pick both of them for my team."

"Your team, huh. Who would you put in centerfield?"

"DiMaggio. Even if he's a Yankee and close to my age. Still the best outfielder in baseball."

"I agree," she said. "Who else would you pick?"

They spent the next twenty miles choosing their ideal teams. Collins was surprised at how much Maria knew about baseball. She chose an impressive All-Star team: Williams, DiMaggio, and Stan Musial in the outfield, Don Newcombe on the mound, Phil Rizzuto, Robinson, George Kell, and Gil Hodges in the infield, and Yogi Berra behind the plate.

"It's great that you picked Newk and Robinson," Collins said. "Glad to see some Dodgers on your team. Did your father tell you that we ran into Pee Wee Reese at the Biltmore?"

"He did. He was quite impressed that Reese came over to you and wanted to chat."

"Great ballplayer. A good man. He married a nice girl, too. Dottie."

"So have you been married, Dennis?"

"No. Never been that lucky, I guess."

"Have you come close, then?"

"It never seemed to work out," he said. "I guess I may not be cut out for it."

"Maybe you haven't found the right woman."

"Could be," he said. "And you? At your age, I figure you're probably fielding proposals right and left. An engagement on the horizon?"

She shook her head quickly, keeping her eyes on the road. "Maybe I haven't found the right man, yet, just like you haven't found the right woman. So we have that in common."

He laughed. "I have to believe that your prospects are better than mine. I'm not the catch that you are. I believe the phrase is 'worse for the wear.' The human equivalent of a jalopy."

"A jalopy. What a wonderful word. It makes me think of the word *galapago*, tortoise. I don't think you are a tortoise, or a jalopy."

Collins looked out at the expanse of blue-green water on both sides of the highway, and wondered how difficult it had been to build the bridges and causeway that allowed drivers to go from Miami to the tip of the Keys. He let his arm hang down from the passenger window for a moment and felt the pleasant warmth of the sun. He found himself yawning and apologized.

"If you're drowsy, take a nap," she said. "The heat always knocks down people when they've arrived from Up North."

"Maybe I will," he said. Collins closed his eyes and felt the fatigue wash over him and he found himself drifting off to sleep.

Maria Highsmith woke him outside Summerland Key, twenty miles or so from Key West, by gently tugging on his left arm. When he reluctantly opened his eyes, he glanced over to the driver's seat and saw the corners of her mouth curving into a smile. Frank Sinatra was singing on the radio, the volume low, "All or Nothing at All," a song Collins hadn't heard in years. She switched off the radio.

"We're almost there," she said. "You were tired. You slept through all the tollbooth stops. I thought I'd give you a chance to wake up before we arrive. How was your nap?"

"Good," he said. "I needed it. I haven't been sleeping too well."

"We can fix that. If you help out around the restaurant and hotel, I promise you'll be tired enough to drop right off to sleep."

"That's the plan, to make this a working holiday. I imagine living so close to the ocean will help with sleeping as well. All that sea air."

She laughed. "You must have read one of the tourist brochures about the sea air."

As they crossed over the bridge into Boca Chica Key, she turned to him. "By the way, you're not what I expected," she said.

"Is that so?"

"I thought you might be more like someone from *Front Page*. Hard-boiled and cynical. The type of New York newspaperman who calls any girl—any dame—he meets 'babe' and any guy, 'pal.'"

"Is that so, babe?" He was rewarded with her laughter. "I'm not cynical enough? I don't want to disappoint you, so perhaps you can tell me when I'm not living up to your idea of a hard-boiled New York newspaperman and I'll try harder."

"I'll do that. It's strange, I feel like I've known you for a long time. Or maybe we knew each other in a past life."

"A past life? Have you been reading Edgar Cayce? I've never been one for reincarnation. I figure we have it hard enough our first, and only time, around. At least that's what the nuns taught us and I wasn't about to argue with Sister Roberta, especially when she had that long wooden ruler in her right hand."

They drove past the Naval Air Station and crossed over the bridge to Stock Island. In a few minutes they reached the bridge connecting the highway to Key West. As she drove them down Flagler Avenue, Maria pointed out the different types of palm trees—coconut palm, travelers palm, and Cuban royal palm—lining the way. Their route took them through a number of side streets until they reached Amelia Street. Maria pulled the station wagon into a driveway next to a two-story wooden framed building painted in yellow and white with a HIGHSMITH INN sign in front.

Collins heard her sigh softly. "Home sweet home," she said. "I have the feeling you're going to like it here, Dennis. I really hope that you will."

Nineteen

After a few weeks in Key West, Collins felt that he had adjusted fairly well to the tropical heat and humidity. He wore a hat and sunglasses for the sun and glare and he paced himself when he was working outside. He had been able to avoid getting sunburned, and his skin had darkened from exposure to the sun.

He liked working with Jim Highsmith, pitching in on chores minor and major, helping his friend repaint the six street-level cottages that made up the hotel and repairing a wooden fence at the end of his property. Collins helped out at the restaurant on the weekends, doing some of the kitchen prep work and occasionally filling in at the bar when Miguel needed a break. He prided himself on not drinking when he was behind the bar.

Collins enjoyed losing himself in the work. He remembered something Karina Lazda had told him about the sense of freedom that came with starting over in a new place. New York and Washington seemed far away when he walked down the calm, sunny streets of Key West, the nearby yards filled with bougainvillea, jacaranda, and oleander; roosters and chickens wandering freely; the graceful wooden houses, many built in the nineteenth century, reflecting a mixture of architectural styles. Some of the larger houses had widow's walks or overhanging long eaves ("eyebrows") or sported Victorian flourishes. Then there were the shotgun houses, the simple structures constructed for the cigar workers. It was unlike any place Collins ever lived and he liked the relaxed, comfortable feel of the town.

He went days without worrying about the world situation. The conflict in Korea had settled into a stalemate, with the Eighth Army and the Chinese locked into trench warfare near the 38th parallel that was reminiscent of the fighting along the Western Front during the First World War. Collins did read the *Miami Herald*, and, when he could, he looked over the *New York Times* at the library, but it was with a new sense of detachment.

He sent Highsmith Inn postcards to Frank and Peggy, Peter Vandercamp, and Beth Winslow. He mailed one to Matthew and Penny, and wrote: "My best to all the Steeles. Give Caleb a hug and kiss. Dennis." He wondered whether Steele had been able to find any more evidence that would connect Philby to the Soviets. Collins figured that Steele would call him with news of any breakthroughs.

At two o'clock most afternoons, after the lunch crowd had finished in the restaurant, Collins and Jim Highsmith would take a break and eat Cuban sandwiches and drink sweet ice tea. Maria often joined them and Collins found himself looking forward to their lunches. She enjoyed soliciting his opinion on the books she had been reading and quizzing Collins about the latest news stories.

He purchased a school notebook from the Kress Store on Duval Street and began recording his thoughts and observations at the end of each day. It was a luxury not to have to write on deadline and he liked filling the page with whatever he had seen or heard that intrigued him.

He found himself writing a fair amount about Jim Highsmith and his daughter. He knew he was attracted to Maria—what male over fifteen years of age wasn't?—but he was surprised, and flattered, by her apparent interest in him. He chalked that up to her relative inexperience. She hadn't met anyone like him, he told himself. The local unmarried men of her age, or the occasional young Marine officer who might stop by to see Jim Highsmith, didn't share her interests. Collins suspected her mix of beauty and sharp wit also intimidated some would-be local suitors.

Collins decided it was best to keep his distance from her. She was the daughter of a friend, and he didn't want to complicate his stay in Key West. His personal life had become messy enough. Why should he create more trouble for himself? Why embarrass himself by mooning over a girl nearly fifteen years his junior? When she asked questions about his past, he sidestepped the more personal ones—which frustrated her—but he knew that keeping some boundaries was better for them both. He tried to imagine how he might explain fathering a child out-of-wedlock to her, and that was enough to convince him to remain tight-lipped.

She had a mind of her own, of course, and she found a way to draw him closer. One Friday she asked him if he'd tag along with her when she went to meet some of her friends at the Moonlight Club.

"Can you dance?" she asked.

"If I'm forced to," he said warily, not sure what she had in mind.

When he first dated Penny he discovered that she loved to dance and that prompted him to take lessons from a dance instructor, a strange, older Austrian woman, Frau Mueller, in her dance studio on West 28th Street. Frau Mueller had muttered critical comments under her breath in German as she led Collins around the dance floor, but she knew how to teach, and Collins found that his years spent perfecting his boxing footwork with Digger Callahan at the Hibernian Club had been well spent. He learned the steps fairly quickly. He and Penny had spent many nights on the dance floor at El Morocco—Elmer's to the regulars—and he didn't embarrass himself even when the band played Latin numbers.

"Good," Maria said. "I need a partner so you can dance with me, then. They have a great little swing band."

He shrugged, not completely comfortable with the idea, but he didn't really have a plausible excuse for backing out. When it came time to walk over to the nightclub, he found her waiting for him in the front room of the Highsmith's small cottage. She wore a pearl-colored short-sleeve sweater, a gray pencil skirt, and high heels. He had never seen her with make-up before and she seemed suddenly older, a beautiful, alluring woman instead of a girl in her early twenties. Collins tried not to stare, carefully keeping his eyes fixed on her face when he talked to her.

The Moonlight Club was a cozy place with a dance floor, a scattering of small tables, and a long marble-topped bar. A sign on the mirror behind the bar announced that "The Moonlight Quartet plays the hits every night except Sunday!" Collins noticed a silver-colored piano standing in a far corner. Maria introduced him to her friends—Henry and Rosalie—as a New Yorker and a friend of the family; she had promised to show him some Key West nightlife and figured they could start with the Moonlight Club.

"Well, you've come to the right place," Henry said to Collins, "and with the right partner. Maria is a great dancer."

"I'm Irish, not Cuban," Collins said. "So unless it's a jig of some sort, I'll have a hard time keeping up with her."

"Isn't there great dancing in the New York nightclubs?" Rosalie asked. She was a tiny girl with large dark eyes and a hesitant smile. "It sure looks that way in the newsreels."

"There is," Collins said. "But did you ever see me up on the screen dancing? There's a good reason I'm not in those newsreels."

"You'll be fine," Maria said. "Don't let them scare you. They're exaggerating—I'm not that great a dancer."

They had a light supper and then the music started. The Moonlight Quartet was made up of a pianist, bass player, drummer, and saxophonist. Henry and Rosalie got up from the table, eager to get on the dance floor, and Maria looked over at Collins. "It's time," she said. "Ready or not."

She took him by the hand and pulled him to the dance floor. She slipped into his arms and Collins was acutely aware of her slim body and the scent of her perfume. The band started playing "The Tennessee Waltz" and Collins and Maria moved about the floor in time to the music. Collins relaxed as they danced and he could see from the growing smile on Maria's face that she was impressed, even more so when he negotiated them through a sudden rumba.

They danced through five numbers, and then, when the band leader announced they would be playing a slow, romantic number, Collins said something to her about taking a break. He wasn't comfortable with the idea of having her body pressed so closely against his, so he led her back to the table. She didn't say anything but he could tell she was reluctant to sit down. Henry and Rosalie stayed on the floor.

"Hey, you weren't completely straight with me," she said after they had returned to the table. "You claimed you weren't much of a dancer."

"I haven't had much occasion to dance the last few years," he said, and suddenly remembered that the last time had been an impromptu slow dance with Karina Lazda in her Upper West Side apartment to a Vera Lynn record.

"What is it?" Maria asked. "What's wrong?"

"Nothing," he said. "Why would you think anything was wrong?"

"Your face. You looked different, suddenly. I haven't seen that look before."

"That's because I was thinking about when you stepped on my foot," he said, recovering quickly.

"Hardly," she said, "but I know the Dennis Collins deflection technique by now and I guess it's something you don't want to talk about."

"And I know the Maria Highsmith interrogation technique by now and I'm going to refuse to answer. I'm taking the Fifth, just like any self-respecting New York politician would."

They danced several more times, with Collins carefully steering them back to the table for the slow numbers, and he got better on the floor as the night wore. He was surprised that he didn't find himself thinking of Penny, but the time and place and partner were so different.

They said their goodnights to Henry and Rosalie just before one o'clock and left the Moonlight Club to walk back to Amelia Street. Collins wasn't happy to encounter scores of drunken young men—many of them sailors from the naval base—roaming up and down Duval Street. He offered Maria the crook of his arm and she smiled at him and took it. He figured that would lower the odds on one of the liquored-up Friday night bravos bothering Maria, and the last thing he wanted was a confrontation to ruin the evening.

"I had a fantastic time," she said when they reached the Highsmith cottage. "I enjoyed the dancing. You're a man of many talents, Dennis. I knew that you were a funny man, but I didn't know whether you could have fun. I think you can."

"I can, even if I felt quite ancient at times. I couldn't ask for a better guide to Key West nightlife, even if you wore me out."

"I doubt that," she said. "If you were back in New York, I'll bet things would just be getting started at the Stork Club or El Morocco and you'd be in the thick of it."

"You can't believe everything you read," he said.

"Do you miss it? All the exciting things going on there and you being here, so far away?"

"I thought that was a selling point for Key West. Southernmost point in the country."

"There you go deflecting again."

"Everything has its season," he said. "Isn't that what the Bible says? For now, the season for me is here, with the Highsmiths. When the day comes that it's time to go, then I'll go."

"And when will that be?" she asked, her eyes lingering on his face.

"I guess I'll know it when the time comes. That's usually the way it works, isn't it? I have a few things I'm figuring out and that will help me decide where I'm going to be."

"Are you happy here?"

"I'm happy tonight. I'll be sore tomorrow from trying to keep up with you on the dance floor."

"You kept up," she said.

She moved slightly closer to him and for a moment he was tempted to pull her to him and kiss her lips. He stepped back slightly, recognizing the danger and realizing he needed to be careful. He wondered what she was thinking, whether she was testing him. He gave her an awkward bow.

"A very pleasant evening," he said. "Thanks for including me."

Maria nodded. "Thanks for taking me. I like that we're getting to know each other better. Even if you insist on being a bit mysterious. It makes it more fun trying to figure you out."

"As long as you're having fun," Collins said lightly. "I'm glad to be of service."

Twenty

A week after his night at the Moonlight Club with Maria, Collins went fishing with her father. Jim Highsmith navigated his boat, the *Marta*, through the harbor to his favorite shallow-water spot near Snipe Key. Collins had donned his long-billed fishing cap that had a flap sewn onto its back to protect his nose, ears, and neck against the unrelenting sun.

"You look like one of Rommel's Afrika Korps wearing that hat," Highsmith said with a slight grin. "Sorry we don't have a camel you can ride."

"Laugh all you want, but I won't look like a boiled lobster later today."

They fished with spin rods under clear blue skies. A soft breeze from the west helped to cool them. Highsmith allowed his boat to drift over the flats, where the water stood only two or three feet deep. They cast jigs into the shallow water, catching and releasing a few jack crevalle. They were alone—no sign of other boats or people in their line of sight. Collins thought that the landscape looked much as it must have when only the Calusa Indians had inhabited the Keys.

"So are you planning to stay with us for awhile?" Highsmith asked during a pause in the fishing. "Missing the big city yet? The excitement?"

"I've had more than enough excitement for the time being. I've been able to relax here and I really appreciate your hospitality."

"You're more than welcome," Highsmith said. "We're taking advantage of you with all of the chores we have you doing."

"No, I like it. Keeps me busy. Less time to brood."

"I'm asking about your plans for a specific reason," Highsmith said. "Because of Maria. She's as happy as I've seen her in years, at least since we lost her mother. She loves talking to you, you know. She claims that she's stumped looking for a subject you don't know something about."

"That's the shallow know-it-all newspaperman in me. I know very little about a lot, and what I do know is a mile wide and an inch deep."

"You're too modest. Maria claims that she's learning just as much from you as she would have if she'd gone off to college and taken a political science course."

"She's too kind," Collins said. "She's a great kid."

"Is that how you see her?" Highsmith asked. "As a kid?"

"Not sure where you're going with this, Jim," Collins said warily.

"I don't think Maria wants to be seen as a kid. Especially by you."

"How does she want to be seen?"

"I think she wants you to see her as a woman."

Collins found himself tensing at the direction the conversation had taken. "She's a beautiful young woman and I'm not blind to that, Jim. I've tried to be her friend and nothing more. I would never cross over any lines."

"I know that, Denny. I respect you for that. But that's the problem. Maria confronted me the other day and demanded to know if we—the two of us—had some sort of a gentleman's agreement about her being off limits. Romantically speaking. You can imagine how I choked on my coffee at that. I told her that you and I had never discussed anything of the sort. So then she started in on how it was probably an unspoken agreement. I told her that I couldn't prove a negative, but that I'd make sure you understood that there were no rules stopping you from asking out my daughter."

"No rules? I can't imagine that you'd be happy about the prospect of that. I'm almost fifteen years older than Maria. I've picked up some nicks and bruises along the way. I have to believe you'd prefer her seeing someone closer to her age."

"Yes, I would," Highsmith said. "I'm not going to lie to you. I'd pick a younger man for her if it was my call. But it doesn't really matter what I think. It matters what she thinks."

Collins shook his head. "She's young. We both know that things look different when you're that age."

"She's old enough to know her own mind," Highsmith said. "She hasn't been sheltered, you know. This can be a pretty wild town, filled with sailors and Marines and cathouses and God knows what. You can't grow up here and not know how the women at the Square Roof make a living. And she had to grow up fast when her mother got sick. She nursed Marta through the last year when she should have been thinking about her junior prom." Highsmith fiddled with the release on his reel. "Let me ask you this, if Maria was thirty, would you feel any differently?"

"But she's not thirty, so that's purely a hypothetical question. I've found that I get in trouble when I answer questions like that."

"You're ducking the question."

"Sure, I am. For once, I'm trying to look before I leap. Think things through."

"I'm not sure it works like that," Highsmith said evenly. "How do you think your way in or out of love?"

"I don't know. I just don't want anybody to get hurt. So where does all this leave us?"

"When we get back I can tell Maria that the two of us talked about the 'off-limits' question and you understand where I stand. No prohibitions. Where it goes from there is between you two."

Collins nodded. He wondered what Highsmith thought about his daughter's interest in his guest. What father wouldn't have reservations? Collins didn't blame Highsmith for hoping that Maria would choose someone younger. She certainly could have. Collins had seen how every man who came into Maria's orbit reacted to her—and how she gracefully deflected their attention in a way that acknowledged their interest but never encouraged it. He imagined she had been dealing with constant male attention for years.

Had his decision to treat her in a friendly, but reserved, way backfired? Had she seen his distance as a challenge, of sorts, to see whether she could make him fall for her?

"While we're having a heart-to-heart, there's something else," Collins said. "There was an episode in Korea that has been bothering me. My last night at Hagaru, a few Chinese broke through the defensive perimeter and I ended up in the thick of it, firing my M1 at them."

"Every Marine a rifleman," Highsmith said.

"Except I'm not a Marine. I'm a newspaperman. I never thought I would be shooting at other human beings, trying to kill them. I'm not sure that I hit anyone, because we were all firing and it was all a blur. I just sighted on these white-coated figures and kept squeezing the trigger. They kept charging and we kept mowing them down. It scared the hell out of me. Still does. I'm having a hard time with it."

"I've heard you yell out a few times in your sleep," he said. "All the way from the guest cottage. So has Maria. I told her that it was pretty common for someone who has been in combat. But you did the right thing. It's very hard to set out to consciously kill another man. Some civilians don't understand that. In boot camp they have to break down our aversion to killing as part of the training."

"I try not to think about it," Collins said. "In the Pacific I was an observer. At Hagaru I was too close to the action. I was part of it."

"You might consider talking it through with Father Gonzalez," Highsmith said and then in response to Collins' frown, added rapidly that the priest had served as a chaplain with the 82nd Airborne in Europe. "He'll understand. With the number of veterans that live in Key West, you wouldn't be the first that he has helped."

"He hasn't converted you by any chance, has he?"

"Hardly. I had to promise when I married Marta that we would raise any children as Roman Catholics. We did that with Maria. I tag along with her now and then to St. Mary's, but the Highsmiths have been stout Presbyterians back to the time of Cromwell. I figure it's all the same to God in the end. Father Gonzalez wouldn't agree with me publicly, but we've had a meeting of the minds privately about the Separated Brethren."

"One other thing," Highsmith said. "I'm telling you this so you understand that Maria is a woman who knows her own mind. She has turned down two proposals of marriage. One came just six months ago. I liked the guy, myself. He was a Navy aviator, originally from Texas. Handsome, tall, ambitious. I thought he had a good chance with her but she told me that she didn't love him and she wasn't going to settle for liking and that was that."

"And the first proposal?"

"A young guy from one of the better-off local families, head-over-heels in love with her. Again, she liked him but she didn't fall for him. She let him down gently. This was a couple of years ago.

So Maria has given more thought to these matters of the heart than you might think. You should know that when I agreed to talk to you about this, I told Maria that you didn't strike me as someone who had taken vows of celibacy, and that I suspected that you hadn't lacked for female attention in New York. You might be one of those men who liked playing the field. I wanted her to have her eyes wide open."

"I've never been much of a ladies' man," Collins said. "I'd be married now if this one girl I dated before the war had cooperated. She had other ideas. It took me a while to get the message. Then I met another woman more recently, before I went off to Korea, and it seemed like it might become serious but we didn't get a chance to find out. Ships crossing in the night."

"I didn't take you for a womanizer," Highsmith said. "If you were, I imagine that you would have already made a run at Maria. You wouldn't have gotten anywhere, because she's been fending the wolves off since she was fifteen."

"No one has ever mistaken me for a wolf," Collins said.

"I didn't think so," Highsmith said. "If I did, I never would have invited you to visit us." He turned and cast his line toward a current near the shoreline, signaling the end of the conversation. "So let's fish," he said. "I can tell Maria that we had our talk."

Collins decided caution was in order—he would wait for Maria to say something to him about the state of their relationship. He wasn't sure what he would say in response, but he knew that if they were to consider moving beyond friendship he would have to tell her about Penny and Caleb. He hated the thought of revealing that to her—for there was a good chance that it would alter her feelings about him. He didn't have a choice; he would have to tell her. Caleb was going to be part of his life in some fashion, and there was no way to finesse that reality.

To his surprise, Collins found the next day that he was uncharacteristically nervous around Maria. She gave him a few sidelong glances but they didn't get a chance to talk. He knew that she was in for a disappointment and he wasn't eager for the conversation that she clearly wanted to have. After the dinner rush at the restaurant was over, they found themselves alone on the back patio. It was still light out, with sunset at least an hour away.

"Why are you avoiding me?" she asked him. "Was it the talk with my father?"

"Why do you say that?"

"It's fairly obvious. You've been hiding from me all day. Is that what you've decided? You're going to avoid me?"

"Of course not," he said. "Don't be ridiculous."

"My father did let it drop that you think you're too old for me. You're not. There are plenty of couples who haven't let that get in the way. Humphrey Bogart was forty-five and Lauren Bacall was nineteen when they met. Leo Durocher was forty-one and Laraine Day was twenty-six. So don't tell me that the difference in our ages should matter."

"You've been doing your homework," Collins said, "but I'm not a movie star or a big league manager, and fourteen years are a big gap in my book."

"But you know there's something between us. Chemistry. Are you going to deny that?"

"No, I won't deny that. But there are other things to consider. Not just the fact that I'm considerably older than you. I told your father that I've resolved to look before I leap. You see, I've had my heart broken before, and it's not something I'm eager to repeat. Or inflict on anyone else. I don't want to hurt you, or be hurt by you."

"I'm not going to hurt you."

"No one ever begins a romance with that in mind. Maria, you don't know all there is to know about me. I know you don't like it when you ask questions and I deflect them, but I didn't arrive here with a clean slate. I guess some of it is vanity. I don't want you to think worse of me."

"You're not going to shock me."

"Before we change anything between us, there are some things you should know."

"A wife you've neglected to mention?" she said lightly.

"No," he said, flatly, with no hint of amusement in his voice. "Not a wife. A son."

They sat in silence for a long moment.

"A son," she repeated, her voice faltering slightly. "You never said anything about a child. Where is he? How old is he?"

"His name is Caleb. He's not even a year old. He lives in Washington with his mother. I didn't know about him, about Caleb, until last month. His mother didn't bother to tell me. It's quite a messy situation, I'm afraid. She is married to another man, now, and Caleb has his last name, not mine."

"Who is she? The mother?" Maria looked down at the patio stones, not making eye contact with him.

"Her name is Penny Steele." He spoke quickly, eager to have her understand. "She wasn't married when we conceived the child. We'd been lovers, years before, and she came back to New York and we both wanted to see if it might work again. One thing led to another and we ended up in bed. One night." He hesitated, hoping Maria would look at him, but she didn't. "A mistake, but a human one. It didn't work out between us. She found someone else and married him."

He waited for her to say something, but Maria remained silent. He spoke to her again, his voice measured. "It's something I can't change. Like I said, it's messy. Since I learned about Caleb I've made it clear to his mother that I'm ready to acknowledge him as my son when the time comes, if the time comes. We're still working through that. Right now it's all up in the air."

She didn't respond for a moment and then Collins saw tears forming in her eyes. They began streaming down her cheeks.

"I'm sorry," he said.

She rose to her feet, still silent, making no attempt to wipe away her tears. Collins stood up as well, but she raised her hands as if to ward him off. He stopped, unsure what to say or do.

"I'm sorry about the tears," she said. "I didn't expect anything like this. It's a bit of a shock. I just assumed that because you never had been married that—" She hesitated for a moment before speaking again. "I never thought you might be a father. I didn't worry about who came before me because you were here now and I figured that would be enough. I guess I was a fool not to recognize that you might have something in your past. I knew you would have had lovers before, but I could deal with that because it happened before we met. This is different." She turned back to him. "Are you still in love with her? With Penny?"

"No. I told you that she's married."

"That doesn't really answer my question, does it? Suppose she wasn't married? Then what?"

"It's over between us," he said. "Permanently. There's nothing there, now, and there could never be again."

"And she feels this way, too?"

"Penny's been married twice now," he said dryly. "And she apparently didn't want Collins as her last name when she had the chance."

"So you proposed to her?" She kept her face turned away from him.

"Never formally, but she could have become Mrs. Dennis Collins if she had shown any inclination. When we first dated, before the war, I was waiting for the right time to ask. We were so hot-and-cold that I never did. Then when I went overseas she met someone and married him. She sent me a Dear John letter, which I don't blame her for now, although I was pretty torn up about it at the time. I realize now that she was just following her heart. Her husband was a diplomat, killed in Greece in '47. I didn't see Penny until two years later, when we connected again in New York." He paused. "That's when we made the mistake of sleeping together."

She looked at him closely. "What's Caleb like?"

"He's a great little kid. He loves to play with blocks. He likes picture books." Collins found himself biting his lip. "It's awkward as hell. It's not clear how I'm going to fit into his life. That's one of the things I've been trying to figure out since I've been down here."

"I don't know what to say," she said. "I feel like I've had the breath knocked out of me."

"You can see why I've kept my distance. You deserve someone without a messy past."

"Does my father know about any of this?"

"No, he does not," Collins said. "I didn't tell him for the same reason I didn't tell you. I didn't want to have him think less of me. Who wants to advertise their flaws and mistakes? It hardly places me in the best of lights." He paused. "So there you have it. I'm not proud of the situation. If there was a time machine, where I could go back and change things, I would. But I can't. I want only what is best for you. I'm not sure that having me in your life under these circumstances would be that."

"I wish that you had told me before," she said.

"To what end? Until your father and I talked the other day, I didn't think we could ever be anything more than friends. I never had a reason to tell you."

"You had to know I was interested."

He shook his head. "Not seriously. You flirted with me, and I was flattered. I figured that I represented somewhat of a challenge, different from the men you're used to. Could you turn my head? I didn't think you could see me as more than that."

"Is that what you thought?" she asked with a flash of anger. "That I was playing some sort of game? To see if I could make you fall in love with me?"

"I didn't know. I didn't want to risk finding out. I was trying not to make a fool of myself, Maria. Chasing a much younger woman? My friend's daughter? Can you blame me for being wary? Keeping some distance? And then there was Caleb."

"How do you feel about me?"

"I don't know that's a fair question to ask. Under the circumstances."

"Why? What are you afraid of?"

"I want only what is best for you. I'm trying not to be selfish. What man wouldn't desire you? You're marvelous—smart, funny, beautiful—a woman with her whole life in front of her. I don't really see where I fit into that future. Now you're seeing me as I am, with a few of my many flaws exposed. I don't blame you for being angry or disappointed with me, but whatever image of me you've carried around in your head hasn't been the real me."

"So I'm all these wonderful things," she said, "but not wonderful enough for you."

"It's not like that. If anything, it's just the opposite. I'm the one who isn't wonderful enough. Haven't what I've just told you demonstrated that?"

"Don't patronize me," she said. "You aren't willing to give us even half a chance. You said you didn't want to hurt me. Why do you think that this isn't hurting me?"

"And if we took this further? And you found that you couldn't deal with the messiness? How much harder would it be?" He took a long breath. "You need to think about all this and figure out what you want to do now that you know about my situation."

"That's courageous on your part," she said bitterly. "I need to figure out what I want to do."

"My circumstances can't change," he said. "So I don't see how I can approach this any other way."

They found Jim Highsmith waiting for them when they returned to the restaurant. "You've had a call," he told Collins. "From Washington. Matthew Steele. He said it was urgent and left a return number."

Highsmith nodded at the phone by the front of the restaurant. "You can call from here." He glanced over at his daughter. "Is everything all right?"

She remained silent.

"We'll give you some privacy," Highsmith said but Collins shook his head.

"Please stay, both of you. After I've made the call, I have something I'd like to share with you, Jim, and I want Maria here when I do."

The phone number was answered by the switchboard at the Georgetown University Hospital, and when he asked for Matthew Steele, he was quickly transferred to another line. Steele answered on the first ring.

"I'm glad you called back so quickly," Steele said. "Penny has suffered a setback."

"She's in the hospital?"

"She is. It's serious, I'm afraid. This morning Bernice couldn't get her to wake up. Penny took too many sleeping tablets. She's had to have her stomach pumped. They just let me see her. She's resting. The doctors want to keep her here for a few days."

"I'm very sorry to hear this. What can I do?"

"She asked about you, Dennis. She wants to see you. If you could come back up here, I believe it would be helpful."

"I will come if you think it will help."

"I do." He paused. "It was not an accidental overdose. She admitted that to me, and she's very ashamed. She feels she has let us all down. I've told her that is just not the case. I would hope you could tell her the same."

"Of course. I'll fly up tomorrow. Let her know I'm coming."

"I will. Call me when you get on the flight in Miami." He was silent for a moment. "God bless you."

After he had hung up the phone, Collins turned back and faced the Highsmiths. He figured that since they had heard his side of the conversation they knew that it was bad news.

"I will need to fly back up to Washington. A crisis. I'm needed there." Collins looked over at Jim Highsmith. "I've just shared some things with Maria that I felt she needed to know. Nothing that I'm proud about, I'm afraid. A few weeks ago before I came to Key West I learned that I have a son, Caleb, who's not even a year old. I didn't know about him before—his mother had concealed the truth from me and only recently decided to tell me. It came as a shock. The man I just talked to on the phone, Matthew Steele, is married to Caleb's mother. I want to be clear about what happened in the past. Penny was unattached when we conceived the child."

"She concealed this from you?" Highsmith asked. He raised his eyebrows. "She didn't tell you that she was bearing your child?"

"We had not parted on the best of terms. She didn't want me in her future, and she wanted to avoid any entanglement. Penny has had a change of heart. At some point she wants me to acknowledge the child is mine and she wants Caleb to know."

"And her husband?"

"He didn't like the idea, but Penny has been fighting depression for the past year or so and she became insistent that I be told. Her therapist thought it might help in her recovery."

"I see," Highsmith said.

"I know what you are thinking, Dad," Maria said to her father. "Dennis doesn't need to apologize to me for anything. He hasn't misled me. He didn't want either of us to know about this situation, and I can't blame him for that. I understand now why he has been so private about some things."

"Does this change anything? Between the two of you?"

"I can't say yet," she said, glancing over at Collins. "We've agreed that I need to think things through."

Collins nervously ran his hand through his hair. "About the phone call from Matthew Steele. There's been a complication. Penny has been sick on-and-off for quite some time and she had a relapse of sorts and she's in the hospital in Washington. She has asked to see me. I told Matthew I would fly up tomorrow."

"I can drive you to the airport in Miami," Highsmith said.

Collins shook his head. "I'll fly out of Key West. That will be less trouble."

"How long will you be gone?" Maria asked.

"I'm not sure. A few days."

Collins knew that Maria might misunderstand why he felt compelled to return to Washington; she would think that he still carried a torch for Penny, no matter what he said. He couldn't do anything about that misperception until he returned. Nor could he ignore Penny's request—he would try to help her in any way he could because of Caleb and because of their history together. It was the right thing to do.

He turned to Maria. "Leaving here is the last thing in the world I want to do, but I need to be there. I warned you that my personal life was messy. This is an example of that messiness. I'm sorry. I wish it weren't so, but it is."

Collins looked at her and Jim Highsmith and managed a crooked smile. "I suppose I should have also warned you earlier about my reputation for disappointing people. Then perhaps all of this wouldn't have come as so much of a surprise. I'm sorry for that and I wish it weren't so, but it is."

Twenty-one

Collins found a gaunt and exhausted Matthew Steele waiting for him at the main entrance to the Georgetown University hospital. Steele stood with his hands jammed in his suit jacket pockets, his face drawn and gray. They shook hands wordlessly and Collins followed Steele into the hospital lobby.

"Penny is awake and alert," Steele said. "She was pleased to hear that you were coming up to see her."

"How did it happen?"

"She overdosed on Nembutal. Thank God that Bernice had the presence of mind to call for an ambulance and the doctors here were able to pump her stomach in time."

"How is she doing?" Collins asked.

"As well as can be expected. She's quite embarrassed by the entire episode. She keeps apologizing. I've consulted with both Dr. Sollers and Dr. Rifkin and based on their advice I've decided to keep her in the hospital for a few days under observation. Until we're sure that she isn't a danger to herself, she needs to be watched."

"Do you have any sense of why she asked to see me?"

"I think the question of Caleb and your relationship with him weighs on her."

"I understand. I told her the last time I saw her that I will never be a stranger when it comes to Caleb. I'm still working things out, but I'm clear about that."

"That's good," Steele said. "You look quite fit. Key West is agreeing with you."

Collins nodded in response. When he looked in the mirror in the morning he could see that his eyes were clear and that he had color in his face. He was not only in better physical shape, but he also felt relaxed, calmer, more at ease with himself and with the world.

"When can I see her?" he asked Steele.

"Now, if you like."

Collins had always hated the smell of hospitals, of disinfectant, waxed floors, and stale air. He had enough of it to last a lifetime when his mother spent the last three months of her life in-and-out of Holy Name Hospital during her valiant but doomed fight against liver cancer. The smell of Georgetown Hospital was no different, even in the psychiatric wing where Penny was staying, so Collins was pleased to find a vase of roses filling her room with a pleasant floral scent.

Penny wore a drab hospital bathrobe over pajamas. She had pinned her hair back and her face looked pale and wan without makeup. She gave him an uncertain smile when he kissed her cheek.

"How are you?" he asked.

"I'm not exactly swell," she said.

"You're always swell in my book." When they dated, she had teased Collins about his use of the word, and it had become one of their private jokes.

"You're sweet to say so," she said. "There's an outdoor patio where we can sit and talk. It's pleasant there."

She took the arm Collins offered and they moved slowly down the hallway until they came to the door to the patio. They sat across from each other on black wrought-iron chairs. The air was warm and scented by the rose geraniums growing in several clay flowerpots.

"You look marvelous," she said. "Healthy, tanned, relaxed. Years younger than the last time I saw you. Did you discover the Fountain of Youth in Key West?"

"Not quite," he said. "I've been working outdoors and taking better care of myself. Cut out the cigarettes and most of the booze. I'm not ready to climb into the ring, but I'm in fairly good shape."

"I'm sorry to make you fly all the way here to see me," she said. "It's embarrassing. I wish I were stronger. I've let everyone down."

"Don't apologize. You haven't let anyone down. What's important is that you get better. Caleb needs you. Matthew needs you."

"I am going to try so very hard to be positive about all this. To get better."

"You will."

"I have been thinking about you and Caleb. I hope you will forgive me for what I want to ask you." She paused, waiting for him to respond, and he gave her a quick nod to let her know that she should continue. "I know this is quite something to request, but I am thinking of Caleb. Would you consider moving to Washington? So you could be here for Caleb? In the future?"

He remained silent for a long moment, considering what to say. "I'm not sure that I can do that," he said. "I have some things that I need to resolve. I don't think I can leave Key West yet."

"Is there someone? Have you met someone?"

"I think so," he said. "It's not clear what's going to happen."

"That's wonderful."

He gave her a wry smile. "It's not that simple, Penny, and I don't know what to do about it. She's the daughter of a friend, and she's much younger than me. Almost fifteen years younger. And then there's Caleb."

"You've told her about Caleb?"

"I felt I had to. If we were going to move beyond friendship, she deserved to know what she was getting into. I told her Caleb was going to be part of my future. She put a brave face on it when I told her, but when she has had time to think about it her feelings may change. So I don't know what will happen between us."

"It sounds like you have fallen pretty hard for her."

"I guess I have."

"What is her name?"

"Maria Highsmith. My friend, her father, runs a hotel and restaurant in Key West. I've been staying with them."

"Your Maria is a fool if she lets anything or anyone get between her and you, Dennis. And you're a fool if you keep hiding behind excuses about her being younger or about Caleb and refuse to take a chance with her. You can work this out with her. You shouldn't let this pass you by."

"This is a strange conversation, Penny. One of the stranger conversations I think I've ever had."

"It shouldn't be. We were lovers once, and I know you, and I know a little bit about your capacity to love. You deserve to enjoy your fair share of happiness. It sounds like Maria could be the woman for you."

"She may be," Collins said. "But that's really up to her now."

"Have you told her about how you truly feel? I know you, Dennis, and I know you're slow to express your feelings. You shouldn't wait. You should tell her."

"You missed your calling," he said. "You should have been an advice columnist."

"No jokes, Dennis. It's good advice. Please take it."

"You're right," he said. "It is good advice."

They walked back to her room together, Collins shortening his stride to match her deliberate pace. He was disturbed by how frail she seemed.

"Thanks again for coming to see me," she said when they reached her room. "I'm sorry about the circumstances. It shouldn't be like this. I shouldn't be like this."

"What matters is that you get better."

She sighed. "I know," she said. "I just wish it wasn't so hard. It's just so very hard, Dennis."

"Would you be willing to stop by the Kremlin and chat with Allen Dulles?" Steele asked when Collins returned to the hospital lobby. "Visiting hours end at four o'clock, and Penny will be sleeping, so there's some time for it."

"Sure," Collins said. "I'm not sure he'll learn anything new from me, but I did say I would drop in if I got the chance."

During the brief drive to E Street, Steele explained that he had made no progress in linking Philby to Yatov and the Soviets. "There is fresh news to report," he told Collins. "Guy Burgess is being sent back to England in disgrace. There was an episode in Virginia involving reckless driving. Burgess had also picked up this seedy hitchhiker who was in the car with him. They say the ambassador was eager to be done with him, that Burgess had been a constant irritant."

"Have you had any contact with Philby?"

"I've been avoiding him, actually. I'm not sure how to handle him. Not yet. I want to be careful about what I say to him when we next meet."

"Is that awkward for you? Having to avoid him?"

"I'm still exiled to the North Building," Steele said. "Little chance of running into Philby there."

Steele escorted Collins to Dulles' East Building office door and then excused himself. "Allen wanted to have a private chat with you," he said.

Dulles came out from behind his desk and greeted Collins with a vigorous handshake.

"I asked Matthew to bring you by so we could talk," Dulles said. "He told me that you had flown up to see Penny, at her request. He was deeply touched by that. It's a fine thing you've done."

"I've known Penny for a long time," Collins said. "I don't know how much you know about the situation, but I'm just trying to help where I can."

"From what I understand, you are doing just that," Dulles said. He motioned for Collins to sit in one of the captain's chairs and occupied one himself, pausing only to light his pipe. "How did you find the trip to Europe?"

"Informative," Collins said. "A more complex situation than I had realized."

"General Eisenhower is an impressive man. He listens and he doesn't automatically assume that he's the smartest man in the room."

"And is he?"

"I guess that depends on who is in the room." Dulles grinned. "Most of the time I suspect that Ike is the smartest, and when he isn't, he's still has the best political instincts. He knows how to get people to do things they initially don't want to."

"I could tell that he didn't like what I had to report from Korea," Collins said. "How the men felt they were let down by the generals in Tokyo."

"A far cry from our finest hour," Dulles said. He cradled his pipe in his right hand for a moment. "I understand the Czechs showed some unwelcome interest in your visit to Paris. I must say I'm somewhat envious that Matthew had the chance to get back in the field while I have to stay here chained to my desk. I miss the action."

"You should have gone in my place," Collins said. "I could do without it."

"The nastiness with the Czechs does suggest that Matthew may be on to something with his theory about Philby. You've met the man. Do you buy the notion that he was involved in this incident?"

"I didn't particularly like Philby," Collins said. "So I don't know how objective I can be. If Matthew is correct and Yatov is his handler, then I can see the logical connection to the attack in Paris. Or perhaps it was just a strange coincidence."

"I never discount the coincidental," Dulles said. "Yet I don't think the Czechs were there by chance. Tell me, do you believe that Yatov is in the picture?"

"I don't know."

"If you had to guess. . ."

"It would just be a guess. Matthew makes a convincing case, but there have been no signs of Yatov since New York in 1949."

"That's a fair estimation of the situation," Dulles said. "I like the way you think through things." He cleared his throat. "Would you consider staying on here in Washington? You could continue to work with Matthew for now, and later perhaps directly with me. We would put you on the Agency payroll." He leaned back in his chair and took a few puffs on his pipe, waiting for Collins to answer.

"I don't think that I'm cut out for your line of work," Collins said quickly.

"Nonsense," Dulles said. "Your analysis of the situation with Philby and Yatov is spot on. You have other qualities the Agency needs. From what I've read in the Trojan Horse file, you showed considerable initiative and courage when thrust into the middle of a complex situation in New York. Matthew says that you saved his life in Paris, and then were of great help on a more recent scouting expedition here in Washington."

"I did what was necessary. Did Matthew tell you that the Czechs were lousy shots? I'd guess that their rounds hit the church ten or fifteen feet over our heads."

"Adrenaline can alter one's aim. Not everyone stays calm in a crisis. You do. Another reason why we could use you here. Why your country could use you here."

Collins shook his head. He couldn't see himself agreeing to work for Dulles. He had no interest in joining the Agency as an intelligence officer. Despite Dulles' confidence in his fitness for the role, he didn't think he would be very good at it. "Unlike Daniel Defoe, I don't think I'd ever be comfortable as a spy. So I'm going to have to decline the offer."

"A shame. You'd make a top-notch intelligence officer." Dulles placed his pipe on a nearby table. "I would have enjoyed working with you."

"I also don't think I could ever accept some of the things that you do, or think you must do," Collins said.

Dulles made a steeple with his fingers. "It's true that we sometimes must employ unappetizing means and methods. How can I justify this? Simply put, we do so only as a last resort. Our adversaries rely on fear and brutality and violence every day. It is a first resort for them. It is all that sustains their system in the end. In the West, extreme acts still shock the conscience. Decency and morality and the rule of law still prevail. No one in New York or London or Paris fears the knock on the door after midnight as they do in Moscow and Budapest and Peking."

"I guess I've seen too often when that last resort starts looking an awful lot like the first resort."

"Yes, we must always guard against becoming the very thing we are fighting. Matthew and I have discussed this at length. He worries that we will be sorely tempted to take shortcuts in the days and weeks ahead, that we will take the expedient course, not the moral one."

Collins was surprised. He didn't think of Steele, so supremely confident in public, as someone who would harbor doubts.

"You're aware that Matthew is taking instruction with Father Loughlin?" Dulles asked.

Collins nodded.

"I'm not unfamiliar with that journey. We're Presbyterian, but my nephew Avery is now studying to become a priest. He entered Harvard as an agnostic and left as a Roman Catholic and it happened because of the smallest thing. He was walking along the Charles River on a rainy day and saw a tree beginning to flower and that convinced him of the existence of God. Are you Catholic, Mr. Collins?"

"Raised as one," Collins said. "I guess you would call me lapsed, although I think much of it becomes part of you."

Dulles nodded in agreement. "I understand." He rose to his feet. "Thanks for seeing me," he said. "It's been quite instructive. And I appreciate all that you've done on our behalf. On the country's behalf. I hope we'll get a chance to chat again at some point in the future."

"You never know," Collins said.

Dulles smiled. "Truer words were never spoken."

Steele wasn't waiting for him at the Packard; Collins strolled around the grounds of the complex until he found Steele sitting on a bench under a tree on the western side of the campus, where there was a view of the Potomac River and Theodore Roosevelt Island. Collins took a seat on the bench and they sat there together in silence for a while. They watched a sailboat below tacking with the wind; whoever was at the tiller was an experienced sailor for the boat came about smoothly.

Steele spoke first. "I assume that you declined Allen's offer?"

"I did. I can't see myself working for the Agency."

"I told Allen that it was unlikely you would join us," Steele said. "He wanted to give it the old college try." His gaze wandered back to the river. "This work isn't for everyone. Dr. Jung believes that the keeping of secrets acts like a psychic poison, alienating those who keep them."

"Do you feel alienated?"

"Sometimes I do. Then I weigh that occupational hazard against what we can accomplish, the cause in which I have enlisted, and I believe the personal costs are worth it."

"Did you know Penny wants me to move to Washington? So I can be near Caleb?"

"She mentioned it to me this morning before you arrived at the hospital."

"Did it prompt this sudden job offer?"

Steele glanced over at him and shook his head. "Believe it or not, Allen has considered recruiting you for the Agency for some time. I won't deny that it would have served a dual purpose if you had accepted."

"Which is a specialty of Matthew Steele, killing two birds with one stone."

"It is one of my weaknesses. Sometimes I can be too clever by half because of it."

"I haven't ruled out moving to Washington," Collins said. "I've thought about catching on with the *Post* or the *Star*, maybe going back to covering sports full time. I could make a fresh start and it would let me see Caleb. But I have some personal matters I need to resolve first and depending on what happens I may stay in Key West for a while. I plan to fly back to Florida tomorrow."

Steele kept his eyes on the river far below them. He seemed distracted, lost in his own thoughts. "I want to thank you for coming," he said finally. "Perhaps we can stop by the hospital later and you can see Penny again and say good-bye."

"I'd like that," Collins said.

"Word has it that the president is going to relieve General MacArthur of command in the next few days," Steele said. "The straw that broke the camel's back was that letter from MacArthur that Joe Martin read on the floor of the House with the line 'there is no substitute for victory.' Truman should have removed him much earlier, but at least he has finally decided to act."

"Who will be his replacement?"

"At least for now, General Ridgway."

"Not Ike?"

"I should hope not," Steele said. "Eisenhower's too valuable in Paris bucking up the Europeans. And I wouldn't want to see him in Asia with a presidential election coming up next year. It will be better for the country if he's closer to the political battlefield than the military one."

Collins didn't wait long to call the Highsmith Inn after arriving back at Steele's house. He phoned from the living room of the carriage house and waited while Miguel went to find Maria to take the call.

"Can you talk?" he asked her when she picked up.

"Yes, I'm alone," she said. "We can talk. Have you seen Penny? How is she?"

"I've seen her. She is very fragile. Apologetic."

"What did she have to say to you? If you don't mind my asking?"

"You deserve to know, Maria. Penny hopes that I will stay in Caleb's life. She has been very anxious about it."

"That was all?"

"She was hoping that I would move to Washington, to be near him."

"I see. What did you tell her?"

"I told her that I had something to resolve before I knew where I would be living. I told Penny about you and how I felt about you."

There was a long silence. Collins thought for a moment that Maria had hung up the phone and he could feel his heart pounding and then she spoke.

"What are you saying, Dennis?"

"I'm willing to give us a chance, if you're game. I wouldn't blame you if you have decided that you don't want to risk it, or that what you've learned about me has changed things."

"Are you sure about this?"

"As sure as I have been about anything in my life. I can fly back to Miami in the morning and we can talk about it when I get to Key West. You just need to tell me whether I should catch the flight or not."

"Fly back," she said. "I'll be waiting in Miami. I need to see your face when we talk. I don't want to wait a minute longer to see you than I have to."

Twenty-two

Collins returned to the hospital after dinner to say good-bye to Penny. Steele had contacted Dr. Sollers and he had arranged for Collins to stop by and see her after regular visiting hours. Sollers also left word for Penny about Collins' visit so she wouldn't be surprised when he turned up.

"I fly back to Florida tomorrow morning," Collins told her. "I wanted to say good-bye. I also wanted to thank you for encouraging me to tell Maria how I felt. I did and that's why I'm leaving, to see her and talk everything through."

"I wondered whether you would act on it," Penny said. "I'm so glad that you did."

"I'll be talking with Maria about Caleb and the idea of living here in Washington. I will be involved in Caleb's life. Matthew and I talked about it in Paris and I know we can figure something out that will be best for Caleb."

"Thank you," she said. "I hope all goes well and I can meet Maria someday soon."

"I'd like that."

"Do you know what is strange, Dennis? When we were seeing each other, before the war, I wondered what it'd be like to have a child with you. And then Taylor came along and I put it out of my mind. Who would have ever guessed that this would happen?"

"All's well that ends well," Collins said. "Isn't that the saying?"

"We did make a beautiful boy," she said. "We did, didn't we? When I look at him, I can't believe that he could ever be considered a mistake. He's too precious for that." She raised her right hand and placed it gently against her chest. "Promise me that you won't have any regrets."

"You know me. I try to keep things simple. Caleb is a great kid and I'm proud he's my son. There's nothing to regret."

"You do keep it simple," she said. "I always admired that about you."

"Don't use the past tense," he said. "I hope you will always admire that simplicity."

"I shall," she said.

Collins sensed that she was somehow retreating from him although he couldn't point to anything specific—she just didn't seem as present and engaged as she had the day before. When he kissed her cheek softly in farewell he saw her eyes fill with sudden tears.

As soon as Collins exited the plane in Miami he began to feel nervous. He wondered if Maria could spot him as he made his way from the airplane across the tarmac to the terminal entrance. He didn't think that she would have come to meet him if she didn't see a future with him, but that didn't make him any less anxious.

Maria was stationed at the entrance to the arrivals area and pulled him aside the moment he stepped through the doors. "I've missed you tremendously," she said and kissed Collins full on his lips, pulling him close to him. "I've wanted to do that for so long." She kissed him again, wrapping her arms around him. "It's been so hard waiting for you to come back. I've been so unhappy."

"I guess this means you're no longer off-limits," he said.

"I was angry at you most of yesterday," she said, holding his right hand in hers. "But I cooled off after I had a chance to talk to Dad. He told me I had a simple choice to make and suggested that I think through what life would be without you. That did it. I realized that I didn't want to live without you."

"There are some other things we should talk about before we leave for Key West," he said and saw a sudden look of concern on her face. "No, nothing shocking," he said. "You need to know more about my past, that's all."

In the back of the small airport restaurant, they found a table that afforded them some privacy. Collins ordered sweet tea and they talked.

He told her about his life in New York with Penny before the war and how carefree it had been, so different from the grim atmosphere in the city after Pearl Harbor. He had met her at a Fifth Avenue society party in 1939 and they had, to Collins' surprise, become a couple. "But I learned a hard lesson for a man in love," he said. "It didn't matter how deeply I cared, or how wonderful it all seemed to me, Penny never felt as strongly as I did."

Then, he explained, they had quarreled over whether he should go overseas and cover the war; he went anyway, despite her objections. He was on Saipan in the summer of 1944 when he got her Dear John letter. She had fallen for another man, Taylor Bradford, and had married him. Collins only saw her twice in the following years, once in 1947 at the funeral of her husband—Bradford, a diplomat, had been killed in Greece by Communist partisans—and then in 1949, during the last week of September when she came to New York. It was then that he had tried to win her back and when they had conceived Caleb.

"There were other things that happened that week," he said. "Things that turned my world upside down. I've thought about how much I should tell you about this, and I've decided not to hold anything back."

He told her how he learned that his childhood friend Morris Rose, an up-and-coming official in the State Department, had been secretly spying for the Soviets. It was through Morris that Collins had been connected to Karina Lazda.

"I had never met anyone like her," he said. "She was a survivor, a strange mixture of vulnerability and toughness. She and Morris had been lovers in Warsaw, briefly, and he arranged for her to come to New York—except the price of admission involved working covertly for Moscow Center. We were together only a few days, but it was as intense as anything I had experienced. In the end, she decided to break with the Soviets and she paid for that with her life."

He stopped talking and studied his hands, trying to compose himself.

"It was different with Karina," he said. "She loved without reservation. I wasn't used to that."

"And you fell in love with her?"

"I did." He paused. "Does that bother you?"

"I'm not jealous of her, if that's what you mean," she said. "Being with her meant that you were open to the possibility of loving again after being hurt by Penny. With what happened, I can see why you've been so reluctant to give your heart to anyone. I'm just thankful that we have a chance now."

Collins explained how Matthew Steele fit into the story, how he had hoped to use Morris Rose's defection as a way to feed doctored information to Moscow Center and how Penny had also been pulled into the scheme.

"It was one of those strange coincidences that perhaps aren't actually that strange," he said. "Steele and Penny's husband had connections through Yale. And Steele had been courting Penny just before she came to New York that fall." When Penny deceived him about her relationship with Steele, and Collins caught her lying, he realized that he had to end it, once and for all.

"I do think she was trying to protect me, to help me," he said. "She thought she could use her influence with Steele. But Penny couldn't level with me about what she was doing, for whatever reason, and in the end I couldn't trust her."

"I'm sure she must regret it now," Maria said. "Who knows what might have happened?"

"I know it never would have worked," he said. "We were wrong for each other. I was more in love with the idea of Penny and all she represented to an Irish kid from Brooklyn than I was in love with her."

"And now? Are you sure you aren't in love with the idea of me?"

"I'm in love with you," he said. "The real Maria. The one who steps on my toes when we're dancing the tango."

On the long drive down the Overseas Highway to Key West, Collins told Maria about what had happened since he had returned from Korea—the unwelcome appearance of Andrew Caldwell at Idlewild, the unexpected reentry into his life of Matthew and Penny Steele, and his trip to Europe with Steele.

"I thought that it had ended in 1949," he said. "That I was done with the cloak-and-dagger stuff. But I learned that there's still unfinished business. The man who ordered Karina's death—Anatoli Yatov—may still be operating in this country. And there is a British diplomat in Washington, an intelligence operative, who Matthew suspects is funneling secrets to the Soviets, including passing them our tactical plans in Korea. His name is Kim Philby. Yatov may be his handler."

Collins sketched out how he had helped Steele with the trip to Paris and London, and how he and his brother had searched Philby's house. "The Agency's counterintelligence officer was unimpressed by the photo equipment we discovered and he didn't lend any credence to Matthew's theory about Philby. There's no appetite to pursue what Matthew has uncovered."

"What will happen now?" she asked.

"With Steele out of favor, they won't listen to him unless and until he has bulletproof evidence of Philby's complicity. So my guess is that nothing will happen."

"And your involvement?"

"I've done all I can. It's a shame that Matthew couldn't make the case against Philby and that Yatov has vanished. In baseball they say that you win some, you lose some, and some get rained out. This one got rained out."

After they had returned to Key West, Collins invited Maria for a walk on Rest Beach. They slipped off their shoes and left them by a street lamp where they could find them later. They could hear the sounds of the night and the constant and reassuring hiss of the waves. Collins took Maria's hand, marveling at her smooth skin, and they walked barefoot through the sand to the ocean's edge.

The sea was calm and the light of the stars above in the night sky reflected off its slick surface. The incoming surf occasionally swept over their feet as they walked through the sand, hand in hand.

"Look at the stars," she said. "Aren't they marvelous? I feel like they are here just for us tonight."

"Of course they are," he said. He stopped and took her into his arms and decided suddenly that there was no point in waiting any longer. He loved her and he couldn't envision a life without her any more than she could imagine one without him. It was that simple and so he asked her to marry him. Maria kissed him passionately on the lips. "Of course, I will," she said.

They continued their walk, planning the future, enjoying the relaxed small talk of lovers.

"I feel so at peace with you, Dennis," she said. "Like I'm supposed to be with you."

"I feel that way, too. At ease."

"Home at last?"

"When I'm with you, yes, home at last."

Collins couldn't remember a time when he had been happier. Now that he had admitted to Maria, and to himself, that he loved her, he felt liberated. He was free to say all the things a lover says to his beloved and he didn't hesitate to do just that with Maria.

They talked at every opportunity, to the point where Jim Highsmith kidded them that they had to be careful or they would run out of topics to discuss long before they walked down the aisle.

Highsmith confided to Collins about his sit-down with Maria after he left for Washington. "We went over her choices," he said. "She could feel wronged that you hadn't told her about Caleb and she could walk away because of it. Or she could decide that the ongoing situation with your son and you and his mother would be too awkward for her. She just had to recognize that if she made that choice, you would be out of her life. Did she want that?" He paused. "For what it's worth, I think she made the right choice."

Later, when Collins called Frank and shared the good news his brother laughed and quickly congratulated him. "Finally, a girl makes an honest man out of you," he said. "She must be quite something. Can't wait to meet her. I hope you can persuade her that New York ain't such a bad place to live."

When he phoned Matthew Steele, Collins asked first about Penny's health and learned that she was scheduled for electroshock in a few days.

"She dreads it," Steele said. "But she knows if she's going to get better she needs the treatment."

Collins told Steele about his marriage plans, and explained that after their wedding in June, he and Maria would honeymoon in New York. "Then we'd like to stop in Washington so that Maria can meet you and Penny and Caleb."

"That would be fine," Steele said. "We'd like that. So I can tell Penny, have you considered moving to Washington or with your getting married is that no longer an option?"

"We're still trying to figure that out," Collins said. "I think that Maria might welcome a change of scenery, but we'll have to see."

"When you visit, we'll do our best to convince her that Washington is a great halfway point between New York and Florida."

"Any progress on the other matter?" Collins asked. He knew Steele would understand the veiled reference to Philby, and would appreciate Collins' caution in talking about it on the telephone.

"No luck yet," Steele said.

"If it's any consolation, Cy Young once said you had to be both good and lucky to pitch a no-hitter."

"I don't think we need to be that good or that lucky. We just need one small break. Whether we'll get it or not, I can't say."

Collins didn't expect to hear from Steele again any time soon, and the phone call from Washington two days later came out of the blue. Collins was fixing a leaky faucet in one of the cottages when Maria came to tell him that he had a long distance call from Steele.

They walked back to the restaurant together and Collins picked up the receiver wondering whether Steele had caught that break he needed in the Philby case.

"Dennis, I have the worst news to relate," Steele began. "Penny took her own life this morning. She apparently had a hidden cache of sleeping tablets. The nurse we had hired to care for her thought Penny was taking a nap. When the nurse couldn't wake her, she called for an ambulance. I drove over to the hospital as soon as they phoned me. She took more tablets this time and the emergency room doctors couldn't revive her."

Collins held the phone, stricken dumb by the news. He found he was gripping the receiver so tightly that his knuckles had turned white.

"I'm so very sorry," he finally managed to say.

"I feared that this day might come," Steele said. "She didn't want to undergo another shock therapy session. This was her way of avoiding it, of giving in to the darkness. I think she just grew too tired to continue to fight."

"She didn't seem despondent when I saw her," Collins said. "Only a bit detached."

"Penny knew how to hide what she was feeling. She had me convinced that she was eager for further treatment because she wanted to get well."

"I'll fly up tonight," Collins said.

"Thank you. I appreciate it."

There really wasn't anything else left to say, so they made their good-byes and Collins hung up, still struggling to accept the news. Could Penny really be gone? It was so senseless—she had been in the prime of her life with so much to live for. Why had she given up? Collins figured that she must have been beyond rescue if she could do such a thing knowing that Caleb would be left motherless.

He sat down on one of the kitchen stools; Maria came over to stand next to him and hold his hand in hers.

"I'm so sorry," she said. "What a tragic thing."

"It must have been unbearable for her. To take her own life when it meant leaving Caleb." Collins shook his head, the tears trickling down his cheeks, and she put her arms around him as he began to cry.

The memorial service for Penny Allen Steele was held at St. John's Episcopal Church in Georgetown on a quiet, sunny May morning. Penny's parents, loyal parishioners, had wanted the service held at St. John's, and Steele had acceded to their request because, as he explained to Collins, Penny had not made up her mind about converting to Catholicism.

"She wasn't ready to see it as the one true Church," Steele said. "I think her parents will find it comforting to have a Prayer Book service with the old standard hymns. Truthfully, I will, as well."

Collins didn't say anything, but he wondered if there were other reasons for the choice of church—Penny's suicide meant that under canon law she would be denied a Catholic burial and Collins figured Steele didn't want to confront the issue with Father Loughlin.

Collins had never met Penny's parents, but he did know her sister, Elizabeth, who lived in California. He also knew that she wasn't one of his biggest fans; she had made it clear that she regarded him as an unsuitable match for her glamorous sister. At St. John's before the memorial service started, Elizabeth greeted him politely and when she introduced him to her parents he could not tell whether they recognized his name or not. Did they know he had been their daughter's lover before her marriage to Taylor Bradford and before Matthew Steele came on the scene? What would the Allens think if he told them that he was Caleb's father?

Collins managed to mumble some brief words of sympathy, but he didn't trust himself to say anything more. Elizabeth made no attempt to continue a conversation with him and he could tell that she disapproved of his presence there.

The service proved to be thoroughly Anglican: brief, restrained, with reminders of the denomination's mixed Catholic and Protestant heritage. They sang "Our God Our Help in Ages Past" and then the mourners read aloud Psalm Twenty-three, "The Lord is my shepherd," and the priest gave a very brief eulogy that focused on Penny's life as mother, wife, and daughter.

After the service concluded, Steele stationed himself at the back of the church and shook the hands of the mourners as they exited the nave. Collins saw Allen Dulles stop to say a few words to Steele. Collins remained with Caleb and Bernice in one of the back pews. He placed the boy on his lap and softly read aloud several of Caleb's favorite picture books. His son sat quietly, occasionally reaching out to stop Collins from turning the page so he could examine the illustration for a moment or two longer.

Collins felt a light touch on his shoulder and looked up to find his brother Frank standing awkwardly by the pew. "I caught the very end of the service," Frank said. "Sorry I couldn't make it down here any earlier. The train ran late."

"How did you know about this?" Collins asked, surprised.

"I called Key West looking for you and Maria told me about Penny and that you had flown up to D.C." He smiled at Caleb, who had remained in Collins' lap, distracted from the book by Frank's arrival. "Handsome kid," Frank said. "Anyway, I thought you could use some company today."

"You're right," Collins said. "I sure could."

Collins drove them back to Hoban Street in the Packard; Steele left with Elizabeth and the Allens for the Allens' home in Virginia. After Bernice took Caleb upstairs, Frank put his arm around Collins' shoulder.

"It's up to you and me to hold a proper wake for Penny," he said. "I asked a couple of cops at Union Station and there's a place over on H Street where we can lift a glass to Penny and to her life and drink to our heart's content. We can grab a cab and be over there in fifteen minutes."

"I've been on the wagon more or less for a while," Collins said.

"Time to fall off it," his brother said. "It's the best way to remember her, far better than singing a bunch of hymns."

Collins nodded in agreement—he knew his brother was right. The memorial service had been too reserved, too constrained, for a proper farewell. Collins wanted to talk about Penny and his memories of her, and he was glad that Frank was there to listen.

On the ride to the tavern, Collins was struck by the beauty of the day, by the soft, warm breeze and the afternoon sun filling the streets with a golden radiance. It stood in stark contrast to his sense of loss—a gloomy, rainy day would have been more fitting.

Fitzgerald's Pub proved to be more than Irish enough for their purposes: a dim-lit place with a dark-wood bar and a mirror above rows of bottles. Dusty framed pictures of Dublin Castle, the Cliffs of Moher, Croke Park, and Trinity College decorated the walls.

They took a booth and his brother ordered boilermakers for both of them. Frank arranged the shot glass of whiskey next to his beer mug. "Down the hatch," he said, and downed the whiskey and then took a large swallow of beer. "Now you," he said to Collins.

Collins drank his shot of whiskey and chased it down with his beer.

"I'm sorry that she's gone and I said a prayer or two for her soul," Frank said. "It's a sad day when a mother with a young child leaves us the way she did."

"I'm having a hard time accepting it," Collins said. "That she's truly gone. I keep expecting to wake up and find out that I've dreamed this and it didn't happen."

"It's tough. No quarreling with that."

"I guess it proves that we can't really know what anyone else is thinking. What they're going through."

"We all make our choices, Denny. She had to be in great pain to do what she did. I hope she has her fair measure of peace, now." He looked around the bar. "We need some music, I think."

Frank went over to the battered jukebox near the back of the bar and fed some nickels into the machine and selected some music. By the time he had returned to the booth, the sound of Dennis Day's tenor voice singing "The Rose of Tralee" was filling the room.

Frank fixed his eyes on Collins. "I don't like to speak ill of the dead, but we closed more than one bar together in the past when she shafted you in one way or the other. Truth to tell, she was always bad news for you, Denny."

"We weren't right for each other," Collins conceded. "But there was always that spark between us, and I kept hoping it would be enough. You know how crazy I was about her before the war, before it fell apart between us. You can't blame me for trying to make it work when I got the second chance in New York. What happened then killed it for good."

"What was it like seeing her in Washington in the past few months?"

"She had changed. Having Caleb, and then the sickness. She was almost a different person. I think she truly regretted what happened before. There were no hard feelings on my part. She wanted my forgiveness and she got it."

"What are you going to do now? About the boy?"

"I'm not sure. Matthew and I have to talk about it. With Penny gone, it's even stranger. And there's the added complication of Maria."

"Maria knows about it? All of it?"

"She does. At first, she wasn't happy about it and I can't blame her for that."

"That's good," Frank said. "If your girl knows, then you start your marriage right."

"I worry I'm too old for her, though."

"Too old? I don't think so. Look at Mayor O'Dwyer. He married that fashion model, Sloan Simpson, and there must be a thirty-year gap between them. That's the grand thing about love, it doesn't have hard-and-fast rules. You know that, Denny."

"I guess I do, because I plan on marrying her."

Hours later, they stumbled out of Fitzgerald's into the early Washington evening and took a taxicab back to Hoban Road and the guest house. Collins could see that lights remained on in Steele's study; the rest of the house was dark.

In the morning Collins spent a painful ten minutes in the bathroom vomiting into the toilet. Frank shook his head when Collins emerged, weak and pale.

"That's what drinking on an empty stomach will do for you," his brother said. "I already called for a cab to Union Station. I need to get back to the city tonight."

"Thanks for coming," Collins said.

"No problem," Frank said. "Just promise me one thing."

"What's that?"

"Call me if Steele asks you to help him out in any more of his schemes. I want to be there. Someone has to keep you out of trouble, and I'm the only one who's going to volunteer for the job."

Collins had started on his third cup of coffee when Matthew Steele knocked softly on the front door of the carriage house. After Collins invited him in, Steele politely declined his offer of coffee.

"I'm sorry I didn't get a chance to talk with your brother and thank him for coming," Steele began. "Please let him know I appreciate the gesture."

"I will."

Steele made no move to sit down. "I must live now with the burden of her death, wondering what I could have said or done to have prevented it, to have stopped her from taking the irrevocable step that she did."

"You did everything you could."

"Did I?"

"You couldn't have known that she would do this. Her doctors released her from the hospital. You had a nurse here with her. You had her scheduled for shock therapy. How could you know what she was thinking?"

Steele covered his face with his hands and groaned. "The worst of it is that what she did puts her outside God's grace."

Collins shook his head. "The church is flat out wrong on this, Matthew. Penny was sick. She was not in her right mind. A just God would not hold that against her, no matter what the rules may say. Canon law is man made."

"Who in their right mind would. . ." Steele's voice trailed off.

"Exactly. She wasn't rational at the end. You have to hold on to that."

Steele removed his hands from his face. His face was drawn and pale. "Thanks, Dennis. I appreciate it. If you could, I'd like you to stay in Washington for a few days. I think we need to talk about where we go from here, what we should do about Caleb."

"I'll stay as long as you need me to," Collins said.

"We should sit down and talk through all of this at length," Steele said. "Not now, though. Let's talk about Caleb later, when we're both a little more rested."

"Whenever you're ready," Collins said. "I'll be here."

Twenty-three

Steele did not raise the subject of Caleb at breakfast the next morning but Collins found Steele's apparent hesitation to broach the topic completely understandable. What they should do about the boy's future now that Penny was gone had to be a difficult question for Steele. Caleb represented Steele's living connection to Penny, but Collins was his natural father. Should Caleb stay with Steele in Washington? Or should Collins take responsibility for raising the boy? Had Steele talked to the Allens about Caleb's future? Collins had no clue as to Steele's feelings about the matter.

Steele had the look of a man who had gone without sleep for too long. Collins had seen it before on the battlefield, the red-rimmed eyes, the sudden lapses in attention, the faltering speech. He worried that Steele might be on the edge of collapse.

Collins knew that everyone grieved in their own way, and that all he could do for Steele was to be there and listen when Steele wanted to talk. That's what you did for a friend, and Collins realized that—to his own surprise and against the odds—he now considered Matthew Steele a friend. It was an implausible development, and Collins never would have believed such a friendship possible even a few months before, but he had come to grudgingly respect, if not admire, the man.

Steele had changed. He had lost much of his surface arrogance and there was a reflective quality about him now that hadn't been there before when Collins had first met him during that strange last week of September 1949. By nature a reserved man—he had never displayed much warmth—Steele nonetheless had a caring side. He

311

had married Penny when she was carrying another man's child, had embraced the child as his own, had looked after her tenderly during her sickness, and then had agreed to let Collins to reenter their lives.

Collins spent the rest of the morning with Caleb and Bernice in a nearby park. Caleb loved throwing a small multicolored ball to Collins, even though he had no control over where the ball would fly. Every so often he would lose his balance and fall to the ground, but he would immediately roll over and struggle to his feet, eager to toss the ball again.

When they returned to the house for Caleb's nap, they found Steele waiting for them. Steele seemed excited about something and he was eager to talk to Collins. He looked much better than he had at breakfast.

"I've had a very productive day," he said. "A new approach to our Philby problem. Since I can't call on the Agency to assist me, I've found an alternative. I credit your brother for the idea. I've hired a private investigator to keep a watch on Philby."

Collins could see that Steele was throwing himself back into work as a way of coping with Penny's death. It was as good a way as any, Collins thought, to deal with the grief. It would occupy Steele, give him something to do.

The idea was clever on its own merits: it put Philby under fairly close surveillance without alerting anyone at the Agency. "What reason did you give the investigator for wanting to follow Philby?" he asked Steele.

"I explained to him—his name is Roger de Groot—that I was concerned that Philby was seeing my wife behind my back. I asked him to tail Philby whenever he went for a drive for the next month and to take photographs of anyone he met with, male or female."

"Aren't you worried Philby will realize that he is being followed?"

"I asked around and de Groot is considered the best in the business, at least here in Washington. A former cop. He's imaginative, though. De Groot Investigations uses teams for most of their surveillance and if you think about it, it's brilliant. Who would ever expect that the couple in the station wagon behind you is actually tailing you, equipped with a camera with a telephoto lens? Of course it's a bit more expensive, but it's effective."

Collins had to smile; it was the happiest he had seen Steele in months. "So you think Philby is going to lead you to Anatoli Yatov?"

"He may, or he may not. Perhaps Philby is employing only dead drops, where he leaves the film for Yatov or whoever else might be his contact. But there's a chance he will rendezvous with his controller, and if he does, we'll have it recorded on film."

"I'm curious. What reason did you give de Groot for asking for photos of anyone Philby meets?"

"I had to give that some thought." Steele paused. "It took me some time, but here's what I came up with. I told de Groot that not only did I suspect my wife was two-timing me, but also that a former business associate, who I fired because he was stealing from my company, knew about the affair and was encouraging Philby as a way of revenge. I gave de Groot the photo of Yatov and told him that he was my former colleague."

"So I take it that you didn't hire this investigator under your real identity."

"No, I did not. I presented myself as Richard Hannay, aggrieved husband and swindled businessman. I paid in cash and de Groot didn't ask for identification, although I had Hannay's driver's license ready."

"One thing is clear about de Groot," Collins said.

"What's that?"

"Either he's never read John Buchan, or he shares your sly sense of humor."

"It's one or the other, I'll grant you that."

"What are the odds that Philby will make contact with his handler in the next few weeks?" Collins asked.

"I think they're good," he said. "The Soviets will want Philby to continue passing them all that he can. What he provides is just too good to shut off. And I'll see what I can do about encouraging Philby to rendezvous with Yatov."

"How will you do that?"

"I plan to appeal to the deep-seated paranoia that plagues all clandestine operatives," Steele said. "The fear of exposure. The fear that you, the betrayer, have yourself been betrayed."

Two days passed and Steele still hadn't raised the question of Caleb's future with Collins. It wasn't surprising, Collins thought, that Steele might hesitate to have what would most likely be a painful conversation. Collins figured he just had to be patient.

Steele had other matters on his mind, as well. That Thursday, he asked Collins to accompany him to the Metropolitan Club. Steele explained that he had arranged to meet Kim Philby there in the late afternoon for drinks.

"I'm prepared for Philby now," Steele said. "I know how I want to approach him. Since I never briefed him on our trip to Paris, I had a ready-made excuse for our chat. He's always delighted to meet at the Metropolitan. I think that Philby likes the place because it reminds him of the elite clubs in London."

Collins knew that the club, located near the White House in a building meant to evoke Italian Renaissance architecture, was considered the most exclusive in the capital.

"I'm sure you appreciate the irony in that," Collins said. "The Metropolitan Club is hardly a place where the workers of the world can unite."

"Orwell had it right, 'All animals are equal, but some animals are more equal than others.' I'm sure like many Marxists, Philby sees himself as slightly more equal. That's how the Communist Party leaders in Moscow justify their caviar and dachas and private cars, you know, while bread is rationed for the masses."

When they arrived at the Metropolitan Club that afternoon Steele nodded to the uniformed doorman who quickly opened the club's imposing doors for them. Before they could make their way through the lobby, a distinguished-looking older man approached them and asked if Steele had a moment for a private conversation.

Collins located a copy of the *Washington Star* and sat down in an oversized tufted-leather armchair in the lobby and read the sports pages while he waited. Both the Yankees and the Dodgers were off to a good start. The Yanks had a rookie right-fielder from Oklahoma named Mickey Mantle who was hitting for both average and power and was said to be Joe DiMaggio's possible successor. Collins would have to catch a game or two at Yankee Stadium the next time he was back in New York to see if the kid was for real.

When Steele returned, Collins tossed the newspaper back on the table next to him. Steele quickly summarized his private conversation. "A friend with connections at the Defense Department wanted to brief me on the Korean command situation," he said. "He corroborated that General Ridgway will become MacArthur's replacement."

"General Eisenhower stays in Paris, then?"

"That's the rumor. Ridgway is a good choice to hold the fort until there's a shift in strategy."

"And it's better for Eisenhower if he decides to run in '52."

"It is. Which is better for the country."

They found Kim Philby waiting for them in a private room that was decorated with photographs of club presidents, past and present. He was already holding a drink, and Steele and Collins ordered their own from a white-coated waiter. Steele asked for a Scotch and soda and Collins for an iced tea.

"Haven't seen you on my visits to E Street, Matthew," Philby said, motioning for them to sit down in the two matching burgundy leather chairs facing him. "Have you been out-of-town?"

"I've been around, except lately I've been sitting in the North Building. Your business most likely takes you to the East Building, so you wouldn't bump into me."

"You were going to brief me on your trip to Paris, weren't you?"

"That I was," Steele said. "Dennis gave General Eisenhower and his staff an accurate picture of the fighting. We talked a bit about the nature of the war. We were in agreement that Korea represents a test by Stalin of the resolve of the West. He seeks to probe, to assess our response." Steele stopped to cough, covering his mouth with his handkerchief. He began again. "I suggested to the general that we need leaders who will directly confront the Russians and make it clear that unless they desist that there will be severe consequences."

"That's rather ominous," Philby said. "You'll make many of our Whitehall chaps quite anxious with that sort of war talk."

"Ominous? I'd prefer realistic. And there are many options short of war. Rearming the Germans. Further encouraging those behind the Iron Curtain who are restive to express their dissatisfaction. Continuing our nuclear research and development efforts. Do you think Stalin believes that the Soviet manufacturing sector can keep up with us and our—permit me the use of the phrase—Arsenal of Democracy? Can he afford to trade swords for plowshares and still feed his people? Those are the questions he'll have to answer."

Philby frowned. "Are you sure that you have not misread his intentions? My sense is that the Russians are more concerned with rebuilding their country now than dreams of expansion and that they see Korea as a problem for the Koreans to settle. A struggle for national liberation."

"I don't see it that way," Steele said. "I don't think General Eisenhower does either. There has been an all-around stiffening of spines. Look at the death sentence passed down the other day on the Rosenbergs. An overreaction in my view, but understandable." Steele kept his gaze on Philby's face. "I think sympathy for Soviet spies will be in short order now. Long prison sentences. The death penalty for more egregious cases of espionage."

The waiter returned with their drinks and Steele grew silent. Collins watched in amusement as both Philby and Steele filled their pipes with tobacco. They were both puffing away by the time the waiter left. Collins took a sip of his iced tea and started the conversation again. "I saw in the papers that Alger Hiss just began his five-year sentence for perjury," he said. "They sent him to the federal penitentiary in Lewisburg, which by all accounts is not a pleasant place."

Philby didn't seem perturbed in the least. His face remained expressionless. "The wages of sin," he said lightly and inclined his head toward Steele. "There was another item on your agenda for Paris, wasn't there? Something about a Soviet agent. Boris something or other. You said the French had quite a file on him."

"Not Boris but Anatoli. A First Directorate man named Anatoli Yatov. The French were quite helpful. They apparently have a source inside the First Directorate in Moscow who is providing them amazing material."

"Is that so? What did you learn about Yatov?"

"Are you familiar with Trojan Horse? It came to a head in September 1949, just before you arrived in the States."

"I believe so," Philby said. He took a quick puff of tobacco. "State Department official who defected with a list of suspected spies, except the list was a contrivance, meant to wrong foot the Soviets and allow us to feed them misinformation. Somehow the Russians caught on to it."

"Exactly," Steele said. "Within six months it became clear that they weren't going to take the bait. At least two of the penetration agents that we had turned suddenly were cut out by Moscow Center. No contact from their handlers. No attempt to reengage. Put on ice. I have maintained that Yatov was somehow tipped off about the operation. The French source in Moscow confirmed that he was alerted to the true nature of the list by one of his agents in Washington. That got our attention, as you can well imagine."

"Any clues as to who this agent might be?"

"We thought at first it might be Homer. Quite ironic if it turned out that Homer revealed Trojan Horse to the Russians. But I don't think it was him. It's a different source, another penetration agent, one still in place and actively passing secrets."

"Any ideas on who that different source might be?"

"Your guess is as good as mine," Steele said. "We're looking for someone well-placed and very clever. I'd guess that he has a surface charm that hides his disdain for his colleagues and superiors. He must also be quite cold-blooded."

"A fascinating portrait," Philby said. "Did the French have anything that could help in finding this Boris Yatov?"

"Anatoli Yatov," Steele said, correcting Philby again. "Yes, there were a few tidbits of some value. I'm still checking some of them, but I can say it has helped us narrow our search."

"How so? It sounds fascinating."

"All will be revealed in good time," Steele said. "Afraid I have to be a bit mysterious for the moment. You understand, of course. Kills the appetite to actually learn how the sausage is being made. I think Bismarck first said that."

Philby brought his glass to his lips and remained silent but Collins could tell from his face that the Englishman wasn't pleased by Steele's refusal to share the details of what the French had told him.

"By the way, Kim, a friend of mine has recently taken up photography," Steele said. "He's one of those chaps who isn't satisfied until he has mastered his latest hobby. You're a photographer, aren't you? Can I send him your way for some tips on shutter speed and lenses and the other tricks of the trade?" Collins could see that Steele was again watching Philby's face intently.

"Must be some sort of misunderstanding," Philby said. "I'm not much of a photographer, I'm afraid. More of a Kodak man." Collins noticed that Philby's right eyelid began to flicker slightly.

"Strange," Steele said. "Somehow I had the notion that you were a shutter bug. Must have been someone else."

"No doubt," Philby said. "I'm not your man."

"My memory's not what it used to be. Too many of these Scotch and sodas."

"Isn't the saying that we drink to forget?" Collins asked.

Philby emptied the remains of his pipe tobacco into the crystal ashtray on the table next to him. He glanced quickly at his wristwatch and rose to his feet. "You must excuse me, gentlemen," he said. "Duty beckons. Thank you for the briefing, Matthew."

"My pleasure," Steele said. "A distinct pleasure."

The following day Collins had returned from a long walk in the neighborhood when he saw a man in a dark suit near the entrance to Steele's driveway. When Collins walked closer, he realized that it was Andrew Caldwell and he knew immediately that the FBI agent was waiting for him.

"What do you want?" Collins asked him.

Caldwell ignored his question. "Quite cozy, I'd say." He waved his arm toward the main house. "I take it you're living in the guest house in the back. You can imagine that it's a somewhat curious turn of events. The man that you should hate suddenly becomes your best friend."

"Is there a point to this?"

"There certainly is. We're making progress on our investigation, but we could always use a little help. We know that you and Steele have become asshole buddies, so we thought you might be able to enlighten us about what you two are up to."

"Still recruiting informers?"

"Call it what you like. The way I look at it, if Steele's above board, he's got absolutely nothing to hide. You should feel the same way. If there's nothing to it, then you can confirm that Steele is one of the good guys by helping us put the puzzle pieces together."

"Are you seriously questioning his loyalty? You are aware of his war record?"

"The OSS was riddled with Reds. Donovan didn't seem to care. In fact, he recruited veterans of the International Brigade. He might just as well as have invited Beria to join up. So if anything, the fact that Steele was in the OSS makes me want to take a closer look. Ivy Leaguers do betray their country. Just look at Hiss and Duggan and Remington. If you ask me, we should start with the country club types first."

"I would hope that no one would ask you."

"Funny. I told you at the Willard Hotel that you're making problems for yourself when there's no need to. Do you really want a bunch of FBI agents digging around in your life? Asking your former colleagues lots of awkward questions? Inviting Major Highsmith to visit us in the Miami field office?"

"If you think harassing me will accomplish anything, you're flat wrong."

"I can tell you this, Collins, when we're done no one will ever look at you the same way again. They'll figure that where there's smoke, there's fire. They'll always wonder about your loyalty. I want you to remember that we gave you a chance to cooperate and you refused. You were warned. You're responsible for whatever happens now."

"I can live with that," Collins said.

"Maybe you can, maybe you can't. Don't think that the assholes at the Agency will protect you. In the end, they won't see you as part of their club."

Collins could feel his anger growing and he decided to cut the conversation short before he said or did something he would regret. "I'm tired of your bullshit," he told Caldwell. "From here on, you can talk to my lawyer first if you have any questions for me. His name is Terry Sullivan. You can find him in the Manhattan phone book."

Caldwell's face now wore an ugly look. "You were warned," he said.

"You've tried appealing to my patriotism and when that didn't work you switched to threatening me, and then to threatening my friends. You get to be more like Frank Costello every day."

"You've got a wise mouth," Caldwell said. "And I've got a long memory. We'll see who has the last laugh."

Collins shrugged and stepped around Caldwell. He walked up the driveway to Steele's house, heading toward the carriage house; he didn't look back over his shoulder. He figured that Caldwell would stop his clumsy recruitment efforts but that Collins would pay a price for refusing to cooperate in the form of continued harassment.

Steele arrived at the guest house ten minutes later.

"So the Bureau has come calling again," he observed after Collins had opened the door and let him in.

"Agent Caldwell thinks nastiness and persistence will win the day," Collins said. "Hoover must be frustrated that they haven't found anything to hang you with—and I guess I represent their last best hope for bringing you down."

"That will all be moot soon enough," Steele said. He sat down on the couch. "So Ishmael, how well did Ahab set the harpoon at the Metropolitan Club?"

"Philby has to know that you suspect him," Collins said. "Bringing up the death penalty. Your questions about photography, the suggestion that there's another penetration agent in Washington, and that you are able to narrow the search for Yatov. I'd say the harpoon went in pretty deep."

"He's a cool customer, I'll give him that. I particularly enjoyed his fishing for what I could tell him about 'Boris something or other.' I suspect that Anatoli Yatov will hear about our progress in searching for him and with any luck Philby will do so in person and Roger de Groot's people will catch it on film."

"Which is what you wanted, isn't it?"

"It is, and I'm delighted that Kim Philby is playing his part the way it was written. Can't have him deviating from script at this point, you know." He shifted his legs and leaned back against one of the cushions. "We should have that talk about Caleb now. I've made some necessary arrangements and it's time that you were clued in."

Collins sat down in the chair opposite from Steele. "I'm all ears."

"I've been dreaming about Penny," Steele said. "My therapist says that's good, there's enough space in my unconscious for dreaming again. In my dreams, Penny's at peace, and she agrees with the course of action I am about to propose. But first I must tell you some things. My health is failing. I'm sure you've seen the signs. The fact is that I have cancer of the prostate gland, first diagnosed last September. Based on the pain I have been experiencing lately my doctors believe the cancer is spreading. I had hoped that some treatments last month might turn the tide, but that hasn't been the case."

"I'm sorry to hear that. Are there other things they can do?"

"They tried injecting radioactive colloidal gold last fall, but it has only helped marginally. I've researched other options. There's a project under way at Stanford to make use of an electron linear accelerator, to bombard the cancer at its source, but it will be several years before they can test it on humans. I'm afraid I don't have that much time."

Collins didn't know what to say. He had lost his mother to liver cancer and he knew the bleak end game of grinding pain and ineffectual hospital stays. It was a grim way to die.

"I'm sorry," he said, knowing that it was an inadequate response.

"I've had the benefit of some time to think about the situation," Steele said. "When I was younger I believed that we could make our own luck, that we could control our own destiny. Now I know better. It's not in our hands. Take Penny's depression, and my illness. Unwelcome, unwanted, certainly not something I expected. Acts of God. It's all become quite simple, you see. Penny would have agreed, not just in my dreams. Caleb should be with you after I'm gone. He's your son."

"What about his grandparents? Penny's sister? What do they think?"

"They're unaware of my situation," Steele said flatly. "Even if they were, it wouldn't change matters. The Allens are too old, and Elizabeth has her own family to worry about. Penny and her parents were never close and it's not like they have been doting grandparents."

"This isn't the conversation I thought we might be having."

"I would like to keep Caleb here with me until the end. I do love him. That wouldn't be fair to him or to you, however. The best option is for you to take Caleb with you, to Florida. The sooner the better. While the Allens may object to your having him, you are his father. That's the trump card as far as I'm concerned."

"Are you sure you want to take this step? You don't want to wait and see?"

"No," Steele said. "It's time to get my affairs in order. We shouldn't wait. Even if a miracle occurred and I went into remission, how could I be sure there wouldn't be a recurrence? No, the boy needs stability. You can give him that. No one else can."

"You're making legal arrangements?"

"We'll approach a judge here to have you declared the father. A revision of the public record." Steele must have seen something in Collins' face that prompted him to quickly continue. "Yes, it would be an embarrassment of sorts if it became public. Although I wasn't cuckolded by you, the world would believe it so. But then again, why would I care? It certainly doesn't matter in an existential sense. It will be 'hail and farewell' for me shortly and I'll be beyond caring about my earthly reputation. As it happens, Penny left behind a long letter. It addresses Caleb's parentage and leaves no doubt that you're the father. I will also provide a sworn statement that when I married Penny it was with the full knowledge that the child was yours. Whalen is confident, by the way, that we can have these records sealed, so the entire matter can remain confidential."

"Did Penny know about your illness? Did you tell her?"

"She did not. I chose not to tell her. I thought she could not have borne it, that it would have deepened her melancholy. Now I wonder if it was a colossal mistake on my part. Had she known that I was sick, that I wouldn't be around for Caleb, would she have fought harder to stay with us?"

"I don't think anything would have stopped her," Collins said. "She knew she would be depriving Caleb of his mother, and if that wasn't enough. . ." He didn't finish the sentence.

"You must be wondering how long I have. That's the question you're being too polite to ask. There's not very much precision in these matters, I'm afraid. It will kill me, and fairly soon, but whether that is one month or six, they can't say with certainty. I'll continue my treatment and hope that it prolongs my stay here."

"Who else knows?"

"Besides my doctors and Whalen? No one else. I'll inform Allen Dulles when it becomes necessary. The only other person who should know about this now, besides you, is Miss Highsmith." He paused. "I'll leave it to you as to how you wish to handle this with her."

Collins nodded. Steele was right, of course, because Maria needed to know that marrying Dennis Collins now also meant becoming Caleb's stepmother.

"I must ask one favor of you, Dennis," Steele said. "Would you be willing to stay here in Washington until the paperwork has been finalized? I'd feel better if you were here, ready to leave with Caleb for Florida once it's possible."

Collins nodded. What had been left unsaid was that Steele wanted him there in the event that his health took a sudden turn for the worse. Collins was eager to return to Maria and Key West, but he couldn't argue with Steele's logic—better for Collins to stay put until he could take Caleb back with him. With any luck that would be sooner rather than later.

Collins reached Maria later that evening by phone. He told her quickly and directly about the developments of the day.

"When it rains it pours. Matthew Steele told me today that he has cancer and doesn't believe that his health will allow him to continue on raising Caleb. He wants me to take him, to have Caleb live with me."

"He's sure about this? What if he recovers?"

"He's dying, Maria. That's the prognosis. Under these circumstances, he thinks it would be best for Caleb to go with me. I can't argue with that."

"Did you know he was so sick?"

"He didn't look healthy, but he never said anything and we don't have the kind of relationship where I could ask that sort of personal question. At least, not until now."

"When will it happen, your taking Caleb?"

"There's some paperwork that needs to be handled. The birth certificate must be changed and Matthew wants his lawyer to make sure everything is legally airtight. I'll need to stay here longer."

"I wish you could come back now, but I understand," she said. "We'll have to find a larger place, with a backyard and more rooms."

"Thank you, Maria, for understanding."

"No need to thank me," she said. "He becomes my child, too. And I can't wait to see the look on Dad's face when I tell him that he's going to be a grandfather. I won't wait too long before I take pity on him and explain that I mean I'm going to be a stepmother, not a mother, and he doesn't have to worry about a scandal."

Twenty-four

Dan Whalen's early optimism about how quickly he would be able to finish the legal paperwork involving Caleb's parentage proved unwarranted. To Collins' dismay two weeks passed without any clear progress on the matter. Whalen was apologetic but the judge he had planned to approach had been on vacation and then had come down with a nasty cold and hadn't yet returned to work.

Late Friday morning the phone rang in the carriage house. Collins abandoned his copy of *Robinson Crusoe*, which he had started reading for the first time after hearing Allen Dulles praise Daniel Defoe, and picked up the receiver on the second ring.

"Hello, Dennis. It's Maria."

"Is everything okay there?" he asked, wondering at the unfamiliar background noise. "We weren't going to talk until tonight."

"I'm at National Airport," she said. "Can you come get me?"

"Of course, I can," he said, surprised that she was in Washington. "What's going on?"

"I missed you so much that I decided to fly up and see you. I'm only here for the weekend, but at least I'll get to see you face-to-face. I didn't say anything beforehand because I was afraid you would talk me out of coming. Dad encouraged me. He said he couldn't stand me moping around anymore. He drove me to the airport this morning. He also made a reservation at the Hays-Adams Hotel for me."

"I'll be there in twenty minutes," Collins said. "I'll try not to get a speeding ticket on the way."

Collins borrowed the Packard from Steele and drove straight to the airport, cursing the traffic, eager to see Maria again. He found her waiting for him in the National Airline arrivals area, a vision of loveliness in her linen suit and sunglasses.

They decided that they would drive to Hoban Road first and that Collins could bring her to the hotel later. Matthew Steele emerged from the house as soon as Collins pulled the Packard into the driveway. He opened the passenger side door for Maria.

"Welcome," he said. "We're very glad to see you here."

"The feeling is mutual," she said. "I want you to know that I'm so sorry for your loss."

"Thank you," Steele said. "You know somewhat of the circumstances from Dennis, and so you know how painful this has been, to be unable to help her, to be incapable of stopping the spiral."

"You did your best," Collins said.

"It was not good enough."

"Dennis has told me of your devotion to the health of your wife," Maria said. "I lost my mother to cancer when I was eighteen. There's only so much than anyone can do. In the end, it's in the hands of God."

"I'm trying to believe that," Steele said.

"Then do," she said. "It's the truth."

"You are kind to say so," he said. He paused. "After meeting you, I can see why Dennis has been eager to return to Key West."

"I consider myself the lucky one," she said, taking Collins' right hand in hers. "To meet Dennis when I did. My life would have been so different if he had not come to stay with us. Completely different."

Steele ushered them into the house and they sat in the side room where he had a light buffet lunch prepared and waiting for them.

"I'm glad you've come now," Steele said. "I want you to meet Caleb, get to know him."

"Dennis has told me what a sweet little boy he is."

"He is." Steele paused. "He'll need a mother in the days ahead along with his father. I know that this is perhaps not what you expected, but it's a blessing that Caleb will have you both."

"I will love Caleb as my own son," she said. "I can promise you that."

"I believe that you will. It makes all of this easier." Steele gave her a slight smile. "I think of you and Dennis as the cavalry riding to my rescue, and just in the nick of time."

Later in the day Collins and Maria sat together on a wooden bench near the side of the guest house. The late afternoon sun bathed the backyard in golden light and a light breeze rustled through the dogwoods and maples around them. Maria held a drowsy Caleb in her arms. When she had begun playing with him in the nursery, the boy had taken to her immediately. Collins had been amazed at how quickly Caleb had gravitated to her for affection but Maria had laughed at him and told him she had babysat for years.

Collins broke the silence to tell her that he could have never imagined the circumstances that would have led him to be there with her and Caleb.

"A few months ago I didn't know either of you," he said. "And now the two of you are my future. Out of the blue. A totally unexpected future."

"We're your future because we're meant to be your future," she said. "It's the same for me. Do you I think that I expected you to appear in my life when you did? Or Caleb? It's meant to be, don't you see? Don't make it overly complicated, Dennis."

"I'm trying not to," he said. "It's so sudden. I'm like the guy at the racetrack with the fifty-to-one longshot bet who can't believe his broken-down old horse has finished first, against all the odds."

"If we were destined to be together the odds don't matter," she said. "There are no odds, then, just what God wills."

"I'm not going to question that," he said. "I'm just grateful."

"I see you in him," she said, giving a quick kiss to Caleb's forehead. The child stirred slightly. "He's adorable. A sweet little boy. I would take him back to Florida with me now if I could."

"That'll delight Matthew," Collins said. "He figured that you would love Caleb once you met him."

"He was right about that," she said, and paused for a moment. "He has lost so much so quickly. It must be very hard for him to relinquish Caleb."

"He sets a great score in doing the right thing. I think knowing that Caleb will be taken care of must be a great relief for him. It's one less thing for him to worry about, and that must be very welcome."

Steele volunteered to drop Collins and Maria at the Hays-Adams; Collins could take a cab back to Hoban Road after they'd had dinner. On the drive to the hotel, Steele explained that he had been on the phone with Dan Whalen and he updated them on the legal situation.

"Dan has been approached by an attorney for Penny's parents," he said. "I informed the Allens about Dennis and Caleb a few days ago. They didn't take it well. Despite the fact that Penny wanted Dennis acknowledged as Caleb's father, they are resistant to the idea and quite upset."

"What did their lawyer have to say to Whalen?" Collins asked.

"Not much after Dan told him that we had a letter from Penny and my statement that I knew you were the father when I married her."

"Will they go to court to try to take Caleb from Dennis?" Maria asked.

"I don't think so. Any legal moves on their part could become public and provoke talk and damage their daughter's reputation. They don't want that. Yet it's possible. I told them about my health so they know that I plan to move quickly and that it will be irrevocable. Now's the logical time for a legal challenge."

"What does your lawyer think?" Maria asked. "If they do go to court. Could they take Caleb away from us?"

"From what Whalen tells me, they have little ground to stand on. Of course, possession is nine-tenths of the law. The sooner Caleb's living with Dennis and the sooner that you are man-and-wife the better."

"I'd gladly marry Maria today at city hall," Collins said. "But I wouldn't dream of robbing her of a church wedding where our families and friends can be there to celebrate."

"I'd gladly marry you today at city hall," she said to him with a smile. "Maybe I should call your bluff and we should get a marriage license."

"I don't think that would go over too well with your Dad."

"That's true," she said. "But he's a Marine. He'd get over it. It's my nieces that I would worry about. I don't think they, or their mothers, would ever forgive me if they lost their chance to be flower girls."

At the hotel, Collins accompanied Maria to the front desk for the check in.

"I'll see you to the elevator," he said, "and wait in the lobby while you change."

"Don't you want to see my room?" she asked. "I don't think even Father Gonzalez could object. This isn't the La Concha in Key West, where everyone would know me, so I'm not too worried about gossip."

They rode up to the fourth floor in the elevator and Collins carried her traveling bags to her room. Maria was delighted with the elegant dark furniture, the floral wallpaper, and the thick carpet.

"Quite beautiful and inviting," she said. She went to the window and peered out. "And a view of Lafayette Square and the White House."

"I'm glad you like it," Collins said. "Why don't you change and we can have dinner downstairs in the hotel restaurant?"

"I think we should stay here for a little while longer," she said, taking both of his hands in hers. "I want you as my lover. My husband *and* my lover. I don't want to wait any longer. It will be perfect. We're alone and it's a big, comfortable bed and I'd be lonely in it otherwise."

"You're sure about this?"

She flushed slightly, momentarily embarrassed by her own boldness. "We're married as far as I'm concerned. From the moment you asked and I said yes. I don't think Father Gonzalez saying a few words over us makes any difference. What matters is that we love each other and are committed. And there are plenty of babies in Key West who were born much sooner than nine months after the marriage and no one says anything."

"You've taken me by surprise."

"I like the sound of that. Taken by surprise." She gave him a mischievous grin and pulled him toward the bedroom. "You don't want to keep a lady waiting, do you?"

He closed the door to the bedroom and she embraced him and kissed him on his lips. Collins placed his hand on the small of her back and pulled her closer until their bodies pressed together. She touched his face gently, tracing her fingers across his lips.

"Turn around, please," she said, stepping away from him. "Just for a moment."

He did as she had asked and a moment later she told him he could look. She had slipped into the bed, and he could see the contours of her naked body under the sheets. "You don't want me to be lonely by myself, do you?" she asked.

Collins fumbled with unbuttoning his shirt and she laughed. "You can slow down," she said. "I'm not going anywhere. Nor are you. We have all night and the morning, too, if we need it."

He stripped his clothing off and when he joined her in bed the moment when their skin touched instantly aroused him. He made love to her slowly, kissing her softly on her face and chin and lips, caressing her body gently with his hands. She whispered his name and then gasped once when he entered her and then clung to him as he grew more excited and moved toward climax.

Afterward, they lay together in bed under the sheets, side-by-side, their legs and arms touching, and they talked.

"I was drawn to you from the start, you know," she said. "I thought that you might be too cynical but you weren't like that at all. My father had told me that you were drinking too much in New York, and it was clear that you'd been drinking when I met you in

Miami. When we drove to Key West together, the more we talked the more I liked you and I was praying that you were not a real drunk, just someone who was in a bad place at the moment."

"I was in a bad place."

"But I could see you coming out of it, getting better. We all saw it. My father thought that you'd be fine once you got some distance from all that had happened in Korea."

"I'm thankful that you were both right."

"I have something else to confess," Maria said. "It's silly. When I saw you get off the airplane in Miami I was attracted to you and I was hoping that you wouldn't have a strong Brooklyn accent. That would have ruined my romantic picture of the dashing war correspondent. When you spoke for the first time, I was so relieved that I almost said 'Thank God' out loud."

"Thank my parents. They corrected us if we started to slide into saying 'dese' and 'dose.' They wanted us to get ahead, and that meant proper elocution, to quote my father."

"I think I could have overlooked it," she said, "if you sounded like Leo Gorcey. I think I would have drawn the line at Jimmy Durante."

"Durante's made a lot of money with that voice."

"I'm sure he has and I'm sure that he's a sweet man. I'm just happy that you are Brooklyn's most handsome and most well-spoken man."

Collins gave her a quick kiss on the lips. "When we met that first time I took one look and figured you were spoken for. A girl as beautiful as you had to have a steady boyfriend if not a fiancé. Not that I thought it would make any difference if you were unattached.

I didn't imagine you'd have any interest in an ancient newspaperman like me."

"That's what made you irresistible. You were different. You weren't convinced that you were God's gift to womankind and that I needed to recognize that."

"Perhaps because I'm not much of a gift."

"But you are," she said quietly. "You are."

They dozed off then, with Maria's head resting on his chest. Collins encircled her body with his arms, marveling at the smooth beauty of her naked back and shoulders.

It was dark in the room when he awoke to her light touch on his chest and this time they made love with greater urgency, and to Collins' surprise she cried out as they moved together in unison, her fingernails digging into his shoulders as she climaxed.

"I didn't know it could be like that," she said.

"It can and it should."

She draped her arm across his chest and kissed the side of his cheek. "If Caleb is without a brother or sister, it won't be for lack of trying. I'll be ready to try whenever you are."

"I think I'll have some scars on my back to show for it, then."

"I'm sorry," she said and giggled. "The feeling caught me completely by surprise."

She propped herself up with one elbow so she could see his face. "I'm not afraid to move from Key West, you know. We spent much of my childhood at one Marine base or the other and it was always clear that we were there temporarily. Living in Key West has been wonderful, but I don't want you to ever feel that we are tied down there."

"What about your father and the Highsmith Inn?"

"That was meant to be his gift to my mother. He could sell it now and with the real estate boom there would be a bidding war. He could actually make some money and spend more of his time fishing." She smiled at Collins. "He thinks you're the right man for me. Considering that you're not a Marine, that's a near miracle."

"We don't have to decide any of that yet," Collins said. "Where we're going to live. I want you to spend some time with me in New York before we decide."

"I'd like that very much," she said. "When we visit New York I want to see where you grew up. The grade school you went to. I want you to take me to all of your old haunts."

"My haunts?" Collins laughed. "I don't know that I'd call them that, but I get your point."

"I want to dance with you in the Stork Club and El Morocco and I want to go to a ballgame at Ebbets Field with you. And you'll have to tell me all your stories from the past when we are there."

"Is that all?"

"Can we go to the Metropolitan Museum of Art and the Central Park Zoo? And to the top of the Empire State Building?"

"I'm going to shock you," Collins said. "I've never been to the top of the Empire State Building. Lots of New Yorkers haven't."

"I'm shocked," she said. "But I forgive you." She grew serious. "Matthew is not what I expected. From what you had told me, I thought he would be very forceful, commanding. Instead, he is very soft-spoken and thoughtful."

"Don't be fooled by his manner. He can be as tough as they come, and I know he can be ruthless when circumstances demand it."

"Perhaps in the past," she said. "I don't know now, though. I sense sadness now in him, that's all. He is so pale, so thin. Does he have the energy for exposing this man, Philby?"

"I don't know. Remember that there's more to it. Matthew also wants to expose Anatoli Yatov, Philby's handler. I would like to see that as well."

"Because of Karina?"

"Because of Karina and because of the damage that he and the people behind him can do to us. I want to do my part, if I can."

He felt her stir next to him. "I know you want to do your part," she said, "but I want you safe and sound."

"I understand. It's becoming less and less likely that Matthew will find Yatov. There's been no sign of him since 1949. I kidded Matthew once that he was acting like Captain Ahab—except the difference is that Ahab caught up to his whale. Matthew has been counting on Philby's connection to Yatov. If he is wrong, then he loses his chance to find Yatov, however slim that chance may be."

"Safe and sound," she said. "Please remember that, Dennis."

"I will," he said.

They spent most of the rest of the weekend in Maria's hotel room bed, talking and making love and dozing off and then making love again. They left a few times—to walk through Lafayette Park and join the tourists standing in front of the White House, and to begin dinner Saturday night at an overpriced French restaurant only to discover that they really wanted to be back in bed. They skipped dessert and Collins hurriedly paid the bill and it was all they could to do to wait until they reached the privacy of her room before they fell upon each other.

Late Sunday afternoon, Collins saw Maria off at the airport. She was the very last passenger to board the flight to Miami, as reluctant to let go of Collins as he was of her, bringing sympathetic smiles from the National Airlines gate attendants. Collins waited in the observation area until he saw her plane take off, and then returned to Hoban Road.

He found Steele settled in an Adirondack chair on the backyard patio, a book in his lap, a glass of Scotch in one hand and a pipe in the other.

"You should know the call with the lawyer hired by the Allens has prompted Dan Whalen to accelerate the legal process," he said. "He's trying to arrange for me to meet with the judge in his chambers."

Collins nodded, pleased with the news.

"There's another development of interest," Steele said. "I've received the official go-ahead to have a chat with Vadim Tolstoy."

"Tolstoy? The Russian diplomat who defected?"

"The very same. Vadim Tolstoy is the only source we have who knows anything about Anatoli Yatov."

"Will he talk to you about Yatov?"

"They tell me that he has been very cooperative since his defection. I met him briefly in January and he seemed tractable enough. A bit of a lost soul, actually. I'd like you to come along with me when I see him. It will be a short trip. No overseas flights. We can get there by car. He's in a safe house in Virginia about twenty miles away."

"When is your visit scheduled?"

"Our visit," he said, correcting Collins. "Tomorrow. I've always believed that the more you know about your adversary, about how he thinks and how he might react, the better prepared you are when the day of confrontation comes."

"If it comes."

"No," Steele said with conviction. "Not if. When it comes."

Twenty-five

The weather was clear and sunny on Monday when they set out for the Agency safe house in Virginia. When Steele drove the Packard down Foxhall Road to Georgetown, he made a sudden right turn before circling back to their original route. He kept glancing in his rearview mirror for cars that might be following them. After another around-the-block maneuver, he seemed satisfied that they had not been tailed from his house.

They took the Key Bridge over the Potomac and followed Route 211 toward Fairfax. Traffic was light and Collins kept scanning the cars around them but didn't see anything that seemed suspicious. Steele kept checking his mirrors as he drove and noticeably slowed once to let a dark-colored sedan pass them.

Steele turned north onto Route 698 near Lee Manor and then drove for three or four miles before he pulled the car into an empty parking lot on the side of the road next to a small, wood-framed Baptist church. He faced the Packard toward the roadway so they could see any vehicles coming from the south.

"While I'm confident that we weren't followed, better safe than sorry," he said. "We'll pause here a few minutes."

Steele checked his wristwatch twice as they sat in silence. No vehicles appeared and the road remained deserted. "Five minutes," he said. "I think we can proceed."

They drove another three miles before he made an abrupt right turn off the highway at a small sign that said SUFFOLK FARM. The Packard rattled slightly as it pulled onto a one-lane dirt road, which was heavily wooded on both sides. A small cloud of dust rose into the air as they drove.

A metal gate appeared in front of them, barring their way. Collins could see a small slate-colored farmhouse, surrounded by meadows, in the near-distance. Steele brought the Packard to a stop and honked the horn three times. The front door to the farmhouse opened and a large young man dressed in a fisherman's sweater and gabardine trousers emerged. Two German shepherds burst out of the house behind him and ran to the gate, barking furiously.

The man strolled toward them and Collins noticed that he was carrying what looked like a Remington shotgun under one arm. He waved in their direction and quieted the dogs with a command, before unlocking the gate. He walked over to the Packard and Steele rolled down the driver's side window.

"Good morning, Tim," Steele said. "Did they call ahead from the Kremlin? Give you some advance warning?"

"That they did," the man said. "We were expecting you. I'm glad you made it out. It's been too quiet and it's made our guest restless."

"Not a lot of visitors of late?"

"They had people out here almost every day for the first two months to debrief him. It's dropped off quite a bit since then. Of course the security concerns are the same. We're keeping an eye out for strangers."

"Good for you."

"You can park closer to the house, Mr. Steele," Tim said. "Over on the right side." He walked over to stand by the gate, ready to lock it shut after they had passed through. The dogs were waiting there for him.

"Tim played center on the Yale football team the fall that the Japanese hit Pearl Harbor," Steele said. "He served with Colonel Evans Carlson's outfit, the Second Marine Raiders Battalion. He's been with the Agency for a few years now. A vigorous young man."

Steele pulled past the gate and parked the car on the grass about hundred yards from the farmhouse. Collins heard the unmistakable sounds of jazz music—Count Basie's "One O'Clock Jump"—from inside the house. Trailed by the German shepherds, they followed Tim up the flagstone path to the front porch. He commanded the dogs to stay, and then he knocked quickly twice on the front door before opening it and leading them into the house. He carefully placed the shotgun by the front door and motioned for them to go into the parlor.

Tolstoy sat by himself with a cup of tea in one hand and a book in the other. Several leather-bound books with Cyrillic titles and a samovar crowned with a teapot sat on the table next to him. The parlor was sparsely furnished with a bookcase and some oak Windsor chairs. An empty fireplace occupied the far corner.

Tolstoy carefully placed the teacup and book on the table and rose to his feet to shake hands with them. He had a long nose and high forehead with brushed-back silver hair that formed a widow's peak.

"I met you briefly in January when you first arrived in the States," Steele said.

"I remember."

"And this is Dennis Collins, a newspaperman from New York who has been researching Soviet intelligence efforts in the West. I invited him along since I believe that he can learn a lot from your story."

Tim returned with a tray with additional mugs and a carafe of coffee. "Help yourselves, gentlemen," he said. "I'll be in the kitchen if you need me."

"An interesting young man," Tolstoy said after Tim had left the room. "Like one of the ancient Greeks. Mr. Tim is an athlete with an intellect." He turned back to them. "What brings you all this way to see me, Mr. Steele?"

"I hoped you could help us with some insights into Anatoli Yatov."

"You are here to talk about Yatov?"

"We are."

"It will be a welcome change from my current debriefing," he said. "That is what they call my interrogation." He turned to Collins. "You're from New York City? Do you like jazz music, Mr. Collins?"

"I do," Collins replied.

"Count Basie? Duke Ellington? Cab Calloway?"

"I like all three."

"Have you been to hear them play in person?"

"I have."

"I envy you," he said. He looked around the bare room. "When they finish with me here I would like to go to New York, to the clubs on 52nd Street, and hear the best jazz. I am hopeful that the terms of my future employment will allow that."

"I'm no expert," Collins said, "but I know some of the club owners. When the time comes, I think I can help with getting you a better table."

"That would be marvelous. It must be amazing to be there when these musicians play."

"It is. My favorite is Billie Holiday. Her voice is quite something when you're in the room with her."

"Ah, yes, Lady Day." Tolstoy smiled. "She is marvelous, her voice is like an instrument."

Steele coughed, clearly impatient. "If we could return to Anatoli Yatov," he said. "I hoped you could tell us something about him, Mr. Tolstoy. I understand that you knew him in Berlin."

Tolstoy shrugged. "I must sing for my supper," he said to Collins with a note of resignation. "I know Yatov. What can I tell you about him? There is nothing about him that would suggest who he is—you might mistake him for a butcher or shopkeeper or tram car conductor. He's a gray man, not colorless mind you, but gray. Nondescript, and yet completely dedicated to the revolutionary struggle of the proletariat. Underneath that gray exterior is a very dangerous man, an arrogant man, one who can justify almost any action in the name of the dialectic."

"Why would Moscow Center choose Yatov to control high-level penetration agents?" Steele asked.

"There is a hardness about him, a capacity for violence, that would give pause to any agent entertaining second thoughts."

"Is that common?" Collins asked. "Penetration agents having second thoughts?"

"It is always a concern. These men operate under the most immense psychological pressure, as you can imagine. They must live a double life. There is the constant fear of exposure. Some men cannot live with this duplicity and they crack. Some become reluctant to continue to take the risk. Yatov recognizes this, and he knows how to keep them in harness."

"How would he react in a crisis?" Steele asked. "Say if one of his agents-in-place alerted him that he was about to be exposed, what do you think Yatov would do?"

"Yatov prides himself on his resourcefulness. He would want to meet with his agent, face-to-face, in a secure place, and decide what to do. Not in the city." Tolstoy looked out the window with distaste. "A place like this, away from the city. At heart he is a peasant, so he would feel safe in the countryside."

"But still cautious."

"Very much so. He has not survived all these years underground without calculation. I played Yatov in chess once when we were in Berlin. He plays defensively. Yatov admires Mikhail Botvinnik, our world champion, and he has studied Botvinnik's best games."

"How was the chess?" Collins asked.

"I lost," Tolstoy said. "Badly. I was too aggressive, too emotional. Yatov played the Winawer Variation of the French Defense, just like Botvinnik. Do you play, Mr. Collins?"

"I don't."

"A shame," he said. "I play here occasionally with Mr. Tim. It would be better to have a variety of opponents. That keeps one sharp."

"So it would be fair to say that Yatov prefers to wait and react," Steele said.

"In chess, that is the case. He does not attack prematurely. But when he counterattacks he looks to smash you. He marshals his forces and seeks a final resolution."

"There is a story about him," Steele said. "From Warsaw. It is said that Yatov walked into a meeting room in the Ministry of Security and executed two officials under suspicion with revolver shots at close range. So quickly that they could not react. And then he calmly left the room."

"I have heard that story. I do not know if it is true or not. Yet I believe Yatov would not hesitate to carry out orders to do such a thing."

"No remorse? No second thoughts?"

"Who knows what is in the soul of another man, but with Yatov I believe that he justifies what he does—if, indeed, he feels the need to justify it—by seeing himself as an agent of history."

"Some history," Collins said. "The mobsters in New York are at least honest that they're killing so that they can control the rackets in the city."

Tolstoy stroked his chin with his hand, reflecting. "These questions have a purpose. You are planning something for Yatov, no?"

Steele nodded. "If the opportunity presents itself. He has a few debts that he needs to pay."

"I would counsel great caution on your part. When they told me I was going to reside near Washington for a time, I became anxious. I did not tell your people this, but I will tell you. I worried that my former comrades might find me here and I wondered if Yatov—or a man like him—would be ordered to locate me and liquidate me. There are many operatives from Moscow Center at our embassy in Washington and if they learned where I was. . ." He took a slow sip of tea. "I'm sure that they also have sources within your government, within your intelligence services. I worry that they will discover this place."

"You're safe here," Steele said.

"Am I? I wish I could share your confidence. Two men to protect me? A few guard dogs barking? It does not seem enough."

"The road from the highway is watched," Steele said. "There are other men patrolling the woods you don't see. And Tim served as a Marine Raider in the Pacific."

"I see," he said. "I must trust then to the Fates and to my Marine Raider." He turned to Collins. "Do you have any other questions? I would imagine as a newspaperman you would never run out of questions."

"I have a few. What caused you to defect? Was there a straw that broke the camel's back?"

"I know this phrase," he said. "In Russian, we say 'the last drop that overflows the cup's patience.' It was not like that. I made a mistake that was going to cost me my life, and I am no hero, you see, so I took the only path left to me. I'm here by accident, a chain of events over which I had little control. I was friendly with one of the younger men at the embassy, Yuri Voronov. Yuri loved the violin and at a recital at the University of Helsinki he met a lovely young girl and fell in love. One thing led to another, and soon he was meeting with her secretly, or at least he believed it was secret. Of course the NKVD knew about this little romance and Yuri was deemed a security risk. He was informed of his recall to Moscow and he came to see me for advice."

Tolstoy interrupted his story to drink from his teacup. "Yuri told me he planned to stay in Helsinki, to defect. He would marry his Annika, he would teach at the university—Annika's father was a professor, there. I explained to him his foolishness, that Moscow would react very harshly and that he would place himself, Annika, and her family in danger. In fact, there was no guarantee that the

Finnish government would allow him to remain in the country. I told him to return to Moscow and admit his indiscretion and plead the folly of youth. Voronov wouldn't be the first diplomat to let his penis—his dick, I think you say—land him in trouble. I believed he would be reprimanded and given a second chance. I knew of other cases where this was the resolution. Good advice, yes?" Tolstoy looked over to Steele for reassurance.

"Good advice based on your experience," Steele said. "The advice any of us would have given."

"I persuaded Yuri that once the cloud over him had been lifted he could arrange for Annika to come to Moscow. I promised to help with the arrangements. They could build a life there, together, I told him." He glanced quickly at both of them and took another sip of tea. "I was lying to him, of course, because I didn't imagine the authorities would allow her into the country. But I knew Voronov would never return without that hope. I offered to take Annika a letter from Yuri explaining the situation."

"And he took your advice?" Collins asked, although he already knew the answer and where Tolstoy's story was heading.

"He took my advice. I delivered his letter. Yuri took the flight back to Moscow and I figured the episode was over. Then a friend of mine, another Soviet diplomat, approached me at a conference in Oslo. He told me that Voronov had confessed to crimes against the state and had been sentenced to ten years of hard labor in Kolmya. A death sentence, even for young man in good health. I assumed that I had been implicated. When I returned to Helsinki, I was resolved that I would not suffer the same fate. A few days later I was told that I was needed for consultations in Moscow. I pretended to be happy, because I would be reunited with my wife." Tolstoy laughed. "I had no wish to die in the camps. I knew I had to run."

"So you defected?"

"What else could I do? I wish it was for noble reasons, because I had rejected Marxist-Leninist thought, or that I couldn't stand that my country is ruled by cruel and vicious madmen, but I defected because I wanted to live. I knew that I would be forced to confess and that I would be sent to Kolyma. My wife would disavow me—as the daughter of a member of the Politburo I knew that she would be protected—and Vadim Tolstoy would die on a winter morning in some distant gold mine when the temperature reached ten degrees below zero, forgotten, unmourned, a victim of his own sentimentality."

"But the ending of the story is different," Steele said. "You're here. With your help we will work toward a day when a future Yuri could marry his Annika."

"Perhaps. I must still live with the present Yuri on my conscience, nonetheless."

"There was no way for you to know that he would be persecuted."

"There was always that possibility. I did not admit it, because of a moral failing. I counseled Voronov to return to Moscow largely to protect myself. I worried that if he defected that I would come under suspicion. The right thing would have been to tell him to run, even if that would have put me at risk." Tolstoy sighed. "I am not an exceptional man. I am not particularly courageous. I accepted the system under which I lived, played by its rules. I could not complain—I lived well. I had spent the war in our embassy in Ankara. It's not that I was blind. I knew of Stalin's cruelty. I rationalized that whatever was corrupt or immoral in Soviet society, whatever compromises had been made, would be transformed for the better when we achieved the next level of socialism."

They sat in silence for a moment.

"When this is over you said you wanted to see the jazz clubs in New York," Collins said. "Anywhere else you would like to go?"

Tolstoy brightened at the question. "New Orleans," he said. "They have good jazz there, too, and it is warm. I promised myself that when I came to the United States I would ask to live someplace without snow. It doesn't snow in New Orleans."

"It doesn't," Collins said. "Not even once in a blue moon."

A phone rang elsewhere in the house, and someone picked it up. They heard a murmured comment or two, and then Tim appeared at the entrance to the parlor to tell Steele that it was a call for him.

Steele left and Collins and Tolstoy talked about jazz for a few minutes. When Steele returned, he explained that he had to return to Washington. He thanked Tolstoy for his time and the Russian stood and gave him a quick bow.

"I hope I have helped," he said. "Anatoli Yatov is a dangerous man so I would again urge that you take proper care."

Steele strode to the car, eager to leave. Collins wondered what the call had been about and why it had excited Steele; he quickly learned the reason once they were in the Packard heading back up the dirt road.

"That was Julian Farnsworth," Steele said. "It's a madhouse in London at the Foreign Office and MI5. They had agreed to begin questioning Donald Maclean today. But Maclean disappeared over the weekend as did Guy Burgess. Julian says the working assumption is that they have both defected to the Soviets."

"Maclean wasn't under surveillance?"

"Only when he came to London, not at his home. That Burgess disappeared along with him is very bad news for Kim Philby. It looks like Moscow exfiltrated both of them. That leaves Philby holding the proverbial bag. What's his defense going to be? I had a Soviet spy living in my house and I didn't know it? It gets worse when you consider that Philby ran the Russian desk for SIS before he came to Washington. You can imagine the concern in London."

"Could this be the end for Philby?"

"Perhaps the beginning of the end. This may open some doors for us. If Philby believes he has been treated poorly by Moscow Center, left hanging while Maclean and Burgess were rescued, he may be willing to work with us. Perhaps even give us Yatov."

"Or the British may bring him back for a proper grilling," Collins said, "in which case his connection with Yatov will be severed."

"They'll move slowly on Philby," Steele said. "They won't want to admit they might have another traitor in their midst until they're forced to. So we'll have some time before Philby leaves the local scene, and I plan to make the most of it."

When Collins called Maria that night she had disturbing news. Although Collins had dismissed the Bureau's investigation of Steele as nothing more than an annoyance, it was clear that Andrew Caldwell and his superiors at the FBI hadn't arrived at the same conclusion.

"We had a strange visitor today," Maria told him. "An agent from the FBI office in Miami came to the restaurant. A young man, very clean-cut. He said he was looking for you. When Dad told him you weren't around, he said he still wanted to ask some questions."

"What did Jim do?"

"He stared at the man for a long time, until it became uncomfortable, even for me. Dad didn't say a word. I don't think the FBI agent had a clue as to how to respond."

"Then what happened?"

"The FBI man broke the silence and spoke first. He said that he would be asking routine questions and that he would appreciate our cooperation."

"What did your father say then?"

"Dad told the man he would be happy to make a statement and suggested he take out his notepad so he could write it down. Then he told him that he would rather have Dennis Collins in the foxhole next to him than J. Edgar Hoover. Dad said that you were a loyal and courageous American and he saw those qualities firsthand on Okinawa. Then he asked the agent if Hoover had ever heard a shot fired in anger."

"How did that go over?"

"The agent didn't write any of that down. He asked my father if you had been visited by any foreign nationals and Dad laughed and told him you had not and that Key West was too damn hot to attract any subversives wearing trenchcoats."

"It doesn't sound like he held back at all."

"That's Dad. No patience for fools. After a few more questions with sarcastic responses the agent must have realized he was wasting his time. He thanked us and then left pretty quickly. I don't think he got the reception that he expected. He must be used to intimidating people by just showing up and flashing his badge."

"Intimidation is what they were trying to do," Collins said. "Caldwell is behind it. He wants to prove that they can harass me through my friends. Thank your father for me. I think he gave them something to think about."

"I hope you are being careful, Dennis," she said, "and I wish you and Caleb could come home tomorrow."

"It won't be tomorrow, but it will be soon enough."

"Today wouldn't be soon enough as far as I'm concerned."

Twenty-six

The next day Steele left the house immediately after breakfast without announcing his destination and without asking Collins to accompany him. When he returned to Hoban Road around eleven o'clock and came to the guest house, Collins found his host was all smiles.

"My long shot that has paid off," Steele said, waving a manila envelope at Collins. "Finally a break."

"What's happened?"

"Weeks into the surveillance and something turns up," he said. "Last week Kim Philby drove out to the Great Falls Park in Virginia. De Groot's team had a very difficult time following him. There's a small amusement park located there with a picnic area and carousel. The falls themselves are quite impressive. I think the river drops seventy-five feet or so." He paused, struggling to contain his excitement. "They spotted Philby's car in the parking lot but no sign of him in the amusement park. De Groot's team decided that they couldn't take the risk of searching for him on the trails that lead to the river and so they left."

"So you think Philby was meeting someone. Yatov?"

"It's suspicious," Steele said. "A drop or a meeting of some kind. But there's considerably more. Roger de Groot's people came up with a jewel. Come, I'll show you." He hurried over to the large oak table in the sitting room and pulled several photos from the envelope and spread them out on the tabletop.

"Monday at lunchtime Philby drove from the British embassy to Union Station," he began. "Not a particularly exciting destination, but it's a logical place to pick up a friend who has arrived by train. Philby heads into the concourse waiting room and stops by a newsstand. He buys a copy of the *Washington Post* and sits down at one of the benches and starts reading the newspaper. It's what anyone might do while waiting, yes? But then something strange happens. A man in a gray hat sits down right next to him. Philby gives him a quick glance, doesn't acknowledge him, but then they talk for a few minutes, quietly."

"Yatov?"

"Yes. Look at the photographs." Steele jabbed his index finger at the first photograph on the table, an image of a middle-aged man wearing a hat. "There's a strong resemblance to the Berlin photo. I'm sure it's him." He handed Collins the Union Station photo along with the smaller image of Yatov taken in East Berlin.

Collins studied them for a long moment. The newer photograph was very clear and the Berlin image was blurry; Collins couldn't be sure he was looking at the same man.

"There are some similarities," he said cautiously.

"I think my harpoon at the Metropolitan Club and the news about Maclean and Burgess spurred this meeting. They must be feeling the heat. When Philby and Yatov finish talking, Philby leaves first. He doesn't take the *Post* with him, though, and Yatov picks up the first section of the paper and brings it with him." Steele pointed to another photo, of the middle-aged man holding a folded-up newspaper.

"You think it was a drop."

"Exactly. Philby probably placed an envelope of negatives in the newspaper. The exchange would normally pass completely unnoticed. De Groot's team caught it only because they were watching closely for anything unusual."

"Did de Groot say anything about that? It doesn't sound like the sort of thing you run into during a routine infidelity investigation."

"I made a joke out of it. Said my ex-business associate was one of the cheapest men I've ever known and he probably wanted to read the paper without paying for another."

"Did de Groot buy your explanation?"

"He did," Steele said. "I paid him what I owed him in cash and threw in another hundred dollars as a tip. Told him I was relieved that Philby hadn't gone anywhere near my wife."

"So now what?" Collins asked. "We know the Great White Whale has surfaced. What's the plan? Will you go back to Guy Myers now that you have something, a photo of your ghost?"

Steele shook his head. "Even if Myers would accept it was Yatov at Union Station, I don't think I can risk involving anyone at the Agency directly now. I don't know who I can trust and I'm afraid the Agency itself may have been penetrated. I'll give Allen Dulles a heads up, but I won't give him details. Allen will be able to deny any prior knowledge of my plans if anything should go wrong."

"If you're not going to involve anyone from the Agency, how do you propose to catch Yatov?"

"I need your help again, and your brother's, if he's willing."

"What do want us to do?"

"I'm convinced that we can drag Yatov into the light of day by applying enough pressure to Philby. If we can rattle Philby, I think he'll lead us to Yatov. He'll ask for an emergency rendezvous. I'll want you and Frank there to provide back-up when I confront them.

Tell your brother: 'Once more unto the breach, dear friends, once more.'"

"The Shakespeare might be wasted on Frank. What happens after you confront Philby and Yatov?"

"I make each a proposition. An opportunity to cooperate. I think even Kim Philby will have a hard time explaining away his clandestine tête-à-tête with a Soviet agent. Can he be prosecuted? I don't believe we will have enough hard evidence for that. Nonetheless, if we can hold onto Yatov for a bit, there's a chance we can bluff Philby into cooperating. It will be his best chance to avoid disgrace and a long prison sentence."

"When you talk about holding onto Yatov, who is the 'we' in question?"

"The three of us. After we intercept Yatov at the rendezvous we keep him only long enough to involve other interested parties."

"I doubt Yatov will welcome that."

"He won't have a say in the matter."

Steele carefully inserted a key in the lock on his top left desk drawer. He reached in and pulled out a revolver and placed it slowly on the desktop. Collins immediately recognized that it was a Luger, the German-made sidearm for Wehrmacht officers.

"I carried this throughout the war," Steele said. "A Model P08. Finding additional ammunition for a Luger was easier in Switzerland and once across the border. I hoped that I would never be called upon to use it again. I begin to believe that I may have to. We'll have to make a citizen's arrest of Yatov."

"A citizen's arrest?" Collins laughed. "That won't hold up for sixty seconds in front of a judge."

"A metaphor," Steele said. "I don't intend for Yatov to ever reach court. The idea is to have some leverage against Philby."

"And if Philby calls your bluff? If he denies any complicity? He may figure that the most you can do without hard evidence is to deport Yatov. You know Philby is damn clever. Don't you think he'll realize that?"

"He may, but he may not. At the very least we can have him recalled from Washington in disgrace. Then we have to hope Julian can talk some sense into his people and if they turn Philby over to MI5 that Feliks is involved in his interrogation."

"And what about Yatov? Would you be satisfied with his deportation?"

"It depends. I'll have to take a different tack with him. Yatov will either accept our control or be hoisted on his own petard. There's some more Shakespeare for you."

"I'm not sure I understand."

"If Yatov refuses our offer, he will discover that there is a high price to pay. We will detain him as long as we possibly can and in the interim we'll pass the word to our friends in London and Paris and Berlin that we have a new and very productive asset who is providing us useful details on Soviet clandestine operations. Then we will happily let Yatov go."

"And you think that will convince Moscow that Yatov has been turned?"

"I do. We need only to raise doubts about his allegiances. We can count on native Russian suspicion to do the rest. This would not be the first time we have manipulated their paranoia to our benefit. Allen is a master at this sort of operation. Convince your adversary that his agent is now yours, that he has been seduced by the riches of the bourgeois West. The agent is placed in the unenviable position of having to prove a negative. How do you convince your paranoid superiors that you are not a Western spy?"

Collins hesitated for a moment. "And would that be the equivalent of a death sentence, if they thought he had been turned, that he was working for the Agency?"

Steele shrugged in response, which told Collins all he needed to know.

"And the morality of it," Collins said. "Would that trouble you?"

"The morality of it? For Yatov it would be a fair sentence for that ugly business in New York and God alone knows how many murders he has committed in the name of dialectical materialism. Is Philby any better? We know that he has blood on his hands. The Dutch resistance agents he betrayed. Volkov in Turkey. The Albanians. And by my reckoning he's also complicit in the deaths of the Marines at the Chosin Reservoir and thousands of other Americans killed by the Chinese. I could make a strong argument that the moral course with Philby is to place this Luger at the base of his skull and pull the trigger."

"Could you do that? In cold blood?"

"I don't know. Fortunately it will never come to that."

"I have your word on that?" Collins asked. "If I agree to help you with this, and I bring Frank into it, I need to know that."

"You have my word." Steele's expression softened. "I'm not about to become an executioner, Dennis, if they refuse to cooperate. I want to see Philby face the music in London, and Yatov the same—but in Moscow. That would be poetic justice."

"Rough justice."

"For Yatov the justice of the system he has dedicated his life to advance. I only regret that Philby can't also be judged by the commissars he has so faithfully served. Nonetheless, I doubt that fifteen years at Wormwood Scrubs Prison will be a walk in the park."

"Is there any possibility that Yatov can wriggle his way out of it once he is back in Russia?"

"There's always a possibility. I'm betting that the paranoia running rampant in Moscow will make his prospects of survival very slim. I wouldn't worry about that."

Steele collected the photographs and placed them back in the manila envelope. "More good news," he said. "Dan Whelan left a message that the judge will approve the change in the birth certificate this week. You'll be listed as the father, and that will in effect give you legal custody of Caleb. Whalen is convinced that it will hold up to any legal challenge."

"Do you anticipate one?"

"I can't predict how Penny's parents are going to react. It will be a further shock when they realize that the boy will be going to live with you in Florida."

Steele put his hand on Collins' shoulder. "This is the best possible outcome for Caleb. I have no doubts about that, nor should you."

Collins made two phone calls that afternoon. The first was to his brother Frank, and it was a short call. After his run-in with Caldwell, Collins couldn't be sure that Steele's phone was secure, although he thought it was unlikely that the Bureau would risk wiretapping an Agency official. Nonetheless, he chose to be deliberately cryptic in his conversation with Frank. He explained that he needed some help again, this time for a moving job, and hoped that Frank could take the train down and spend a day or two with him in Washington.

"Actually it's Matthew who needs us both," Collins said. "It's his move. He needs some strong backs and weak minds."

"I see," Frank said. "He's too cheap to hire some local movers?"

"That's it. He also doesn't think they're dependable."

"He's probably right. How heavy will the lifting be?"

"We'll have to watch out for our toes, some of the furniture may come from overseas."

"Okay," Frank said. "I'm in."

"Thanks. By the way, I think it would be best if you come fully prepared."

"I will." Frank paused. "You know that Irish saying, Denny— 'If it's drowning you're after, don't torment yourself with shallow water.' It sounds like Matthew wants us in the deep water."

"That's where the larger fish swim," Collins said. "And I'm going to say good-bye before either of us tortures another metaphor. It may only be a day's notice for you to come down here. I'll phone."

"I'll be there. I wouldn't miss this for the world."

Collins phoned Maria immediately after he had finished with his brother. He told her the good news, that he would soon be listed as the father on Caleb's official birth certificate.

"I'm going to bring Caleb with me when I come back to Key West," he told her. "I have one last thing that Matthew needs some help with. Frank will be coming down to join us."

"Does it have to do with the Great White Whale?"

"It does," he said. "Matthew is ready to take action, but he can't do it by himself. Frank and I'll be there to back him up."

"This is something you feel you must do?"

"It is."

"When will this happen?"

"In the next few days. It's better that we don't talk about this on the phone. I promise to call you once it's over."

"Promise me that you'll be careful, Dennis."

"I promise, Maria. I learned back when I was a boxer that if you didn't keep your guard up you'd end up on the canvas counting stars really quickly. So don't worry. I won't drop my guard."

Twenty-seven

Now that he had hard evidence that Anatoli Yatov was nearby, somewhere in the vicinity of Washington, Steele moved quickly and decisively. On Tuesday he asked Collins to arrange for Frank to join them in Washington the following Thursday. Collins noticed an alertness and enthusiasm present in Steele that had been absent for weeks.

Steele had decided to confront Philby at the British agent's home on Thursday afternoon. Steele would present him with an ultimatum—either admit his role as a Soviet agent and cooperate with the Agency or face exposure and prosecution.

"I'm giving him until the following morning to decide," Steele explained. "I expect Philby will deny everything. After I leave his house, that's when I believe that he'll arrange an emergency meeting with Yatov either at Union Station or the Great Falls Park. My guess is that Yatov will want to meet at the park."

"And if he doesn't contact Yatov? Or they meet somewhere else where we can't easily follow?"

"My gambit will have failed." Steele paused for a long moment. "Then I must persuade General Smith to demand Philby's recall from Washington with just the facts we have now. A tough sell, but not an impossible one."

Early Thursday morning, Collins watched as an aging Chevrolet sedan pulled into the driveway of the Steele residence and parked next to the Packard. Collins walked around to the front yard and found Steele exiting the driver's side of the car.

"Philby might recognize the Packard as mine when it comes time to follow him to the rendezvous," Steele explained. "The Chevy shouldn't attract any notice."

Just after three o'clock, Steele drove the Packard over to Union Station and Collins followed in the Chevrolet. They waited outside for Frank to arrive on the New York-Washington train. When his brother emerged from the terminal, Collins waved him over to the Chevrolet and Frank climbed into the passenger seat.

Steele left the Packard and got into the back seat of the Chevrolet. After he had welcomed Frank, he asked him whether he was armed.

"I've got my service revolver."

"Good," Steele said and tapped Collins lightly on the shoulder. "I have a weapon for you, as well, Dennis." He produced a Luger from inside his suit jacket pocket and carefully handed it to Collins.

"I can't take this," Collins said. "You need it more than me. I'm along as backup."

Steele shook his head. "I'm loaning you my spare," he said. "I'm carrying my own. The safety can be a bit awkward to operate. It's a lever on the left side, and when it's down the gun will not fire. If you can see the word *gesichert* the safety is locked. If you push the lever forward and up, you can fire. If you are called upon to use it, remember to squeeze the trigger slowly."

Steele explained that they should park north of Philby's house on Nebraska Avenue, where they could see his driveway but wouldn't be too conspicuous. He told them that after he confronted Philby, he would leave and drive the Packard past them and turn left and park on Van Ness, a nearby street. Then he would walk back to the Chevrolet.

Steele checked his wristwatch. "There's no point in delaying this," he said. "It's time to test my theory."

As he followed Steele's Packard through Washington's late-afternoon traffic on the way to Nebraska Avenue, Collins was surprised to find that he wasn't nervous. Instead, he was eager—eager for Steele's confrontation with Philby and for a final resolution, one way or the other.

Collins parked the car on Nebraska Avenue as Steele had instructed, and then he and Frank sat in the front seat, watching Philby's house. Steele's Packard was already in the driveway. Collins turned the car radio's volume down low and they listened to a jazz station playing Charlie Parker, Dizzy Gillespie, and Charles Mingus. Frank smoked a few Chesterfields, tempting Collins who hadn't smoked in months.

They saw Steele emerge from the front door of Philby's house, get into his car, and drive past them. He turned left on Van Ness and disappeared from view. Five minutes later Steele, breathing heavily, slid into the backseat.

"How did it go?" Collins asked.

"I pitched him only fastballs," Steele said. "I threatened that if he didn't show up at the Agency in the morning prepared to make a clean breast of about his involvement with the Soviets that we would alert both Ambassador Franks and London about the traitor in their midst. Philby tried to fob me off, claiming that I had been infected with witch hunt fever and that I was imaging things. I told him that I had enough credible evidence to make a very strong case against him. That seemed to set him back somewhat. I told him the time had come for him to make a decision. I warned him against trying to make a run for it, that we were watching the airports and train stations."

"Which you aren't," Collins said.

"Of course not, but he doesn't know that. Now we'll just have to wait, and when he comes out of the house we can follow at a discreet distance. Philby will operate under the assumption that his home telephone is tapped. He'll head elsewhere to make the call to Yatov and arrange a rendezvous."

"If he comes out of the house," Frank said. "You're counting on him panicking."

"That I am," Steele said. "I'll concede that he is a cool customer, but I think I rattled him. We'll know shortly."

Collins kept the car radio switched off and they sat in silence, each lost in his own thoughts. He wondered whether Steele's stratagem would work. There was no guarantee that Philby would seek an immediate meeting with his Soviet handler.

A misty rain had begun to fall, and Collins had to start the car twice to run the wipers so they could see through the front windshield. Just when Collins was ready to lose hope, he caught a glimpse of Philby in the backyard near the garage and they saw him back out his car, a green Lincoln sedan. They waited until he exited the driveway and drove down Nebraska Avenue.

Collins followed the Lincoln at a distance through the city streets until Philby pulled over into a parking space by a pharmacy on Massachusetts Avenue. "Keep driving and go around the block," Steele instructed Collins. "He'll use the phone in there."

Philby emerged from the pharmacy moments later, got back into his car, and sped off to the south.

"It's the Great Falls," Steele said. "I'm sure of it. Dennis, give him plenty of room. Once he crosses the Potomac to the Virginia side of the river we don't need to keep him in sight. We know where he's going and we can't risk being spotted."

They followed Philby to the Canal Road and then over the Chain bridge, into Virginia. Collins allowed several other cars and trucks pass him so he could drop well behind Philby's Lincoln. It had begun to rain intermittently, and the road became slick. Philby picked up speed when they reached the Georgetown Pike, and Steele grinned.

"Yatov wanted the Great Falls," he said. "Outside the city, just as Tolstoy predicted. He wouldn't have felt safe at Union Station for an emergency meeting. Too many people around."

They drove along the Georgetown Pike in silence. Philby's car had long since passed out of sight. When they came to the turn-off to the Great Falls Park, Steele spoke up. "Keep a lookout for his Lincoln. It'll be there someplace."

When Collins pulled the Chevrolet into the parking lot, he heard Frank exhale sharply. "Philby is here," his brother said, pointing to the far corner of the lot where a green Lincoln sedan sat. "A Ford next to it. Dollars to donuts the other car is Yatov's."

Steele surveyed the parking lot. "Not many visitors today because of the weather. Yatov and Philby will look to avoid people, so I think they'll meet somewhere closer to the river, south of the Great Falls. The Patowmack Canal was dug parallel to the river and there are ruins of several canal locks there. No water, now. The canal ran southeast down to the Potomac where there's a cut that allows access to the river. Anywhere along the dry canal bed would be a logical place to meet."

"How do we get there without alerting them?" Collins asked.

"There are several trails that lead there," Steele said. "We'll have you remain on the main trail from the parking lot. Frank and I will push ahead and try to maneuver behind them."

"If that's where they are," Frank said.

"They are there," Steele said. "Trust me."

As they moved down the trail from the parking lot they could hear the roar of the falls in the distance and, through the trees, Collins caught glimpses of the Potomac below. They came to a fork in the trail, and Steele told Collins to follow the left branch for about five hundred yards and then to stop and wait at the top of the first canal lock. If Philby and his Russian handler somehow evaded the initial trap, Collins would be there to block their escape. Steele and Frank would take the right branch of the trail and hope to work their way behind their quarry.

When Collins glanced over he saw that Steele had his Luger in his right hand and Frank was also carrying his service revolver at the ready. They slowly walked down the right path and soon disappeared from sight.

Collins took the Luger out of his suit coat pocket and held it by his side, ready to quickly conceal it if he ran into any innocent hikers. In a few minutes he came to a clearing and he recognized that it had to be the canal bed, a grassy, sunken depression in the ground. There were two ruined masonry walls that must have been part of the canal locks. He could see that the canal sloped down toward the river with what looked like a fairly steep drop.

He felt a light mist and glanced up at the overcast sky, wondering if it would turn into a heavier rain. That might drive Yatov and Philby back to the parking lot.

Then he heard what sounded like muffled shouts in the distance followed by the distinct but instantly recognizable sound of gunshots. Collins counted at least four shots and quickly adjusted the safety lever on the Luger. He checked—the German word was covered and the gun ready to fire. Collins took several steps back and raised the pistol, pointing the tapered barrel of the weapon toward the clearing. He heard someone approaching and he tensed.

A stocky middle-aged man dressed in a dark raincoat came running up the canal bed toward him. When he saw Collins he stopped and raised his arm and Collins saw in his hand an ugly looking revolver with a long barrel.

Collins didn't hesitate, squeezing the trigger on the Luger, aiming for the man's midsection. The revolver jumped in his hand and then he heard a whizzing sound, and what felt like a tug on his upper left arm, followed by bark exploding from a tree behind him. Collins pulled the trigger again and watched as the man suddenly collapsed to one knee and then awkwardly toppled, face first, onto the trail.

Collins felt his hands shaking and he carefully lowered the gun down to waist level. He clicked the safety on and took a deep breath. He felt a stinging sensation on his left arm and saw that his suit coat sleeve was stained with blood near his bicep.

"It's Matthew," a voice called out. "Don't shoot, Dennis."

A moment later Steele appeared, his own Luger in hand, accompanied by Frank and Kim Philby. Frank had his Colt pointed directly at Philby and Collins could tell by the look on his brother's face that he wouldn't hesitate to shoot the Englishman if he tried to escape.

"Are you alright?" Steele asked.

"I've been nicked on the arm," Collins said. "It stings a bit, but I don't think it's serious."

Steele walked over and quickly inspected Collins' arm, gently examining the spot where blood was staining his coat sleeve.

"Looks like a flesh wound," he said. "There's a first aid kit in the car. We'll get a bandage on it once we've finished business here."

Steele turned to the body sprawled awkwardly in the canal bed; he walked over and squatted next to it. He rolled the body over and Collins looked away for a moment, not wanting to see the man's face.

"He's finished," Steele said and bent down and picked up the revolver lying next to the right hand of the man. "A Nagant with a silencer. Exactly the weapon a Soviet assassin would carry." He reached inside the man's coat and retrieved a leather wallet from an inner pocket. He straightened up and took a moment to examine its contents carefully.

"A passport made out to Vladimir Bodrov," he said. He glanced over at Philby. "I doubt that this cover will hold up under any extended examination. We're looking at Anatoli Yatov of the First Directorate, Moscow Center, illegal *rezident* for New York and points south. We've interrupted his meeting with his prize agent-in-place, a man who has been working for the Soviets for decades." Steele addressed Philby. "I take it that you weren't going to make a clean breast of it at the Agency tomorrow?"

"You have this all wrong," Philby said. "This man, whose name *is* Bodrov, was an agent that I have been running, a driver at the Soviet embassy. When you confronted us, he must have thought that you were security from the embassy and he panicked. No wonder he began shooting. He knew that he was dead for certain if he was caught in these circumstances."

"Russian agents speaking English?" Frank asked. He spat dismissively on the ground. "That's a good one."

"A rather flimsy story," Steele said. "It won't hold up. You have to know that, Philby. Why would you be running a low-level Russian? That's not your job."

"I don't think you're the one who decides what my job is," Philby said. "Bodrov was my asset. Since you've killed him, and he's the one person capable of corroborating it, it will be my word against yours. I would hazard the guess that this operation of yours wasn't sanctioned by those in authority. It if was, you wouldn't be relying on a newspaperman and this other chap as your backup." Philby smiled thinly. "And now you'll have to figure out how to handle the messy aftermath. Mr. Collins has killed a member of the Russian diplomatic corps."

Steele casually raised his weapon until it was pointing directly at Philby. Collins felt himself tensing, discomfited by the motion. "You're forgetting the evidence I have that implicates you as Stanley, a Soviet agent-in-place," Steele said.

"Stanley? Who's Stanley? I have no idea what you're talking about." Philby waved his right hand in peremptory dismissal. "If your evidence was credible, I'd already be in custody on my way back to London."

"We know who you are and what you have done," Collins said.

Philby shook his head. "I'm afraid that you have lost all sense of proportion about this. I'm not Homer or Stanley or any other code name that the Soviets are using for their agents. You've mistaken me for someone else."

Steele kept his weapon trained on Philby. "We have photographs of you meeting Yatov at Union Station. And this rendezvous with the same man, after my ultimatum earlier today. We have quite a dossier on Yatov, by the way. There's no logical explanation for your connection with him, other than that he is your handler."

"You're quite wrong, Matthew," Philby said. "And now you face a choice. You can detain me, alert the local police and involve your Agency and of course my own people. The FBI will insist on becoming involved. Then you'll have a lot to explain. Your friend Mr. Collins will face charges of some sort for killing Mr. Bodrov, the Russians will insist on that. The newspapers will have a field day. Shootout at the Great Falls. A botched operation. There will be calls for an investigation. I can't imagine General Smith will be happy with that turn of events."

"So what do you suggest I do?" Steele asked.

"Allow me to walk back to my vehicle, unhindered, and drive away. It'll be up to you to dispose of Mr. Bodrov in whatever way you deem fit."

Collins was surprised at his own anger. "You're a cold bastard," he said. "With bloody hands."

"Matthew, what do you say?" Philby asked Steele, ignoring Collins.

"There is the river," Steele said. He waved the muzzle of the Luger in small circles, keeping it directly aimed at Philby's chest. "We could consign you to its depths as easily as we shall Yatov. Properly weighted, your bodies might not surface for weeks, if at all. There would be the mystery of your disappearance, but I suspect that after Burgess the assumption would be that you had defected."

Frank grinned and glanced over at Philby. Collins didn't care for the ugly look on his brother's face but he understood where it came from. "Mr. Steele has it right," Frank said to Philby. "As far I'm concerned, there's no reason to deal with you any differently than Yatov. In fact, there's more reason, because you're a fucking traitor to your own country and the Russian at least was loyal to his."

Philby ignored Frank's outburst, and shifted his gaze back toward Steele. "Liquidating me would be a hollow victory, Matthew. You would have proved absolutely nothing. The mystery of Homer and Stanley would remain unsolved. My disappearance would certainly be suggestive of complicity, but when I don't turn up in Moscow to join Maclean and Burgess then it becomes an open question. Did Philby defect? Or was there foul play of some sort? It would forever be a mystery and you would have the murder of an innocent man on your conscience. Don't I deserve my day in court, as it were, a chance to refute the charges?"

Steele stared at Philby for a long moment, weighing his next move, and Collins thought that there was a good chance that he would pull the trigger. Instead, he slowly lowered the Luger.

"You're right," he said. "The world should know your true nature. You should stand trial and be exposed as a traitor. When we visited Paris we made a side trip to London. One that you and your Russian masters were not aware of. We spent time with some interested parties at your Service and at MI5. They're fully briefed, including your history of betrayal—the Dutch resistance, Volkov in Istanbul, the Albanians."

Philby shrugged. "Blind alleys. Nothing there. They'll be wasting their time."

"I don't think so. You're finished. When you're sent back to London in disgrace you will be cut off from the Service, shunned as a pariah, prosecuted, and sent to prison. You've done a very poor job of covering your tracks. Arrogance, I suppose. It won't take very long for them to build a case. And even if you did somehow manage to wriggle out of this, what sort of life awaits you? One of disgrace in England, snubbed in public, reviled, considered the worst of blackguards. Or if you decide to follow Burgess and Maclean you'll have to actually live in your false Utopia. In some ways I think I'd prefer that you do bolt for Moscow—I like the idea of you trapped in a dreary Marxist prison of your own making. If you believe that you'll be seen as a hero of the socialist state, you're mistaken. Behind your back they'll despise you—because while you may have been useful to them over the years, they'll see you as a Judas, a bourgeois Judas, and you'll never be trusted. They will watch your every move."

"Rubbish," Philby said. "I didn't take you for a McCarthyite, Steele, but it seems your fantasies are just as bizarre and paranoiac."

"Go," Steele said, waving the Luger in the direction of the main trail leading to the parking lot. "Take your car and leave now before I change my mind. Start packing when you get back to Nebraska Avenue because you'll be on a return flight to London within days."

Philby muttered something and turned on his heel and walked back up the main trail.

Steele didn't move, lost in thought for a moment. He returned to Yatov's body and bent over and rummaged through the man's trouser pockets, retrieving a set of car keys. He handed them to Collins and explained how they would handle the situation. Collins and his brother should drag or carry Yatov's body down the sloping canal bed to the river.

"Load his jacket pockets with stones," Steele said. "It will help submerge the body. Push him into the water as far from the riverbank as possible. With any luck it'll be several days before it surfaces and is discovered."

"What about the guns?" Frank asked. "The Luger that Denny used and Yatov's gun. Should we toss them there?"

Steele checked the safety on the Nagant before handing it to Frank. "Yes, throw them into the river, as far out as you can. Find the spent shells from the Luger, too, and dispose of them."

"Then what? What about the car?" Collins asked.

"Drive to Griffith Stadium. Take Fifth Street through the city. You know where the field is?"

Collins nodded. "I can get us there."

"Park the Ford on one of the side streets near the field. They should be relatively empty, because the Senators aren't playing tonight. Leave the keys in the ignition and the car unlocked. Wait at the corner of U Street and Fifth Street. I'll swing by and pick you up no later than seven o'clock."

"This would have been a lot less complicated if Philby had caught a stray round back in the clearing," Frank said. "Right between the eyes. I don't like the idea of letting him go."

Steele shrugged. "That's neither here or there, now. I made the decision and I'll have to live with it. We need to get moving." He turned to Frank. "I'll leave the first aid kit on the hood of the Ford. Just make sure there's no fabric left in the wound after you've cleaned it."

"I used to help out as Denny's cut man when he boxed in Golden Gloves," Frank said. "I'll get him fixed up just fine."

"That should be it," Steele said. "Time to move. The longer we stand around here with a dead body at our feet, the more likely we're going to shock some birdwatcher out for a walk. We don't want the Virginia State Police showing up."

"We'll see you at the ballpark, then," Collins said.

Frank lifted the lifeless body of Anatoli Yatov by the shoulders and Collins took his feet. Collins felt some light rain on his face as they started down the sloping canal bed. It took ten minutes for them to near the opening where there was access to the river. The sound of the Potomac rushing past grew louder as they moved into the cut, rock walls on both sides, and Collins felt the sweat dripping from his face as they negotiated their way down. He ignored the burning pain in his left biceps where Yatov's bullet had clipped him.

When they reached the Potomac, they laid Yatov's body down on the bank right next to the water and silently went to work loading his jacket and pants pockets with small stones. Collins tried not to think about what he was doing. He avoided looking at Yatov's face, with its blank stare and open mouth.

They took off their shoes and rolled up their pant legs and, cautious about their footing, waded out into the river with the body. Frank counted to three and then they gave it a hard shove further out into the current where it immediately submerged into the muddy water and then disappeared from view.

"Let's hope that he stays at the bottom of the river," Frank said. "Even if he does float up, there won't be much in the ways of clues." He patted Collins on the back. "Now the guns. You toss first."

Collins took the Luger from his front pocket and took a step back to give himself some room. He grasped the revolver by its grip and threw it as high and as far as he could. He saw it splash when it hit the surface of the river.

"Duke Snider couldn't have done better," Frank said and proceeded to hurl the Russian revolver out into the Potomac. "Now, let's get out of here. No second thoughts, Denny. You did the right thing. We did the right thing."

"I know. There were many others besides Karina. It wasn't only revenge for her."

"Don't think of it as revenge. It was simple justice. Tell me that the world isn't a better place without Yatov."

Collins remained silent.

His brother hadn't finished. "It would be a better world without Philby as well. Much better. It burned me up to watch that bastard walk away. I know the type. Sneaky. Smooth about it. The type that never gets his hands dirty, but is more than happy to help the real killers like Yatov. Don't forget that Philby has been passing our military secrets to the Reds—which makes him a Judas in my book. And he has gallons of blood on his hands from all the poor GIs and Marines in Korea who were butchered because the Chinese knew our plans."

"I don't forget," Collins said. "How could I?"

"Don't forget. Like I said, you made the world a better place tonight."

Scattered raindrops started to hit them as they waited at the corner of U and Fifth Streets, near the entrance to Griffiths Stadium. They had parked Yatov's Ford three streets away, the keys in the ignition and the front windows rolled down, and then walked over through deserted streets to the Stadium. By the time Steele arrived in the Packard, at five minutes before seven, the rain had picked up and their clothing was damp.

"Sorry to be late," Steele said, once they were in the car. "It took longer than I had thought to drop off the Chevy and catch a cab back to Van Ness to retrieve the Packard. Everything squared away at the Great Falls?"

"There are no traces left of what happened," Frank said. "I got Denny patched up and we left Yatov's Ford up the block ready for a teenager to take it on a joyride."

"Have you alerted the Agency about Philby?" Collins asked Steele.

"I called Allen and requested a meeting with General Smith as his first order of business tomorrow. I'll present my evidence for Philby's guilt. After I convince Smith that Philby is the Third Man, the idea is to call Sir Stewart Menzies, the head of SIS, and make it clear that we regard Philby as a Soviet asset. As long as Philby remains in place in Washington, we can't share any intelligence."

"Are you going to fill him in about Yatov and his meeting with Philby tonight?" Frank asked. "Isn't that damn convincing proof of Philby's guilt?"

"No, nothing about Yatov or the rendezvous," Steele said. "I think I have enough circumstantial evidence. If Allen and General Smith learn about Yatov, they may feel compelled to mount an investigation, perhaps even drag the river to retrieve the body. I won't take the risk of implicating you, or Dennis." He paused. "By the way, remember the Luger that killed Yatov is mine. I'm the most likely candidate for having pulled the trigger. If I was ever asked, I would plead the Fifth."

"But I shot Yatov," Collins said. "I wouldn't shirk from admitting that."

"That's not my recollection," Steele said. "I'd bet that your brother doesn't remember it that way either. Do you, Frank?"

"He has you, Denny," Frank said. "I'd testify that I saw Matthew shoot Yatov. That's two of us saying that he did it, not you."

"No need to argue about it," Steele said, holding a hand up to forestall Collins' angry response. "It'll never come to that."

"What if Smith balks at accusing Philby based on your circumstantial evidence?" Collins asked.

"I play my last card. I tell him to reconsider or I will resign on the spot and go to the *Washington Post* and *Washington Star* and reveal that Kim Philby is a Soviet spy who is being protected for political reasons."

Collins was astonished. "I can't believe that you would do that."

"Why not? It would be true. I'm hardly concerned about any personal repercussions. Let Philby sue me for libel. I have nothing to lose at this point. I'm free to do whatever I need to."

They were silent for the rest of the drive to Union Station. When they arrived, the rain was coming down in sheets and Steele pulled under the covered entryway so Frank could exit the Packard without being drenched.

"I'm hoping this is my last overnight train trip from Washington to New York for some time," Frank said.

"A promise," Steele said. "This is the last one you'll take on my behalf."

Frank turned to his brother. "You should get back to Key West and that girl of yours."

"I will," Collins said. "But I do have one more favor to ask."

"What's that?"

"Can you take some more vacation time this summer and come down to Key West in June with Peggy and Brendan? I can't get married without my best man there."

Frank smiled. "You bet. I was wondering when you were going to get around to asking."

Twenty-eight

It rained much harder on their ride from Union Station to Hoban Road, a sheet of rain drumming down on the Packard's convertible roof. It would have made it difficult to talk, but Steele remained silent and Collins was grateful for that. He felt tired, played out, drained of emotion.

He found himself replaying the scene from the Great Falls in his mind: the moment when Yatov first appeared, running up the canal bed toward him, and Collins' sudden realization that he was in danger and had to fire his weapon. He had been acutely aware of everything around him—the slight mist in the air, Yatov's gray raincoat, the abrupt percussive sound of Collins' Luger firing, and the strange, whizzing noise of the bullet from Yatov's revolver just before it grazed him. Then the recognition that he had been hit, if only slightly, and that Yatov had dropped to the ground in a heap. Collins remembered his heart racing and then feeling an immense sense of relief when he realized that he had not been badly wounded. He had been suddenly, and intensely, conscious of his own breathing as he took deep gulps of air.

Steele waited until they had reached the comfort of his study before addressing the evening's events. He poured a glass of whiskey for each of them and motioned for Collins to sit across from him. They could hear the sound of the wind sweeping the rain against the windowpanes and Collins caught the far-off rumble of thunder.

"How's the arm?" Steele asked.

"Sore. Frank did a good job of cleaning and bandaging it. I'll have an ugly scar to remind me of tonight."

"You did a very hard thing," Steele said. "But the right thing."

"It doesn't seem real, somehow," Collins said. "It happened so quickly. It took a few moments before I realized that I had hit him. Then I saw Yatov on the ground and it was clear that he was badly wounded or dead."

"Yatov commenced firing the moment your brother and I stepped into the clearing near the canal lock," Steele said. "He must have been on edge, to react like that. It may be that Frank or I winged him, but it didn't keep him from making a run for it. Fortunately you were there to stop him."

"Stop him? Kill him, you mean."

"You had no choice. He would have killed you. In fact, he tried to kill you. If he hadn't been moving, his aim might have been a bit better and you might not be here for this conversation."

"There's no disputing that. I'm thankful to be alive." Collins paused to take a small sip of his whiskey. "It bothers me, though. After Korea, I never thought I would be the direct cause of another person's death."

Steele rose to his feet, gingerly, and walked over to his bookshelf and stood there, looking for a book. He selected a slim volume and returned to his chair. "I'd like you to have this," he said, handing Collins the book. Collins read the title, *Man's Search for Meaning*, and waited for Steele to explain.

"It was written by Viktor Frankl, a neurologist and psychiatrist who survived Auschwitz," Steele said. "Frankl decided that the world was divided into two races of men, the decent and the indecent. You're a decent man, Dennis. The fact that you're troubled by Yatov's death, that concern alone places you in that category. Yatov belonged to the indecent race." Steele paused. "Despite all that he saw and experienced, in the end, Frankl concluded that our salvation is through love and in love—a sentiment that I'm sure Father Loughlin would endorse. I know that you will love Maria and Caleb in the days and weeks and months that follow and if you do nothing more than that with your life, it will be enough. More than enough."

"I'm pleased that you turned Allen down when he asked you to join the Agency," Steele said. "I fear that we will have to do many more hard things in the years ahead, that we will begin to match the brutality of the other side. We'll justify it, of course, by the ends, the need to resist the evil that their system represents—but it will come at a considerable spiritual cost. Some of us will even join the ranks of the indecent. I'm glad that you'll not be drawn into that, Dennis."

They sat in silence for a few minutes, each lost in his own thoughts. The rain had increased in intensity as the storm moved closer and the sound of thunder grew louder. Steele stirred, finally, and turned to Collins. "Do you have any questions? Anything that you've wondered about?"

"I do," Collins said. "When you threatened Philby tonight, did you consider killing him?"

"I was tempted. I decided against it, and not because it would be a hollow victory to secretly execute him. No, I had more theological concerns."

"Theological concerns?"

"I'm about to be accepted into the church. And sometime in the not-too-distant future I will have all of my questions about the afterlife answered. I desire to die in a state of grace. If I had killed Philby, I would not be able to say, in good conscience, mind you, that I truly repented the act. No remorse or guilt, nor could I feign it, not that it would fool my final judge. In the end, I would not risk that loss of grace."

Steele rose to his feet. "We could use some music," he said. He moved slowly behind his desk and placed a disc on the record player. "Vivaldi," he said. "One of my favorites. 'Concerto for Two Cellos in G Minor.'" Steele returned to his chair as the first movement began to play. "Whenever I listen to it I'm reminded of the great beauty that we are capable of creating. A shame that we get only glimpses of it."

"I'm more likely to glimpse it in Billie Holiday singing the blues," Collins said, "but I catch your drift."

"You do appreciate the small wonders in life more in circumstances like mine," Steele said. "The small things. You're probably feeling the same way tonight, with what you've experienced." He drank from his glass of whiskey and then hesitated for a moment before he spoke again. "It's unlikely that Caleb will remember any of his life here with us. He's too young."

"Perhaps he won't have any conscious memories, but he'll remember that he was loved. And 'Steele' will remain one of his names. Caleb Allen Steele Collins."

"Thank you," he said. "I'm touched by that. I've instructed Dan Whalen to establish an account for Caleb's education. It will be there when he reaches eighteen, for college."

"You don't need to do that," Collins said.

"I know I don't, but I have. After I'm gone, this desk will be put into storage and I want Caleb to have it when he becomes an adult."

"So you know, Maria and I have agreed that we'll tell Caleb about his mother when he is old enough to understand the situation. Is there a photograph of Penny that I can take with me to show him? I know he'll be curious."

"Of course," Steele said. He glanced over at the photograph of Penny by the window. "You can take this one. I have a duplicate of it next to my bed." He finished his whiskey and put the glass down carefully on the table next to him. "I did love her, in my own way. She doubted that. She accused me of marrying her as a gallant gesture, not as an act of love. It was both, I guess. That doesn't matter, now, of course." He shifted in his seat. "I dream of her almost every night now. I walk down a long dark, corridor and she is waiting for me at its end, a smile on her face. My therapist has suggested that these dreams are a way of preparing me for what is next. I pray that he's right about that. It's comforting to think that there's someone waiting for you, expecting you."

He looked over at Collins, suddenly all business. "When you get back to Key West, you'll hear from a friend of mine, Norris Jennings. He's at the North American Newspaper Alliance. They need someone to write some travel pieces for them. Cuba, Bermuda, the Bahamas, at the start. They'll pay well. Don't say 'yes' or 'no' now, before you've talked to Jennings. The money should come in handy and you'll be able to keep your hand in with the writing."

Collins thanked him. He might very well need to freelance in the future, and Steele's friend could prove helpful.

"I do owe you some explanation about my actions of the past few months. I began to realize last fall that the clock had begun to wind down for me. I had a few things I hoped to accomplish with the time I had left. I needed to bring you into our orbit—Penny's and mine—so that she could tell you about Caleb. I knew that you would accept responsibility for him. I never questioned that. I hoped that you might also look after Penny when I was gone. I never imagined that her illness would progress as rapidly as it did, or take such a horrifying turn."

"Was the meeting with General Eisenhower on the level, or a pretext to keep me in your orbit?"

"It was on the level. I welcomed the opportunity to keep you close, to have you spend time with Penny and Caleb, but I also wanted you to tell your story to Eisenhower. He needed to hear the truth about Chosin from someone who was there. And there were other reasons."

"Other reasons?"

"I wanted Moscow Center to know that you and I had visited Ike and discussed Korea. Remember our discussion with Philby at the Metropolitan Club? A message to his masters. They know Eisenhower. Stalin met him in Moscow in August 1945 and Eisenhower and Marshal Zhukov got along quite well. Eisenhower is, in their minds, first and foremost a military man. They will think long and hard about what his election to the presidency might mean. A tougher, more calculated line on our part. A recognition that we know that Europe is the prize, and a willingness to take whatever measures necessary to resolve the Korean situation."

"So the trip to Paris served multiple purposes," Collins said. "It flushed Philby into the open, it briefed General Eisenhower on the Korean situation, and it allowed you to send a message back to Moscow."

Steele laughed. "I plead guilty. Always thought that killing multiple birds with one stone was a Yankee virtue. And they say Ike is going to run for president next year. I'd like to think our visit played some small part in encouraging him to do so." He moved again in his chair, clearly in discomfort, wincing at the pain. "There really aren't any mysteries about the rest of it. Everything else that happened. When Penny took her own life, it became very clear what I needed to do. I had to satisfactorily resolve the legal situation with you and Caleb. That's been accomplished. There are few loose ends, now, if any."

Steele reached into his pocket for his pipe and matches. He lit the pipe and took a slow puff. "You must still be careful, Dennis. Keep an eye out for the next year or so. Remaining in Key West for a while would be prudent. It's a long way from Washington, and you'll be out of sight. Moscow Center is aware of your and my connection and may very well conclude that we're responsible for Yatov's disappearance. That could make both of us targets."

"Will Philby tell them what happened?" Collins asked.

"I don't know," Steele said. "Probably not. Why should he? Moscow wouldn't know about their emergency rendezvous—there wasn't time for Yatov to communicate about it and most agents in the field learn the less that headquarters knows, the better. I should think Philby would be very careful about what he tells his masters when he returns to London. The episode doesn't place him in a flattering light. We followed him to the rendezvous spot, and that doesn't say much for his tradecraft. He also knows how paranoid his colleagues in Dzerzhinsky Square are and he certainly wouldn't want them to start questioning his own loyalty."

"Any advice on staying out of sight?"

"Simple things. Keep your name and address out of the local phone directory. Be wary of strangers, especially curious strangers. Explain the situation to the Highsmiths in very general terms—there's no need to reveal everything, of course—so that they can stay alert as well."

Collins nodded. "I can blend into the background," he said. "Maria and I were planning to find a small place up the street from the hotel. Close but not too close."

"One other matter. I won't close out Anatoli Yatov's file. As far as the Agency is concerned, he's still out there somewhere. Your involvement should never come to light."

Steele paused to listen to the dark and frenetic final movement of the Vivaldi concerto, closing his eyes for a moment.

"I thought you might want to know that we've made arrangements for Vadim Tolstoy. A new name, a new life, in Santa Fe, where he'll own a record store, which he can stock with jazz records. Tim will be accompanying Tolstoy on a visit to the jazz clubs on 52nd Street next month—a reward of sorts for his cooperation—but it's too risky for him to stay in New York for any extended length of time."

"What are your own plans?"

"My plans? I've decided to spend time at Arlington Hall, working with the cryptographers on the Soviet cable traffic, decoding some of the more abstruse cables, putting real names to code names."

He poured himself another glass of whiskey and held it up to the light, admiring its amber color. "I have set things right as best I could," he said. "The books are balanced. Philby removed, Yatov finished, the leaks plugged. My doctors have warned me that they can't predict with any accuracy how long I will last. Apparently the growth of the tumors can accelerate quite quickly. I have my affairs in order, so I have no worries on that account."

He put his pipe down and took a sip of the whiskey. Steele reached into his coat pocket and produced a small red-covered book and opened it to a bookmark. "I had been reading this today, before I left to confront Philby, and I found this one passage that spoke to me. It's by Epicurus." He looked at the page and then read aloud: "Against other things it is possible to obtain security, but when it comes to death we human beings all live in an unwalled city." He gently closed the book. "I marvel that a Greek living centuries ago could capture the essence of my current situation so well. I know now that I am living in that unwalled city." He looked over at Collins, a trace of a smile on his lips. "But we all live there, you know. Some of us are just reminded of it sooner than others."

Two days later at the Key West Airport, Dennis Collins made his way down the ramp stairs of the National Airlines Lockheed Lodestar with Caleb in his arms. The child clung to him, burrowing his face into Collins' shoulder to avoid the bright sunlight reflecting off the polished exterior aluminum skin of the aircraft.

When they reached the tarmac, Collins smiled when he saw a slim dark-haired young woman moving toward them. Collins carefully put Caleb's feet on the ground and the boy looked around, his hand firmly grasping his father's. Maria Highsmith enveloped Caleb in a hug, and to Collins' delight the boy clung to her.

"Welcome home, Caleb," she said. "We've been waiting for you."

She straightened up and gave Collins a quick kiss on the lips. "Home at last, Dennis. For good."

Collins gathered Caleb in his arms and followed Maria across the tarmac to the terminal. Once inside Collins could see the tall figure of Jim Highsmith through the windows, leaning against the Highsmith Inn station wagon in the parking lot. He waved to them, smiling.

Caleb rested his head on Collins' shoulder and Maria rubbed the boy's back affectionately.

"He's already very sleepy," she said. "A tired little boy."

"I'm tired, too. It's been a long day. I'm so glad to be here."

"Not too tired, I hope," she said with a slight smile, tucking a strand of hair behind her right ear. "I've missed you tremendously. Perhaps once we've put Caleb to bed we should find out how much energy you have left."

"I'd like that," he said. He gave her a long, lingering kiss. "Somehow I don't think this old man will stay tired for very long."

Part Three

Twenty-nine

The man entered the Highsmith Inn from out of the bright midday sun. Once inside, he hesitated for a brief moment, letting his eyes adjust to the darkened interior of the restaurant.

He wasn't a tourist. His well-tailored tan suit, tightly knotted tie, and straw hat would have been overly formal attire for anyone on vacation. His slow, measured appraisal of the nearly empty dining room and bar of Highsmith's suggested that he also wasn't a local. Conchs knew the place well—it had been on Amelia Street long enough for it to become a local fixture.

The man's pale complexion provided further evidence that he had recently arrived; it would be nearly impossible for a fair-haired man to live in Key West for any appreciable period of time and not darken from the sun.

The stranger walked over to the otherwise unoccupied bar and sat down on one of the stools, nodding briefly to Miguel, the regular bartender. Miguel acknowledged him with a polite smile. The man asked for a beer and Miguel opened a bottle of Schlitz and poured it carefully into a glass.

The man drank his beer and glanced around, taking in the mirror behind the bar, the long shelf of bottles, the framed photos of Ted Williams and of Lauren Bacall and several of clusters of men in uniform. His gaze settled on a photo of three smiling men in Marine utility uniforms in a tropical setting; he studied it for a long moment.

"Excuse me," he said, looking over at the bartender. "I was wondering whether Dennis Collins is around. I was told that he works here."

"So you know him?"

The man hesitated for a moment. "Sure."

The bartender considered his answer; he had registered the pause. "Let me get Señora Maria. She's the person you should talk to."

The man sat and drank his beer while he waited. He watched a couple finishing their lunch and a family—father, mother, and two children—at a larger table in the corner, but he quickly lost interest.

A few minutes later a striking dark-haired young woman dressed in a white shirt and khaki pants strode into the dining room and made her way to the bar. She fixed her brown eyes on the stranger and frowned. It was clear that she wasn't happy to find him there.

"I am Maria Collins," she said, not offering to shake hands. "Miguel tells me that you've inquired about my husband."

"I have. I'm Cliff Wittingham. I was hoping to find Dennis and I was told that he works here." He tried not to stare at her. He hadn't expected to encounter such an attractive woman and there had been nothing in the file about Collins' being married. Now that she was closer he could see that she was pregnant—there was a telling rounded bump under her loose white shirt. Wittingham guessed she was in her mid- to late- twenties.

"You're his friend?" Her tone conveyed skepticism and Wittingham flushed.

"Not exactly. We have mutual friends."

"I was under the impression that you told Miguel that you knew Dennis." There was a sharp edge to her voice.

"Well, I know some of his friends. His lawyer, Dan Whalen, told me that I could find him here, at Highsmith's. I came down from D.C. to see if he could help me with some research."

"Research? What sort of research would that be?"

"With all due respect, Mrs. Collins," Wittingham said, "I'd prefer to discuss it with your husband. It's a private matter. I only need to have a brief conversation with him."

"Mr. Wittingham, with all due respect, I know how much my husband values his privacy. If you can't be more specific about why you're here, this conversation can't go anywhere."

"Perhaps I can help?" A tall, older man with a crewcut had walked over and joined them. "I'm Jim Highsmith," he said. "My daughter is correct. We try to guard Dennis' privacy, at his specific request."

"Major Highsmith," the man said. "Pleased to meet you. I'm Cliff Wittingham, State Department. Flew into the Naval Air Station this morning courtesy of Uncle Sam."

"That's a long way to come to see someone you don't know," Maria Collins said. "For the purposes of research."

Her father frowned. "Maria, please, let me handle this." He turned to Wittingham. "I guess that we're a bit protective."

"I do need to talk with him. As you might imagine, I wouldn't have made the trip if that weren't the case."

"Why would the State Department want to talk to Dennis?" It was Maria Collins. "He hasn't been overseas in well more than a year. How could he possibly help you?"

"I'm sorry, Mrs. Collins. That's something I can only discuss with your husband. Security reasons."

Highsmith stared at him directly. "Dennis won't be by the restaurant this afternoon. I'll pass along the message and I'll explain that you know Dan Whalen and that you're conducting some research. Then it will be up to Dennis. Why don't you come by tomorrow, after the lunch rush, say at two o'clock. If Dennis is interested in helping your research, he'll be here. If not, you can have another beer on the house, before you head back to Washington."

"I'm staying at the Casa Marina if you need to reach me," Wittingham said. "I'll stop by tomorrow."

He caught the quick glance exchanged between Major Highsmith and his daughter before he stood up and left the restaurant and went back out into the afternoon sun.

Dennis Collins was waiting at the bar in Highsmith's at two o'clock on Wednesday when Wittingham returned. Maria Highsmith Collins was sitting with him and when Wittingham appeared she got up from her seat and left the dining room. She didn't bother to greet him.

Collins looked like the man in the photos Wittingham had studied so carefully after he was given the assignment. His skin had darkened from the Florida sun and there were some lines around the eyes, but Wittingham could spot the resemblance to the black-and-white images in the Agency's file on Collins, and to the young man in uniform in the framed photo behind the bar.

"Glad to meet you," Wittingham told him after introducing himself. "I appreciate that you're taking the time."

"Would you like something to drink?" Collins asked.

"What are you having?"

Collins motioned toward his glass on the bar countertop. "Unsweetened ice tea. We can get another from the kitchen if you want."

"No, a beer, please," Wittingham said, directing his request to Miguel, who silently produced a beer glass and a bottle of Schlitz.

Collins nodded to Miguel who moved from behind the bar and left the dining room.

"So who exactly are you, and what is it that you want?" Collins asked.

"Simply a conversation, Mr. Collins. There were some unresolved questions when you left Washington, and I'm hoping you might fill in some of the missing blanks."

"You told Major Highsmith and my wife that you were from the State Department."

"In a manner of speaking, I am. I've held a few embassy posts. But I think we both know that I travel in the same circles that Matthew Steele did. Regrettably Steele's not around or I wouldn't be bothering you."

"I haven't been in Washington since last December. I went back for Matthew's funeral and to attend to some other business. It's almost a year later now and frankly I have no interest in talking to you. I'm done with all of that."

"I had hoped for your cooperation. Steele apparently didn't leave much of a paper trail, and you're the only one who knows what he was up to at the end. There are some things we don't understand and we need to."

Collins laughed. "So Matthew went to his great reward with some of his secrets intact? You could have figured that. He didn't care much for paperwork or for bureaucracy. He liked to improvise. I'm sorry you wasted your time flying down here. I've got nothing to say to you or anyone else from your Agency."

"If you thought coming down here was going to take you off the radar, you were wrong. Is that why the major and your wife are so overly protective? You must know that Mrs. Steele's parents aren't happy about the situation. They question whether you are fit to be the guardian of the boy."

"I'm more than his guardian," Collins said. "I assume you know that, too."

"I know that. I've seen the legal paperwork. The grandparents don't accept it, or at least they don't want to accept it. They believe that Steele wasn't in full possession of his faculties at the end. I'm surprised that they haven't filed a lawsuit."

"Is this supposed to be some kind of veiled threat?"

"Of course not. I'm just suggesting that you need all the friends that you can get. I've reviewed your file, and I don't think you'd want your background introduced into any legal proceedings. It's not the record of a model citizen."

"I guess that depends on how you define 'model citizen,'" Collins said. "I've got nothing to apologize for. And your superiors apparently thought I was of some service to the Agency in the past."

"That's what I wanted to talk to you about. There are two unresolved matters. The first concerns a meeting with General Eisenhower in Paris last year. We think we understand your involvement in this episode, but we'd like to hear from you exactly what went on."

"Do the election results last week have people in the East Building worried? Concerned about Ike's intentions and his attitude toward the Agency?"

Wittingham remained silent.

"And the other matter?" Collins asked.

"We understand Steele had placed Kim Philby under some sort of surveillance, without any authorization, just before Philby was recalled to London. We're curious about that."

"Matthew knew he had limited time left," Collins said. "He turned to a private detective because he wasn't getting any support from the Agency. He may have cut some corners. Expediency being the mother of invention. Something like that."

"I'd like to hear more about those corners," Wittingham said. "The ones he cut."

Collins shook his head. "I was willing to meet you today because I was curious. I'm sorry you spent taxpayer money on the trip down here. It's clear we have nothing to discuss."

Wittingham frowned. "What could convince you to tell me your story? Are there any, let's call them incentives, that could encourage your candor?"

"You're not offering to pay me, are you?" Collins gave him a thin smile. "Do you really think that would interest me?"

"There might be other inducements."

"Such as?"

"A promise that you will be left alone in the future. No further contact with anyone in the government. A letter of appreciation from the director of Central Intelligence in your file. Should the Allens ever seek legal action, the Agency would be willing to vouch for your character with the judge."

"You're offering me something I already have. Caleb isn't going anywhere. It's been almost a year and a half since I've had Caleb with me. I don't see the Allens going into court. And why would anyone in the government bother with me now?"

"One other incentive. We can very helpful if you decide to go back to writing for newspapers. We can help remove any impediments that might stand in the way of your employment."

"You mean the blacklist, or whatever it's called now. Don't bother. I'm done with newspapers."

"You don't miss New York? Didn't miss the Dodgers and Yankees? The World Series?"

"Watched it on television, WTVJ out of Miami."

"Not the same thing."

"Maybe. Reception wasn't very good. On the hand, it's nice to just be a fan. And now that DiMaggio has retired, everyone is telling me that baseball will never be the same. You're shooting blanks, Wittingham."

Wittingham reached into the inside pocket of his suit jacket and produced an envelope. He handed it to Collins, who retrieved the folded letter inside and read it quickly. It was from Allen Dulles, on Central Intelligence Agency stationary. It stated that: "Mr. Wittingham has been authorized to act on the Agency's behalf in making certain assurances and I am prepared to provide written confirmation of these assurances at the appropriate time."

"You should have started with this," Collins said. "I trust Dulles largely because Matthew trusted him." He waved the sheet of paper. "May I keep this? If Dulles is behind your visit then I know it's not part of some posthumous witch hunt."

"The letter is addressed to you. Keep it."

Collins glanced over Wittingham's shoulder at the light cascading through the front window of the restaurant. He thought about his choices. Letter or no letter, he had no guarantee that talking to Wittingham would end it—Dulles could fall out of favor at the Agency, and whoever followed him might very well want to reopen the file on Matthew Steele. On the other hand, if Collins provided some answers, he believed that Dulles would follow through on those "assurances." It wouldn't hurt to have a favorable letter in his file if things got ugly later on.

Collins stood up. "There's a small dining room where we talk in private." He checked his wristwatch. "I can give you the rest of the afternoon. That should be more than long enough." He looked directly at Wittingham. "Where do you want me to start?"

"From the beginning," Wittingham said. "From the very beginning."

Thirty

Collins had been surprised; Cliff Wittingham proved to be a good listener, instinctively sensing when to let Collins talk and when to interject a question or two. He was a study in neutrality, keeping any judgments to himself. How much Wittingham already knew about Steele's pursuit of Kim Philby and Anatoli Yatov, Collins couldn't tell.

"A few things still bother me about your story," Wittingham said after Collins had finished. "Steele never told you what he said to General Eisenhower when they were alone? He didn't give you any idea? Drop any hints on the flight back?"

Collins shrugged. "Matthew was tight-lipped by nature. He once quoted the English poet George Herbert to me that 'the life of spies is to know, not be known.' He didn't open up to me until later."

"But he did open up to you eventually. Why do you think he did?"

"I think he wanted a witness. Against the day that the Bureau came after him or that someone in the Agency like you wanted to review his file. He thought that our history together—what happened in New York in 1949 and his marriage to Penny—would suggest that I wouldn't lie on his behalf. If anything, I had an incentive to do the opposite."

"You think that was his reason, then? To make you his witness?"

"He wanted someone to know the truth. Near the end, he wasn't sure who he could trust."

They were interrupted by the sounds of a gentle rapping on the door. Collins opened it to find his wife standing there with a shy smile. From behind her came the sound of a radio playing the mambo music of Pérez Prado and the muffled voices of the cooks from the kitchen as they readied for the dinner hour.

"We're going to have supper soon," she said. "I didn't know whether you were going to join us."

"I am," Collins said. "But please come in. I was just finishing with Mr. Wittingham."

She stepped into the room and Collins closed the door. She glanced over and saw that Wittingham had placed his wristwatch, an expensive one from the looks of it, on the table next to a notepad. He had a silver pen in his right hand. He rose when she entered the room and he waited until Collins had seated her before he sat down again.

"I've just told Mr. Wittingham the story of my time with Matthew in Washington," Collins said. "He has been sent here by Mr. Dulles, the deputy director, a man Matthew trusted."

Maria looked over at Wittingham warily.

"Your husband has been quite helpful," Wittingham said. "He has cleared up a number of matters that had been obscure. We're particularly pleased to be able to set the record straight before too much time passes."

"And this is it?" Maria asked, her hand unconsciously moving to her stomach in a protective gesture. "You won't need him to go to Washington?"

"This is it. He won't have to come to Washington. And Mr. Dulles will place a letter in your husband's file noting his cooperation and assistance to the Agency."

"Will Dennis receive a copy of this letter?" Maria asked, fixing her gaze on Wittingham.

Wittingham shifted in his seat. "I imagine we could arrange that."

Collins gave him a slight smile. "It would be even more helpful if you could arrange for a carbon copy of the letter to be placed in the Bureau's Dennis Collins file."

"That would be a mistake, I think," Wittingham said. "It's best to let sleeping dogs lie."

"I never liked that saying," Collins said. "But I get your point."

Wittingham picked up his watch and placed it back on his right wrist. He closed the notepad and looked at the two of them. "I'll take my leave now. I'm due back in Washington tomorrow. Should we have any follow-up questions—which I doubt—I know where I can reach you."

He shook hands with Collins and nodded to Maria, but then hesitated, making no effort to move toward the door. "I never met Matthew Steele," he said. "I'm fairly new and what I know of him comes from others in the Agency. He apparently was a strange mix of intellectual and swashbuckler. After hearing your story, Mr. Collins, I'm not sure what to think."

"Why is that?"

"He took some significant risks, all on his own initiative. In the end, it worked—Philby was removed and recalled to London—but I understand why there would be questions about Steele's methods, and at the end, even about his stability."

"His stability?"

"Some believe his thinking was negatively affected by his health concerns, that he became overly fixated—perhaps even obsessed—with finding Anatoli Yatov. Maybe he began imagining connections that weren't there."

Collins shook his head. "There was nothing wrong with his mind. He thought that Yatov was controlling Philby. Logic suggested that the way to find Yatov was through Philby."

"And he was dead wrong," Wittingham said. "There have been no signs of Yatov in years and certainly no traces of him in Washington. We've asked the British, French, and Germans and they say he hasn't been in Europe."

"Perhaps he went back to Russia."

"Perhaps. Did Steele come to that conclusion as well? He left nothing behind specifically about Yatov. I looked in the file and there isn't much there, which is surprising considering how important Steele thought he was and how much time he devoted to searching for him. There are no notes or memos concerning Yatov after May 1951."

"Perhaps Matthew concluded he was wrong, and that Yatov really wasn't in the country. One of his colleagues accused him of chasing ghosts. Maybe Steele decided to quietly end the pursuit."

"What do you think?"

"I don't believe in ghosts of any kind," Collins said. "Matthew told me once that when he caught up to Yatov, he wanted to see justice done. He had faith that would happen, that the scales would be balanced, if not on his watch, then by someone else down the road."

"That might explain one loose end," Wittingham said. "In his Yatov file, Steele left one scrap of paper with a Bible verse on it. Undated. Seems he became a bit of a mystic at the end. They say he converted to Catholicism before he died."

"He did. Which verse?"

Wittingham retrieved his notepad from his jacket, opened it, and flipped through the pages. "Here it is," he said. "Handwritten, not typed. 'Though hand join in hand, the wicked shall not be unpunished: but the seed of the righteous shall be delivered.' It's from Proverbs. Wishful thinking on Steele's part, I'm afraid. Punishment of the wicked, the righteous rewarded. Too bad it didn't turn out that way."

"That could be," Collins said. "On the other hand, I guess that we'll never really know, will we?"

Author's Note

In June 1951, CIA Director Walter Bedell Smith informed the Secret Intelligence Service that Kim Philby represented a security risk and was no longer acceptable as the British liaison officer in Washington. Yet after his recall to London, Philby led a charmed life. Despite the considerable evidence pointing to his guilt as the Third Man, Philby brazened his way through interrogations by MI6 and MI5, sticking to his story that he was not a Soviet agent. One of MI5's top interrogators, Buster Milmo, failed to elicit a confession from Philby in 1952, and the British government—in the form of Foreign Secretary Harold Macmillan—publicly pronounced him innocent of espionage in 1955.

Separated from government service, Philby went to Beirut in 1956 as a stringer for the *Observer* and the *Economist* and, it was rumored, was asked to assist MI6 intelligence efforts in the Middle East. In 1963, the defection of KGB major Anatoly Golitsyn gave the British more information on Philby's clandestine involvement with the Russians. After an interview with an MI6 colleague sent from London, Philby fled Lebanon and surfaced in Moscow, joining Burgess and Maclean in exile.

Over time the story of the Cambridge Five (Philby, Burgess, Maclean, Anthony Blunt, and John Cairncross) and their betrayal of crown and country has fascinated historians, playwrights, and novelists. They have been portrayed as England's best and brightest—elegant, gentlemanly spies. To a surprising extent, however, the damage caused by Philby, Burgess, and Maclean to the United Nations cause in Korea has been downplayed.

While there a number of excellent histories of the Cambridge Five, I found two books especially insightful: *Treason in the Blood* by Anthony Cave Brown, a study of Kim Philby and his larger-than-life father, St. John Philby; and Verne Newton's *The Cambridge spies: the untold story of Maclean, Philby, and Burgess in America*. Both Brown and Newton rightly indict the British intelligence establishment for its cover-up of the breadth and depth of the spying involved.

How much of the blame for Chinese military successes in the winter of 1950–51 can be assigned to the leaking of American war plans and how much to the strategic recklessness of General Douglas MacArthur?

There have been dramatically different answers to that question. While conceding that the Cambridge spies may "have been one of several factors in the dismal outcome," military historian Roy E. Appleman has argued that errors in generalship by MacArthur were "the main causes of the Korean disaster." Appleman concluded that MacArthur's "decisions and policies were militarily unrealistic and unsound in the circumstances and conditions that prevailed in Korea and its border territories and in light of the conventional military resources available to the United States and the UN."

MacArthur's mistakes, Appleman maintained, included not unifying the Eighth Army and X Corps in one command, dispatching the X Corps to Wonson by sea instead of by land, not establishing a defensive line at the narrow waist of Korea, failing to employ units of X Corps so they could support each other, and advancing to the Yalu River despite clear warnings of a significant Chinese intervention.

Joseph Goulden has questioned whether the secrets passed to the Russians by Maclean, Philby, and Burgess ever reached the Chinese. In *Korea: The Untold Story*, Goulden maintained that the Chinese responded to the UN's fall offensive in 1950 as if MacArthur planned to invade China itself. The most plausible explanation for this overreaction, Goulden argued, was that the Soviets had not alerted Beijing to American intentions: "The Soviet Union was happy to tie the United States down in a proxy war in Korea, with the Chinese and the North Koreans suffering the casualties. The war increased China's reliance upon the Soviet Union; it prevented China's growth into a significant world power, and the Soviets could sit back and watch with assurance that the United States did not wish global conflict. Thus the value of the material gathered by the Philby-Burgess-Maclean ring."

The historical record, however, suggests that the Soviets did indeed inform the Chinese. MacArthur and other U.S. commanders complained repeatedly in 1950 and 1951 that their adversaries appeared to have advance knowledge of their plans. William Manchester in his biography of MacArthur, *American Caesar*, wrote: "James M. Gavin, an officer untainted by McCarthyism, recalls that during his service in the last critical months of 1950, the enemy repeatedly displayed an uncanny knowledge of UN troop deployment." According to Manchester, Gavin became "quite sure now that all of MacArthur's plans flowed into the hands of the Communists through the British Foreign Office."

General James Van Fleet told *U.S. News and World Report* in 1955 that: "The enemy would not have entered Korea if he did not feel safe from attack in Northern China and Manchuria. My own conviction is that there must have been information to the enemy that we would not attack his home base."

Anthony Cave Brown noted in a 1994 interview on C-SPAN that many officials thought that "through Philby, the Soviet government learned enough about the deployment, the limitations of the force, the lengths and breadths of the strategy in Korea to be able to launch the Chinese counteroffensive at the right place, at the right time with the right weight and with terrible destructive force. If my opinion was asked for—and it often is on this case—I would say that Philby did, in fact, provide the Soviets with that type of information."

A fair reading of history would suggest that the advance intelligence provided by the Cambridge spies gave the Chinese leadership a significant battlefield advantage. At the same time, General MacArthur's arrogant recklessness played directly into the hands of the Communist invaders, leaving the rapidly advancing United Nations forces vulnerable to counterattack. It should be noted that President Truman and Defense Secretary George C. Marshall approved MacArthur's bold pursuit of the remnants of the North Korean Army, so they must share in some of the blame.

President-elect Dwight Eisenhower visited the frontlines in Korea in December 1952, fulfilling a campaign pledge. Then, after concluding that "[s]mall attacks on small hills would not win this war," Eisenhower rejected calls for escalation and pursued an end to the fighting through a combination of diplomacy and military saber-rattling. Whether or not Eisenhower threatened the Chinese with the use of nuclear weapons is a matter of historical debate, but his efforts to forge a peace paid off. An armistice was signed in July 1953, some three years and one month after the start of the Korean conflict.

As Stephen Ambrose noted in *Eisenhower: The President*, Ike regarded the armistice as one of his greatest accomplishments as president. "He took great pride in it. He had promised to go to Korea; he had implied that he would bring the war to a close; he had made the trip; despite intense opposition from his own party, from his Secretary of State, and from Syngman Rhee, he had ended the war six months after taking office." Ambrose added: "The truth was that Eisenhower realized that unlimited war in the nuclear age was unimaginable, and limited war unwinnable."

Historian Jean Edward Smith has observed that after the Korean armistice, not a single American serviceman was killed in action during the remaining seven and a half years of Eisenhower's presidency.

The North Building depicts a number of actual historical figures, including Eisenhower, Philby, Burgess, and Allen Dulles as well as Pee Wee Reese, Toots Shor, and others from the period. I've tried not to stray far from the historical record in their portrayal.

A disgusted Lt. Col. Don Faith did throw the Silver Star awarded to him by General Almond into the snow; whether a combat correspondent would have heard about it from contemporary witnesses is debatable. Faith was awarded the Congressional Medal of Honor posthumously for his bravery during the doomed breakout attempt by Task Force Faith.

Valeri Mikhaylovich Makayev was Kim Philby's Soviet controller, not Anatoli Yatov. After arriving in the U.S. in 1950, Makayev taught musical composition at NYU and reportedly became friendly with the family of Senator Ralph Flanders of Vermont (who were unaware of Makayev's true identity). Flanders, a distant relative of mine, introduced the motion of censure of Joseph McCarthy on the Senate floor in 1954. Makayev was a bit of a bungler, becoming entangled in a love affair with a Polish ballet teacher in New York and later losing a microfilm with operational instructions secreted in a hollow Swiss coin. He was eventually recalled to Moscow and cashiered.

The Great Falls of the Potomac would have been a logical choice if Philby had called an emergency meeting with his Russian handler. It is near the location where Philby says he buried his photographic equipment when he realized that the authorities were closing in on him in the spring of 1951.

Guy Myers, the CIA counterintelligence official in *The North Building* who doubts that Philby is a spy, is my fictional creation. His real-life counterparts in the CIA had a mixed record on the Philby question. William Harvey eventually came to suspect Philby; James Jesus Angleton apparently did not, even after being directly warned by Israeli intelligence officer Teddy Kollek, who had attended Philby's marriage to Litzi Friedmann, an Austrian Communist, in 1934. Kollek later became mayor of Jerusalem.

Allen Dulles met Carl Jung in Switzerland during the war and greatly admired him. Jung became Agent 488 for the OSS, analyzing the psychology of the Nazi leadership for Dulles and senior American military commanders.

Whenever possible, I prefer to write about places that I have visited. There are telling details—sights, sounds, topography—that I've learned are best discovered and experienced in person. Unfortunately the political situation in North Korea made any "on the ground" research about the Chosin Reservoir campaign impossible. I did have the benefit of discussing the battle with my late brother-in-law, James Ng, who served with the First Marines at Chosin. I also found the moving testimony of Chosin veterans in *Chosin*, a 2010 documentary film directed by Brian Iglesias, to be both informative and inspiring.

I relied on a number of excellent books for background including Margaret Higgins' *The War in Korea*, David Douglas Duncan's *This is War*, Robert Leckie's *The March to Glory*, Gail Shisler's *For Country and Corps*, Roy E. Appleman's *East of Chosin*, Martin Russ' *Breakout*, Shelby L. Stanton's *America's Tenth Legion: X Corps in Korea, 1950*, and James Brady's marvelous fictional treatment of Chosin, *The Marines of Autumn*, which Kurt Vonnegut described as the Korean War's *Iliad*.

Once again I turned to the scholarship of John Earl Haynes, Harvey Klehr, Alexander Vassiliev, Steve Usdin, Ron Radosh, and Allen Weinstein for an understanding of Soviet espionage in the United States in the 1950s.

For their insightful feedback, I want to acknowledge and thank Steve Flanders (for his observations on matters military), Michael Conniff (for sharing his memories of the world of Toots Shor), Christian Flanders (for reconnoitering the Great Falls Park and Key West with me), and Linda Salisbury (for her thoughtful wordsmithing). A Cuban-American friend from Key West, and his mother, helped with all things Conch. Mick Wieland ably fashioned the map of the Chosin campaign as well as designing the cover of *The North Building*.

Any errors of historical fact or flaws in interpretation found in *The North Building* are mine alone.

Researching and writing a historical novel requires a significant investment of time and energy. That time—often spent alone—comes at some cost: things left undone or placed on hold, priorities shifted, experiences delayed. I'd like to thank my loved ones for their support, understanding, and patience and for bearing with me as I fashioned this story.

About the Author

Jefferson Flanders has been a sportswriter, columnist, editor, and publishing executive. He is the author of *Café Carolina and Other Stories* and of *Herald Square*, a novel of the Cold War described as "Jimmy Breslin meets John le Carré" in the *Huffington Post* and as "well-written, action packed and engrossing" in the *Washington Times*.

11/13

CPSIA information can be obtained at www.ICGtesting.com
Printed in the USA
LVOW10s1832051113

360106LV00016B/960/P

9 780988 784086